SECRET INTELLIGENCE

DARK RIM

ENOCH CHANG

PARTRIDGE
A Penguin Random House Company

ISBN:	Hardcover	978-1-4828-9307-6
	Softcover	978-1-4828-9306-9
	Ebook	978-1-4828-9308-3

To order additional copies of this book, contact
Toll Free 800 101 2657 (Singapore)
Toll Free 1 800 81 7340 (Malaysia)
orders.singapore@partridgepublishing.com

www.partridgepublishing.com/singapore

For my mom, Alice.

Contents

Prologue

SECRET INTELLIGENCE

It was dark. There may be no demons at night but there was always secret intelligence going on. No light. No public. It was a perfect venue.

Jacobi Parr had been working for the Central Intelligence Agency for more than 15 years and he was now 35 years old. They had recruited him when he was barely 20. But this was a completely new experience to him. It was an experience not known to many people in the entire globe.

The car he was sitting was black, he didn't have the chance to identify the model or anything else. In the car, one of his partners wasn't an undercover agent, but worked for one of the world's largest criminal intelligence organizations. They were now doing business with another illegal enterprise that's even bigger and more lethal than any other. Some people we will call them 'Ventures' but in reality, they had no real names at all since, so little was known about them.

The driver was lethal as well, he could kill someone with his bare hands in three seconds. The place they're going was a sea coast location. Here the Ventures will trade something radioactive in metal cases to his criminal organization for somebody very important, and he had no idea who he was. The person was in the car behind them, following. Although Jacobi Parr was an undercover double agent, they never tell him much and it's better not to ask questions and risk his life being taken silently.

The car roamed along a black road with trees lining the path. No one talked during this time. After about 15 minutes, they reached their destination. To their left was an expanse of blackish water and sand. A big private ship stood in the dark water.

The ship stored the uranium, 50 kilograms. If made into nuclear missiles, they could bring the world down. The two cars pulled up to the side of the coast near a metal gangplank. They got out of the car as soon as the wheels stopped turning.

The air was cold and the sky was clear, he could see stars, he missed his family who were a few thousand miles away. He could never mention them when he's on any mission. It's better not to think at all. There was still no signal.

The people in the second car came out. There were three men from the organization and another man with a black bag on the top of his head. He was handcuffed. Two of the men guarded him while another stood looking for any signs of danger.

The Ventures agents must had seen the men in blindfold and they signalled them with a torch light. Three blinks, the third lasted for five seconds. It was their code.

They walked up the gangplank in a line. One guard in the front, then the man in the blindfold, and Jacobi Parr next, followed by the other four men. He could smell that the prisoner stunk, he probably hadn't washed for weeks.

He had a feeling of nervousness as they ascended the planks to the ship. No one except a completely cold-blooded serial killer could avoid having this kind of feelings. But he wasn't a serial killer. He was an undercover agent of the CIA. and he won't simply kill without examining his self-conscious. It will always be his weakness and he knew that well.

He still wondered who the unknown man was with his face concealed, standing just in front of him. What was so special about him that he was worth 50 kilograms of illegal uranium?

The door of the ship opened as they neared. A Japanese man in his twenties urged them in. They all entered, leaving the cars behind, which wasn't a good thing. The interior of the ship was plain and normal with white-washed walls and metal decks.

They made their way as they followed the Japanese man up to the highest deck of the ship. It was probably the top-deck because nothing was covering their heads. That was good. The CIA. had sent agents as snipers on the hills of the jungle, and they will not fire until he gave them some special signal.

He had a sensor inside his shoe, just under the small of his insole of the right foot. If he stepped on it hard enough longer than 10 seconds, it would call the back-up team and this mission will end. Whatever planned trade of uranium for the unknown man would be over. But he would not do it until the uranium was first checked by them.

The place was furnished with a large square table and two chairs. One of them was occupied by a man in his twenties with brilliant eyes and a gun tied to his belt visible. He was Japanese as well, but he looked like the boss.

They walked towards him and the man that escorted them left the place without being told. The men guarding the unknown person just in front of him manoeuvred him to the remaining chair and forced him to a sit.

All of them stood, waiting for the Japanese man to check the person he wanted and to get them the uranium they all wanted. But he just sat there and looked at them. He needed to be careful if the man tried to use the gun but that wouldn't be possible. They all had guns and there was a six to one advantage. A man in his right mind wouldn't even consider it.

But as time passed, they understood that he only wanted to talk to Jacobi's criminal organization's representatives. It was Parr and his partner. That was already negotiated. The other men left the area without a word being said.

Now there was just the Japanese man, the unknown man and the two representatives. The man sitting removed the bag of the unknown man. He was an English about 50 years old, with fair hair, fear was clearly visible on his face.

"Are you Mr. Doyle?" the Japanese man said for the first time. The English was heavily accented. "Yes," the man answered after looking around at the three people.

"Our trade is for uranium, fifty kilograms," his partner said in the simplest of terms. Although he could speak English better than the Japanese man, he didn't show it.

Once they checked the uranium, Jacobi will call the CIA. Their first priority was to get hold of the radioactive metal as it could threaten national security, not mentioning humanity itself. And they needed to make sure this Japanese man had really brought the metals. He could be cheating as well.

"Wait for a moment," the Japanese man spoke slowly. "Are you all followed?" he asked. That was weird, if he suspected that, why wouldn't he ask the question earlier.

"No," his partner said again. For the moment, Jacobi thought that his cover had been blown and the CIA's back-up team had been noticed. He resisted the temptation to activate the sensor. The man could just be asking as a matter of course. But everything changed in an instant. Without any signal, two guards with guns dragged another two men from the door they had used to exit earlier. The men were covered in raincoats with forest camouflage of leaves and branches.

The guards threw the men down onto the floor. They were looking terrified and knew their end had come. But in what way would it come? The man named Doyle looked at the new presence uncertainly and once again looked at the Japanese man.

"Snipers," the Japanese man said again. Jacobi Parr immediately activated the sensor but he showed no sign of it. His hand near to the gun strapped to his waist, ready to use it. The CIA's snipers' cover had been blown but they still didn't know his real identity.

Silence stretched on for 10 long seconds and Jacobi knew that the back-up team will arrive in three minutes. The Japanese man took out his gun slowly, not showing any interest in the two criminal representatives, and they drew theirs, too, but didn't aim at anyone.

The Japanese man then looked at one of the snipers and shot him once in the head. The report was only a shudder and a hiss, the gun was suppressed, The dead man dropped to the floor.

He once again looked at the remaining man. The sniper struggled and the guards held him. He resisted like a bulldog and ran to the railings of the deck, but before he could jump, the man killed him with another silent bullet into the back.

Two men had their covers' blown. Jacobi Parr didn't wish to be the third. Suddenly, the guards that brought the snipers in raised their concealed AK-103 assault rifles up.

"Drop your weapons," the Japanese man pointed his gun and said to the two representatives. They could aim at the Japanese man, and one could have managed to shot him, but they both would have died as well. His partner looked completely calm, though he was barely holding himself together. They both dropped their weapons.

"I wasn't talking to you," the Japanese spoke to Parr's partner. "You can get your gun back and I'll hand you the stocks," he said again.

With hesitation and time, his partner slowly picked up two of their guns and stood aside. Two of the assault rifles and a handgun were now aiming at the undercover CIA agent, there's no doubt this was his last mission.

His partner will not even consider helping him. Why would he, they just met in the last 12 hours and they only knew each other's coded names. But he did say he will give his partner the stock. That meant the uranium was here and the CIA will get them, although he didn't stand a chance to watch.

"Jacobi Parr," the Japanese man called his real name. "You work for the CIA and have a wife and two kids. You live in Paris." The agent then froze. They knew about his family and they will kill all of them. He now regretted joining the world of secrets. He prayed to undo his action or at least let his family go.

Parr looked at him in the eyes, begged him in eye language not to do anything to his family, but the Japanese man didn't show any expression. The man smiled and raised the gun.

The agent had already decided, he spun around, the Japanese man shot at him and missed. Jacobi aimed his gun towards one of the guards but he was too late.

The guards opened fire, the sound of chattering rifles broke the night's silence and the agent was killed instantly. Before Jacobi died, he knew that the back-up team must had heard the shots and they will be faster on their way, knowing that stealth wasn't needed any more. He was thrown to the deck, a pool of blood widening around his body.

Just at the moment the Japanese turned to the dead man's partner, sirens of police marines and helicopters filled the air. The agent had somehow contacted the back-up team but that wasn't the most important thing now, he had an escape plan.

"We'll need to get out of here. It's your choice to follow. I'll give you the uranium on another day but let's escape first," the Japanese man said to the partner.

He stood up immediately and headed for the door that led to the inside of the ship. The man followed. Guards held the other man named Doyle and moved quickly.

The Japanese led the way forward and descended a few steps to the last floor of the whole ship. There was scuba-equipment and he put it on. The guards did the same, in turns, with one always looking after their prisoner.

"We're not swimming out of here, they have Marines!" the partner said.

"No. We'll just be in the water for a while. The swim is not more than 50 meters. Follow or die," he said as he hooked the oxygen tank to his back and secured it.

He jumped into the water, not making much sound. The guards helped the unknown man to put on an oxygen tank. They told him how to breathe correctly and manoeuvred him together into the water. The man was handcuffed and he couldn't swim, so they had to help him. If the man tried to escape, he'd die.

The Japanese man and the guards were in the water, half-floating. They were waiting for him. They saw the CI.A's elite forces were already boarding the ship and they will reach him in not more than a minute. The partner immediately buckled up the scuba-suit in 10 seconds, and jumped into the water.

Although the suit did fend off a little of the coldness of the icy water, he felt like he was in the Atlantic. The little knives of icy water pricked his flesh and into his bone.

The four men had disappeared into the blackish water, into the depths of the sea. The guards switched on their torches and led the way ahead. The partner worried that they may get lost, but he had to trust these people that chose not to kill him.

But as they descended deeper into the waters, the light of the torches made out a very big and long fish. It wasn't a fish, it was a submarine. The dived and landed on the top of it and got hold of the metal railings. He was already very cold and would favour to get inside fast. Fast, before hypothermia came.

The Japanese man opened a door and they all got inside a room filled with seawater washed with green lights. The guards closed it. For a moment, the partner thought they had something hidden under their sleeves and would kill him now, but the man just pressed a few buttons and the water started to drain out of the room.

After the air-lock room had been cleared, he opened a door to the interior of the submarine. It was white-washed metal with green lightings. They all climbed to a seat along a pathway and the Japanese man took off his scuba-diving suits with the guards.

The place felt warm with a ventilation and radiator. He felt relieved as the coldness started to leave him, but not completely, there was still numbness. The man named Doyle sat slumped and exhausted on the seat. He looked like his body was confused, both scared and exhausted.

"Where am I?" the partner asked. He also took off the suit, as it made it easier for him to move. He didn't sit down, his hand ready to reach for his gun if anything went wrong.

"You're in a submarine. The uranium is here but I doubt you alone can take so much back to your boss," the Japanese man said.

"You broke the deal," he said again.

"No. Your undercover partner broke it. Your organization should take care of their own issues before trading with us, we don't want any mistakes and attention from the intelligence," he replied.

"If you know he was an undercover, why didn't you say that earlier? Why must you wait until the last moment? A lot of our men have died," he said again.

"We already said that we wouldn't contact you before the trade. We only knew about the agent during the last few hours and we wouldn't cancel the mission," the Japanese man simply replied.

"But why didn't you just cancel it despite what your boss said? The CIA already knew this and you might just not show up. You're crazy!" the partner said.

"I'll explain this. First, the undercover agent had known that we already been dealing a uranium trade and so did his agency. I admit that it is the first Ventures' mistake in 10 years. We cannot change the fact that the CIA had already known this, but we can at least recover something," the Japanese said.

"What the hell is happening? You just lost a ship and men. I hope the uranium is on this ship and if not, you lose another thing. And now you said you're recovering? You're kidding me, I've heard the wrong thing. I'm insane!" the partner said.

He wanted to shoot the Japanese man sitting in front of him but that wouldn't do anything good to him or the man.

"The uranium is here if you want to know. My meaning of recovery means an improvement. Intelligence is knowledge and the ability to use it. The CIA already knew about us and the uranium and we had to do something to improve the situation rather than doing nothing. We could find a new spot but it'll take too much time and it's what we don't have," he paused and continued.

"You see, the ship and the men I lost are nothing because I wanted them to believe that they had succeeded in trapping us, it's just that their agent's cover had been blown in the last minute. And that we were desperate to run like just now. Plus, why would they come after you arrived to receive the uranium? Why not just take control of the ship when you're not here? You all aren't valuable and they'd no intention to lure you for your little lives," he spat the words out and licked his lips.

"They wanted to confirm the existence of the uranium and then get hold of them. It wasn't what we that they wanted, they just wanted the metals. On the ship, there is opium worth 50 million Euros and I think the police will be delighted to have them. It will be a success and a big gift that I personally gave them.

"Why would I put the 50-million-thing on the boat?" He let the words hang in the air. "Distraction . . . Yes, a price for every desire. I want them to forget about the uranium. I want them to focus on the drugs they got. Why would someone bring so many drugs for a uranium trade? Why would they even bring it in the first place?

"I tell facts, I'm now making reasons and doubts that our uranium didn't ever exist. They do not know about this submarine or our escape. So, the 'drug trade' looks like it completely failed. They win, we win. The difference is we win two times.

"Why would I say two times? The first time is we managed to pursue them to forget our real plan of trading uranium and we succeeded.

"The second is, after they really convinced themselves that the uranium really didn't exist, that they blame the CIA for the 'wrong information'. After all, they hadn't confirmed the existence of the metals. So this makes them feel even more unconvinced about any radioactive stuff." He stopped as if to ask questions but said nothing.

"What happen next? We locate another coast and insert the uranium into the country and we had virtually almost succeeded. We win the second time. We are now inside the borders of the Australian coast. After our intelligence tells us and confirms that the CIA had given up on the 'non-existing' uranium, we will dock and win for the third time. The metals will be inside and that's not much to worry about.

"I know you are weighting possibilities about why I'm doing so much for your organization and telling you so much, but I'll now explain. But it wasn't for your organization. Our real plan didn't even do anything good to your side. We wanted this Mr.

Doyle. One of our leaders is very addicted in meeting him under some circumstances that I don't know. And it's better not to know.

"We use you all to get this man named Doyle since you all already had him in custody, it made things easier. You wanted to smuggle the uranium into Australia but we also wanted to. This was a great coincidence. It is just as easy as this. And I just remember that it was we who broke the deal, not you. Sorry for mistaking just now.

"We have a grand plan. After we got into the country with the uranium, there are a lot of things to do. We cheated you. You won't get any uranium at all. If the CIA somehow thinks that the uranium still exists, which wasn't very convincing as I'd told you, they will hunt for your organization and not us.

"You all are the buyers, right? You all 'have the uranium', right? So why look for the seller? They may involve us but that is after they got you. You all will be their primary targets if this plan to convince them that the metals didn't exist fails, do you understand?"

"You're full of bullshit! You get the man and everything else. And then put the main blame on us. You threw away the amount of money that could buy a few tonnes of drugs to do this? You're insane," the partner said. But he thought of one puzzle still not in place.

The Japanese man showed nothing that he was offended. The swearing was like praises and he was enjoying it with everything he could.

"Why did you tell me all this?" he asked.

"A great plan deserves to be known," the Japanese replied and raised his own gun, the guards did the same. "This is the power of the Ventures. One more thing, I'm only honest to people that will die because dead man tells no tales, and you'll be one of them."

The partner scrambled for his gun, but before he could even aim the guards and the Japanese man pulled their triggers. Bullets and sparks ricocheted in the confined space, leaving a undesirable sight of a human with more than 30 holes filled with blood.

He turned to the hostage man that was now wide-eyed. "Mr. Doyle, don't you be afraid. You're too valuable. I'll not kill you, at least not yet. But you'll reunite with your son soon. And then, the real plans start," he said.

Mr. Doyle struggled and begged and then cursed him not to even touch his 14-year-old son, but soon was held tightly by the guards and yanked into a confinement room elsewhere inside the submarine. The Japanese man was alone now.

He took out a paper written by computer and read the few underlined words to confirm his orders. The Japanese smiled and murmured to himself. "I'm coming to get you, little boy."

Target: (First Name Unknown) Doyle. Fourteen. Central London. Custody.

Chapter One

SAPPHIRE AND MEMORIES

He sat in the Tube roaming through the dark tunnel. Fourteen-year-old Nathan Doyle knew today was different from the after-school days he experienced before. His aunt had asked him to come back early without any questions, it wasn't a good thing.

Nathan was lean, wearing his school uniform of polo shirt and ironed coat, now of course crumpled, his dark brown hair attractive and neat in a way.

Clutching his fake-leather backpack to his stomach, he waited impatiently for the Tube to bring him back to his home somewhere in Central London. School wasn't a particular good day with extra history lessons and a whole bunch of mathematics homework demanding the simplified algebraic expressions, not to mention an essay. Westminster School, yeah, he studied in it.

After about 15 minutes, the train reached the stop he wanted and he quickly left the train and got beyond the hustle-bustle of people in the station out into the afternoon sun. It was about 2:30 p.m., and the fumes from vehicles weren't the best thing to greet him.

Nathan hurried passed slow-moving pedestrians with his backpack flying in his hands. Honestly, the extra history class meant detention for him and that wasn't needed to get home early. He quickly hailed a cab and yelled his address out and pre-paid him in case he refused to take him.

The cab man smiled and the car was speeding off before he'd even closed the door. He asked the cab to stop not far from his double-story house along the streets, not wanting his aunt to see him in such a damn rush.

He thanked the cab man and ran in one moment and slowed down before the gates. He scrambled for the keys while trying to calm his heart, which seemed to be shattering his ribs. He found them, unlocked the gate, got in and locked it again.

Nathan stood in front of the doorway, removed his sports shoes and moved quickly into the house. "Aunty! I'm back!" he yelled, afraid she might not hear him. "Nathan, you're almost late, I told you to come . . ." She was cut off. "Sorry, traffic jam!" Nathan said.

He threw his backpack onto the sofa and lay down beside it, tried to remove his shoes with his legs and resting his pounding heart. His aunt, Veinna came out and saw him, her hands holding plates. "Go and bathe, Nathan," she said in disgust.

"Are you cooking?" Nathan asked curiously. Of course she was cooking, he could smell black pepper and meat from the kitchen.

"Surely, Nut," Veinna answered. His nickname for every time his aunt thought he was late. "Please, stop that!" he pleaded. "Not for a late boy!" she replied.

"When can I eat?" Nathan asked, changing topics.

"That's for dinner, if you dare touch it without my word, I'm not going to let you get away untouched," she said while looking at him with his devilish eyes. Nathan wasn't scared neither did he want to provoke her. Without being told again, he retrieved his socks from the floor and bag and got to his room, passing the open back door leading to the garden. Veinna had green fingers for plants, she even coloured her nails green.

Nathan got into his room, threw the bag for the thousandth time in his lifetime and got to the bathroom, he hit the showers on, lathered the soap into foam and made his spa. Well, not too long this time, he quickly scrubbed his body, his dark-brown hair and whatever skin he could find and got out of the comfort of warm water. He turned off the shower and began to towel himself dry.

Then he got into his room and finished the idiotic history and algebraic work in an hour. His aunt continued cooking something like sweet sauce, but he didn't dare moved out of the room. He couldn't be sure he could resist the smell.

Well, why did she tell him to come back early, especially on the day of his detention? It wasn't as if he'd done badly in her class. Mrs. Gotham's favourites were to detent students for getting *good* marks but the *lowest* in the class. Nathan blamed himself for not looking at his homework at least twice before handing up. He'll ask his aunt later, after dinner, all right?

He finished the work and dumped it in his backpack and ran down the stairs to the smell the sweet sauce. He peeked inside the kitchen, his aunt was cooking and fine, no chance. Then he went to the back garden and looked at all the plants once again, which was his daily routine. He turned on the pipe and watered the plants, then stole a just ripen tomato and cleaned it.

The daisies always made him felt like a girl and vegetables provoked him to get them, he mostly only ate his aunt's vegetables, they were sweeter than anyone's. He looked at the small pond with fat fish swimming, some of these fish were for decoration only and he didn't see the point in that, others were for future seafood dishes and then he noticed one of them was missing, his dinner, perfect.

He ended the watering with spraying some of it into the pond, which scared the small freaking brains of the fishes and they retreated into the depths of the pond. It wouldn't hurt them, it was just reminding them to be energetic. He heard before fishes slept with their eyes open because they had no idea how to close them. He polished the tomato he'd picked earlier.

He waited while switching on the evening political news, sports and comedy, well, it wasn't as good as he thought so he decided to try and *help* his aunt in the kitchen, but she waved him out and away.

The evening dimmed at around 5 p.m. and welcomed the night. His aunt finally came out with plates of food and sauces on a tray. Nathan's gleaming eyes reached her. "We'll eat in the garden," she said and Nathan followed her beeline to the Zen marble table beside the pond.

"Aunt, why did I have to come back early today?" he asked in a tone he thought was innocent. His aunt settled the tray down and began to place the dishes, she looked tired. Nathan knew she worked in some sort of bank as an accountant and somehow decided to apply a leave for today.

"Because I don't want you to be too late," she just replied. The answer took Nathan off guard, he didn't know *what* to say. He just sat on the rock stool and glanced at the food, special that she'd sacrificed one precious fish that she yelled and beat Nathan for throwing rocks at it while he was 12.

The plates for two held delicious-looking food like grilled beef with black pepper sauce and a fish salad with the sweet sauce he'd smelled earlier. Veinna took her seat and set the tray aside. She handed over utensils and somehow looked hesitant or worried. What was she thinking? What was all this about?

Nathan touched the steak with his knife and made sure Veinna saw it, she didn't utter a word, safe. He began cutting it and feeding himself, the sauce warm and the steak soft and both melted in his mouth as he chewed.

Just as he touched the salad, his aunt called his name in such tenderness that shocked him. "Nathan . . ." she began. Nathan placed his fork and knife down and looked at her. She hadn't touch her own food yet and looked at him with a serious face.

"I want to tell you something today," she continued. Nathan waited for her. "You are 14 since last week wasn't it?" Why she was speaking like his? Something weird must have happened.

"I didn't mention this because of you birthday last week, so I will tell you now," she said. "Your parents did leave something for you and I kept it for a long time without telling you. It's actually yours but I want to make sure you're mature enough to hold it without missing," she said and produced a pendant. It was blue and translucent, the size of a coin and tied to a silver chain.

Nathan casually took it from her hands and made a closer look. The thing was actually beautiful, not the *cool* thing he mostly adopted to describe. There were patterns of some kind of flowers at one side and a horse, well, maybe a Pegasus at the other. A silver frame wrapped the edges of it. When he looked closer, he saw cracks inside it. It was made on a purpose somehow, the cracks were uniform and nice in some pattern.

Well, back to the point. She said his parents gave this to him. His parents had died in a train crash or that was what they told him. That's when the lawyers and government workers helped him to arrange the procedures to be adopted by his aunt seven to eight years ago.

"I think you know about the train crash that killed your parents in southern France. Before they died, a week ago while you were sick, they asked me to take care of you and gave me this, said something about giving it to you if anything happened to them. Well, something tragic did happen. I kept this for seven years and now's the time to give it to you," she said.

Nathan pocketed the pendant and looked plainly at her, they seldom brought up the topic about his parents. "Why cook this dinner then? You could just hand this to me," he said, feeling there was something more to it.

"I want you to appreciate this last thing your parents gave to you," she said and kept the silence going on for a moment, hesitating something. "I know the train crash wasn't any pure accident. There might be someone that did that. But my sister and your father didn't ever make any enemies, they even thought twice about killing a bug. The train coached more than 50 people and I wasn't sure about anything, maybe I should stop making assumptions," she said as if regretting about the words.

"Tell me more," Nathan said. He'd lost his appetite, a rare thing to happen. He really wanted to know more about his parents in a particular time but always decided against it. And now, he wanted to know more but at the same time hoped she could stop all this. He pushed himself on, willing his mind to accept.

"I investigated about the train crash seven years ago. I think something had to do with the pendant but your father told me not to show anyone else about it and I didn't. However, I wanted to find out who killed them but without the crystal, it was almost impossible to start. At last, I just accepted the facts the police told me," she said, her eyes looking at a distance as she remembered the pass.

Nathan narrowed his eyes, he never heard about the things she said earlier. "Nathan," his aunt called his name. You know this is very important. If I could somehow *speak* to describe the look in your father's face as he handed me this important pendant, I would tell you. His eyes were enough to tell me how substantial this is. You are 14, you should keep it as me and your father did. All right?" she said.

"Yes," Nathan blankly replied, in his mind trying to picture the face of his parents and the moments when he last met them, hoping the moment could last longer.

"Good boy," she said and ruffled through his brown hair. At that moment, he was the 7-year-old Nathan trying to get attention from his aunt and succeeding. Then, reality came back and his cheeks became rosy red, he pulled away, embarrassed.

His appetite took the express train back to him. He began polishing off his beef steak and fish salad, the sweet sauce a combination of tomato and butter. His aunt ate her food as well, but he noticed her throwing subtle glances at him.

They ate in silence and as Nathan finished the food and got every drop of the sauce, satisfaction eventually came. He chatted with his aunt about the events in school, about how strict and yet funny discipline teachers' distorted faces in disapproving expressions when students left their shirts un-tucked and everything else.

Nathan noticed the change in her as well. She was as if ill at ease, worried, and not being natural in her speaking. She kept showing false interest in every topic. However, Nathan just let that go, he say good-bye and retreated to his room. Before that, he caught a glimpse of his aunt watching him leave.

He took out his crystal, well, so fast in indulging in the possession. He lay down on his bed with the crystal on his chest. For the few moments, he missed them, his parents, maybe even more now than when they had just died. Nathan didn't notice he had slept, teeth un-brushed, just waiting until morning.

Neon lights decorated London's streets. It was night time and he felt the warmth of safeness in his small jacket and with his parents holding his little hands. They looked at him. Was it his birthday? Yeah, he was going to be 6 today.

They guided him as he roamed through the entertainment outlets and played all the things he wanted. He could hear the giggles of a child, not exactly, it was from himself. After what seemed like an eternity, he felt tired and noticed strong hands scooped him to his father's shoulders, he lay on them, exhausted.

They brought him to a restaurant, one of the most formal in London and settled him down on a chair. He remembered he took in the nice carpeted floor, the linen curtains, and the opulence of the wooden furniture lit with the soft yellow light from candles.

He heard voices whisper from the people around and his parents told him a funny story, he giggled again although he couldn't remember what it was about. A waiter came and served a large cake, ice-cream, biscuits and other delicacies, he giggled again.

Soft hands, he thought were his mother's, fed him a big slice of cake and praised him for eating it. The taste was chocolate and milky. It was a taste he will never have again. They fed him more until he felt so full and he finally turned his head away. A pair of hands ruffled his hair, strong but gentle at the same time, his father's hands.

Then, two faces approached in his vision, a masculine and protective face beside a vulnerable and soft look. Both were happy and smiling. His father and mother were together. The parents looked at him longer then walked away without him, gradually vanishing into thin air. Nathan wanted to say good-bye but they just went away, never once did they turn around and say a word.

Chapter Two

AFTER SCHOOL

Nathan handed in the mathematics homework and said good-byes to his friends. He will be staying a bit late in school, not because of the history teacher, but for his swimming hobby.

He remembered about his aunt, she made breakfast for him of toast and tea and didn't mention the matter that happened yesterday, perhaps already wrapped them up to Nathan. She'd said what she had to. Nathan removed the pendant around his neck and kept it in his bag.

He ate a slice of sandwich and drank some water, and then headed for the pool in the school. Nathan will have swimming lessons on the weekends, but he decided to swim for fun, doing the strokes he liked himself instead of being controlled by Roberts, his swimming coach since his was 12 years old.

He went to the lockers and avoided a few big bullies. He brought his backpack. Nathan got to the toilet and changed into swimming shorts and proceeded to the pool. The place was empty except for his friend, also a kid who loved swimming.

The kid was a year younger than Nathan. The younger boy saw him and waved his hand, Nathan replied him with a smile. Nathan took off his shoes and socks and sat beside the pool, Joe Pryor joined him.

"Hey, Nathan, how's school? Got yelled at by teachers yet?" he asked. His clear blue eyes and yellow fair hair was attractive, and the girls in school started to make him their choice. Joe looked small but he was fast in the water, like a speedboat.

"Barely, but the bell rang and she needed to prepare for her next class," Nathan joked and they laughed. He was just joking actually, he never got scolded by any teacher more then once for a week, except *that* history teacher. And he didn't have her class today.

"Did you see Roberts? He gave me forms to pass it to you and James," Joe said.

"What's that?" Nathan asked.

"They're forms for a state competition. Somewhere in Edinburgh, he asked whether our parents agree or not. Hope mine will. I'm tired of going to school," he replied.

"When?"

"Two more weeks and that's it," he replied. "Do you think that James will go or not? We won't actually stand a chance against him, except being his shadow," said Joe.

"I just don't care about him." Nathan waved him off. James Lane, a 17-year-old big bully had pushed Joe into the pool with his school uniform still on when he first arrived. He did this for no clear reason. Nathan got the bully back by hiding his bag containing his clothes and leaving him a note. So he'd to travel all the way to the other side of the school to get them with his muscular body in trunks.

The students took notice and some laughed, some girls thought he wanted some attention, but the discipline teachers wouldn't come without calling his parents. Until today, he still had no idea who did it. Lesson learnt.

"So, tell me more about the contest," Nathan said to Joe.

"Three days if we make it to the final. We go by train with Roberts. And nothing more except more practice," Joe simply replied.

Well, Nathan didn't call forty laps non-stop something like *nothing more*.

"I'm going to warm up," Nathan said and stood up from the edge. He done a few stretches and runs and gone back into the water. Joe tailed him.

They swam together with the whole pool theirs. After about an hour, Nathan swam to the edge and got up. He looked for Joe, he was still doing breast strokes. Nathan called for him and he slowly manoeuvre his way to him.

"What's up?" Joe asked.

"I'm tired," he replied and tried to think about a topic. "Are you free tonight? Tomorrow's Saturday, so my aunt would probably let me stay late," Nathan said.

"Where do you want to go?" he asked. "How about our old place," Nathan just said.

"Wait for you at 4," Joe replied. He stood up and retrieved his small pack of clothes and towels.

Nathan did the same and they walked together to the showers. Nathan washed the chlorine from him and tried to find Joe, but he'd probably gone elsewhere. Joe had left the form near his bag. Nathan dressed into jeans and a jersey.

He called his aunt to ask her if he could go, but surely knew she would agree. He then went to the lockers and got his wallet. Nathan hanged around the library, looking for comics and finished his homework early because there was really nothing to do.

He waited for the hour to pass and finally took the Tube to their old place. It was one of his favourite streets in Central London, they often hanged out there since they were friends.

Nathan was already waiting at their old street. It was 3:45 p.m. The sun was beginning to set below the horizon. The sky was like orange-yellow liquid, slowly changing the colour from yellow in the west to orange in the east, forming an eye-catching display.

The traffic had settled, with only a few cars heading home, the drivers tired of the whole day's work. The traffic lights seemed to be useless for the moment, flashing red lights while the entire street was so empty. Any car could speed 80 kilometers an hour without needing to worry much. But surely no one would dare.

Nathan was waiting in front of a bicycle shop as they decided to meet, old place where he was taken for his 13th birthday. The smell of rubber was strong. The shop was packed with new and branded bikes on the front and old ones behind. There were also spare-parts, bulbs and riding equipments.

He stood in his T-shirt and jeans that he'd changed into at the school. He had brought 10 pounds with him, just in case he needed it, he felt comfortable in the cooling environment with an occasion breeze.

Central London swarmed, it was filled by a lot of people trying to cheer up in the entertainment area. And sure, although his parents did bring him here before, he didn't recall the past memories, but he was in a fine mood, and good things seemed to happen today. His watch told him that five more minutes and Joe would arrive.

As a few minutes passed, Nathan felt a little uneasy, as if being watched. This occurred sometimes, but mostly when he was outdoors. He didn't want to be paranoid, but this was like every person and car that passed had something to do with it. It was a feeling of suspicion. In other words, he might have been followed.

This feeling vanished as he saw a small figure heading across the road towards him. It was Joe, smiling and waving a hand towards him. He wore a collared black jacket, and black long trousers. He walked over and spoke to him.

"You're just in time, good evening Nathan. Have you been waiting long?" Joe said as he glanced at his watch.

"Evening Joe. I'm just early today," he replied.

"Come on, let's go."

The two of them walked deeper into the streets. He just wanted to throw all the weird feelings away, they may spoil the mood. The middle of London was especially fun and entertaining, with places to hang out. They had a good time.

First, they went into the freaking ghost house that had just opened. The tickets were cheap. Inside it was dark, with just a few lights posted on the wall to show the way. The ghost figures seemed to come out of nowhere and gave them nasty looks. But Nathan admitted they were close to reality.

There were ghosts, zombies, vampires and nasty creatures. Nathan knew they were fake beings, but in the dim light with smoke, they really made him shiver. Plus, the make-up and costumes were the work of professional dressers. The ghost house ended after a few minutes of walking through and screaming. The two of them had fun. And that was the point of ghost house.

Next, they ate finger food and played various games, winning a bunch of prizes and girlish teddy bears. Joe said that the toy was a waste of a prize, so he dumped it right into the trash bin.

They enjoyed the games for an hour, targeting ducks on platforms with fake guns, grabbing something they like in the glass cube with a steel arm, riding a roller coaster until they yelled their heads off. At last, they decided to watch a movie in the cinema.

"That was fun Joe," Nathan said as they walked.

"Do you remember the look of the worker when we shot his yellow ducks? He just lost a fortune." They both laughed.

"You remember the event in the ghost house, I accidentally put a fist into the worker's face when he scared me with the vampire costume. I hope he's fine," Nathan said.

"Oh! Did you see the expression in his face when the mask drop, ridiculous," laughed Joe.

"And he dropped his vampire's teeth!" added Nathan.

"Do you think he'll resign from the ghost house, your knuckles are hard?"

"No, he'll scare people more with the bruise in his face," chuckled Nathan.

"So, let's go to the cinema business, which movie is nice today?" asked Joe.

"Anything, you choose."

"So, I buy the tickets and the food's done by you. Order me a Sprite and butter pop corn." They entered the cinema. There were people there all around, mostly teens and some adults.

"Let's meet at the cinema entrance."

They both went in their respective directions and Nathan lined up as he enjoyed the decoration. The ticket counter was on the left of the entrance. It had a chest-height marble wall and fixed glasses supported by a few bars of metalwork.

A few workers sat behind the counter, dressed in black overalls with ties hung neatly down to their waists. They were trying to be as polite as they could but Nathan knew that asking the same questions over and over again. "Sir, which movie and what time. Ma'am, which cinema room and what seat number? Is your son older than 12? If yes, then there's an extra fee."

There were 20 more people lining up. Watching the schedule of the movies projected on the screens screwed in place on the ceilings. Joe was already ordering the tickets at counter seven.

The entrance to the cinema units were guarded by big-sized men, armed with iron batons protruding out of their belts. Their bloodshot eyes were hidden behind their dark shades.

It was Nathan's turn. He ordered the food from a cheerful female worker in her early twenties, she was still new. He then paid her. He took the drinks and popcorn with him and waited at the entrance. Joe was already on his way back with the tickets.

"Which time did you book?" Nathan asked as Joe approached.

"Eight fifteen, half an hour from now," Joe replied as he handed the ticket and searched for his Sprite. He drank a little from the paper cup.

Nathan retrieved the ticket as something caught his attention in the side of his eye. He noticed someone outside the cinema down the street, it was an American man in his late twenties. He wore a waistcoat with and long jeans.

He was staring directly at Nathan, his eyes were bloodshot and serious, surely overworked. He stood with his back leaning on the brickwork of a shop, reading The Times when Nathan looked at him.

He was sure that the American tried not to be suspicious, pretended to be reading the newspaper and looking at the advertisement board of the cinema. He only glanced at Nathan when he was facing the other side.

What was this man doing? Was he spying on his every move? Anyway, Nathan knew they must often changed shifts when following him to avoid being suspicious, he hadn't seen him before. But this one was new, perhaps.

Every instinct in Nathan's mind told him to follow the man if possible, he may not have the chance again. No one stood near the cinema with a newspaper in their hands.

Nathan turned to Joe. "Do you see the man in black attire, with The Times in his hands? He looks like he's watching over us." He turned to Joe for confirmation.

Joe looked around and craned his neck. He glanced back at Nathan. "Who? I don't see anyone with a newspaper here."

"Not here, outside the cinema. He's down the street." Nathan was careful not to point any finger towards him.

Joe looked outside and laid his palm over his friend's shoulder, he looked concerned. "Are you feeling well, I don't see anyone you're talking about," he sounded sympathetic. *No one?* Nathan thought.

He looked out of the cinema again. The man in black was gone. Nathan rubbed his eyes and massaged his temples. But he wasn't imagining, he noticed The Times thrown on a pile of rubbish in the nearby trash bin, just a few meters from where the man had stood.

"I'll be back, just give me 10 minutes," he said as he handed the drinks and food to Joe.

"Wait! Where are you going?" He scrambled the packets unstably.

"Give me some time, I'll be back."

The next thing he knew, he was running to the street. He apologized as he knocked a woman. Nathan glanced left and right and he saw the American's back, the same black overalls and the same height. He followed him.

Nathan ran quickly while trying to hide as much as the sound of his trainers hitting the road and slowed down, making 10 meters of distance between the man and himself. The man was walking along the buildings.

Despite his bright shoes and laces, he could hide very fast into the shadows, with a perfect camouflage of black jersey and dark blue jeans, just in case the man turned around.

There were only a few people on the streets and that was a good thing, the man will always be in his sight. The only bad thing about this was if he were caught, there were not many people around to help him.

This disadvantage changed as the man headed to the central square, the place was still filled with people. Nathan glanced at his watch, three minutes had passed.

The man stopped and turned around. Just in time, Nathan threw himself into the shadows near the single-story building, lying flat on his stomach.

After a few seconds, he heard the man continued walking and let out a sigh of relief. It was so close. He got up on one knee watched. The man looked left and right, ensuring no one was following him. He quickly walked into a narrow and quiet street with no lighting.

Counted five seconds, Nathan stood up and followed that American, careful not to expose himself in the light, just for precautions. He was aware not to be taken by surprise if he realized his presence.

The path was only 15 meters wide and full of large trash bins, the smell of sewage and dust. It was dark and uninviting.

Nathan leant flat on his back against the wall, ignoring the dirt, just prepared for hiding behind the bins if needed. He proceeded side by side, like walking on a railway. His heart was beating twice as usual, afraid that the man would look back. If he did, Nathan would be in big trouble.

The man walked to the dead end of the back street. There was a door and he knocked on it. Nathan hid behind a trash bin, crouching and hiding his bright-coloured trainers.

Nathan couldn't see the figure properly, it was dark. It was something like man in his late twenties, maybe French, wearing the same black attire like the American.

"How's it doing?" asked the French in thick accented English. They were not so cautious, talking outside instead of inside the house.

"Watching the boy, you mean?" the American spoke, heavy in his own country's accents. Although they were whispering, it was clear enough for Nathan.

"Sure, tell me all about tonight's watch," the French asked, emotionless. Nathan was now worried about his escape, if he snuck back to the main street now, he surely be spotted, but if the two of them walk towards the streets, he'll be dead. There was no retreat now.

"He's quite happy today, hanging out in the streets of London with a friend like his own age." Nathan was shocked to hear that.

Someone had watched him and Joe from the start, so his suspicious feeling was right. But he was still not perfectly sure, many other boys were just like them, hanging out after school. But the problem was the man had been spying on him just now.

"Do your work precisely, do you have a gun?"

"Model 18, with a 33 bullet capacity chamber," said the American. Nathan felt a wave of coldness ran up his spine, someone with a gun had work to do with him.

Nathan now regretted his decision. If he'd just ignored the American, he would be in the cinema, enjoying the movie with Joe. The public and police will protect him and they would not dare to hurt him.

"Good, make sure you bring enough ammunition, just in case," said the Frenchman.

"I heard he will be going to Edinburgh next week, you want to add more men?" the American asked.

Edinburgh, next week? Cinema and game stalls? A friend about his age? Nathan confirmed that they were talking about him. He needed to listen more.

"I have news from spies that the Ventures may interrupt our work. Request Region Force for back-up, I can't handle them myself. Also, remember to send me a teammate," said the Frenchman, sounding more serious than before. And what was Region Force or even who? What? Where?

"Where's boss, we are reporting this to him. He needs to know this changes," spat out the American.

"I'll lead the way," the French said.

Nathan eyes widened, his worst dreams had come to reality. The both of them will spot him in seconds! He had to hide no matter what, but with this trash bin and in this narrow road, what can provide cover.

Running was the last thing he would dare to do, not so fast with only a few seconds and without making any sound. He thought of throwing himself into the trash bin, but it wouldn't work, there wasn't even enough time.

He looked around and noticed two pages of a newspaper. Immediately, he snatched it up and covered himself, minimizing his body size by curling into a ball with head close to tight, hands around the legs and body bent. The newspaper was just in place when they turned around.

It was only just enough big for him. He felt the pressure of his knees compressing his lungs and ribs. He hoped the newspaper won't fall off when they came.

Now all he could do was to stay in place, seconds deciding his fate between life and death. Nathan held his breathe, his heart was pounding against his chest, threatening to jump out.

"Hey, do you hear that," asked the American. He must have heard the noise when Nathan snatched the newspaper. Nathan froze in fear.

"Maybe it's a rat eating cockroaches. Be quick, you don't want the boss to wait," the French said, feeling very annoying to work with that guy, new and inexperienced. Anyway, Nathan thanked for him to not be suspicious.

The American glanced around, he saw a pile of old newspaper beside a large trash bin in the dark corner and hissed at it, then unhappily followed that French guy. The two of them passed Nathan with only a few centimeters and a piece of paper separating them. Nathan breathed out in relief as they went into the streets. His luck was not that bad.

Nathan thought back about the conversation, he was annoyed that anyone would spy on him. It was about life and death after one week in Edinburgh, and he didn't want to sit in the train, worrying about everything suspiciously.

Even if he cancelled his participation in the contest, the condition was not better and the facts were the same, it was only the matter of time and place. He could report to the police, but they would just laugh at him, or be annoyed with and teenager trying to play with them. He wanted to know the meaning of Region Force, who was their boss and what was happening. At last, he decided to follow them to their boss.

Chapter Three

FROZEN FEAR

Nathan got up to his feet, threw down the pieces of dirty newspapers and tip-toed to the streets again. He felt grateful about his rubber trainers, with the combination of the concrete pavement, his footsteps were barely audible.

He saw the two men walking together. They were very aware and suspicious, looking sideways and occasionally backward. This forced Nathan into the buildings' shadows and the trash bins for cover. Nathan was worried about getting caught and the thought made him tingle, and shiver ran down his spine. He stayed about 20 meters distance between him and the men.

Nathan glanced at his watch, eight minutes had passed, he was scared he wasn't going to make it back to the cinema, it'll surely disappoint Joe. But he had to know more about this, this also involved Joe's safety as well, they'd mentioned him in the secret conversation.

The weird thing about the conversation was about the Frenchman saying that he requested backup to do the work. If they wanted to kill him, one killer was enough, he was not one of the superheroes on television. And that didn't include the weird army force called Region Force.

It took Nathan a minute to realize that the two men were heading to the square, where the roller coaster and game stalls were located. Nathan passed the cinema and looked for Joe, maybe he could change his mind and head back and just ignore everything. However, Joe was not in sight, he'd probably gone somewhere else.

Despite the thought of giving up on what he managed to find out (except the inexperienced American), he insisted on following both of them to their boss.

Nathan and the men reached the square. The place was getting quiet and people were starting to go home. However, he would have enjoyed the scene of relaxing and fun if he wasn't following two men with guns.

The men didn't give out any emotion, just the pale and empty eyes with grey pupils behind the shades. The two men had no fun in their lives at all. Their mornings were spent spying, their afternoons revolved around paperwork. The evenings saw more training, and then report in at night. Finally, they'd go to sleep with a gun under their pillow. Nathan was sure they had been teenagers before like his own age, but what did they do to enjoy? He couldn't figure out anything.

Nathan quickened his steps, nearing 10 meters. He didn't need to worry about the sound he made, the roller coaster and the voices of the remaining people were helping a lot. On the other hand, getting spotted wasn't that biggest problem now, he could turn to one of the game stalls if the men turned around, he just looked like a teenager playing. Their guns were not so useful now with so many witnesses around, and shooting a 14-year-old boy in the public for only suspecting him following them would be nonsense.

Nathan reckoned that would not happen. The two men walked along a fleet of shops, some entertainment types, some selling food and lastly, a larger one isolated from the others. It was opulent with its large and inviting entrance with a counter selling tickets. There was an advertisement poster and a board at the entrance, trying to tempt anyone who passed by.

Nathan had been in this place, just a half an hour before. It was the ghost house. The place was already closing, the entrance door was half closed with workers coming out in groups, chatting and half-awake guards preparing to end their miserable shift, leaning against the wall. The place was dark, as only a few dim lights lit it.

The men stopped into a halt just in front of the entrance. Nathan hid inside a food supply shop, about 30 meters away from them, opposite from the house. The two men looked, waiting.

Nathan brought a packet of chocolate milk and drank slowly. It tasted milky sweet, he was thirsty after following them. Nathan positioned himself near the store's entrance. The owner of the shop didn't care much, he's sleepy and counting time until the working hours end.

Nathan assumed they were waiting until all the workers had gone, and then they could seek in. It wasn't pleasant for Nathan if he needed to follow the men into the ghost house. The building was too quiet and he'll be shot dead if they spotted him. He told himself not to panic and cooled down, then concentrated on the drink.

After five minutes, with the ghost house empty, the men took a last glance around and went to the back of the place.

Nathan drank the last sip of the drink and throws the bottle into a nearby trash bin, he counted a few seconds, making sure that the men were inside. Certainly he wanted to avoid being ambushed in a backstreet of London.

He didn't want to be a boy found dead in a backstreet with a bullet in the chest. Or even worse, a schoolboy found missing after playing at Central London with no reason. What would Joe think about it? And his aunt, school friends and teachers, no one will ever find the truth if he were dead. Nathan shivered at that thought. Somehow, he knew he'll not die in such way. Bracing himself, he headed for the backstreet.

The street was dark and uninviting, with only one bulb giving out light. The air was full of dust and the air smelt of sewage and trash. Nathan felt the presence of mice and cockroaches by the occasional weird sound and movement. He crouched behind an abandoned car and watched as they unlocked the back door and went in. He waited for a few moments, there was no sound of the door being locked again. He went near it.

On the door it read: **STAFF ONLY.** Someone had pasted a car engine oil advertisement. Somehow, no one ever bothered to enter the back door or buy the oil, so the writing and poster seemed useless. He put his ear on the wooden door, trying to make sure no one was guarding near it. At last, he twisted the handle, and the door wasn't locked.

Quietly, Nathan slipped in and closed the door again. He was in a store room lit by four naked bulbs. It was full of a stockpile of boxes and cardboards, along with empty beer cans, burnt cigarettes and trash. The boxes contained make-up equipment, clothes and beer. They were all stacked up in the metal selves untidily. Nathan saw a door that led into a better lit corridor. He went for it.

The corridor's sides were constructed with several rooms on each side with doors. One of them was a large make-up room. The room contained a series of mirrors, tables with seats, various make-up creams, face powder and a comb. They were all scattered on the table, with caps unsealed and filthy mirrors, ghosts didn't need to be clean. Anyway, the make-ups of the human vampires were close to reality even being prepared in this non-immaculate room.

Surprisingly, Nathan heard three voices. He recognized the French and American speaking and another unknown masculine voice nodding occasionally. Immediately, he hid himself behind the door frame and peeked out at them.

The boss wore a dark green T-shirt advertising beer and jeans, he was in his late thirties with bloodshot eyes and a muscular body. He drank vodka slowly, balancing the bottle in his gigantic hands. There was a box of guns on the nearby make-up table. Five handguns with ammunition. Nathan must be more careful.

The two men explained the same issue to their boss that he had eavesdropped. After finishing, the French sat down on the chair and wrote something onto a stack of papers, frowning sometimes. He cursed the pen and shook it hard, it must lack ink. He then threw it away as if it had bitten him. It looked like he was having a hard time writing a report of the day's work in English instead of French.

Meanwhile, the American took a black thing, a gun, and slipped it into his belt, then he walked to the corridor. He was told to guard this place for the night. Nathan hid in one of the unlocked rooms as he approached, then spied on the boss and the French for one last time. The boss was drinking the remaining vodka and checking the box of weapons. For the moment, nothing happened.

Nathan was bored and wanted to know more. He rapidly passed the room, staying as low as possible. The line of sight between the boss and him was blocked by the other table, he didn't need to worry much about crossing over.

He continued down the corridor where the American had gone. It was darker and scarier here. After a few meters of silent walking, he passed an unlocked door and realized there were a few constructed gaps on the wall of the corridor. There were metal steps he could use to climb up and pass through the gap, if he needed to escape out of sight.

He understood that it was made for the "ghosts" to hide and surprise their customers. However, he didn't realize that this existed when he was with Joe.

Suddenly, he heard a metallic *click* and saw some iron gears attached to the metal steps working. The metal steps moved aside to reveal a trap door. It opened. In seconds, he knew the American would spot him.

He couldn't fight with him, the man had a loaded gun, even if he overcame him with an immediate knock-out-blow, the boss and the French may suspect some intruder's presence and search for him.

Nathan quickly looked for any cover but failed. There was only one way to get out of sight. He climbed up another metal step near him and passed through the gap. He was now in the customer's passageway. It was so dark and unlit until he failed to see his five fingers. Only the dim light from the gap made him felt better.

He heard approaching footsteps and then they gradually faded, it must be the American. After making sure the footsteps gone faint and eventually vanished, he returned to the corridor, Nathan was interested in the trap door and what was beyond.

He looked for the trap door, it was still open. The American must be carless again, thinking it was impossible for anyone to enter here without being noticed. Risking his own safety, he entered. The trap door was built on the floor, there was a metal ladder that led to underground. It was 10 meters deep.

The hidden room was lit by a red bulb on the wall. It was a small department with boxes on a bare floor. Surprisingly, the place was clean, but not decorated so lifeless. Nathan focused on one of the boxes. It was plastered by a black logo. The logo was about a dove accompanied by four stars with a name written on it.

REGION FORCE

Nathan opened one of the boxes, he needed to tear the tape plastered onto it. The box contained a few sets of uniform. There were blue helmets, dark green, long trousers and green army shirts, bulletproof jackets and a few badges, printed by the same logo and words on the box.

Nathan felt a slight feeling that the puzzle in his head had moved a centimeter. The secret conversation became more relevant. And they rented this ghost house to conceal the uniform of Region Force Army. But he still did not know why they wanted to kill him. He heard the metallic sound of shoes brushing against metal.

The American was climbing down! There was no way he could run or hide here and the man was armed. He turned around and faced the American. He was half climbing down the metal ladder and stopped, with a gun readied and aimed at his chest. He saw the serious face of the American in the red light.

"Don't move," he hissed. He climbed down the last step, still aiming at him. "Lie on the floor now, if you don't want me to shoot you!"

Nathan knew any aggressive movement made will make his heart into a burst packet of blood, certain death. The American was aiming steadily at his heart. He might be inexperienced but he knew where the trigger was and how to pull.

But Nathan had a slight knowledge about handguns. The safety clip wasn't released so the man needed one second to pull the clip before he could open any fire. Nathan was forced to obey what this man said, so he didn't remove the safety clip as a warning, but lying on the floor and waiting for him to tie his hands was as good as being dead. One second, one hope. He needed his best.

Nathan forced some tears out of his eyes, they must be exactly real. It was hard, he wasn't the type that liked to cry, but he thought about everything that was sad in his life. Somehow, the tears he squeezed were enough and they filled his eyes and then spilt onto the floor. He sniffed and distorted his face in sadness and fear. He tried to pull the sympathy out of the man.

Luckily, the man relaxed a little, knowing he was dealing only with a schoolboy. He walked a little forward. But he wouldn't take any risk, the handgun was tightly held in his hands. In a moment, Nathan gathered all the possibilities of survival. First, one second, the safety clip. Second, his act of fear distracted the man, thinking he was only dealing with a young boy and that made him letdown his guard a bit. Third, he had learned a little self-defence techniques in the taekwondo class and he could prove it was worth tonight, but attacking now wouldn't help a lot. The last one will be revealed soon, after the man got closer to Nathan. His calculations were perfect.

He waited until the man got close onto him, until three meters separated them. Nathan could see the sympathy in his eyes, but he was enough alert to fend off any surprises at that time.

Nathan now directed his eyes direction to the ladder and widened them, he then inhaled air, making a sound of surprise. It distracted the American a little but it's not enough, he just moved his eyes a little, the gun was still in his hands.

"It's that you boss, Spassky. I've got this boy. Come and help me," said the American. Now Nathan knew the French's name but it may be coded, "Looks like our job is done here, our cover's blown, no more spying!" he said. His voice hung with a heavy French accent. Nathan shook his head and backed off a little, he flattened his back against the bare concrete wall. The man may be clever not to turn back when he suspected his friend was behind him by the look of the boy's eyes, just not to be distracted. He could be taken by surprise. But Nathan was cleverer, the American was talking to nobody. Nathan now breathed heavily and fast, making as much sound he could for the American to hear.

There was still no reply. And there would not be one, either.

Chapter Four

GHOST TRICK

Nathan hardened his muscles, preparing to strike when his only hope came true. The man froze, suspecting there was a ghost behind him but he didn't believe in ghosts, they were just stories made by adults to fear children. Anyway, his curiosity overcame caution, he risked a look. He was shocked that there was no one behind him, not even a ghost. He knew he had been tricked but that it was too late.

At that moment, Nathan slammed the hand holding the gun away from his direction and side-kicked the man in the chest, he felt something break from the immense impact, the ribs, probably. The man staggered backwards and hit the wall, not even shouting, and rolled his back down and sat on the floor. The gun was still in his hands and he still had consciousness.

A stream of blood flowed out of his mouth. Nathan pulled one of the bulletproof jackets out of the opened box and held it in front of him.

The man removed the safety clip realizing keeping the boy alive was a blunder. And he looked for revenge for being tricked him and breaking his ribs. One second.

Nathan then snatched two helmets with the strip and braced for the impact. The man fired. Nathan could feel the force of the bullets hitting the bulletproof jacket. He felt as if something had stabbed his chest and stomach and he staggered backwards, falling down. He then threw the two helmets at the man. One helmet hit him in the chest, breaking another bone, another slammed into his temple, making a gash-type wound and knocking him out on the spot.

Nathan clutched his chest and stomach with both hands, the bullets somehow bruised him but none made contact with his flesh. He coughed and regained his breath.

He was lucky that the man didn't shoot him in the leg or head because the bulletproof jacket wasn't enough big to cover either part of his body.

Then he examined the unconscious American, lying on the floor with broken bones and the gun still in his loose grip. Nathan cursed him, he had just shot five bullets at a 14-year-old unarmed boy, such an idiot coward. If the jacket wasn't in place or even late a second, the man's shot would have killed him.

He'd never been shot at and this was his first deadly experience, he was lucky to successfully get out with his life on this one. He realized that the gun didn't make much noise when it fired. He now saw a silencer on the gun's muzzle. The shots just produced and puff of smoke and a hiss, very quiet. That gave him a few minutes before the Frenchman and the boss found out what happened, thank God, his luck seemed to be continue. And now he possessed the Model 18 handgun.

No time to examine his bruise, he grabbed the gun from the unconscious man, he didn't want to encounter the other two men unarmed. He climbed the ladder while taking one last look at the American and said, "I hope you were really talking to ghost just now, have some bad dreams tonight. Get a headache."

Nathan climbed up the ladder and closed the trap door. He found a hidden lever and pulled, then some gears worked and the metal steps disappeared automatically. He counted 28 bullets left, as five had been used on him.

An evil part of Nathan now hesitated to kill, the knock-out-blow lasted only a few minutes, he didn't have another bulletproof jacket, it was too bulky and heavy for him to wear. However, he didn't intend to kill anyone in cold blood. Since the man had given him a chance by not shooting him immediately when he was found, to be generous, he repaid him this once.

He couldn't risk being here, he wanted to get out of there, and every second counted. Nathan wouldn't take the risk of going back and sneaking out using the back door, and he didn't have much time to hesitate. He decided to continue, he may have a chance if the front door was locked from the inside. He still could run to London's streets and vanish into the crowd, staying away from this underworld.

He walked along the corridor and reached another room a few meters away. There were no more routes to proceed except the room. He pushed the creaking door open. The room was very dark. It was a dressing room from what he could tell by his first look.

The place was messy with costumes and clothes hung by metalwork nailed to the walls. Those costumes only worked in the dark and scared people. If someone ever dared to wear one in the day before the public's eyes, he surely would be one of the topics in the news: Insane man pretends to be a ghost.

Nathan's attention shifted onto the masks tied to strings, which hung down from the ceiling. He had seen some of them before. But only one he could never forget: the black and red mask with only one vampire tooth. He punched the person who wore it. He wanted to laugh out loud but all the humour wore off as he heard Spassky shouting.

"Boss! Someone had been here, Rave has fainted," he shouted. The American's name was Rave. He'd been discovered, no, not yet but soon.

After a few moments, he heard a pair of footsteps rushing nearer to him, and then stopped. "What the hell! How did anyone enter, we guarded it? I don't care if Rave suffers a brain damage or comma. The problem is our job's crushed. Now, you go and find the person before he gets away. Do you have a gun?" yelled the boss.

"I handed it to Rave just now," said the French.

"The where is it now?"

"I'm sure he has taken it!"

"Idiot! Now we have to deal with him, armed, it's all your fault. The Region Force must fire us and you will be a hotel cleaner again!" said the boss.

"It's not my fault. Rave is responsible for all this. He must be careless in the field, someone became suspicious and followed him here and I don't know how he sneaked into here!"

"I told you all to be more careful when following that boy."

"What could he do? He is just 14 years old, just a child."

"He may call for reinforcement or the police. Hold this gun, go and find him in the customer's passageway, I'll search the corridor," ordered the boss.

Nathan knew they'll not suspect him to be here but time was getting short, there was no more exit from this dressing room except the door he gone through, and boss was getting nearer each second. He couldn't go out now, the boss would spot him immediately.

There was no place to hide, the hanging clothes were too close to the wall and couldn't conceal him behind them, even though he could fit, the risk was too high. The mask concealed his face only, it was surely not working. He could hide in the dark around the corner but his fair face didn't help a lot. But the combination of darkness and the mask may help.

Nathan had only one escape chance, he noticed that the masks were in the dark. He quickly positioned himself in the dark behind one of the masks and bent his waist, it was just enough to conceal his face and his body was in the dark with the camouflage of dark-coloured shirt. He made sure that his shoes were hidden far into the dark, just in case.

Now, only one thing was left, the lights. He pointed the gun towards the switch near the door and fired two shots, he heard a hiss and the plastic cracked.

Not wasting anymore time, he went back into the hiding position. After a second, he heard the door bust open, it was just enough time for him to shut his eyes. He heard the boss hitting the switch several times and become frustrated. He was lucky for not getting electrocuted for touching a spoiled switch. The boss swore and kicked the door.

He walked into the room and scanned at the costumes, and then at the masks, Nathan guessed. He felt a slight breeze when the boss brushed passed him, his heart beat so fast like something ramming into the chest. He relaxed as the man went farther. He didn't even notice he was standing just a few centimeters from who he was looking. What a fool!

Nathan now hesitated. If the boss didn't find anyone here, he'd return to the make-up room and lock the backdoor. If so, Nathan would never have the chance to escape with both routes guarded. He couldn't wait longer in the ghost house, they may call for reinforcement. Nathan waited until the boss' back was facing the door, when he'll be temporally out of sight. Then he sneaked out of the room quietly.

Unfortunately, when he was at the door frame, he heard the boss yelling and a deafening sound. Waves of heat passed him and they were bullets. Some hit the doorframe and the wood fragments smashed into Nathan's shoulder, tearing his jersey and cutting his flesh. But he was lucky the bullets didn't hit him.

Now he didn't have time to decide where to continue. The madman was only meters behind him. Running along the corridor and escaping from the back door was crazy.

The corridor was now lit with a few bulbs and that was not good, sure they had switched on the switches when Spassky found Rave unconscious. If he used the corridor, he seemed like a dummy in a target practice field, with a straight corridor and no cover, completely suicidal. The costumers' passageway may have no cover but it was dark, making the man harder to target Nathan.

Left with only one survival chance, he climbed up the metal steps and slipped through the gap, he then ran as fast as he could, hoping the boss with not shoot him and he'd not meet with Rave. He examined his wounds while running, they were not serious, only a few gashes and mild bleeding.

Nathan now hoped he didn't follow them. He turned left, trying to dig all his memories about this place, he needed to escape fast. He could hear boss's heavy footsteps and shouts of pursuit.

After a several turns, he reached a figure, it was Spassky. He tried to retreat but boss was already there. Spassky cursed and pointed the gun at him. The boss smiled.

At the last moment, Nathan threw himself onto the floor and lied flat on his stomach. Spassky opened fire. He was the third cruel man trying to kill a schoolboy. Hot air rushed pass him, just a centimeter closer, his brain may burst. Nathan picked the right choice, the costumers' passage way was darker and the bullets missed him.

Nathan was unhurt, but the boss was not so fortunate. One of the bullets hit boss's arm, penetrating flesh and bone. He yelled. He heard a disgusting sound and a snap, which was a bone. Boss staggered backwards and fell, groaning and cursing his friend. Spassky was shocked by the surprising event, he'd shot his boss.

That's the time when Nathan made a 150 degree horizontal, butterfly stroke kick. His leg hit both of Spassky's and the Frenchman stumbled. Nathan quickly pulled out his own gun and pointed it at the vulnerably positioned Spassky.

"No!" he begged. Nathan didn't intend to kill anyone, he just wanted to scare him and escape in one piece. He brought the gun down and rammed it to the right side of the head, not very hard. Spassky was unconscious before he registered what hit him.

Although one arm was injured, the boss was still strong and offered more resistance, he was muscular. Nathan noticed the boss was unarmed, he had lost his gun in the dark. Nathan ran but was surprised about the man's speed. The boss rammed his good shoulder into Nathan's, making him lose a little balance.

Then, he caught his hand and turned his wrist. A flash of pain ran up to Nathan's shoulder and he shouted, he must have dislocated it. Nathan was disarmed.

Knowing he was distracted by pain, the boss positioned himself right in front of his opponent and lashed out at his knee, he hit Nathan's chest and stomach and threw him a few meters away. That was a front kick, one of the most lethal ones.

Nathan felt sick now, his dinner rushed all around him. Every laboured breath rewarded him with a flash of pain in his ribs, but he hoped they would be fine. He lay on his back, semi-conscious and in pain.

"Okay, let's start. Why are you here, young boy?" asked boss, a palm clutching his wounded arm, blood was soaking his sleeves and dripping down. Nathan hoped the boss would faint from loss of blood.

"You should ask your men when they are out of bed," said Nathan, grasping for air.

"Don't be funny. I know you're quite good in combat, three against one and you knocked down two in a cunning way."

Nathan was trying to find for Spassky's gun just a few centimeters behind him beside the unconscious body. In this position, he was too vulnerable to attack or defend. If he could get the gun in his hands, he may stand a chance to escape.

"By the way, how did you come here?" asked the boss. He wasn't even trying to pick up the gun that he had disarmed from Nathan.

"Your friend Rave was a bit new I think, he made me suspicious," Nathan said.

"So, you're Nathan Doyle. How did he make you felt suspicious?" He knew his name and that wasn't very shocking.

"No one ever takes a newspaper into the cinema, his actions were not natural."

"You have good potential, very alert, looks like they didn't choose the wrong person."

"You mean who? Some kind of army called Region Force."

"Looks like you have known a lot of things, you had been busy in the hidden room. Tell me more, clever boy."

"You and your workers and the army are trying to kill me." He had found the gun and tried to wait for the right moment to use when it was the most surprising to use it. "If you want to kill me, why do you need an army to do it?"

"But we are not here to kill you. We thought you were an intruder. You don't expect us to see in the dark"

"Then what are you doing? Don't tell me you're doing some job spying me like James Bond. I have watched enough of his movies. Anyway, he's more handsome than you, you are a freak, ugly."

The boss brought up a hand to protest. "Hey, boy, we were trying to deal some other army that wanted to kill you. And we are not interested in you." Nathan felt weird about the word *protecting* but it didn't matter, they were harming him just now.

"Well, I don't care what you say, those guys followed me just now and you shot at me, I was saved from the first shot by your Region Force bulletproof jacket and you call that protecting me? You are an insane, fake James Bond!"

"Enough! I'm doing a favour for you and you are now making a fool of me! Damn y . . ." yelled the boss. It was the moment when Nathan revealed the gun, when the target was angry and let down his guard. The boss threw himself to the floor, unharmed as Nathan fired. Then Nathan sprang to his feet and ran for his life. He heard the boss shouting in pursuit.

Nathan found the main entrance to the ghost house after a few turns. He fired at the door locks and pulled the fire alarm. Red lights filled the darkness and the bell rang. There was even water spraying down from the ceiling. He saw the boss running towards him.

There was a cylindrical trash bin and Nathan picked in up and threw it into the air towards the boss's direction. Then he fired a few shots to the ground near the boss, distracting him. By the time he registered the trick, the whole dust bin's contents spilt all over his body, with the spraying water mixed with trash. The boss yelled and cursed him.

Nathan put down the gun and headed for the main entrance's door and ran away, putting as much distance between him and this underworld, which claimed to protect him but actually shot at him. Leaving the boss into a miserable condition, he smiled.

He also noticed a fire engine in the distance moving towards the ghost house and eventually stopped, the alarm must have called them here automatically.

Anyway, how was the boss going to explain about the false alarm? Nathan couldn't imagine how he would handle this. He wanted to report this to the police but they'd think he's just too free after school and making fun. They wouldn't trust him somehow. He still didn't want too much attention from anyone, his aunt would kill him.

Now, Nathan thought of himself, wounded and exhausted. He didn't know how to explain all this to Joe for being late to the movies for almost a half hour, and how to explain the wounds to Veinna. He decided to explain that someone robbed him in the backstreet. He went to the nearest 24-four hour supply shop and brought bandages, medicine and a new jersey.

Surely, it must affect his swimming lessons and the contest in Edinburgh. Now, he could just relax for those insane guys had claimed to be protecting him, they were out of their minds, nothing to do after work and pretending to be some sort of spies. He decided to ignore them completely, it just spoiled the entire mood.

He headed to the cinema and apologized to Joe and used the robbing excuse. Joe seemed to be more concerned rather than disappointed. He barely enjoyed the show after the events in the ghost house, his shoulder was still sore and the wrist hurt, too.

The both of them finished the movie and headed home. Veinna helped him with the wounds. He had to lie that the medicine and jersey were brought by Joe because he had been robbed, luckily she trusted him and didn't report it to the police after Nathan convinced her. He had gone into a deep sleep after that. It was a restless and uncomfortable sleep but he somehow managed to grab a few hours of rest for the next day.

Chapter Five

EDINBURGH'S RIDE

THE LAST TWO WEEKS WERE occupied with swimming lessons and school. Nathan's wounds were healing well and his aunt found a Chinese medical doctor to repair his dislocated wrist.

The doctor examined his wrist, then even without hesitating, he used some technique and twisted the wrist again. Nathan felt the same sort of pain he had in the ghost house, but this was different, the pain lasted for a few seconds and was gone without a trace. His hand recovered completely, despite the soreness.

Somehow, the miracle cost 50 pounds and demanded fast cash. In school, Nathan was a bit shy when there were swimming lessons, with him being naked to the waist and all those bruises and the gash. These wounds provided him more attention from his swimming mates.

Meanwhile, Mr. Roberts seemed unconcerned as Nathan approached him for explanation, "Learn some self-defense technique and the robbers won't snatch your sweets!" That's what the coach said.

Veinna and Joe accepted the false robbing excuse and didn't ask a lot and that relieved him.

Nathan resisted going to Park Grand for a period of time, he needed to be away from that place, especially the ghost house.

Every time this matter disturbed his mind, he would think about the worn-out boss and his unconscious friends. He'd left a big problem for the boss as a souvenir, it was humour to him when the fire brigade arrived called by the false alarm. The boss must have had a hard time at the moment, anyway, he deserved it.

Now, Nathan, Joe, James and Mr. Roberts were at the train station located on the border of London, preparing for departure. Nathan heard the announcement of an emotionless feminine voice coming from the speakers. These speakers faced all directions.

The train station was large, opulent and immaculate with many facilities. The roof was constructed with glass, which shocked Nathan. Something so heavy and not stable can be on top of thousands of people's heads. But the engineers calculated well, the glasses were a quarter of meter thick and supported by a huge metalwork frame. There were more than 10 railways running through the station, gleaming tracks hid humbly underneath the high-voltage cables.

Nathan sat in the second-class carriage while Roberts and James were meant to sit in another one somewhere behind. The carriage they were in was comfortable enough for him. Joe sat beside him, and kept looking at the scenery outside. There were windmills and wooden houses dotting the paddy fields.

Nathan checked one last time and placed his luggage in the overhead compartment. He looked at Joe and tried to talk to him. The train will be leaving in half an hour's time and they were a few hours to kill. He wanted to take his portable Playstation, but Roberts warned him about confiscation. His mobile was low on battery and what else he could do?

He took in his surroundings inside the train. Yellow lights lit the place with comfortable cushioned seats, he was on one of them, built-in televisions showing BBC world news at the moment and some boring headlines and announcements.

Roberts was nowhere to be seen, nor was 17-year-old James. They were probably in their own coaches. James had been Roberts' favourite student and he insisted to isolate Joe and him. It wasn't as if Roberts was happy with him but he just allowed it.

The people were filling the train and settling down their luggage. There were a few children swarming back and forth and being told by their parents to behave. He stole a glance at Joe, he was probably sleepy, must had been too worried for his first-time participation yesterday.

Nathan landed a hand on Joe's shoulders, shocking him from the thoughts he was in. "Hey, I didn't know you're a fan of those windmills?" he teased.

"Err . . . nothing." He looked away and countered. "You must be more careful, the thief may follow you all the way to Edinburgh, you know? You don't want your wallet emptied again, don't you?"

Nathan came up with a false excuse. "No, so I didn't bring a lot of money in there, and I kept it somewhere else," he answered simply, trying to be normal. Nathan took out his comics and picked one of them, Marvel's. Good, he read it again to distract himself but Joe wasn't over with it.

"Why did you follow the man back then?" he questioned.

"He looked at me. Not just that, he stared at us. I wanted to know what was going on and tried to, and when he entered a back alley way, the plan backfired. Luckily, I didn't get killed," Nathan answered.

Just at the moment of awkwardness and guilt for lying to his best friend, Roberts approached them alone from his coach, walking obviously towards them. "Nathan. Joe," he called out. His fair hair and brown eyes looked at them, his muscular body was like one of a former police or Marine. He wore his trainer T-shirt and long trousers.

"Yes, sir?" they both replied in unity.

"I've something to advise you. Just remember about the doubled trainings the week earlier, I'm not choosing you all because you're really great or what, but the school is lacking of really good swimmers, so just don't tell the whole world about that," Roberts said. It must be the talkative James blaring and emphasizing or telling stories for his lovely coach to hear.

Joe opened his mouth indignantly and defiantly and tried protest, but Nathan just pulled his hand and squeezed it, he then threw him a warning look. It wasn't good to go against Roberts. He may immediately disqualify them with a single phone call.

"Sorry, sir. Just got a little nervous and too interested," Nathan apologized and tightened the grip on Joe's hand. His friend looked dissatisfied but just allowed it to happen.

"Better if you know that. Mind yourselves next time, boys," Roberts said and retreated back to his carriage.

"Why?" a single word demanded from Joe's mouth.

"Just don't care about the silly Jamey Lane-lee. I'll have a word with him when the train stops," Nathan said in a tone that frightened him.

"But just don't end up in a fight okay?" Joe said timidly.

"All right, I'm not sure there will be a win for anyone if it really breaks out. That Jamey wanted to stay in this tournament so he'll probably just continuing poking our backs, no direct assaults," Nathan replied.

He tried to engross himself in the comic and thought the villains were Jamey Lane-lee, who was once walking three quarters naked across the school a good few 100 meters.

After reading the last page of the chapter, Nathan saw someone in the corner of his eye through the window, staring at him in the train station. It was boss. He wore black overalls, a jacket and trousers. He could imagine the bloody bandage tied around his arm. He had wrapped his head in a bandana.

Boss stared at him with serious eyes accompanied with vengeance, not even minding that he had been spotted. There was a look of promise that he'd get payback from the encounter two weeks ago. Nathan looked back in disbelief, taken back by the furious stare. But then there was a shudder and he heard the wheels started to roll. The train picked up speed, pulling them out of the station.

Nathan watched the boss as the train rushed out of the station, both in eye contact until the last moment. He didn't notice that boss was such a type who liked revenge and now seemed like threatening his life.

But nothing could change now, the train was already moving and he couldn't just shout at the driver, they surely would tie him to the chair until arrival, an insane child. He may even be disqualified for the tournament and yelled at by Roberts.

But there was only one thing that concerned him, in the seriousness of those eyes, only pure hatred and vengeance could be found.

"Are you okay?" concerned Joe as he shook him a little by the arm.

Nathan looked at him and tried to think what he was saying just now. "Yes, what's up?"

"I noticed you staring out of the window, who was there? You don't even realize I patted you on the shoulder," Joe said. Nathan didn't even know that the stare actually hypnotized him until his five senses were paralyzed.

"I'd mistaken someone who was an old friend," Nathan lied.

"How long was the last time you saw him?" Joe seemed unconvinced, probably by his look.

"A few years ago," Nathan lied again, and that wasn't his friend.

Nathan tried to change the topic, he wanted to quit talking about the things he'd already left behind. *Or you could not*, something in his mind reminded him. Anyway, about friends, he made up some conversation. Nathan didn't want Joe to suspect him anymore. Since they were in Central London and he'd disappointed Joe by following Rave, he seemed to be silently angry at him. Well, Nathan did say five minutes but it was more than six times that. "Do you remember how we first met?"

Joe's eyes squinted as if trying to see something and he said. "That was when you saved me from the discipline teacher, they like to slander everyone, every student is suspicious to them. It was a year ago when the canteen had a food fight, throwing everything edible like snowballs. A student threw a creamy thing at me, he was probably 17, a big bully.

"But at the last moment I ducked and it hit another person, and then there was something like this repeating and it formed a chain reaction. I tried to run out of the canteen but that was when the miserable head discipline teacher Mr. Colfer chased me, you know running makes a person look suspicious.

"I ran to the school's backyard into the sports area and you saw me for the first time. You gestured a hand to me, telling me to hide under the water and hold my breath for a minute. I was wearing a light T-shirt and shorts after some sports, so it wasn't very bad.

"Then, Colfer lost me. I was lucky he didn't recognize me, if he did, I'm dead for the next day. And that time, Mr. Roberts saw me trying to be curious, he then asked me to join the swimming club instead of the boring table tennis club. We met every lesson and sometimes after school, then we are good friends," Joe said.

The little flashback conversation released a little tension between them, and the invisible thin wall completely vanished. Nathan felt more comfortable after the story, instead of worrying about the stare.

"Well, that time you were clever not to jump into the pool and make a splash, you just rolled your body sideways. If not, you'd had been spotted," added Nathan.

They both laughed, ignoring the protesting passengers.

"Okay, enough of those laughs, I don't want the passengers to call the security guard. Anyway, the people in this carriage want silence. I want to take a nap. It's a long journey," Nathan whispered as he yawned.

"All right, I'll call you up when I'm really bored. The snack I brought won't last long."

Nathan kept his comic aside and curled himself and relaxed on the seat, seeing and enjoying the countryside scenery as he once again thought about the vengeful stare from Golem. Maybe his motive was only to scare him and nothing else, something like a fake James Bond, yeah. He just pictured the image of the rubbish spilt all over Golem a few weeks ago and silently chuckled, he then focused on sleeping.

Nathan was awakened by several violent shakes on his shoulder. He thought that it was the boss but it was only boring Joe.

"Wake up! *Wake up*! You have slept an hour and a half. You don't want to have insomnia tonight. Wake up!"

"All right, stop shaking me, I'm getting dizzy," Nathan rubbed his eyes. His mouth was dry. "What do you want, Joe?" Nathan glanced at his watch. The sky was getting dark, it was 5 p.m.

"I'm bored. How could you sleep for so long?" Joe murmured and took a long breath.

"Could you endure it? Could you endure it for just a few more moments?"

"Ah, are you thirsty?"

"A bit," Nathan said and licked his dry lips.

"I want to go to the pantry and get a drink, you want to follow?" Joe cheekily got up and stirred a few passengers that first looked at him, but then gone back to their work after a second.

"Yes, I'm right behind you." Nathan lazily got up and tailed his friend.

Nathan followed Joe as they passed a few carriages and reached the kitchen. By the way, they noticed people were very bored and uneasy in the third-class carriage, the seats seemed to be made of plastic and everything was smaller and cheaper.

The pantry was lit by fluorescent lamps and occupied by a few stoves, trays and a few kitchen appliances. They found an automatic drink machine and Nathan fed it a few coins to produce two cans of drinks.

"You see the room behind the door, it is the main generator on this train. It manages the electricity supply and transfers it from the cables to this train. A few thousand volts a second, interesting," explained Nathan as he casually pointed.

Joe peeked through the examination window on the door into the generator section. There were a few big devices constructed on the roof. These were fed by cables connected to a machine with a big disc turning slowly. Light indicators and meters complicated the design.

"I wonder how these generators receive electrical energy from the cables when the train is moving, they can't make switches all over the cables, this seemed not so logical," proclaimed Joe.

"Maybe you will be an engineer one day. I could imagine the yellow helmet on your head and blueprints in you hands," Nathan said as he giggled with Joe looking at him with disapproval and embarrassment. "Hey, swimmer," proclaimed Joe.

"Hey engineer. How about . . ." Nathan didn't even finished the sentence when they heard a deafening sound from the carriage they were in just now, an explosion sound. The shock made them drop their cans of drinks onto the floor, spilling root beer and coke all over the place.

The fire licked and consumed the materials in the carriage while destroying it. Meanwhile, in the driver's room, someone rammed the emergency brake. The wheels of the train locked in place, firing sparks and slowing the track. They jerked and fell as an invisible force wave spread out by the explosion and struck them.

Chapter Six

DERAILED CARRIAGES

NATHAN GUESSED SOMETHING BIG AND hard from the exploded carriage made had forced the train off the tracks. The wheels ran over it and derailed, pulling off the cables and electrifying the roof, producing more sparks and fire.

The whole train lost control and rushed towards a farm, destroying crops and shocking farmers. Chickens, cows and pigs ran for their dear lives and at last the huge vehicle rammed into a wooden house and stopped.

The house crumpled to the ground, left with the remains of broken wood fragments. This was the consequences for pulling an emergency brake at the speed of more than 100 kilometers per hour.

He only knew one thing to do in this situation, which was to make as much distance between him and this generator. He dragged Joe with him and got out of the kitchen then heard another smaller explosion, the generator exploded into flames, converting electricity into heat and light.

They entered the third-class carriage, the passengers were either half-conscious by the mega shockwave or too frightened and rooted in their seats.

A man in a white waistcoat stood and pulled out a gun from his belt. He was in his mid-twenties, shaven chin and short hair. Nathan thought he wanted to attack him and escape but the man was also in shock and acted defensively.

The emergency door bust open with a kick, an emotionless man in black overalls entered the car. Nathan thought he was a security guard, until he took in the machine gun, PK-P model code. This man in black pointed his weapon quickly at the other man. There was a flash of light and a continuous deafening sound. The man with the handgun staggered backwards and lay on the floor. His clothes pierced by bullets, a series of holes and crimson liquid spreading on his clothes.

Nathan lunged forward and punched the machine-gun man in the temple and it was rock-solid. He didn't even cared if the man was his enemy or not, but he had just killed a person. Nathan couldn't take the risk of finding out that he was one way or another.

The man didn't even flinch, he immediately responded, he brought the gun down onto Nathan's shoulder, sending a flash and a spasm of pain down to his wrist. Nathan dropped to the floor, agonized by the attack. He was lucky his shoulder was hard enough to withstand the blow, no cracks were heard.

Now the vulnerably positioned Nathan provided an easy kill. The man targeted him but Joe threw a red cylinder-object, a flame extinguisher at the man, it hit him in the neck. The man staggered backwards and the gun went off, making holes in the ceiling. Joe was luckily standing to the side, and the bullets missed him by inches.

Nathan now picked up the fire extinguisher up and activated it, spraying white foam into the man's face. The man rubbed his face and eyes violently like a monster shaking off something disturbing. He was temporally blinded. Joe took the gun and sent it flying to one of the corners, disarming him.

The both of them now ran for the emergency exit, borrowing time from the blinded man. They now noticed it was opened and the passengers had fled, all cowards to have let two boys fight with an armed man.

They knew the man could see again as the fire extinguisher flew passed him, hitting Joe in the shoulder, he should hit the man in the head hard with the red cylinder. Joe staggered in front and laid on his stomach as the man side-kicked him in the back. The blow sent him into unconsciousness. Nathan's respond was slow a bit as he turned, shocked by the man's demonic eyes. The man lunged forward and hit him in the chest with an elbow. The blow knocked Nathan to the floor, in agonizing pain.

The man now retrieved his machine gun. Nathan knew he'd not survive if the man had no sympathy. The man must have killed a lot of people without mercy. He couldn't fight him as he was out of arm's reach, but the gun could shoot far. Fear of death rooted him on the ground, waiting for a miracle to happen.

He couldn't believe he would die like this, like the first victim. The man aimed, Nathan closed his eyes, trying to forget what was going on. He heard a deafening gunshot sound and a window smashed, glass shattering all over him like rain. Some blood sprayed on his face.

He opened his eyes and examined his body, but nothing was wrong. There was not even a scratch or a tear. The blood wasn't his. He looked at that man with the handgun, the man's eyes were closed, probably dead. Joe was still unconscious. The man's temple bled out a steady stream of blood that poured to the floor. His gun came off his grip and he stumbled.

Nathan wiped the blood with his sleeves and scanned the area outside the smashed window, it was an open area with grass and vegetables planted, far away was a hill with a forest. He looked for somebody but failed.

There was no police and the passengers were gone, maybe running in fear. A reflection of sunlight glared his eye for a second. It must have been a sniper shot! The glare came from a sniper's scope far in the hills.

Whoever was there had saved his life, he wanted to say thank you but no one could hear him. Nathan didn't know if it was right or wrong to be so grateful for his own survival after two men had just died a few seconds ago, and many more had been killed after the explosion, it just seemed so selfish. Anyway, the man was a terrorist and wasn't meant to live long, some evil part in Nathan said that. The marksman must have had potential, it had 5,000 meter in distance and he had managed a headshot, precise weapon accuracy.

Nathan examined the man, he was certainly dead. He couldn't think that boss had sent a man with a machine gun and an explosive device just because of the events that previous night. He was such a coward, trying to kill a boy and he destroyed the entire carriage with 30 passengers on board, there must be even children. And they were now ashes.

He went and helped Joe but on the way he heard a weak voice, it was the innocent victim that the man had shot.

"You, come here," said the man. His face was pale and blood poured out of his chest. Nathan knew he'd soon die of blood lost, there was no way to save him. Nathan knelt down beside him.

"Listen, Nathan Doyle." He was surprised that the man knew his name.

"I don't have any time to waste so don't ask questions. Someone had betrayed us, we have a parasite in the organization. It must be Golem, you had met him two weeks ago. And you were quite clever to enter the place, they didn't even know your presence until the last moment and that was when you took down two of out three armed man alive, brilliant!" he said as a stream of blood started to form under his lips.

"The Region Force had made the right decision to keep you alive. But Golem has provided our enemies with information and blown our covers. He killed everyone on that carriage you were in with 20 kilograms of C-4 radioactive explosive. But they failed to kill you, just the guards like me, we often die in our mission," he murmured the words out desperately. He looked incredibly pale and coughed several times before continuing.

"You were lucky to be in the kitchen, not in the exploded carriage. On the higher grounds, a marksman saved your life, but there may not be a second chance anymore. The Ventures are hungry to kill you, someone paid them enough money and they have the determination.

"You must be careful, leave this place at once. Edinburgh isn't so safe, thanks to the parasite. Now the whole unit is unable to secure that place because they themselves aren't secure. I told the authorities to lock you down for your own safety until they return you to the headquarters but they don't listen. They just say it's too early. So people like me die." Nathan knew a person talked a lot when they lost blood.

The man handed him something, a metal rectangular with a dove logo crafted in the middle with four numbers. "Tell Fibiano I hate him, best wishes from agent RF6373. And remember, Edinburgh is not longer safe. Don't feel sorry about my death, I live to protect you and I die to do the same. This is my passion and my destiny. Be clever." The man closed his eyes and rested his head on the floor.

Nathan couldn't believe that he witnessed two deaths in a few minutes. Edinburgh was not safe, but why? The man said some kind of organization had tried to kill him and he had an exploded train as a solid proof, he was not lying. And who was Fibiano? The man only told him what happened but without proper explanations, he didn't have enough time.

He hoped he listened to the explanation in the ghost house but the boss had attacked him. Boss claimed to protect him two weeks ago but maybe he changed his mind after what Nathan did to him. But the events seemed so illogical. Why would someone want to kill a schoolboy and risk the entire carriage of passengers? Golem's vengeance couldn't be so deep that he needed to do it like this, there must be some more reasons and he didn't know them. The man said Edinburgh was unsafe. But he demanded to go back, Mr. Roberts will go mad.

Mr. Roberts, could he be dead? It wasn't convincing, luckily James Lane had chosen to sit in a different carriage from them, if not, they would have died in the explosion. As they were in another carriage, the explosion did not hurt them badly.

Quickly, he checked Joe's condition, he was unconscious but fine. Nathan placed him in a more comfortable position and reduced the risk of any injuries or any deterioration from injuries if there were any. He wanted to go for help and reached for the exit.

Footsteps could be heard as a man approached from the carriage door, he wore a simple black collar shirt and military jeans with a leather belt. He was in the mid-20s with watchful eyes. The man noticed the two dead men and a boy standing between them, what on Earth had happened?

Nathan positioned himself defensively as the man came nearer but he seemed to be less interested in him. The man crouched beside the innocent victim and checked his carotid pulse rate in the neck. He shook his head in disappointment as he failed to detect a pulse.

"Did he say something to you?" the man asked as he turned to Nathan.

"He did. He said someone betrayed him, Golem. Golem set explosives to this train. He mentioned some organization is after me but I don't know why," he trembled as he spoke.

"Don't be scared, I won't hurt you." That was the most comforting sentence he heard since the train crash and a terrorist came in with cold blood. "You still don't understand a lot of things but I don't have so much time to explain, there are men with weapons outside the train and it's only the matter of time before they find us. Okay, I'll try my best to bring you to safety. The police are on their way."

"Who are you?" Nathan asked, he didn't trust him.

"I work with the dead man that talked to you, the same organization on your side."

"I'm sorry. He died because of me. He protected me," Nathan apologized, he felt bad, all the people in the carriage had died *because* of him more or less.

"Don't be. It was his job and it's also mine." Nathan felt like something weird in his voice, like a soldier saving his captain. "We're paid and contracts were signed. So indirectly, his left hand killed him."

"Are you Fibiano?" he asked but the name didn't suit the man, he was an American with the look and accents. "He asked me to hand you this." Nathan produced the metal tag and handed it over. The man examined it and slipped it into his pocket, "Thanks, my name is Shaun, not a code name, it's real." He snatched the machine gun and tore the man's jacket to take the ammunition.

"My name is Nathan."

"I know, Nathan Doyle." Nathan felt less impressed as so much people knew his name. "Do we have anyone helping us? The other terrorists must be armed."

Shaun jammed the cartilage and checked the machine gun. "There's only you and me. When we go outside the train stay close to me. We'll run for cover like houses and walls, there is going to be gunfire."

A question Nathan wanted to ask all along since the ghost house incident popped up at the wrong moment, but he asked it anyway. "Actually, why are the terrorists hunting for me? I didn't do anything. They even blew up the entire carriage to kill only one person, but a dozen of innocent people died. This seems irrelevant and insane!"

"Stop asking! I will tell you later. My job is to prevent you from being killed and the terrorists have no self-conscience. They're programmed to kill for money only!" Shaun replied as he checked his weapon.

This was when there was a shout in Russian and a gun outside the train went off. Nathan was forced to the ground as hot, angry bullets passed over him. They hit the wall of the train, smashing some wood into fragments and breaking glasses and plates. Shaun crouched below the window, the machine gun ready to fire at anyone that got near them. But he was outnumbered and the ammunition wouldn't last for long.

"Are you all right?" he asked.

"I think I am," answered Nathan, he had just recovered from the shock. That was the second time he was being shot at.

"Try to get over here. Lie on the floor and climb, keep you head low. Quick!"

Nathan lay flat on his stomach and used his elbows and legs to drag himself there, the terrorists were still firing, looking forward to keeping them under cover as long as possible.

He reached Shaun, now he could see the look in his eyes clearly. He may be under control but he knew he was afraid.

Nathan risked a look, there were at least 20 terrorists outside. They made a semicircle formation around the train.

"Be ready to move!" Shaun pulled out a black ball and deactivated the pin with a click. He threw the grenade out of the window. There was a small explosion and coal-black smoke rose from the ground rapidly. "Move now!" he yelled as they ran out of the door and charged.

Chapter Seven

SMOKE AND GUNS

Now Nathan could feel the chemical-stinking gas and his eyes watered, but he was grateful to obtain cover. The terrorists didn't dared to open fired because they might hit their teammates without aiming since the semicircle formation they made wasn't meant for situations like this.

They ran out of the smoke, Nathan was relieved that they didn't split in the blurred situation. He could see hills on the far horizon, two-story countryside farmhouses and a river feeding a windmill, and there were golden paddy fields, which seemed to go on forever.

Shaun led the way while the shouts of pursuers got louder behind them. They couldn't be in an open area for long, or they might as well be sitting targets for 20 guns. After half a minute, half of the terrorists found their way out of the smoke and leading the others with them.

A terrorist, probably Russian, smiled and took an aim with his Famas short-range rifle equipped with a high-power scope. He may get extra income if his boss found his bullet in the target. He pulled his trigger and cursed as the first shot missed.

Nathan felt something flying 300 meters per second brushed passed him and he looked back. A terrorist was aiming him but there was a "bang" and an echo from the hills, the man held his chest and fell to the ground. Nathan thanked the sniper, he had saved him twice.

There were more sniper shots, picking the terrorists off in their open position helplessly, they deserved it. The sky was getting dark, and probably it might be harder to aim. However, the pursuers behind them were distracted and desperately taking cover in the open area, all in vain.

Some were running, hoping they'd survive in one good piece. The two of them were making great process as the distance between they and the gunmen increased.

They were nearing the farmhouses, which were packed together. There were ten farmhouses in one group and most of them rising two stories high. The farmhouses each had four pillars rising half a story. Nathan noticed a van, black and modern, it must have come from a city.

Several men with khaki jackets came out armed with rifles. Shaun fired at them followed by a deafening chatter of continuous shots. Some of the men dived to the ground, some were not so fortunate. He noticed there were a dozen villagers running down the stairs while screaming in fear, he worried they may get hit but he couldn't do anything to help, he was unarmed and useless.

Shaun rested behind an old jeep, it was rusty and the paint had worn off a long time ago. He reloaded the gun, ignoring the villagers. The remaining five men near the van fired back, bullets shattering the steel of the jeep, creating sparks. They couldn't hide here forever, the surviving terrorists in the smoke were catching up as the smoke began to clear, the sniper had somehow stopped his good work, was he out of bullets?

There was no safe place. Nathan noticed a staircase leading up to a farmhouse, but climbing up it would be the last thing in his mind to do. They may be trapped again if the enemies surround them. Shaun was out of smoke grenades. The terrorists can make it very bad for them by setting the farmhouse on fire until they come out. Then they could easily shoot them both.

But suddenly the worst place gave them the best chance at surviving. Something gave Nathan a good idea, a slanting elevation wooden board was fixed from the ground to the first floor near them. The farmers must have used them to transport carts up to the houses.

Suddenly, the desperate condition seemed to change after things combined together—the elevation board, the cart and most important of all, time.

"Shaun, we're going up into the farmhouse, trust me. I have a plan," urged Nathan.

"Are you crazy, we'll be trapped," he said while firing off a dozen of bullets into the van, damaging its metal sides with ease.

"You have to trust me, look at the terrorists behind us, once they reach us, we will be surrounded and probably dead. Please, listen to me," begged Nathan, his voice barely heard above the guns chattering sound. The jeep cracked and fragments of glasses sprayed into the air. They sheltered themselves from the glass rain.

Staying there was the worst option, he just nodded and yelled over the gun shots. "Al right, I'll cover both of us!"

Shaun raised the gun and fired while they ran towards the stairs. They didn't dare to look back until Nathan shut the door and barred it.

"What now?" said Shaun.

Nathan scanned his surroundings, it was a living room with dim lighting, a wooden table and an old-fashioned radio. There was a corridor that led into several rooms. He walked into one of them the kitchen. It was filled with oil stains, high piles of dirty plates and a large stove with two big cuboid canteens of yellow cooking oil.

He looked into another room, it was bigger and dark. The air was damp and full of stench and dirt, 10 more cube-shaped hay piles were stacked untidily in an old cart. The farmers must have kept them here during rainy days but he was fortunate today.

"What's your plan, they're going to slaughter us!

"Please help me to fill the cart with that hay. Make sure it's heavy enough to make a person faint, just do it. I'll help you later," said Nathan, it was like he was commanding an army. Shaun looked around in confusion, half knowing what the boy was up to, and half thinking he was mad. But arguing was just wasting precious time, and he chose not to.

Nathan grabbed one of the oil cans, it was heavy with 10 liters in it. He held it but the whole thing slipped off his grip as it was coated with oil, and really slippery. He wiped the oil onto a cloth and hung it on one of the door nails. "Gross . . ." He then took the cloth and tied it around the handle.

He lifted the can, he took one step and dropped the can, it was very heavy but the cloth helped a lot. He was lucky the oil hadn't spilled. He tried again with all his energy, and the can left the ground. He moved it while holding his breath. The weight was straining his back and his muscles.

He reached the hall and left it on the floor, relieved. He ran into the storeroom and saw Shaun was almost finished with the hay. How much time had passed? It was weird that there was no angry pursuit and violent knocks on the door.

"Help me to push he cart to the doorway."

Without questioning, Shaun accompanied Nathan to work the cart. Perhaps he knew the plan and preferred to be silent. They pushed the cart 20 meters away from the door.

"Light the hay up, quick!" urged Nathan. Shaun swigged the can up into the cart with the cloth and tried to turn the cover but failed, it was too slippery with oil.

"I have an idea." He pointed the gun and fired three shots at the can, oil split into the hay while the bullets made contact with the metal, producing sparks fed by the oil. Soon the hay was burning. Sparks and fire swallowed it.

"Push the cart hard into the door, we'll run it over them with fire!" laughed Shaun, as the idea was his one but that didn't bother Nathan.

Nathan and Shaun pushed it. The first few meters were used to pick up speed and it was getting faster. The floor was creaking under the weight of four heavy wheels. Ten meters more, the flame was very big, greedily consuming the hay and oil.

Fire was licking into the steel handle of the cart, hurting Nathan's hand, but he braced and concentrated to smash the "visitors" behind the door. Five meters more. The intense heat warmed Nathan's face, he closed his eyes and faced away, afraid it might cause a burn, but Shaun seemed to enjoy this very much.

The last two meters, they used their final strength and charged the cart into the door.

The terrorists were waiting outside. Two of them were just outside the door, another three surrounding the farmhouse. They seemed to prefer to wait for further commands from their boss over the radio.

Anyway, a fire could burn the whole house down, there were no survival chances. He had to admit that working as a terrorist was the most successful criminal job and two years had proved it.

Just storming something or killing someone can allow you to make a fortune, $20,000 cash to set a bomb, $50,000 to kill someone or storm a security system. And the best thing about it was the fast cash with no bargains, he just needed to survive an operation and there was the money. He looked at his partner, code named as Saul. He looked uneasy and always shifting his position.

"What was that buddy? You look shot by a bazooka!"

"I'm just feeling uneasy. That's all."

"The both of them are zero threats to us, they don't stand a chance. Come on, we'll enjoy a beer after this. They're so idiotic to hide inside the . . ." he didn't even finish the sentence when the door of the farmhouse was suddenly smashed open by an incredible force.

He sheltered himself from the wood fragments and swore. By the time he regained his sight, a cart with an enormous fire on it charged out of the entrance like a cannonball. He and his friend were shocked and rooted on the spot, what on Earth had happened? The cart charged towards them and knocked them to the ground as if some giant had thrown them in anger.

They yelled, screaming as they flew a few meters away and landed hard on the dirt, probably breaking several bones. His friend caught fire and rolled on the ground, begging God to for mercy to spare him.

He now knew what the feeling was of being hit by a bazooka, the bullet was just a little bigger. He saw a boy and a man running out of the door, and then passed out. The cart exploded, sending mushrooms of flame into the sky.

Shaun fired at the other three men who were also shocked. Nathan ran for his dear life, the terrorists in the smoke seemed to be catching up extremely fast. Only half of them survived the sniper assault. They heard rifle chattering and a hiss.

Twenty meters away the ground seemed to blow itself up. There was an explosion five meters high, a deafening sound followed by a ball of flame. Nathan shielded himself.

"They're using grenade launchers—HM20 models, I guess. Be careful. Stay apart, we may survive, we have a chance."

At least they have two directions to fire, instead of one, Nathan thought. Nathan braced himself but his whole body was trembling.

They heard another hiss, the grenade hit the earth only some distance of not more than 20 meters away from Nathan. There was an explosion and his head was ringing. Then his eyes became blurred. He fell to the ground while an arm secured him around his shoulders. His legs were half running and half dragging the soil.

"Are you all right?" Shaun asked. Nathan didn't answer, he was very dizzy but otherwise unhurt. "I'll take you to the windmill there. Reinforcements are coming, they asked us to take cover. They're striking from the air. To Hell, floor-flushing idiot terrorists," Shaun smiled. Nathan wondered whether he had received the news from the small radio transmitter attached to his shoulder just now.

Nathan limped with Shaun's support into the windmill with the terrorists chasing them. It was painted red and white, but still looked like it was working, fed by a clean river. Shaun slammed the door and sealed it with a metal bar. He helped Nathan to sit down and crouched beside him.

"Are you really fine?" he said while examining his body for any wounds but found none.

"I'm okay, I'm just a little dizzy. It's been my second deadly experience. One more meter nearer, I lose my whole leg!"

Shaun did care more than that for a brief moment, he needed to hold the terrorist back before air strikes came. He hold up the machine gun, placed it on a frame of a large window to stabilize it, and fired in the direction of any incoming terrorist, not even caring about the gun's poor accuracy.

The chattering of the gun was deafening and vibrating in Nathan's ears. The terrorists couldn't take any risk, they ducked and laid flat on the earth, taking an inappropriate cover of uneven ground and the dead bodies of their teammates. Some of them tried to fight back but were taken down by the furious Shaun. He emptied his chamber and took cover.

The commotion of fierce firing had created a horror scene for the gunmen outside. Although there was no more attack, they feared too much to even crouch up and examine the area.

"Listen here, you're very brave at the farmhouse. Anyway, where did you learn that? Thanks very much, you save both of our lives," Shaun said.

Nathan didn't know what to say. "Not without your help," he said casually.

There was chatter in his walkie-talkie, a voice of a military soldier. "This is Silver Wing 2, to Zero Alpha, do you copy? We are requested to supply reinforcement in air," the masculine sound came from the radio transmitter.

Shaun brought the black equipment up and said, "Zero Alpha copied. There're terrorists assaulting on us, they're equipped with firearms. Declaring red code situation. Requesting for immediate air support. Rescue mission's target is safe with me," Shaun barked to the transmitter.

"Request is received and accepted. What is your current position?"

"The red windmill is near a river. I don't have smoke indicators.

"I see you. Position is confirmed. Delivering air strike now."

For a while both of them kept silent. The sense of fear hung in the air. Nathan could image the gunmen outside, peeking and crouching up after nothing had happened. The time went by painfully slow. After a moment, they heard a roar of the Silver Wing 2's rocket-powered blaster engines.

"Close your ears, it may hurt," Shaun shouted above the noise.

After five seconds, they heard another blast and a deafening sound of the air strike. The missile hit the land with an immense explosion, which killed all the terrorists immediately. A ball of flame and smoke mushroomed up into the atmosphere.

"Target is destroyed. Zero Alpha, we're sending you a transport in the forest. Spot for a black helicopter, the access code is Winter's Evening."

"Thank you very much Silver Wing."

Shaun turned and looked at Nathan, his voice was serious.

"Look, I know you're very confused but I can't explain anything to you now, we have no time and this is not the right place. I know you're on the way to Edinburgh. But just don't trust anybody that you don't know there, we may give you cover for a moment. If anyone says winter's evening to you, I beg you to trust him, he is one of us.

"And the last thing, stay safe. There's some corruption going on in our organization, but we'll handle it. Remember, only trust the person if he knows the code. There may be enemies pretending to be us. Good-bye." He unlocked the door and ran.

Nathan watched as he disappeared into the paddy fields and into the forest. He sat on the ground and enjoyed the countryside scenery and the sun setting. Despite the large destruction that the air strike made, everything else suited the nice environment. The police are going to be shocked at the hole.

Nathan didn't want to think about that for a moment. He was tired and worn out, he only wanted to have a good rest and prepare for the swimming tournament.

Things looked like they were getting out of control and he felt like a piece on a chessboard, forced to be pushed here and there, or being captured. Region Force was protecting the worthful piece in chess while Ventures attacked it. The game's faith hung in Edinburgh.

Chapter Eight

PANIC IN WATER

ONLY A FEW MINUTES LEFT before the swimming tournament. Nathan sat on the hall's bench, thinking and trying to comprehend everything that happened since the ghost house until the train explosion. He was lucky to survive both near-death experiences. When he was being shot at those several times, he felt he was dead, or half-dead.

Roberts had called all of their parents and told them about the issue, although he thought the police had done it. Veinna was shocked to the nerve but Nathan managed to convince her he was fine and well. After everything settled down for a few days, they got to participate in the tournament.

Nathan thought back about everything. First, Rave, Spassky and Golem, known as boss, claimed to protect him in the ghost house in conjunction with some unknown organization known as Region Force. However, they threatened to kill him and hurt him.

Now, there were two possibilities, they couldn't recognize him in the dark and accidentally opened fire. Next, they were paid to eliminate him.

About Golem, maybe he was too angry after Rave accidentally shot him in the arm, maybe he blamed Nathan all along, and betrayed his authority, Region Force. The dead man in the train said he was betrayed, too, by Ventures.

Next, the furious stare of Golem at the train station. Nathan and Joe were the only survivors in the exploded carriage. All thanks to Joe waking him up for a drink, if not, they would now be dead with boss licking his fingers. Golem tried to kill him even though there were so many innocent and uninvolved people in the carriage. The organization—Ventures, the dead man in the train had also mentioned must be very cruel and cold-blooded, they were certainly not on Nathan's side.

The question was: Why did Golem and the Ventures group want to kill him? Maybe he had made them very angry. Even so, they did not need to murder him over getting angry. If Shaun wasn't there to help him, 20 terrorists and a bomb may have certainly been more than enough to do the job. And thanks to the sniper as well, he did help a lot.

Everything made sense: Golem betrayed the good people and accepted corruption, the dead man in the train said. That told the whole story about the bomb and the terrorists. Winter's evening. He'd been waiting for that day but no one ever said this, not even a faint sign.

And about the police, they claimed that no official army force delivered the air strike but Nathan knew it was Silver Wing 2. He couldn't imagine how Region Force infiltrated the airways.

Unfortunately, the government was starting to suspect other countries. The British Intelligence said it could be the Mafia, but even without much evidence insisted that it was true. But the Mafia didn't have aircrafts, t that Ventures was the real answer.

After Shaun went away and things settled down, Nathan and the other passengers were sent to the hospital for treatment or medical check-up although he didn't need it. Mr. Roberts and James were silent and deep in thoughts like everyone else after the near-death occurrence. While Joe woke up from unconsciousness on the hospital bed, he boasted every five minutes on how he threw the fire extinguisher at the terrorist, but the nurse told him to lower his voice.

The police interrogated Nathan and Joe about the dead man. However, Nathan said he knew nothing about it and answered only basic questions, no one will believe him anyway. They said the sniper model was PSG1, German made and used in the World War Two. But it's still popular in the army nowadays.

Joe saw him and joined him on the bench with the other participants from other states. The swimming tournament would start in five more minutes. The stadium was large, with more than 1,000 seats surrounding the crystal blue pool in the middle, with gentle currents and small waves hitting its edges.

There were high-definition cameras everywhere, with cameramen setting up the brightness of the flash and testing them until satisfied. A few surveillance cameras were switched on too.

Nathan trained and swam a few laps before lunch. He remembered the advice that his coach told him, *just don't care if your opponents swim faster than you, don't even look. The most important thing in this tournament is stamina, not speed, this is a five-lap swim, and they'll get tired before they reach the end. And remember, no panicking, this makes your heart race faster than normal and you'll breath more than you swim. Keep them in mind.*

The audience was murmuring in interest, he could hear the faint sound in the distance. It was just the grumbling of the other team's coaches that annoyed him. It was as if they booked the whole place. He looked at the clock hanging in the far end of the pool, three more minutes to go.

Joe hadn't said anything since they entered the stadium, it was not his usual character, just staring at the water beside him like a silent companion. Nathan and Roberts had convinced him to cool down, but that only worked a little, at least he was not shivering anymore. Nathan laid a hand on Joe's bare shoulder, "Don't be scared, you're looking great."

"Thanks," he looked at him while replying.

He heard an announcement demanding them to follow all the rules, stating how important this tournament will be and at last telling them to prepare. Roberts signaled them to be ready, the tournament begins in a moment. The participants walked to the platform rising a meter high and waited. All of them were staring at each other once a time as if trying to tell them something. The murmurs loudened.

The referee stood around the corner and waited for the precise second. He was in his fifties, a retired coach or an ex-police maybe, with well-built muscles and masculine body. He didn't shave well, leaving white fine hair on the chin. He wore a blue jacket and long trousers, the whistle hung on his chest back and forth, like creating some temptation.

The referee took a last glance of his watch and blew the whistle. Nathan and the other participants jumped into the water. He powered his first kick, propelling into the never-ending blue wall of water. He felt the current pressing on his goggles as he glanced at the far end, not even looking at the others as his coach had advised.

He performed free-style as his hands sliced the water surface again and again like the others. He turned left and right, longer on occasion to take a breath of chlorine-accented air.

He reached the end and turned, breaking the rule he made for himself as he looked only once on his progress, two swimmers had long ago overtook him and now were a few meters in front of him, the others were chasing up with Joe just behind him. He quickly came into focus again, not forgetting what Roberts said.

Another slice and push of the stroke brought him forward, not too hard to maintain the stamina. He turned and took a deep breath and saw some of the surveillance cameras, as dead as statues, rooted on the ceiling while staring at an area lifelessly. It was just one of them had an extra screw just below the lens. Why had he never spotted these kinds of things in the first place?

Nathan didn't care, it was just a coincidence to notice this kind of strange thing, and it was no doubt a waste of time. He came back into complete focus and pushed all those thoughts out of his mind.

That was the time when someone in the control room switched on a remote control powered by a weak battery, which only supplied a few volts of electricity for a minute. As long as there was light, no matter how little, he didn't care about anything else. He flicked on the green button, activating the device's only use.

The black device antenna sent a signal, weak and difficult to detect but effective for half a second. One of the surveillance cameras was bugged, the one with the extra screw received the signal. It'd been connected to the camera lens, tracking the image that had been programmed precisely. The screw couldn't aim so it must be at the most precise moment when it deployed the secret needle dipped with a type of special serum.

The screw produced the high-powered needle flying into the air. It took only one point two seconds before it met with the target. Nathan felt something small and sharp hit him in the arm, he felt its coldness as it entered his flesh. What was that? It was like being bitten by a big ant. He didn't stop to think, perhaps it was just his imagination produced by the effect of the unfriendly chlorine, nothing much more than that.

A minute passed by as he felt that the coldness wasn't just anything normal, he felt very tired and was breathing faster and faster. Suddenly, he felt a jerk from his body and every muscle in him went into a spasm and cramped.

By the time he noticed something was wrong, he was struggling in the water, trying his very best to emerge for air but it seemed in vain. Suddenly, his mind came into a thought, like a devil from the dark world spoke to him, he remembered what the dying man on the train said, about the danger of the organization known as Ventures might cause, they had tried to kill him without caring other innocent lives for no clear reason.

The ant, or whatever thing it was that managed to make him cramp must be high-tech, he never heard of anything like this. The needle was not made by metal but something else hard, it now dissolved in the water incredibly, without anyone seeing or knowing how.

Nathan came back to the thought that he was going to die, if the Ventures were serious, they will be clever enough to distract the lifeguards away and perhaps kidnap the coaches.

He thought about the events of their last practice and breakfast this morning, they seemed to be fine but now this. It was a terrible mistake since he followed Rave and Spassky into the ghost house, he now regretted it but it was too late.

This thought of death vanished into thin air as someone wrapped a hand around his shoulders, the lifeguards kept the casualty's head above the water. He thought it was Mr. Roberts but it didn't look like him, the arm wasn't dark but slightly fair, different from his coach's skin that liked to be under the sun.

He just relaxed and put away the thoughts of what might have happened after he was on dry ground. He was pulled to the edge slowly and was relieved as he reached the pool's edge, away from the cold water. His muscles were still hurting and spasmodic as the serum still tried its best to paralyze him. He could still feel it in him, the uncomfortable feeling of cold flowing liquid. He lay down there for a while and coughed water, regaining his breath while preparing to face the worst.

He could see the lifeguard's face properly, he was in his thirties with fair hair and blue eyes that seemed to be telling something, the dark complexion similar to his hand he'd first seen. He said thanks but the sense of sour defeat and unfairness made his voice sound ungrateful, he was sorry for that. The other participants were still swimming, not going to be interrupted by such a small problem, less one participant to compete, more chances of winning, they were delighted as Nathan guessed. Joe looked concerned from his movement, he craned his neck to look for a few times but was waved away by Roberts.

Nathan sat up as Roberts approached, he could hear the murmurs of the spectators now, some protested, and some sympathized while others wondered what had just happened. Nathan didn't know how to explain, he didn't attempt to. The coach surely will scold him louder if he did explain, no one would believe the nonsense.

The cramp gone without a faint trace as Nathan confirmed it to be triggered by the serum. Mr. Roberts came near him and crouched down. "What was wrong with you? The judges never listen to such excuses, cramp! You are disqualified from the match," scolded Roberts.

Nathan lowered his head, he felt ashamed and angry about the cramp, it wasn't his fault but he was forced to take all the blame without any effective explanation.

"Did you done your warming-up exercises? How many times do I have to teach you? I was wrong to choose you in the first place, you're wasting our chances!" scolded Roberts, and he sounded more disdainful.

Some of the nearest spectators were looking at them. Nathan was fed up, he had had enough about those matters between whatever Region Force and Ventures, why did they have to include him in their conflict, a 14-year-old child. Why was he even worth their efforts?.

They paused for a while. Nathan decided that he should apologize even though it wasn't really his fault, things seemed on the opposite side and he didn't want to make them worse. "I'm sorry Mr. Roberts. I didn't mean to spoil this, but I really had done the warm-up exercises."

The coach softened a little, maybe he was being too hard on his student. "Fine, you better show your best in the future training sessions, if not, you're kicked out from the school representative list, understood?"

"Yes, Mr. Roberts," he tried his best to sound grateful.

"Good, now go and wash yourself up and think again about your mistake, I noticed you weren't so focused just now as you were in school. I'll have you stay after tomorrow when we return to school." He turned around and walked away, as if feeling all his advice had been neglected by the boy that he gave hope to.

Nathan got up and packed his things, he dressed up in shorts and a plain T-shirt. The hotel was just beside the stadium, just a minute walk. He made his way to the hotel and showered in the warm water, hoping those thoughts might flow with the shower water, away from him.

After that, he went out of the bathroom and dried himself with a blue towel his aunt brought for him. He dressed in a simple collared T-shirt and knee-length shorts.

This was the first time Nathan really looked around his room. There was a bed with sheets, dim yellow lighting, a bouquet of elegant red roses in a vase on the table just beside the bed, and a picture of the Edinburgh Castle for decoration on the wall.

There was also a plasma TV with DVD players but he was in no mood for movies. This room was nice and comforting but sadly it may be his last time here. Mr. Roberts may not be confident in him anymore.

He looked out of the window, the sun was cheerily shining a bright yellow light onto buildings and tarmac, it was 3 o'clock in the afternoon. Joe and the other participants must have finished the tournament by now, it was the prize giving ceremony and the qualified names for national level will be announced.

Unfortunately, Nathan didn't stand a chance. He wanted to be home as fast as possible, he felt safer there. He missed his aunt but calling her with that kind of bad news, he didn't want to mention it to anyone, let alone her. It would make her more worried, plus the incident at the train, nothing good, might as well wait until he returned.

He was eager for a good rest, but as he uncovered the sheets, there was a pamphlet advertising The Modern Art Gallery of Edinburgh. He remembered no one had ever entered his room except Joe since his stay, after all, he'd hung the **DO NOT DISTURB** sign on the door.

This pamphlet didn't look to belong to Joe, he hated everything about art or modern art. He was shocked to find a note printed in the second page—**THIS EVENING, walk there.**

It must belong to the organization Shaun was working, Region Force, or someone that specially sent this letter to him. He surely wanted to go there, he wanted to know why the Ventures had attempted to kill him and made a fool of him in the tournament. And the most important thing, he must tell the guy that he's only a 14-year-old kid, so why even bother with him.

The place wasn't very far from the hotel and he was requested to walk, perhaps they wanted to see if anyone was following him. There was no coded password on it like "winter's evening" or something else. He turned to the last page and there was another small note—**ELIMINATE EVIDENCE.**

Surely Region Force didn't want anyone else to find it, he decided to tear it into pieces and threw it into the toilet bowl, and then flushed it with satisfaction. He was going to meet with those guys and perhaps an explanation and the promise to get out from this kind of world will do.

Nathan waited for an hour, wandering around the hotel pointlessly to kill time, then he redressed into a green polo shirt and long black trousers. He probably won't be meeting Joe or his coach, they wanted him to be alone for a while.

He made his way down to the hotel's entrance and started walking, knowing that somewhere, an agent will examine him from far and could alert back-up if anyone was following him. The streets were full of pedestrians making their way back home after work, the traffic jam long and frustrating.

After a 30-minutewalk, he finally reached a huge, elegant with a few white polished pillars supporting the tiled roof in the front. The place looked finely cared for, but years had eaten a little of its colour.

He stepped up the worn stone steps that led to an inviting entrance with two oak doors guarding the place. The decoration was modern and comforting. A few local and French tourists stood by the walls and took pictures, nodding in satisfaction as the image appeared on their screens.

He paid the worker and entered. He took in what looked like wood-crafting. Each of the people involved with the class were protected by a glass panel or surrounded by protective banners. A small bulb shone a soft light to attract more attention.

There were a few boring descriptions beside them, which seemed to indicated only the dates and names were changing, everything else remained the same. He enjoyed some of what he saw, but some of the items were very common with wood like twisted metal and smelly dull varnish. Maybe he hated anything about art after all, not for any particular reason.

He proceeded to the next section, a visual drawing gallery. He looked at the drawings of nature, humans, animals, plants and old buildings. Each of paintings was protected by thin, invisible glass. Nathan noticed them because of the fingerprints left by curious tourists.

A picture attracted him the most. It consisted of bald oak trees and bushy Christmas trees with snow to contrast, white crystals and cotton raining down from the dim winter sky. A frozen river sliced down the horizon portion of the work, accompanied by far mountains and larger ranges.

The paintwork was drawn in wet paint, varnished with dried egg white that made it shiny. He scanned around the gallery, this was the only picture with snow. Could it be a coincidence?

Chapter Nine

110

He knew the answer as a man walked near him. He wore shades, a multicolour collar T-shirt and white shorts. A straw hat covered his face. He removed his shades and folded them. He blinked his right eye once unwillingly as he was making promises to a kid to be obedient.

At once, Nathan was shocked about this, he expected someone to come near and give the code then tugged a letter to him, but this was completely unpredictable, a paintwork. Region Force must have somehow managed to persuade the manager to hang the picture, it was nice for exhibition to be honest.

"Nice to meet you, Nathan, you'd grown tall, boy," greeted the man as if they were uncle and nephew on fishing trip. But Nathan could see the professional disguise. "I'm Fibiano, we met before in France when you're just 5." He was great at his job. Nathan knew it was the name the dying man had mentioned on the train. "Yeah, a little faint memory," he tried to suit his 'uncle'.

"Follow me, I have something to show you," he had a cheerful voice, rather American accents. While this sentence seemed to be commanding, not asking, Nathan was meant to accept, not decline.

Nathan obediently followed him out of the gallery, wondering what was playing in Fibiano's mind, it might be his coded name, too. A car was waiting 10 meters from the entrance. It was a Peugeot 508 four-seater, pure white with a lion logo above the car number. Fibiano led him as he made one last look at their surroundings, and then he entered.

Nathan sat in the back seat, alone with the two agents looking at him, and then at each other. The driver was in his thirties, well-shaved chin, dark skin and bald. He noticed a sidearm attached to his belt, half-concealed by his blazer.

Inside was very comfortable, with luxurious soft leather seats, inviting air-conditioned air. But an uncomfortable aura told him that this wasn't a holiday and not to be too relaxed and be happy.

Fibiano nodded at the driver, he immediately took out a cuboid box with a few lights and glass panels and scanned Nathan from head to toe, it was the same equipment that immigration agents use at the airport, just a little smaller than usual.

"He's clear," he driver said, he had a warm Southern American voice. He then locked the doors and stepped on the accelerator and the car moved on, frightening a sleeping cat near it.

"Where are you taking me?" Nathan asked.

"Somewhere safe. You don't want to be assassinated, do you? I know you have many questions to asked but please wait for a moment. I'll only tell you we're really protecting you, not killing you. So don't use any of your fists or we will beat you to a pulp." Fibiano said and turned his attention to the road, he didn't sound as friendly as just now when they were in the gallery, it was meant to remind him that they were willing to protect him, but to talk as little as possible. Fibiano was a person who wanted authority over someone else.

"The dead man in the train asked me to give you this," Nathan said as he handed the metal tag to Fibiano, he remembered he kept it well-hidden in his wallet. The man took it without a word as if nothing had happened.

After a few turns, accelerations, breaks, traffic lights, they finally reached the place. It took about just five minutes of silent journey. Nathan went out as the doors unlocked.

There was a building just 20 meters in front of them. The building was huge and in English tradition, with a wooden roof that stood more than five stories above the ground, and a chimney protruded from it.

A soft yellow light lit the whole place and made it glow like a gift from heaven. It may be a mansion owned by an English millionaire and now converted to a hotel after some renovations. But the only weird thing was there was no one in sight. Region Force must rent the entire place, indeed.

"Follow me," Fibiano said, leaving the driver behind. They made their way into the building.

Nathan noticed this in the guidebook, one of the high-class hotels in Scotland and the landmark of Edinburgh City. It was known as the Northern British Hotel until the late 1980s. It was located in the heart of the city at the east end of Princes Street.

"Why are you taking me here? I can't afford to stay," asked Nathan.

"You are not going to stay here. It's the only proper place that we can find here, to isolate you from the public while someone briefs you. I hope you didn't expect to find a haunted old warehouse or a broken-down chemical factory for the meeting," answered Fibiano. He really didn't like Nathan from the start.

"Your organization seems wealthy, booking this entire place," added Nathan.

"Don't be so talkative, kid, you don't want the superior officers to slap you," warned Fibiano.

They reached the entrance. Fibiano pressed his hand against the door as trying to push it but failed. He pushed the second time, and the door opened. It must have been some concealed fingerprint scanner or face-recognizing cameras hidden on the door.

The place was lit by chandeliers and hidden bulbs of soft yellow lightings like the outside. The floor echoed as they walked on the old wooden floor. There were only a few furniture pieces and a large living space in the lobby—a few English-style sofas, a coffee table with magazines and a huge flower pot with plants on each part.

A few guards stood there, dressed in blue jackets and helmets with a re-enforced face protectors, like the uniform he saw in the secret compartment at ghost house. They were wielding Famas battle rifles and stood in a defensive position.

If anyone somehow managed to point a gun at them, they could easily duck to the nearest pillar and return the fire. Fibiano gave him his ID as a guard came forward, others ready on their guns if anything weird happened. Their captain eyed Nathan carefully as if trying to read his mind. The guard nodded almost reluctantly and returned the card.

Nathan was led to the left side of the reception desk to the lift area. There were six lifts, each guarded by a soldier. This time they were wearing black blazers and trousers, a small earphone plugged into one of their ears. They had no visible weapons but who knew what there was hidden in their blazers.

Fibiano went into the second lift as it opened, like it was as if it was waiting for them. They entered the lift while he produced a key and activated it. Then he pressed the button to the highest floor. Nathan felt a shudder as the lift pulled them up.

He saw a series of identical rooms as the lift door opened. Fibiano led him out of the lift and walked left to a corridor into an outdoor area. It was a five-star dining place. There were no candles on the tables, more guards looked at them, but they didn't say a word or stop them.

Fibiano led him to the middle of the place were a square table stood, a man in brown coat with a stripped tie sat there. He was surely the head here, sitting so comfortably with the entire world standing. He stood up to greet Nathan.

"Nice to meet you Nathan Doyle, I hope you don't mind if I introduce myself later, there are more confusing things that you must understand first before I can tell you anything," said the man, he was in his mid-forties, looked like an Irishman who liked to think and write. He had the style of a world-class chess player.

"I don't mind," replied Nathan. He was shocked to find that the head was more polite that Fibiano.

"Please, take your seat. Would you like to have anything?" asked the man.

Nathan sat down on the cushioned chair, which seemed too soft. "I prefer nothing, thank you." Nathan didn't dare to take anything from those guys, it may sedate him. He still didn't trust them very much.

He signaled a hand, Fibiano and the other guards immediately left them. "So, I want to know how much you know about us, first," he asked.

"You're some kind of secret organization, Region Force. Fibiano said that he was protecting me, but Golem, Rave and Spassky, their names may be coded, they this said before, but none of them even hesitated to open fire when they first saw me. I know that you're hiding uniforms in a place in the London," said Nathan.

"About the names, you're exactly correct, we are really protecting you, it was just there is some bribery going on in our organization. Golem and his teammates are a few of the traitors," he paused.

"About the uniforms, we were organizing an outpost in Central London to look after you, but there's something going on there. I heard the Ventures are high on your trails, they even tried to kill you and almost succeeded." He drank a little of his milk tea and swallowed.

"Who or what are Ventures? Why are they attempting to kill me or even make a fool of me in the swimming tournament? I didn't stand in their way or do something that offends them. And why it is so hard to kill me?"

"The Ventures, an organization that had been formed since World War Two, they're a group of cruel people who robbed the riches from other countries and people, and helped the Germans. No one ever knew them much, not like the other famously large organizations like Mafia or the Triads. This is because they're well-concealed, they sometimes even rob from the robbers."

He looked at his arm and said, "I'm really sorry about the needle, we were forced to do it like this. I didn't mean to ruin your tournament or make a fool of you."

Nathan narrowed his eyes, he was getting frustrated about this nonsense, he wanted an explanation. "The Ventures tried to electrocute you in the water, they had spoiled some of the light cables," he said slowly, as if he were biting a rock to make out those words.

"These is nonsense, they can kill me and the lifeguard and everyone else in the pool before I even got out of the water! I'm really tired of this, please, leave me alone! You're ruining my life!" shouted Nathan. He didn't care if he attracted attention.

A few guards looked at them, the man sitting in front of Nathan signaled them as to order them to stay back.

"You don't understand, things don't seem to be as you think. Those people are professional and they do as they plan precisely. They accept no changes. They wanted you die in a method that looks to be an accident so the police will blame the swimming pool's management. And if someone is cramped while the lifeguard's saving him, and they die together in an electric shock, the risk is too high for them. I hope you understand," the man said in a normal tone, he was incredibly calm as if he were facing a little kid asking for an ice-cream.

"Then why do they want to kill me for no clear reason?" asked Nathan, he lowered his voice a little, he was scared of Fibiano, the French may lose his temper.

"We're investigating this issue, I'm doing my best. I don't like to involve kids in this kind of job, we've tried to make deals with them but they ignored us," he paused, waiting for Nathan to cool down, he seemed to understand him more than Nathan himself did.

"Now just think about the things that happen before the ghost house, did anyone give you anything special or tell you anything weird?" asked the man, he leant forward as interested in the answer.

Anything special, the pendant, or the coin-size crystal that Veinna told him to keep it well and not to tell anyone about this, was it related?

But he was not going to tell the man that he didn't even know his name and betray Veinna whom took care of him after his parents passed away, there was no way he's going to tell. He forced himself not to touch or look at his chest, it will immediately tell the man where it was. Fibiano may be forced to take it out surely. The chain was tied around his neck with the pendant hanging down.

"No, nothing weird," Nathan answered calmly.

The man looked in his eyes carefully as if trying to read his mind. He seemed to succeed but said nothing, perhaps respecting his decision, but why did he need to?

"I think I should introduce my real identity to you now, since you treat me like a complete stranger, we may need to meet often in the future if things get worse. My name is Harvard Norman, the chief of the Elite Division in the International Intelligence Organization. Please, don't think that I'm talking nonsense again, almost everyone doesn't believe it when they first know me, but most of them have regretted it," he paused, "you may not have heard of us or the Ventures, neither your friends nor your aunty have . . ."

Incredibly, he knew everything about Nathan and decided to prove it. ". . . but the world I'm in is made to be concealed from the people that aren't meant to be involved. This is the world of criminal and anti-criminals, no one can be pure here. The bad guys kill and rob and we often have to kill to save more people's lives. One bad guy can slaughter 10 innocent lives in a day, we kill him first to prevent more.

"We have to bribe for the truth, it was the hardest thing when I started my career. I thought it was fun, like some sort of high-class police, chasing thieves and work for righteousness, but I found I was wrong as I got higher in the ranks. There's always politics among the organizations, a word with hidden meanings, sarcasm.

"Those matters are making me very tired, I wanted to get out of this ugly world but once you're in, it's hard to get out, or perhaps impossible. The criminals know your name and you have to keep working until you've caught them, and then, surely, their teammates will want revenge. The cycle keeps going on and it never breaks. Okay, enough of this, what I wanted to say is I want you to stay out of this world for you own sake," he said.

Nathan didn't know how to reply, this man seemed to be talking to himself.

"Do you mind if I tell you more about the International Intelligence Organization and the Ventures?" asked Harvard.

"No, I don't mind," answered Nathan, he thought of nothing to ask since there was no answer, maybe lies if there was any. He hoped that the man in front of him could make things better, but nothing convinced him.

"Actually, Region Force and Elite Division are under the IIO. We just make things neater. Region Force is mostly responsible for external issues and they communicate with other intelligence agencies and certain governments all around the world. They care for external things such as serious terrorism in certain countries that trust us or know us since World War Two.

"We earn our profit from anti-terrorism and external security management like keeping the Triads and Mafia controlled since they cannot be swapped out of the world, they have seconds in command to replace their leader after he's dead and another to replace if their new leader dies. While the Elite Division is meant to train new recruits, and manages the shares and business that the IIO owns in the world. They also control the internal security and look out for corruption. The Elites is kept completely from any people in the world, unlike the Region Force.

"The special thing and the most important weapon we have is the element of surprise, when we take down one criminal organization, they didn't know who did it, or how. And so they won't be able to prepare properly for the next assault." He took his tea cup and finished the remains, a waiter came to collect it without any signal.

He continued. "Unexpectedly, the Ventures and IIO were the same organization in the past. We were formed as a communist organization during World War 2 around Europe. We divided after 11 years, when there were two different ways of thinking in one society. They tried to change each others' minds but mostly failed, so a fight came.

"Almost all of them were tired of the war, they hated to be looked on. They wanted pride, they wanted revenge. Some of them were rich businessmen and they thought they had to do the right thing.

"We brought and made weapons and trained women to fight. The women we trained were deadly, they attempted to be sympathetic until they found the enemies' defences were low, they attacked, fatally.

"None of the people who joined our organization had self-consciousness anymore, their sons and husbands had died in the war, they just wanted to kill, it was quiet scary." He stared into the distance, thinking back as if he was there. "Slowly, people around Europe knew our presence, we were just like the anti-Japanese Army in Asia but rather the anti-Germans. People from Scotland, Austria, Belgium, Czech, Ukraine, United Kingdom, Italy, Ireland and Iceland joined us, we expanded our power until the Germans had to do something about us, we made our presence something to contend with.

"We managed to survive the war without a person dying from starvation, but there was then a serious conflict as I told you a bit about just now, some members wanted to form a group to take half of the government down when they were weak, while some thought it was a bad thing. They fought and fought until the remaining ones decided to stop, but the conflict hasn't ceased and may go on forever.

"Until now, both sides had long ago rebuilt and seemed to have vanished from the world. The government decided to forget about us and chose to care about their development and economy. It's a long story."

That was the end of it, Nathan couldn't take this Harvard Norman anymore, he was here to tell him not to care or bother him but now this grumbling man . . . "I'm not here for history lessons, tell me how can I stop getting myself involved in Ventures," asked

Nathan, he was frustrated about things that he never ever before bothered him.

"Just keep yourself safe, stay around with your friends. We'll send agents around you but just relax, you won't feel their presence. And one more thing, be honest to us, lying to the people helping isn't good," reminded Norman. Nathan was sure he was talking about the pendant, he shivered accidentally.

"Do you want my agents to send you home? That's enough for today. I hope we need not meet again, it will be bad news," said Harvard. What a weird good-bye. Nathan wondered whether or not the man had finally finished talking.

"I think I can hail a cab myself, I know the way back," answered Nathan. He wanted to be alone for a while, especially from these guys.

Harvard signaled a hand to Fibiano. "Send him to the door, and leave him."

When Nathan made his way out, a few guards looked at him impressively, maybe it was the little quarrel he had with their boss. Harvard Norman seemed to endure him for some time. But that wasn't Nathan's concern, he just wanted to care nothing about their business.

He and the Frenchman used the lift to get to the ground floor and when there were no guards around for the moment, something flickered in Fibiano's eyes. Suddenly, Fibiano pulled Nathan's collar into a corner and pinned his body to the wall. With his muscular hands securing Nathan's shoulders, a leg came up to knee his stomach, just below his ribs.

The other guards didn't notice. He tried to shout but Fibiano pushed his leg into his gut harder, creating pressure that hurt and silenced him. "You're quite brave just now, talking to a man that could kill you with a signal of the hand," whispered Fibiano.

"He didn't seem to look like you, mentioning to kill someone just when you're angry," replied Nathan, his voice was just not more that a whisper.

Fibiano, used his elbow and pierced it into his shoulder, a wave of pain travelled down to his waist and arm. "You better mind your manners starting from now, if we're not here to help you, you're either shot dead or electrocuted in the pool with your baby friends, understand?" said Fibiano, but he still hadn't release the pressure.

"But it's not me," Nathan couldn't finish the sentence. The man pinned his shoulder harder, hurting him even more, "Just say you understand or not."

"Yes, let me go . . . ." He was finding it harder and harder to breath, the pressure around the shoulder and stomach was compressing his lungs, starting a burning sensation and suffocation. Nathan couldn't fight him and release himself. He just wanted to go home and pass through his last hours in Edinburgh.

Fibiano eyed him carefully and finally let go. Nathan felt relieved from the pressure, he massaged his shoulder slowly but didn't say anything.

"I think you know the way out boy, you don't mind if you show yourself out," said Fibiano, his voice had changed to normal as if they were just chatting. Nathan looked at him for a while and went out of the five-star luxury hotel, just a piece of gold with dirt inside.

He hailed a taxi and made his way back to the hotel, tired of the commotion. He went straight into his room without finding Joe, he wasn't in the mood to chat. He showered then watched a bad Scottish movie and read a magazine about cars, killing as much time as he could.

Chapter Ten

NIGHT HUNT

It was a cold night as if Edinburgh had become an ice castle, the wind brought not only cold to Nathan, but also the sour defeat and confusion about the recent matters. It was unpredictable, something called the International Intelligence Organization. It could be a replica of the Central Intelligence Agency, but they were completely different and ridiculous if he thought again. But they were not out of a comic that he enjoyed, it was the real world, real secrets and real enemies.

It wasn't that he wanted to care or be involved, it just seemed that they were coming nearer him one step at the time, urging him to join the world of secrets.

A schoolchild may think of the world like that as an entertainment, but it's real with bullets entering real flesh and death that cannot be undone. A person could just disappear from the surface of Earth without anyone even knowing or missing the deceased, it could be made as if he never existed. It was the world that you have to be aware all the time and accept one danger after another. Perhaps Hell was not any different.

Nathan was exhausted when he took a rest in the hotel earlier. He went down at 8 p.m., and ate dinner alone. He then read a magazine in the lobby. He came out for a late walk, thirsting for fresh air. It gave him some energy and calmed his mind.

It wasn't that he enjoyed the chilled, icy wind that acted like needles digging into his skin, it was the quietness that he really needed in this situation, he urged himself to think, comprehend, to decide the next move that would avoid putting innocent lives in danger. People that weren't even involved in this issue—like the passengers on the train. This included himself. He shoved away every thought of Roberts or Joe, they were not helping a lot since none of them understood or even knew anything.

He was told that Ventures had a very strong influence in the world of criminals and intelligence. It was an unknown to him for them to take his assassination serious as if he radiated numerous threats.

The time to hide was over, he decided to face them, not hiding from them but he needed help from Harvard Norman. The man he just met was potentially powerful in the organization that claimed to help him, some chief officer in the division. He could supply financial support, contacts, weapons, resources and information. Nathan regretted as he didn't take down any contacts from him.

Between those thoughts, his legs were just going one step after another. He'd walked nearly two kilometers from the hotel without noticing. It was already late, almost 11 p.m. The traffic had slowed to one or two cars passing by every 10 minutes or so, he thought of home sweet home after a long day. How pleasant if he had an ordinary life, away from secrets. The words that Fibiano said hung in his mind as if he were just behind him, repeating the sentence. *He's a man that could kill you with a signal of a hand.*

He took in his surroundings, there were a lot of shops selling products, a new flat still in construction and a shopping complex with a car park outside. Suddenly, he felt something pushing down onto his shoulders, some kind of invisible force, it wasn't physical but some kind of old instinct. It was the same feeling he had in the cinema with Joe, there was an urge to look around and everyone seemed to be an enemy. It was the sense of being followed.

The thoughts of danger and the furious stare of Golem came back, filling his vision with his muscles urging him to run.

Just as he turned accordingly to his instincts, the muscular shape of boss appeared in the half-lit area near the complex parking lots, he was sitting in his car, both hands on the steering wheel as if waiting for Nathan to notice him.

There was something rather sinister, rather than furious. Golem came out of the car, as the moonlight shone dimly in the dark. He had something in his good arm, something formed out of several complicated pieces of twisted iron equipment, a golf stick? Nathan wasn't in the mood for this. Was it a weapon? Was it a firearm, a MK-5 submachine-gun equipped with a variable scope and front grip? Nathan made out the black cylinder on the muzzle, just producing a hiss when it fires, he surely needed a silencer to avoid waking the public or getting the attention of the police.

Acting on impulse, Nathan started running back to the hotel, but it was a world away. He was sure Golem was hot on his trail and Nathan had a huge problem, as there was no one around to help, and he was horribly exposed and in clear sight. Nathan ran along the buildings, searching for backstreets that led into another road that may provide cover. He could imagine Golem aiming with his scope. A volley of bullets would send pain all around his back—and certain death. The stores were locked, no backstreets or gaps were where he hoped to find them.

He felt hot air rush passed him as a window shattered, spraying fragments of glass onto him. Golem opened fire for the first time. It was lucky for Nathan that a post box as big as a car was between them as this predator fired the second round of bullets. The postbox flew off the ground like a toy being thrown by a small kid, with torn papers and envelops exploding into the air.

Nathan prayed, he surely won't stand a chance against Golem, until he reached the hotel. He needed to lose him on the way, but in this kind of condition, clear sight and neat shop lots, it was impossible.

The odds were in Golem's favour-after all, he had a gun. But Nathan had watched many ghost stories and movies when he was still a kid, when he couldn't go into bed without Veinna hugging him. And Golem was the ghost now. But why had Golem chosen this moment and wasted time to chase him? He could fire at him in the dark before Nathan even noticed him. Maybe he wanted him alive and to suffer. It was as if they were playing a chess game with Nathan on the losing side, there was no need to go straight for a neat checkmate. He could make it worse by killing him slowly. Golem smiled, his lips twisted in a cruel turn and several folds of the cheeks compressed below the temples.

Nathan noticed a building under construction, not the flat, with green nets and the skeleton of bare wood and metalwork coated with damp concrete around them, forming a structure of five stories. That could provide cover and he had a plan of losing Golem, but it was double-edged, if he succeeds, he wins. But if he fails, it was the perfect position for the devil to do anything he wanted. It was a very risky plan.

After all, he was going to run out of postboxes. He needed to get on the other side of the road and he needed to pass a grass field after that. He was not willing to take too many risks. It was already probably suicide but he had an idea, there was a less risky way to slow down Golem or maybe destroy him, but it was extremely dangerous. Nathan had taken physics classes in school and they were related to some basic common sense. The gun could aim and shoot far, but it's not so easy when something was fighting with the gunman in close range with a weapon.

The street now was more familiar to him. Nathan passed a backstreet and there was the building he saw earlier with a restaurant. The hotel and immediate area was much more familiar to Nathan than to Golem.

Advantages will come when the enemy is fighting in your area without any knowledge of the place, he was going to keep that in mind. He needed to enter and there was a plan nagging him in the back of his mind.

The door and elaborated floor-to-ceiling window were made of glass. He wanted to throw a rock or something hard at the glass, but there wasn't enough time and he was empty-handed. He braced himself and charged into the glass, something like a sensation of jumping into the pool naked when you're 10 stories high. The glass broke into fragments while he was in between the eruption of glass shards.

He landed painfully and hard on his stomach. The sharp fragments cut into him. He quickly stood up again as an alarm broke the silence of the night. He noticed a box with an illuminating red bulb in one corner.

He quickly examined himself, his legs were protected by the long jeans, but he noticed the front of his shirt was stained with blood as his left arm and forehead had suffered nasty cuts. He didn't know whether it was worth it to raise the alarm by hurting himself badly. But surely, the alarm system was set to send a signal to the police automatically, they were on their way soon. Things didn't seem to go as he planned, he thought Golem would just run away and he could somehow squeeze out an unbelievable, desperate explanation, but those thoughts were far on the horizon of his mind. It was time for a plan, a real plan.

Golem was even angrier but didn't panic at all, he only seemed to bring out his own classical kill-and-flee plan faster. He sprayed a wave of hot bullets, which forced Nathan to duck while Golem came closer. Nathan then went into the kitchen with Golem just seconds behind him. He locked the door and re-enforced it with a blockade of heavy crates.

Nathan wiped his forehead with the back of his hand, it was full of blood and sweat. The wound was getting worse and he didn't know how to explain it when he got back to the hotel, but that didn't matter, he needed to be alive first.

The restaurant served crabs, lobsters and delicate world-class cupcakes, what a weird combination to the plan. Nathan took a gas cylinder from the cabinet near the stove after a quick search, it was what the chef used to create a little fire to roast the surface of cupcakes as an art of food, this, this may be as an art of defence, too.

The cylinder was twice as big as his palm and curled into a ball. He never thought of burning Golem directly, but he would be shot before he succeeded. He heard the door being kicked by the man several times while the crates shook.

Quickly, he searched the refrigerator and eventually found a crab in the freezer. He thought of a funny idea of throwing it into the man's face, but it was not very possible. He was lucky the crab was not as fresh as he thought, it was frozen. He removed the bindings on the creature and tied them together, forming only one rope.

The process was a bit long and frustrating, the bindings seemed to be frozen, too, and he needed a pair of scissors. It wasn't that he wanted to trouble himself but where could the restaurant keep ropes? Time wasn't in his favour for a search.

Golem gave up on kicking the door and decided to waste more bullets, Nathan heard the door giving in, it was cracking and most of the crates were dropping. He tied the rope around the muzzle of the gas cylinder while he found a few liters of sluggish oil and dipped into it. His stomach churned at the smell of oil and the anxiety on what he was going to do next.

He managed to grab the lighter and headed to the back door. He couldn't light the explosive he made, once muzzle was removed, flammable gas will leak out of it and as the fire licks it, the whole thing will go off before he gets out. Golem had almost finished with the door and took his time taking the lock down with the hilt of the gun. Nathan headed to the back door, it took him about 20 seconds to open it from inside with his oily hands.

Then, with the lighted ropes tied to the cylinder, he unlocked the muzzle and threw it near the kitchen door and made his way out. Golem didn't even think to himself that the boy could have escaped through the kitchen, he could use the back door but it will be locked probably, and he could find him later. Or, he could be hiding underneath a table crying quietly. *Looks like the boy's not so brave as before*, he thought. But any easy thoughts of making the boy suffer vanished as the door he was trying to take down finally opened. But the weird thing was that some powerful force burst through it. The door crashed into Golem's body, followed by an explosion and flames making their way out of the kitchen and burning Golem. He was thrown to the floor and the blow nearly killed him. If he had entered the kitchen one second earlier, he would have been in Hell by now.

What was the boy up to? The explosion was almost like a grenade's, which Golem had experienced before in previous missions.

Nathan forced himself to the floor as he heard a deafening explosion inside the kitchen and a rush of flames burning out of the building through the windows. He was sorry for the restaurant's owner.

Was Golem dead? It wasn't very convincing, he may escape or the gas cylinder went off too early. It wasn't as strong as a grenade, it may be about half as powerful. A little gas remained to burn the place, also consuming everything.

Nathan didn't care, if he spend time finding out, it'll only waste time and such risk could be fatal. He didn't want his efforts and wounds to be in vain, his plan was to slow Golem down. This would give Nathan enough time for the journey to the construction side, since the shop lots offered no cover and the apartments were too far away. He could make his away back to the hotel if Golem was really down.

He kept running across the grassy plain. But that thought shattered as he heard loud swearing from the inside of the restaurant.

Chapter Eleven

BACKFIRED GETAWAY

He kept running as fast as he could. He looked back once, measuring his own progress. Golem was panting on his feet, recovering from the explosion. His clothes were embroidered with burnt rags with holes in the middle, but the submachine gun was firmly held in his hands as if he was born with it.

He kept an eye on Nathan, as if trying to tell him he was going to tear the boy into pieces slowly. Nathan turned his head back and could see the anger in his wide eyes, he brought up the gun and fired uselessly, he was out of range and it was too dark to aim. As the man was overtaken by anger and impulse, Nathan had successfully increased the distance between him and the predator of at least 100 meters.

Nathan kept his head low, and the inaccurate bullets never reached near him. He could hear the sirens of the police far away, but he'd be dead before reaching them if he dared to try. Golem stood where he was, firing and reloading the gun.

Nathan decided to head to an old castle connected to the construction side, if he wanted to get to the hotel using the fastest route, he needed to run along the construction area and Golem would easily intersect him or come in closer range for the gun. But if he entered the place, he could loose him easily then find another way out. By the time Golem reloaded his last magazine and decided the bullets may not be enough, Nathan had reached the gates of the old construction built in the olden days by the Scottish forces.

He tried the gates and thanked God it wasn't locked. He entered and closed the gates, then bolted it with an iron rod. He stopped a while to catch his breath while his muscles were complaining under the strenuous activity. He decided to get out of here in any exit as long as he lost Golem in this place. There were too many exits for the devil to guard.

He was shocked to find a figure on the dark floor. He went nearer, the body was lying with the head facing down, a pile of blood around it. The man was in his fifties, had a white moustache and half-bald head. He wore a blue guard uniform with a patch of blood soaked through the fabric material near his heart.

He was shot and it wasn't convincing that the guard came out for air and accidentally gotten hit by one of Golem's stray bullets.

The pool of blood proved it, there wasn't enough time to bleed a meter diameter in less than a minute. Nathan examined the man, brushing the back of his hand against the neck without leaving fingerprints. No pulse. The pale skin was still warm but looked pale and dead. He had no time to care.

Nathan regained his breath and energy then continued his way of finding an exit, he must be careful, of course. He burned all his effort to open the arched back door, which seemed to be a story high, wooden and decorated with old empirical signs.

He ran deeper into the castle, not waiting for Golem to shoot the gates. He walked along the luxury furniture, sofas, wooden tables with elegant teacups and pots. He imagined the relatives of the royal family once sat there, chatting in perfect manner with servants ready to come at a snap of two fingers.

He made his way along the wooden floor and turned right into a larger corridor. The furniture and decorations seemed to be the same and placed in the same pattern everywhere. Nathan thought it was like buying several connected apartments and decorating them equally.

After one and another, pictures of the royal family staring in the dark, radiating some sort of authority and sinister feelings all over the place as if classifying Nathan as an intruder, one could argue that. He didn't stop to look, in case Golem was near.

He passed a dining room, a few dishes, forks, spoons, knives and various utensils stood on a large and long varnished oak table. He picked up a knife with razor-sharp teeth and slender point, it might be useful later.

The area in front was covered and blocked by wood panels. He looked into the kitchen with an old cooking stove and firewood. There was another small corridor made for the servants to travel through without being seen. It made an impressive impression on the royals that servants appeared when they were needed and vanished when they weren't.

Nathan had definitely lost Golem, he just needed to find another escape and make his way carefully back to the hotel. And then he could think what to do later on. He hoped he could avoid meeting Golem in such a big place. He reached a barrier that read: **CONTRUCTION IN PROGRESS. SAFETY FIRST**. There was no other way out except this. But there wasn't much time for "safety first" since "alive first" was more important. He decided to proceed.

The place was completely different from the castle, it was dusty, dirty and some pathways had holes with only unstable wood panels covering each of them. It was the construction with five stories that he seen just now. Nathan grimly made his way down the flight of stairs, it was incomplete and not as stable as a normal one could be with creaking panel wood and nails.

It led into a room of sluggish and thick air, an underground construction section with the unventilated air being trapped there for months. It smelt of sweat and dirt. There were hoarse endings of cables and nails protruding out of the walls and incomplete ceilings. Piles of bricks and wet cement with grime and dust littered the entire place.

Nathan's throat was hoarse and dry, his head aching at the lack of oxygen and the weird scent. He wiped the blood off his forehead gently, not wanting to scratch the skin and checked whether his bleeding in the front had stopped.

While walking, he made out the patterns and shapes of slender walls and arched door frames, all still under construction, it could be a gallery or a speech hall. And about the workers, how could they stand the environment like this every day? It was suffering and lifeless, nothing more than an amount of space between the combination of concrete, bricks, wires and metal.

He proceeded into another section through the arced frames and eventually found a way to the first floor with an unstable ladder. The air was cooler there, with some naked bulbs willing to share enough light for the way ahead, it was definitely better. He went through a section of more complete corridors with rooms about the size of miniature galleries.

The smell of paint mixed into turpentine hung in the dust of the air. He noticed a collection of bricks and tiles lying in the corner with spades and a cement mixer. A weird contrasting of a clean wooden table and a box of pens and papers stood on one side.

The image of it blurred as something hard hit him square in the shoulder, sending him sprawling onto the dirty floor. The knife fell out of his grip and a wave of pain ran up from his shoulder and down to his waist. He groaned and turned slowly, the person who ambushed him was Spassky, the one Nathan had tricked by using the secret compartment in the ghost house, but he was not allowing any escape possibilities this time.

The man took out his gun, the same Model 18 he'd used before and pointed it towards Nathan's head, he then kicked the knife away that Nathan had dropped, out of range.

"I could kill you if I want now, right here on this damn floor, which a boy out of ideas and in pain is laying," he said and swore. "But I will have a huge benefit just to reserve that part later. The Ventures promised to pay us more if we keep you alive for the moment. Alive is better than dead."

He was in a black T-shirt, dirty jeans and yellow boots. Nathan now knew how the guard died near the gate.

Just at he let the words hang in the air, Golem appeared on the other far side. He walked slowly along Nathan's body and turned around, letting it be clear that there was no escape for a mouse in the corner. He handed the submachine gun to his partner, the black muzzle still billowing sulfuric, dark smoke.

Golem crouched with one leg and whispered, the voice poisoned and spitting out venom in the form of words. "You will experience a bad way to die and probably the worst pain before it. I will kill you with pleasure after this.

"If you are concerned, I already caught your nanny named Veinna this morning and tried to squeeze as much information out of her tied on the chair. But she kept secret, so I . . ."

"Leave her alone, she didn't even know what is going on," warned Nathan, his voice not more than a whisper. The pain had weakened him. The devil must have been asking whatever secrets about the crystal his father passed to Veinna before him. But he had no knowledge about it, not at all. But the devils in front of him knew something.

"I don't think she knows anything about this. It is you that don't know a lot and there are lots of things for you to know before you and your secretive nanny go to an unmarked grave," he chuckled a cruel voice. It was one that may have been formed in the deepest bowels of Hell.

"Scared now? Looks like you're a coward when there are no ideas in your worthless brain. You should care for yourself more than that nanny. She gave you the pendant, didn't she?" His hand crawled into Nathan's chest and pulled the crystal out.

Nathan tried to defend, but Spassky brought down the spade another time with a slap in the face from Golem. He accidentally bit his lower lip. His visions were blurred and he didn't have the strength to get up or care.

Golem retrieved the knife that Nathan had possessed. He balanced it in his hands with pleasure. Then, without even hesitating, he cut the boy's arm, sending out a weak groan and pain up to his neck.

"This was how I felt when they took the bullet out of me, you should have known it by now," he said then stood up and walked away.

Nathan clutched his arm defensively, he bit his teeth to hold back the pain.

"I think this will soften you, since you had so many tricks the last time, you deserved it!" Spassky spat the words out.

Suddenly, just after the last word, Rave came in, dragging a small human figure and threw him onto the floor. He turned around and kicked back but missed.

Golem angrily took out a handkerchief and a bottle and poured the contents onto it. It smelt like chloroform, he covered it over the boy's mouth and nose, resisting with a few struggles and then the boy slowly relaxed, surrendering to the chemical.

"What the Hell is this brat doing here?" demanded Golem.

"I caught him eavesdropping outside. He may be the boy's friend, following him here," Rave said.

For a moment, Nathan froze, the pain had suddenly subsided, could it be Joe? But there wasn't enough light for him to see the face. How did he come here? The stupid boy must be following him when he took a walk or when the devil was chasing him. He hoped someone else knew about their whereabouts.

"Okay," murmured Golem with the accents of cruelty. "We can make him suffer for the boy to spill out everything he knows." Golem suddenly froze and asked urgently. "Is anyone following him? Did he call the police?"

"Relax boss. No one knows he is here except us," Rave said in a high-pitch voice. "There's no phone around for a least a kilometer and if he did make for it, how can he follow him?" The three devils exhaled dusty air in relief.

"Now drag them into somewhere secure and give the boy some bandages so he will not get infected and die before we pass him to the Ventures. I'm contacting them," Golem eventually said.

Spassky took out a white cloth and a bottle of cheap brandy from his jacket pocket. He came near Nathan and tore the fabric of his arm then smiled while pouring the alcohol on the wound. Nathan yelled and kicked but was intersected by Rave. He caught him and held him down, watching the bloody fluid flowed to the concrete floor.

After 10 seconds, they stopped. Nathan was still in pain, his back and hand throbbing and waves of pain radiating from the wounds. However, the alcohol had prevented infection. Rave then took the cloth and tied it around his hand roughly, pulling the knot so hard and tight until Nathan yelled another time.

They chuckled and smiled. Golem had finish watching his drama and walked out, leaving the four of them there.

Spassky dragged the unknown figure, it was too dark to see who, probably Joe. Rave pulled Nathan's good arm, tied his hands behind his back and forced him to stand and walk. "You better do as we say and accept you fate or we will kill your friend that will not bring money to us dead or alive," Spassky said.

They dragged the unconscious and semi-conscious boys through another wide corridor with wooden poles that needed to be avoided, but they did hurt his arm indirectly.

Eventually, they reached a small doorway into a construction of a library or it looked like one. It was small inside with no books, but Nathan could make out the counter and concrete shelves supporters weirdly built and attached to the walls. Spassky and Rave pushed them in, both landing hard on the floor with Joe in unknowing heap.

"We'll pick you up before dawn. You better sleep well instead of thinking of ideas that will not work this time. You will need all your wits for the coming days. Don't try anything we don't want, just to remind you about your friend," Rave warned them casually.

The two of them took a few wooden panels and secured them to the door frame with nails. The ugly sound of a hammer hitting the brickwork ached Nathan's ear.

"Sweet dreams," Spassky said. Rave dragged a steel container and sat there, a gun in his hands while the Frenchman walked away.

Nathan quickly examined his surroundings, the library was wet with cement, otherwise not more than an unfinished room.

He looked at the figure nearer him. Despite the dim light from one of the ventilation veins, probably the moon was bright, he could make out the small nose and thin lips. These were the features of Joe, especially his fair yellow hair. Talking about holes in walls, they were too small for anyone as old as 6 and barred with metal rods.

Nathan was exhausted and hurt, it was likely almost midnight and he needed sleep. The throbbing wounds and surprises had worn him out, sucking whatever energy that was left in him. Nathan supported himself into a sitting position and helped Joe with one hand.

Then he carefully placed his own hand so that it hurt the less and curled into a ball to at least fend off the cold of the night. Most of the time he was half awake with his skin numbed cause by the temperature, but he eventually entered into a deep sleep without knowing it.

Nathan woke up with a few kicks to the back, reminding him of the spade-inflicted wound. Rave and Spassky had removed the woodwork. He uncurled and sat straight, the wound full of dried blood and alcohol, but the pain had at least subsided.

Rubbing his eyes with the back of a grimy hand, he saw Joe had long ago awakened and wondered about the wounds on Nathan, he didn't say anything, probably still taking in what had happened when he passed out.

For a brief moment, both of them were locked in eye contact. They didn't know what to say or couldn't make out the words because of the two devils standing in front of them.

The two men escorted them out of the construction side area through a series of corridors, rooms and turns. They went out through the back door, not the one Nathan had gone through the day before. Nathan felt like night walking all the time, but he just continued moving and did as he was told to switch directions by words or a rough pull.

Eventually, they got out and inhaled the fresh cold night air. Fighting and breaking through was out of the question with their backs at gunpoint and hands tied with a cord. He saw a gate half opened with Golem standing beside it. A jeep, military green-black painted stood in front of them. They were told to enter the vehicle.

It was a four-wheel drive vehicle. Golem and Spassky got to the front seats. Golem, the driver, started the ignition key and the engines jerked and shuddered in a repeated vibration.

Rave urged them into the back seats and climbed into the space used to contain hiking equipment and goods. They pulled out with the gates open. The men had probably came into the place at night uninvited and shot the guard. And with such coincidence, Nathan had stumbled into their nest. At least there was an advantage, the missing guard could be a trail for the police while bloodstains were probably cleaned off except the one in the library, he didn't see them entering it again.

They took a small street north. Nathan simply glanced through the quiet city's concrete scenery, with blocks of colourfully painted houses, metal skyscrapers, and granite banks.

The streets were lit by the yellow lamp posts, silent witnesses to the boys' fate. It was about 4:30 a.m., everybody was still fast asleep. Occasionally, their eyes met Nathan blaming himself for following while Joe simply looked away, slightly ignoring him.

Nathan recognized Princess Street that they took, the whole way vacant as if they were in an abandoned area. They passed the stadium and the landmark of Edinburgh City, Balmorals Hotel. He wondered whether Harvard Norman was still inside or was someone watching and following them, but his instincts told him nothing.

He thought what Roberts and James would think about their missing students. They will report this to the local police. It would only do a little with such slight evidence at the burnt restaurant, the dead guard and some witnesses, before the police would actively start looking for them.

As the journey went on, the buildings became fewer and fewer. Even the tarmac was faded and weather-beaten. They may be exiting Edinburgh City.

The wounded arm had gotten better. Although the bandages were soaked with dried blood and plastered to the wound, it was better not to remove it. He was lucky the bleeding had stopped while he slept.

The presence of trees and wheat field told them that the outskirts were near. Soon, as they guessed, both sides of the road were guarded by clumps of trees and vegetation. The road led into God knows what place, which began to worry the both boys. He hoped it wasn't so bad after all. *He hoped.*

Chapter Twelve

FIRE HEAT

AN HOUR HAD PASSED AS the jeep made its way to an alternative turn on the right onto a bare road. The trees were guiding them instead of dividers or white painted lines. The journey was still and accompanied by the rhythmic hum of the engine.

Occasionally, herds of goats and dogs ran with the jeep. The dogs soon became tired, realizing the driver wasn't generous to share some fragments of meat.

As far as the two boys were concerned, they had reached an abandoned town. Every section of land was separated with barriers of straws and bamboo wood, a stack of untidy hay covering each of their tops. The barriers were creaking under their own weight and looked not so solid as if in one kick of a human foot, it could go tumbling down into a heap. They were old and uncared for perhaps at least 10 years. Since the barriers were low enough for Nathan to see the surroundings, he made out the houses in it. The woodwork wasn't either with fading colour and crumpling pillars.

Weeds and whatever plants that had grown over and around the archways, door frames, pillars and every infrastructure of the place, performing their greatest embrace and making their own decoration as if they were nice. *They weren't.*

The humming vehicle drove through the abandoned land for about five minutes, same and familiar sceneries flashed passed all the time. The car suddenly broke into a halt as if Golem knew what landmark to stop at.

The driver looked at his hostages and stared at them for the moment as if trying to pull all the fear out of them and meaning—you are free to cry in this place where no one will notice. But he gave them a signal to get off the car. Spassky and Rave independently got to the outside, their boots brushing and stomping on the dry ground. Golem followed next after turning off the engine. He opened the door for the two boys but said nothing, the message was clear.

Nathan and Joe helped themselves out through the same door. The cold morning air pressed onto his bare skin and promised to go through the fabric that wasn't suitable for his kind of weather, it was just a matter of time before they really felt cold. The first light was successfully breaking through the night sky.

Joe stood beside Nathan, trying to hide but somehow didn't show it. The three men escorted them through the village for a hundred meters, this time there was no need of gun pointing, they could slowly bring out the weapon and pull the trigger with pleasure if anything unexpected happened. No any other people would witness.

They passed along a lot of countryside houses like the ones they saw earlier, abandoned stalls and a dried wells near the village square or what the remains that was left of them was. The place seemed to be echoing some sort of past joy with friendly neighbors or nostalgia and no-one-you-didn't-know-that-live-in-this-place type of scenario. Heavy hints of anguish radiated from the houses. However, something bad happened and now they radiated senses of horror and the past happiness seemed to become a type of sinister feeling in a ghost story.

They made their way to the edge of the abandoned town, along a series of familiar sceneries replaying on the not-existing television screen. Until something different finally appeared on the far end of the town, which was the place they were meant to be detained.

They surely didn't want to keep them in an unsecured house that was identical to the rest, there may be a funny possibility of forgetting or mistaken the prison's location.

A warehouse stood in front of them, high up to three stories but with only one floor-to-the-ceiling area. Rave opened the huge metal sliding door after unlocking two different pad locks and a tied chain. Spassky pushed the two boys in roughly as if fearing the may flee. Both of them turned and watched helplessly as the door shut and the *click* echoed through the warehouse.

The place was full of bundles of straw, stacks of rice, flour and wheat that were a decade from the selling date. Leaking bottles of oil piled up on the other side. The place wasn't as big as the warehouses in cities and not as spacious. But still, big stocks made them stuffy and packed. There was a failed ventilation system and a few gaps in the ceiling.

After a minute or more of observation, taking in the resources that were worthless for an attempt of escaping, they finally couldn't ignore each other's presence. Joe had already known Nathan's wound on the arm and seemed concerned, but he didn't show it. Nathan was the first to break the silence.

"Joe," he said. "Why did you follow me? It's dangerous."

"I'm worried about you since the swimming tournament. I didn't have the chance to meet you. Mr. Roberts told me something bad happened, he asked me to give you some time alone but I was impatient," Joe explained.

"When did you start peeking on my back?"

"I started when I saw something burning in the restaurant, which caught my attention. I was determined then to find you."
"You could have alarmed the police when the madman was firing at me, why didn't you?" asked Nathan. His voice was high-pitched as if someone had let him down.

"I left my mobile in the hotel and there weren't any visible public phones around. And the incoming police was too far away. I couldn't leave you alone, you may need me," his voice was shrinking.

"But following me won't help anything. You couldn't fight him," said Nathan. He already knew what the reply was but kept silent.

"I just can't leave a friend behind and get away like that. I'm not that kind of coward, and I at least have to be on your side and know where you are. I'd rather be caught with you than to be worrying in the police station," he answered in a loyal voice. Nathan kept silent, a little of his emotion had spilt out.

"Since the train incident or perhaps earlier, when I saw bruises all over you two weeks before, I knew something bad happened. You were in danger and got out of it in narrow way somehow. You had been quiet most the time. What actually happened?" his voice got a little louder and faster as it was mixed with anger and disbelieve of his friend questioning his loyalty. "Why didn't you tell me?"

The events in the train with the dead man replayed again, the man's last words, the tag, Shaun's rescue, Balmorals Hotel, IIO with Harvard Norman, the way Golem stared at him the night before and the surprise by Spassky, and then the unconscious Joe on the floor.

Could Nathan tell him about all that? Or he could just say I don't know with further unanswerable questions. He gone through a sharp decision, since Joe was already with him, hiding all those things will only make things go from bad to worse.

He needed his friend to be united with him, to make the last hope possible and to stop being suspicious. It wasn't only involving him, he was his best friend. Now, two lives were virtually in his hands and he needed to tell Joe who or what he was facing.

"All right. I can tell you the things I know and how far I understand about those nuts," he said. He took a break, deciding where to start with Joe relieved from convincing him. "First, I met or I noticed someone following us when we were at our old place, it was the American, Rave.

"Or sometimes I could feel it, just I didn't know who. He pretended to be an ordinary pedestrian reading the Times but you know, I seldom notice someone reading a newspaper near the cinema, not at night, it was inappropriate.

"So, I left you and followed him. He met a person called Spassky in the backstreet and reported what happened. Both of them then went back to the hideout and met the boss, Golem. All along they didn't notice me on their trails. The hideout was in the ghost house we visited," he stopped for a while and swallowed. His throat was sore and lacked of water, talking made it worse.

"What happened afterwards?" asked Joe.

Nathan had no idea how to continue about those sneaking and fighting and tricks. It's wasn't easy but he tried his best.

"I somehow was a bit over curious. When I eavesdropped on them for the second time, everything was the same as the first time. I felt my effort following them to the ghost house had been wasted if I didn't investigate further. I'm given a chance to leave the place quietly but I didn't. I continued to examine the back part of the place, where workers used to make-up and dress. I made my way without being noticed, they each had a gun and it was extremely dangerous, even more without me being armed. I followed the trail Spassky made, he was told to guard the place. I saw he opened a safe department, a small room. He left it and I went in using a lever without needing any key.

"I found boxes written with a weird name—REGION FORCE and they were full of army uniforms, helmets and bulletproof jackets. I didn't understand why it was useful.

"After that, my worst fears became reality when Spassky returned with a gun. Lucky I managed to knock him out with some tactical trick and escape with his gun. It is too hard to tell you.

"Moreover, when I tried to make my way out, things didn't seem to be in my favour. Golem and Rave noticed the unconscious Spassky. They predicted where I headed since there was only two ways out and one of them was guarded by Golem. I was forced into a room, a dead end, too. I concealed myself in the costumes and Golem failed to find me. I was nearly shot when I'm forced to run out of the room. For a reason, I won't let the devil lock the door with me on the inside.

"I forced my way out of the workers' passageway using hidden metal steps to the customers' passageway. By the way, Rave and Golem closed in from both sides and they trapped me. In the commotion, everything seemed to be happening so fast. Rave missed a shot and hit Golem in the arm and I escape from the ghost house, nothing much more than that."

"Why did they want to follow you?" asked Joe, the puzzles in his head were still far apart.

"Unbelievably," Nathan said slowly. "They claimed to be protecting me."

"They said Region Force sent them. It must be they are angry with me as I made them look like fools. I had fooled Spassky and indirectly hurt Golem and then they switched sides. They switched to the criminal organization that existed after World War Two named Ventures. They intended to kill me for no clear reason. It may be the pendant my aunt gave me, Golem mentioned it the night before," Nathan continued.

"Until then, I met a person after the swimming competition. He was one of the most powerful men in an organization claimed to be protecting me. They'd been betrayed by Golem and the International Intelligence Organization (IIO). I met him in a hotel, booked specially for our meeting. His name is Harvard Norman. He told me about Ventures, himself, and some boring history, I want to skip that.

"Although Norman said he's is helping me, I didn't show him the pendant. I don't trust him still, I only knew him for less than half an hour."

He mentioned the Ventures decided to take this more seriously, they want to kill me," said Nathan. It was like cursing himself to say that so many times.

"And they tried to drown you in the pool somehow." He was confirming, not asking. He already knew the answer. He massaged his head.

"They didn't care if hundreds of people died, they just want to kill me. And about the pool, Norman said the Ventures spoiled a cable supplying power to the lights underwater, they wanted to kill me with what looked like an accident. But the IIO agent sent a paralyzing needle into me, he needed a reason to pull me up," replied Nathan.

"It's not very clear Nathan. You said they wanted to kill you and make people think it is an accident, but how about the bomb on the train with the terrorist?"

"They may rob the wealthy businessmen in the first-class carriage. So no one would think the bomb was for kid like me," he replied again.

"What about the pool. They could electrocute you with the lifeguard, why not?"

"Harvard Norman said they wanted everything to look as an accident. They don't expect impreciseness."

For the moment, both of them looked at each other. Nathan felt exposed after all the secrets he had been hiding finally broke out. Joe was trying to accept what he had just heard.

"Let's find a way out of here, before the men come back," Joe broke the silence. Nathan didn't know whether Joe had accepted his explanation or not, but he seemed to put aside what wasn't important to saving their lives.

Nathan looked around, taking in the hundred packets of flour, wheat and grain. Some oil and shattered glasses from the broken bottles.

A window, built over them, stretched across the three-story high ceiling. Brilliant sunlight was trying to break through the long accumulated dust, but only some managed to shine brilliantly through the holes. It was perhaps 7 a.m.

"We need to untie our binds first," Nathan suggested as both of them examined the firmly tied ropes. Death knotted several times and sticking to the hands so tightly until it disturbed the circulation. It was close to impossible to get them out without a sharp edge.

"Try the broken glasses," Joe said, looking at the pile of half-shattered glass of bottles in the dark.

Nathan went and crouched down, he tried to grab a sharp shard, but it slip off his restrained fingers as he attempted to use it. They were too slippery, coated with oil.

"Too oily?" asked Joe.

"Yes, I can't get them."

"I hope we can just burn them without hurting ourselves," he joked but there was time for humour.

"Even if we can find something flammable, how are we going to escape?" murmured Nathan.

"We can blow the door down but that won't help if three armed men are after us and they said they're going to kill me first!" demanded Joe.

"We need to find loose parts on the walls, they're patched up with metal slides, not very thick. We might be able to find and unscrew parts around the perimeter. And if I didn't meet any usable sharp edges, I going to use petrol from the engines or something else," Nathan said as they moved in different directions.

Nathan decided a look at this place and see what possible resources they had. As soon as Nathan walked between the countless piles of grain packets, he went and took a brief look at the materials they had, looked like Golem was leaving no chances, there were no sharp metals or rubble from some spoiled machineries. The binds around his wrists were hurting now, leaving red scratches from the hoarse ropes that limited the blood flow.

While Joe stayed at the metalwork closing in the warehouse, strolling and examining each piece that made up the whole part. He needed to hold his frustration from kicking the walls, it'll do no good anyway.

Eventually, Nathan found a lifter, used a decade ago to transport rice stacks through the warehouse without using human energy. It stood abandoned in one corner near a collection of miserable spades and cutters.

The farmers may have kept them for some of the constructions of their houses using wet mud and straws from the river a decade ago. The cutters won't work a lot since the restrained fingers couldn't open to use them. They now were useless. He struggled to open a fuel tank beside the lifter, using the fingers of his hands that were in bindings slowly. It was full of petroleum's smell. It might be three quarters full or more.

The petrol would help them to blow the way out and they could have a little chances in the jungle or set chaos in the warehouse and provoked Golem to think that they had been burned alive if they had another way out.

He memorized the location of the lifter and spade and returned to Joe. "There weren't any loose screws. But there're some narrow gaps of the metalwork just above the ground, some were wider but we can't get through it. A little hope just blinked in Nathan's mind, he just stumbled upon a few spades they could help them escape very quietly, but first—the bindings.

"Do you have any more ideas to remove this?" asked Nathan as he showed him the binds.

"We can't cut it with our hands like that even though you found some cutters. But I'm not joking just now about burning it. There must be a safety precaution for that plan," Joe said as trying to tell something but failed.

"What do you mean? The petrol, I don't think that's a good idea. And what safety precautions can we make with our hands tied?" asked Nathan.

"I don't really get what I'm thinking. But sometimes the sunlight and the glass can help. If we can magnify the sunlight to burn the ropes, we don't necessarily need flammable substance," said Joe as he pointed at the leftovers of shattered glass bottles.

"Even though it works, we could burn our hands and that plan may take a decade," replied Nathan.

Joe stood there, repeating several times on looking at the window above, the bindings and the glass as if expecting them to make a comment.

"I'm still thinking about safety. If we don't hurt ourselves, it's a perfect plan," he paused. Don't you get it? Help me find a way," said Joe.

"Water? Fire can't burn water," replied Nathan.

For a moment both of them looked at each other.

"We need to wet three quarters of our binds except the upper part, so the fire will only consume a quarter of the binds, it's more than enough," Joe came up with the sentence quickly as he had already had the idea. No one knew whether or not it was a good or crazy idea—a double edged sword. If it works, then they may get away after all. If it didn't, someone may be burnt to death. The both of them examined their surroundings again, this time more precisely. There was a canister, used to collect water from the broken roofs, but they didn't notice it before. Perhaps no one thought water and fire will make out a plan.

The fortunate thing was they have more than three liters of rainwater and could use it if anything else unexpectedly caught on fire. Burning the binds requires only one person and the one that was freed could use the cutters. It wasn't a great plan, but no one could figure any better one, so they agreed. But who was going to burn and who was going to *be* burned?

"I'll try to wet my binds as we said, take the glasses," volunteered Nathan.

"Why not me? I could fail and no one could imagine the consequences, I'll wet my binds," said Joe. He moved as to stop Nathan from saying another word.

"Don't," Nathan said as he stopped him. "Think again, I brought you into here. It's me to be responsible if anything happens. Just . . ."

"I followed you, it's nothing to do with you," Joe cut in, his voice was urgent.

"It's no use arguing, Joe. My arm is hurting now and it can't hold the glasses in the correct place for a long period of time," Nathan tried to reason with him. It was a good enough argument, even a lawyer will have difficulties with it.

Joe thought for a while. "All right, but if I burn your hands, don't blame me," Joe said unwillingly. His voice sounded like a younger brother talking to an elder one.

Nathan went near the canister and dipped half of his binds into it. He had to be careful not to wet the entire thing. Joe crouched down beside the pile of broken glass, examining the best ones. The glass was oily and he only managed to hold slightly, but with a little more friction they'd slip.

The both of them then met below the hole of the big window, sunlight pierced down on them. Joe came with a few pieces of carefully selected glass in different sizes and shapes and a handful of dry hay. Nathan sat down with crossed legs, Joe wasn't tall enough to do the job if both of them stood.

Joe crouched down and examined the glasses again in the pure sunlight, combining them to make the most magnified line of light. He needed to use both hands to grip them.

"What are you doing," asked Nathan curiously.

"I'm trying to put the best light rays into one line. I used to play dry leaves when I was 8 years old," Joe said. He applied the handful of dry hay found from the stacks on the binds.

"Don't move," he warned. Joe slowly brought up the combination of glasses, three altogether and placed it over the hay. He elevated and lowered them until a line of red appeared on the hay.

When the light heated up a single point on the hay, a little grey smoke flew up but it didn't catch fire. During this time Nathan thought about the sound of the door unlocking and Golem looking at them with vengeful eyes at what they were doing. Nathan's wounded arm was already throbbing and the pain starting to go through him again. He bit his lower lip.

But that didn't seem to be happening, they thought there was no escape and perhaps there was. After 10 minutes or more, there was a flicker of small sparks. Joe's hands were already shaking although the glass was light but gravity was failing him.

That was the most exiting moment for the two boys as a couple of sparks and the dry hay lighted, and a small fire licked the hay. It began consuming the hay a little more and spread to the dry parts of the binds.

The fire intensified, and Nathan stared at it. Whether this was a good idea or not, this is the time to prove it.

Chapter Thirteen

UNINFORMED BACK-UP

THE FIRE WAS BURNING THROUGH the bindings. Nathan felt his wrists were scalding and the heat had spread throughout his entire arm. The heat was intense with the bindings beginning to burn . . . Joe was already dragging the water canister nearer with his restrained hands and was ready to pour it out if anything bad happened.

Nathan waited for the exact moment and tore the weakened bindings apart. The remains of the ropes fell to the floor, still burning a little. Nathan treated and examined his hands, they were raw and red, but otherwise unhurt, just overheated by the fire.

"I will get the spades and cutters," Nathan said. He looked at his wounded arm, he'd accidentally slightly opened the wound and blood soaked through the dirty bandages. He needed to get it wrapped again, no one wanted any infection.

After a minute, the two boys were released from the bindings and looked for where they should dig along the metal panels. They didn't have enough time, but Nathan finally chose a spot that seemed to have the most space between the panels and the ground, a good 20 centimeters, some mice must be finding their way through this spot for the entire decade.

Nathan brought up the spade and started with Joe next to him. They formed a pile of earth beside them and the gap was getting larger, it showed their exhausting progress. The sense of

Golem opening the door was stronger than just now but it didn't happen. Perhaps they were close to escape and failure will surely make their effort in vain and this bothered Nathan more than anything else.

Soon, the gap became a meter wide. Joe put down the spade and struggled then rolled out of it. Nathan followed next, almost stuck but Joe helped to manoeuvre him out with the ground and metal rubbing against his body. They took a deep breath, leaving the unventilated warehouse's atmosphere away.

Joe used a pile of dry branches and leaves to conceal the gap. They took in the surroundings and examined the area. There was nothing guarding them except the same houses made of straws, dried mud and bamboo, trying to make their last stand. A bare road led to the end of the outskirts, opening into the forest.

The town ended with a few lots of shops and a wooden fence filled with gaps and spoiled by curious animals. The morning sunlight was striking down, intensifying the heat on their heads and shoulders.

"I noticed a river when they were driving, we could follow it downstream and we could reach the sea, follow the coastline east and get ourselves to civilization or any harbour near city. We could go to the police station and tell them all about this, whether they believe it or not, as long as we are alive," Nathan recommended.

"Yeah, we should stay alive. We better keep moving," replied Joe in agreement.

The both of them made their way as quietly as possible along the straw houses, keeping low and trying not to attract any attention. Their escape seemed to be still unnoticed by the three men, as no one raised the alarm, they let out a sigh in relieve.

As they entered the forest, leaves and branches blocked their way and they needed to shove them away, making sound that wasn't good if the any of the men were near. Their sight was blurred by the moisture from transpiration of the plants.

They searched for the river by testing the ground's moisture, which didn't seem to work out well. Finding the plants that could only survive near a water source, something from geography lessons they learned in school suddenly became a lifesaving resources of navigating their way through the woods.

They heard a shout—rough, angry, disbelieve and urgent. Someone had found out the boys' had escaped. They quickened their paces, Golem and his teammates will take time to find out where they had gone.

Surprisingly, they heard men with heavy footsteps hurrying to the forest on the east and north, the way they were heading. Golem must have alerted the Ventures and around 20 armed men were on their way. From the boys' vantage point, they could see these men wore green khaki uniforms of forest camouflage and looked well-disciplined. A commander in full authority was shouting without questions being asked.

They hurried across the landscape of pine trees and bushes and saw what they were looking for, the gleaming river, reflecting the sun emerging from the horizon. The river was clearly in sight without any trees or big bushes blocking their view.

"We can't follow the river directly, it's too open. Just keep it in sight and move with it," Joe said and his partner nodded. They ducked as four men nearly saw them. They were catching up pretty well and soon would surround them. This type of forest had too many open areas and the pine trees had fine leaves that didn't hide anything well.

The men were taking every chance of Nathan's whereabouts, every direction was being checked by men. But the area was big and only four men headed in the correct direction, but the others could join in with just a shout or a gunshot. They boys continued on their way carefully.

The sun was merciless, shining furiously. Nathan's shirt was plastered onto him by the sweat and dry blood, a wound that Golem had caused by hurting him the day before. The wound was throbbing right now and he feared it might be infected.

They heard another shout and a gunshot, the tree beside Nathan creaked. One of the men had spotted them and began firing, the other three chasing.

"Run! Quickly! Our cover's blown," shouted Joe.

Both of them rushed through any possible bushes, keeping themselves low behind trees and leaves. The vegetation was mild and open. Another gunshot scared all the birds away, it hit the earth a few meters away, not so accurate this time.

Now, the men had chosen a better position to flank them, one behind, two on the right and the last one on the left.

For the moment only the gunman behind was firing stray bullets at them. The others wouldn't take risk of shooting one another. But soon, three men will overtake them and close in, surrounding them.

They were running at maximum speed but not fast enough, avoiding any open area of the forest. Nathan felt the burning sensation in his legs, his throat was dry and hoarse, lacked of water. He couldn't go on like this any longer.

They saw a cave ahead, about five stories high and 500 meters wide. Spiky plants and weeds climbed around it accompanied with a family of unknown animals hiding in it. Behind, more men were following, the number had doubled. Soon, their chances would be zero. Nathan and Joe were near the cave, passing a steep landscape. Someone pulled Nathan and another pulled Joe, they closed their mouths tightly. Their hands were large and the small body of the boys looked pathetic. In the same movement, they retreated into the dark cave with their captives.

"Don't shout if you want to live, we're here to help you," the man said, his voice was rough but just enough to be heard as a whisper. Nathan looked at his face in the half-lit cave, his head was wrapped in a black fabric, two holes for his eyes.

Nathan was already unable to breathe with the large hands over his nose and was suffocating. He nodded and the man let him go, pulling his arm and guiding him into the cave, away from the entrance. The man with Joe did the same, but brought out a gun and shot some of the men outside, a whisper of the gun's muzzle and two shouts, they probably had noticed the unknown men.

"Follow us," the first man said as he led the both of them deeper into the cave. His shoulders were strapped with SCFW battles rifles, stealth equipped. Both of them followed the men, surprised by their approach. The light of the cave began to disappear as every step measured its progress.

Neither of the men or boys had said a word, afraid it may give them away. The cave walls narrowed, compressing them and they'd to move in a single line. They heard occasional shouts outside, barely audible through the rock a meter thick.

Soon, there was water beneath their shoes, black in the dark until ankle deep. It could be some of the river's water. Nathan felt relieved as a faded light pounded through the darkness with the sound of the river. They followed it and reached the other side of the cave.

The two men held them back, then made their way to the entrance, keeping low and taking each boulder as a cover and a break. Their guns were tilted away from their eyes, ready to shoot fast and accurately if anyone approached. After a minute, one of the men returned to them, his face half-lit in the cave.

"We don't hear any enemy voices, this means they've completely surrounded this whole area. They're now waiting for reinforcements, and we have to break through before they arrive. Eight versus two and we have liability, that is you two," he said, rather like explaining to them what they were rather than blaming.

"How can you be here? Do you know about the warehouse?" Nathan asked.

"Yes, but don't ask too much, my previous mission was compromised before it even began. The Ventures might know of our presence already, we were forced to shoot two men outside just now. Listen, follow us close and don't attract any attention. No accidentally kicking a pebble or falling, soldiers hate this. We will get out of here silently, in one piece," the man said again.

Nathan honestly never predicted such things, who were these men, could he trust them? Since they took the risk of killing two Ventures men, they were probably Norman's men and he hadn't had much of a choice right now.

The men led them out of the cave, in a formation of two soldiers guarding the front and back and they moved with half crouching. Nathan had to adjust his eyes to the sudden light.

There were topography of pine trees and slender landscape of hills. The running river was the only source of sound since any animals present were quiet after the deafening gunshots.

The formation of men and boys made its way slightly uphill, they hid among the pine trees while keeping in track with the river. They soon saw three men facing them, but they were far away and well-hidden with camouflage. The man that held Nathan urged them silently into a halt and then lay on their stomachs, keeping in contact with the forest floor, full of dry leaves and branches. They boys did the same.

"They outnumbered us by one and they're very alert, we must be extremely careful. They're well-equipped with assault rifles and a direct gunfight will kill us sooner or later. The sound of it will alert their entire force. We can't creep behind them without being seen," said one of the men, his hoarse voice just audible.

Nathan couldn't name them, they seemed almost identical from the uniform and weapons, their faces were concealed and he then made his own nicknames of Hoarse and Silence.

"Could we avoid them? We can take another way and return to the river's track," asked Nathan, his voice equally soft.

"It is not possible, they've guarded a perimeter of this area near the stream. We reached their corner and the other guards will be not far away. I'm afraid they have been increasing the number of guards from eight to 15 by now. We need a better plan," said Hoarse.

"We could make a distraction, disorganize their formation and take them by surprise. They may open fire and alert the others but we could make it out through the far eastern end and eventually meet our regrouping team at the harbour. There's a lot of cover in this side of the woods for the moment," Silence recommended, speaking for the first time.

"This is a dangerous plan, we don't know how far the other guards will be and how much distance we could make between them when we're on the run. I'm afraid these boys will be tired, it's a few miles of running," said Hoarse. They seemed to be completely calm with not a sense of argument, even though their opinions were different.

"We must risk that, you've heard how serious the Ventures are treating this plan, they could increase to 50 men of reinforcement if we keep waiting. It could be too late and more risky. The Scottish government wouldn't even know what is happening here, their gunshot sounds being contained in the forest," Silence said again, waiting for his partner to reply.

"You've convinced me well enough. We need a distraction," he said rapidly after a slight hesitation.

"Throw some rocks into the river," Joe said, still cheeky after being chased by so many armed men.

"Good, now go and hide behind one of those pine trees," he said to Nathan and Joe. "Distract and kill, I'll finish with the other two," ordered Silence.

"Here, take this first," he produced two army-grade knives with the slender shape and metal teeth, which could make any incised wounds even worse and cause infection faster. He passed them to the two boys.

"We could help or do something. Don't treat us like a liability," Joe said.

"Idiot. You can just run outside and distract them and I'll finish the job with you dead. You don't know how to aim well or even fire a gun, so just hide," said Hoarse. His voice low but was a sharp blow of annoyance.

Silence already had crept into a nice position and aimed, waiting for them to prepare. The boys unwillingly followed Hoarse's orders while he took a few pebbles and threw them into the air, landing with an unmistakable splash into the river. It wasn't a sound that would come from nature.

One of the guards saw it and took a look in the direction, and then went to check it out. "Stay here, I'll see what happened, it may be the boys," the guard said.

Chapter Fourteen

FOREST CHASE

The moment the guard stuck his body out, his eyes widened, scrambling for the rifle. Hoarse expertly fired five rounds into his torso. The sound wasn't audible from far but enough for the other guards to notice what was it. The poor man screamed and knelt in a final prayer then slumped down to the ground.

The other two guards were alerted, one of them ran over but was shot by Silence without knowing what hit his back. The other immediately fired in the direction of his attacker, forcing him into cover, but that was soon in vain as his magazine was empty, Hoarse ran forward and saw the guard scrambling with his pouches to reload and put him out with a knock of the gun's hilt in his head.

With the deafening, unsuppressed gunshots by the last guards, perhaps 10 or 15 men began to shout and detecting the sound's source, started tracking them. The soldiers signaled the boys to regroup. They continued moving in formation as a uniform of footsteps stomped on the ground behind them.

Nathan and the others made their way rapidly across the river, the water splashing below their feet. The place was even more dangerous than ever, they needed to run as fast as possible to maintain a good distance between themselves and the men. The intensified heat was affecting Nathan, the sweat on his palms lessened the grip on his Rambo knife.

They reached a place that looked to be an old wooden house for hikers. Small blocks of abandoned houses stood there, delighting the climbing tenders and clasping roots of plants and mushrooms, the green vegetation embracing it back into nature. A manmade pool surrounded by wooden barriers that was used to warm the hikers' feet now became one of the forest's small ponds.

"It's too open here, get back into the greens," shouted Hoarse as they turned right into the forest.

It was an exhausting 10-minute struggled running without rest, for the soldiers, they could move as quietly as they wanted or move in maximum speed for more than an hour. However, Nathan and Joe were burning full glucose in their leg muscles, their body begging them to stop.

It was a relieving sight of yellow sand and blue sea gleaming with the river feeding it. Far beyond, the harbour stood there, a few ships from fishing boats to millionaire private cruises stood with the waves.

They had to keep themselves concealed in the bushes to avoid being spotted. They followed the border of the jungle along the seacoast, every step measuring their progress of surviving. But that wasn't very smooth, their tracks had been noticed by the gunmen and they were very close, a minute later one of them noticed them, the others started to surround them.

It was difficult to lose them as they followed the coastline northeast, the predators were coming straight from west towards them. They would sooner or later meet and there will be direct assault with each soldier outnumbered by six. Their chances of survival were not good. Silence was taking no chances of that happening, he searched his vest and brought out a grenade, pulled the pin then threw it towards the enemy position. Three seconds later, there was a deafening explosion, followed by a ball of flame bursting through trees and consuming the close-by trackers. There were several shouts before it, and at least five men and their commander had been killed or injured, but now their allies wanted revenge.

Three of the left gunmen managed to climb their way forward and another four surrounded them almost completely and randomly behind trees, they did this so that a grenade couldn't kill them all, afraid of the same mistake. They left their prey with two dead-end roads. Fight to the death or run out to the beach and be shot dead there.

Hoarse and Silence were fighting their way through, shooting and keeping the enemies low while they proceeded. They were well camouflage in the forest and the surrounding enemies were not in formation. This would buy Nathan's group some time to get organized and be in a better position to fire at their pursuers.

But Nathan and Joe weren't wearing any camouflage so they were east to sight. Both of the soldiers reloaded and one of the three guards took the chance to throw a grenade, but Joe threw his Rambo knife, it hit the man in the side. He screamed out in pain, but failed to launch the grenade.

The explosive dropped onto the ground. His teammates managed to take a look at the grenade, but it was too late and they were thrown into the air by a mushroom of flame and an immense blow of destructive energy.

Hoarse and the three others had already stopped and took cover behind a clump of trees, out of breath and panting on his feet.

"We need to fight a direct assault against them, they are too close already. One to two," shouted Hoarse.

The other four gunmen didn't even flinch from the explosion, they'd sworn to die if the mission fails anyway. But the second in command sergeant had organized them into formation and they were not letting anymore chances go by.

One of the gunmen opened fire, the burst of machine-gun firing kept them in place behind the shattered pine trees. The other one joined the shooting and the sergeant and a guard made their way towards them, their bodies low and taking cover behind every tree.

"They're flanking us, be ready!" yelled Silence.

The sergeant had already approached behind Hoarse, he swung the rifle into his back and the victim dropped to his knees.

Hoarse clenched his teeth to hold back the pain and countered the attack with a swap, his body reflexed and turned backwards with a kick to the legs of the sergeant.

But the gunman was fast and without recovering from the kick, he threw dismantling blows to Hoarse. Both of them struggled on the forest floor. They struggled to be in the driving seat. Silence kept the other guards under cover behind the pine tree, firing randomly, probably saving what was left of his ammunition.

But the guards behind were already tired of shooting, they were in close range and their rifles were bulky, the soldiers could quickly manoeuvred their handguns and picked them off. Knives were also more suitable. They couldn't fire from far without hitting their comrades.

The enemies knew that and they dropped their heavy guns down, took out small firearms and prepared themselves for close combat. Hoarse was dealing with the soldier that flanked them, both of them had lost their weapons and were struggling on the forest floor, punching and kicking each other. Hoping their enemy would fall first.

Joe ducked and took cover behind a tree as the two soldiers fired their officer's side arms. Nathan wanted to join him into cover but one of the men intersected them, blocking him. Another ran across the brittle pine tree to help the battle against Hoarse, but Joe took him by surprise. He tackled him to the ground, and then they both scrambled for the gun.

Nathan looked at the guard in front of him. He was a man in his early thirties, with bloodshot eyes that were desperate to win. He smiled, his unshaven chin barely noticeable. But he was also a bit concerned about his teammate behind. Nathan gripped his Rambo knife tightly and ran forward, stopping as he pointed the gun at him.

"Put down the knife," he ordered, the gun aiming at Nathan's head. But he forgot one basic rule he learnt as a trainer, never stand too close when you're aiming. He didn't notice that the gun was just 20 centimeters away from the boy.

With the man's distracting concern about his sergeant and teammate, Nathan turned to one side and ducked, and the man fired late. It was deafening, so near to his ears. He didn't care. He took the knife and swung it violently at him. The guard backed away, surprised by the boy.

Another swing and it caught him in the wrist that was holding the gun, blood flew out and he yelled, dropping the gun. Nathan assaulted the guard with whatever move he knew, knocking, kicking, punching, but the guard only flinched a little by the cut and the combos of blows, he had been in worse situations.

As soon as he recovered from the shock and knew that this wasn't easy, he punched out, hitting Nathan in the chest, sending him sprawling onto the ground with the knife flying away. Nathan thought his heart stopped.

Nathan was adrenaline-filled, he didn't feel much pain as the blow hit him. The guard didn't even care about the gun or his wrist, he went forward and put his huge hands around Nathan's neck, suffocating him. Immediately, Nathan felt breathless, the air supply cut off. He didn't know what to do, the grip was incredibly tight from a madman. His vision was blurred and the remaining oxygen in his lungs was burning out. For the moment, Nathan thought of an idea, he had to do it. He kicked out a foot, hitting the man in between the groin. He did that several times, each one getting desperately harder.

After a few times, the man suddenly awoke from his madness, he looked more shocked and pained, and the grip loosened as if a release button of a machine had been pressed. Nathan pushed him with all his strength and he was thrown back, the ugly fingernails hurting his skin, leaving five bloody lines.

Nathan took about a minute to recover from the suffocation as well as the man's madness. He soon got back into reality and looked for a weapon, the knife or anything sharp.

The sidearm was still on the grass. Both of them saw it and went to get it. The man retrieved it first but Nathan threw him to the ground, pinning his hand. Someone shouted out his name and he looked. It was Joe, standing on lower ground with the other guard unconscious. Nathan could only make out his head and chest.

He felt a shudder ran through his arms and then a few wild gunshots. Joe was thrown back by some invisible force and lay there. The shots came from the gun on the ground. The guard under Nathan managed to grip the trigger and pulled it a few times, firing three stray shots.

For the moment, nothing moved. The past events of meeting Joe came to Nathan's mind, the day they met, lunch in the canteen, swimming tournament . . . everything up until now.

He hadn't noticed that he let loose the pin on the guard. He swung the slab of metal into him, Nathan crumpled to the ground, mentally and physically stunned. But it was the moment when Hoarse won the fight between him and the sergeant and took a few precise shots towards the guard. With Nathan on the forest bed, he had to be clear and careful.

Just after half recovering from the dizzying blow, Nathan forcibly got to his feet and ran over to Joe, ignoring whatever pain he was feeling. He saw the small figure laying there, a circle of blood surrounding him. Nathan went nearer and crouched down. The boy's face was pale and covered with blood. He was hit once in the side of the head by one of the guard's stray bullets. He was already unconscious, his life hung by a thread.

"Joe . . ." Nathan murmured, he didn't know what to say. Nathan applied pressure on his wound with torn fabric from his clothes. The red liquid absorbed by the rag widened every second. He couldn't let his friend die, he needed to do something instead of standing there uselessly.

The wounded boy was breathing rapidly and heavily. It was entirely Nathan's fault, he shouldn't have gone out for a walk from the hotel. He shouldn't have escaped the warehouse, he shouldn't have pinned the gun in Joe's direction. He took all the blame but his friend wouldn't wake up. Joe was his best friend, and now the one that was closest to him in school was dying in his arms.

His hands were now wet and soaked with sticky blood. Silence prevailed for the moment as Hoarse stayed guarding the area.

"Get aside," he said urgently. He took out huge cotton balls and heavy bandages from one of his many pouches. His placed the cotton on Joe's head, then wrapped it up with bandages and tied it tightly, applying pressure to the wound.

Without delaying, he carried the boy in his arms, and made sure that his head was placed comfortably to prevent the wound from worsening. Then quickly he gave a move-out signal and hurried back into formation. Silence still somehow prevailed as they made their way on. "We need to take him to the medical centre and our ship has one. They're perfectly equipped for this type of trauma, maybe he can be saved," Hoarse said. He's lost a lot of blood, we need to move fast," said Hoarse as he ran. His back covered with blood from Joe's worsening wound.

Nathan followed them like a rope that had been tied. He was seriously worried about his friend and time seemed to drag on for hours. At the back of his mind, he still had a missing aunt and a shattered future. But it was the least of the worries right now.

Chapter Fifteen

WHAT'S NEXT?

"It's bad news that you have to meet me again." The room was warm and comforting. There was modern furniture placed in a spacious area. Harvard Norman wasn't pleased with people knowing his favourites, personalities or whatever things that could represent him. As a result, he kept metal furniture at all of his offices and showed little emotion when he spoke. Sometimes, he forgot what he liked to do and what he didn't like. Or if he didn't like them anymore, it was virtually the same.

Things went wrong all the time and this was one of the worse moments. It was a crisis. He was facing the only teenager that could bring so much attention to both his organization and the organization he was working against, probably the only one in history. He didn't intend to put all the blame or trouble on Nathan, but his heart vaguely did. Perhaps there wasn't any trouble, there was just more work to do.

"We've found more information on what the Ventures want from you and your aunt. And for some reassurance, what we can do to help you," he continued. Nathan and Joe had boarded the Atitlan yesterday, the ship owned by IIO. It had set sail with two army destroyer vessels and a nuclear-powered submarine to France.

For what reason, Nathan knew not, he knew nothing about what was going to happen next. Joe had been in the operating room for the entire day yesterday, and surgeons did their best to save him. Nathan had worried for the day and seven hours after sunset until a psychologist, a battle and medic trained, came to reassure him. A few more experts convinced him to take sleeping pills for the night.

It was 7 a.m. now, and the pills' effects had worn out. Again, he couldn't believe about what that had happened, and he soon went back into depression, regrets, uncertainty and sometimes hatred. He wanted to delay the result of Joe's injury from being told to him and so Harvard put it in the end of this briefing.

"From a little evidence, we believe the Ventures want the crystal, but not because of its quality or anything else except what is engraved onto it. They want patterns, some code that had to do with your late father," he said. Immediately, Nathan lowered his head, holding back tears, grief and bad memories. He remembered Golem had confiscated the pendant from him, and how he put up just futile resistance against him.

"I'm sorry to mention that. I've sent agents to investigate the incident of the train crash in France where we will be heading to keep the momentum going on of the overall investigation about the Ventures' clear initiatives.

"Before that, as far as I know, nothing significant will happen." He stopped to take a good look at the boy, sat hunched on the chair with huge eyes and a worn-out look, he could see a clear difference from the one he met in the Balmorals'. The ship's rocking had made him looked even more pathetic. He had unmistakably changed.

"Well, about Golem, we have a chronology of his actions after he betrayed us. First, he was angry after what happened in the ghost house. He walked out from our group and joined a criminal organization in southern Europe, not the Ventures to be clear, not yet," Harvard Norman said.

"Second, the train explosion wasn't meant to kill you but to terrorize and rob the businessmen in the first-class carriages. Golem somehow persuaded the terrorists to put the bomb in your carriage. And for more evidence, the Ventures wanted you alive, not dead, so, it's surely not them. We still don't know why they attempted to kill you in the pool in Edinburgh. Anyway, they could be doing unclear tricks and make us think the opposite of what they actually want. About Shaun, the terrorists thought he was a police agent so they chased him, nothing more.

"Third, the Ventures hired Golem to grab the crystal since they didn't want any of their own agents' location and identity to be detected. These silly guys always use other man's hands to do the hard work. Since Golem knows you clearly and hates you, he must be one of their suitable choices. The both of them could pair up. Anyway, I'll tell you more about why the Ventures *must* work with Golem. Just wait until I've finished this.

"Fourth, Golem succeeded in getting the crystal but a lot of Ventures' men died in the forest. We managed to arrest Golem and his teammates and . . ." He stopped as Nathan opened his mouth to speak for the first time.

"Did you find the crystal and my aunt somewhere there?"

"Regrettably, no. He may have passed it to another Ventures agent earlier, since it's important. Despite this, there's some positive news. Almost unbelievably from our early confirmed investigation, it seems that all your locations and identification references that the Ventures possessed have been *destroyed*.

"Since the big bad guys like to keep their hands so *clean*, they have to risk losing information that was meant to reach them. On the other hand, the small bad guys don't have that kind of power and weapons to keep it fully safe, like Golem.

"Why could this happen? Why could all their information they have be *destroyed*? Actually, the Ventures don't know *exactly* who you are in the first place. They just know that a *person* has a crystal they want, and they started searching for the *person*, you, using this very limited resource. That's why the Ventures needed Golem to work for them, because Golem knows what they want after all. However, we are lucky for the IIO had somehow found out who they exactly want, much earlier than the Ventures and so we intercepted them.

"I'll make this clearer. First, the Ventures have interest in a crystal with that kind of pattern, they want to know who possesses it. So, they made a search for the *person*, you. However, we managed to receive intelligence information on what they are really looking for. Second, we sent Golem and his teammates to protect you if anything happens, but then they betrayed us, unfortunately," Norman continued.

"Third, as I'd said, the Ventures are very eager to know who possess such a type of engraved crystal. After the Ghost House incident, after Golem and his teammates betrayed us, the Ventures sought help from Golem, since he knows who you are with the info we provided him. They wanted him to expose your identity to them.

"However, Golem wanted to protect his own policy so that the Ventures don't have everything they need about you from Golem and just have an option to terminate him because all his *assets* have switched hands. You must understand that Golem has betrayed us and he is now our enemy, so he needs the Ventures to give him some support and shelter. But this doesn't mean that he has to tell them everything he knows and risk being killed. Anyway, he won't be contacting the Ventures from now onwards, we got him in the maximum-security jail.

"About the small army of men on the outskirts, it's a little risk that the Ventures decided to take to secure what they have got from Golem's help. They were prepared to negotiate with Golem to hand you over. But that didn't have the chance to happen after your near escape.

"As for now, the Ventures know *someone* owns the crystal but don't know who he is for the moment. And with Golem being arrested and interrogated, we confirmed the information about your animosity to them. Golem did lie at first and then regretted it and decided to cooperate," explained Harvard.

Nathan leant forward and suddenly a flash of pain made its way from his arm to his shoulder. The line-shaped wounds in his neck stung. He couldn't just forget about the wounds. In the back of his throat, a little sense of nausea had begun, perhaps it was a mild case of seasickness. "How's my aunt and where is she? What about me?" Nathan asked. Too many questions to ask but he only managed some. It always seemed to be the case.

"I'm sorry to notify you again that your aunt is still in their custody. They may force her to declare your identity and whereabouts to recover as much information that they had lost to us. The possible location of your aunt isn't clear, but agents are making good progress. What we could ensure you that your aunt will not be killed but may be . . . ill-treated," he said and paused for Nathan to accept what he had just heard. He backed away to his chair and looked away, uncertain about anything.

Harvard Norman had to say this, he needed to keep the schedule going and work out other things. Now was the end of his briefing. "About Joe, doctors said he's in a stable condition but due to the blood lost and insufficient oxygen supply to the brain, he's in a medically induced coma. They managed to take out the bullet lodged in his head and provide treatment to the injured part," he declared.

For the few minutes, Nathan sat there and started thinking about everything that happened in his life and those things that will happen. Harvard broke the silence. "Joe is a good person, which I could see. I'm sorry for your loss."

Norman felt he needed to state that, the hardest part.

"Didn't I say I would send you an agent without bothering you the last time we met?" Harvard spoke his words slowly hoping whatever he said can be accepted in this sort of bad situation the boy was facing.

"Yes, and who was the agent?" demanded Nathan again. Something in the back of his mind was bothering him, but he couldn't be sure what it was.

"It's your friend, Joe. With him beside you, you wouldn't feel suspicious and nothing will bother you." He had waited for this moment to declare the truth and finally he did it. In his eyes, there were sympathy and guilt. He wouldn't have chosen to tell him at this moment if his superior officer wasn't pushing him all along.

"This can't be true! That friend of mine on that bed is my friend. Not whatever agent you are talking about!" yelled Nathan. He was already standing, ready to leave the room to avoid the truth. Could the man he knew for a few days have cheated him? But what was the reason?

"Wait Nathan! This wasn't my idea, I didn't even agree with it but I'm forced to." Nathan reached the door. "Could you just sit down and listen before you go?"

He was already holding the door knob but somebody opened it first. The door swing outwards. It revealed a man in his fifties in a perfectly ironed grey coat and trousers. His hair was combed with gel to show his high forehead, what men often did in the eighties. He looked calm but there was an unpleasantness in him, like a father annoyed by a child's behaviour.

"If you keep on going like this, nothing is going to proceed. Not the plan to save your aunt and whatever things left by your father will be recovered. Instead, I will have you forced to take psychological assistance and pills for you to sleep and calm down until you make up your mind to cooperate with us or at least understand the situation and position you are in," the man said. His voice was warm and welcoming as lecturing a class, but the words were harsh. "Joe isn't like you at all, he's not secretive and kept everything to yourself. I know him myself," Nathan said again, looking uncertainly to both directions of the powerful officers in the IIO.

"No. You do not," the man said. "How could a discipline teacher chase a boy after a canteen food fight, instead of asking the others about his name and dealing with him at the assembly? How could a coach accept a student who had just vaguely rolled into his swimming pool?"

That had pierced Nathan right into the fine memories that he will never repeat. He couldn't accept more of these things anymore and tried to walk round the obstruction at the doorway, but the man insisted to hold him there.

"Face the truth. You must accept everything, no matter how astonishing or unbelievable today, and then I will give you time to comprehend it all because thinking of something that you can't do anything to improve won't help you. Why don't you stop ignoring something that will help your future and improve things?" He paused. He mercifully gave him a minute to digest rocks in his brains.

"Joe was the only teenage agent we have. We have trained him since he was 4 years old, and I must admit he's brilliant at everything. When he was 12, we sent him to a mission that is classified as not dangerous somewhere in the States. His job was to look after someone small. And then after a year he was switched to the U.K. to look after your safety and report to us."

"You have no proof about that and don't show me the files that you made in the last day," Nathan said urgently, holding his pace.

"You forced me to be even more uncivilized. Don't blame me," the man in grey coat said. "Just don't do it," Harvard cut in. "He needs more time, Argent." The man's name was Argent.

He just ignored him.

"Did Joe ever tell you about his parents? No, he's got nothing to tell. Or, about his childhood about burning leaves when he was 7 to save you and get out of the warehouse. He had been trained and had memorized a script to make natural explanations. Don't be stupid, Nathan Doyle," Argent said slowly, almost not aware about the piercing words.

"Think again, think for the entire night. Just to find out the best move and decision that is for your own sake. Meet me tomorrow, Harvard and I have plans for you," his voice was equal. He stepped aside to let him pass and Nathan walked or ran (he wasn't sure of himself) back to his room. He wrapped himself in a blanket and swore at Harvard and the idiot scumbag Argent for a thousand times.

Before he realized it, tears had wet the sheet and he was having difficulty breathing. The wound was throbbing badly but he ignored it, it was the truth that his friend wasn't his friend anymore that pierced straight into his heart, and the way Argent told him polluted whatever sanity that was left of those memories.

He felt tired and disengaged, every breath was an immense effort. He was cold, like being thrown into a freezer, but in reality, his body temperature was 40 degrees Celsius. He lay on his soft bed in a room, with a furry blanket covering him from neck to toe. The fan was switched off.

Someone was stroking his hair gently, he could make out the blurred image slightly. There was a look of concern and sadness in his eyes. He heard someone speaking politely on a mobile phone outside the room, occasionally looking into the room, the voice was masculine, it must be his father's. He only heard some part of it.

". . . Veinna, I'm Nathan's father. Could you take care of him for a while? Your sister and I have work to do, it's very important. Nathan is sick and his body temperature is high, I had taken him to the doctor and gave him medicine. However, I'm still worried about him. Could you please just stay in my house for a few days and take care of him . . ." Then there were a few nods. ". . . thank you very much, I will fetch you from the train station in the evening . . ."

Then, darkness pulled him away.

The next thing he recalled was when he got down from his bed, he had been lying on the bed for a few days but he was somehow better, able to move at least. He pushed the blanket aside and limped to the corridor outside his room. He knew he wasn't meant to get down from bed but something managed to persuade him, an instinct. Both of his hands were holding the door frame, supporting him from losing balance. His head was spinning because of being suddenly awake.

He could listen to his own weak and slow breath in his head, his body temperature was still high. Now, he looked across the corridor into the hall, his sight was blurry, but he saw a woman in her thirties, English, with a kind and concerning-looking face. She had fair yellow hair, which hung neatly to her shoulders, and red lips. She wore a green shirt with embroidered morning glories all over it, and a brown, knee-length dress. She looked sad and sat on the leather sofa. That was his aunt, Veinna.

Accompanying her was a man in a neat black coat with a red necktie with yellow strips. He looked like a lawyer in black overalls, emotionless, with empty grey pupils, short grey hair and a lifeless face. Both of them were discussing something important, their eyes were serious. No one knew he eavesdropped, not yet.

"Mrs. Veinna, I feel sorry for the death of your sister and her husband, Mr and Mrs Doyle." He didn't even feel sympathy or sorry, there was almost 10 cases of death that needed him to arrange the procedures in a day or two, people died and that was not a big deal for him, as long he wasn't involved in the deaths and received enough money for the arrangement. Anyway, this was only his work to earn a living.

"According to the police authorities, they had both died in a train accident in southern France. Some technical problems happened and the train derailed. Meanwhile, there was another train coming from the opposite way. The two of them were sitting on the front seats. There was no chance of survival. Both of them died on the spot."

The woman who was called Veinna looked shocked, with eyes wide in fear, she brought a handkerchief to the side of her eyes and then to the nose. But the lawyer still showed no emotion. There was a pause.

Veinna broke the silence. "How about the child, he's only 6 years old." Her face showed sympathy and worries. Nathan guessed they were talking about him, he was the only child that was 6 in this house, he wanted to listen more.

"He is quite fortunate that his parents left enough money for him to survive an ordinary and reasonable life until he finishes his basic education, high school at least. The only thing he doesn't have is a legal guardian. I hope you realize that the only relative to him is you, as an aunt. But you can decline to adopt him.

"He'll live in the orphanage with the money to support his living expenses. Or until someone adopts him," said the lawyer.

Veinna's a widow and didn't have any children, her parents had passed away long ago and now her only sister, too. On the other hand, she had seen Nathan often and liked him very much. She even treated him more like her own son than as a nephew. She decided for a while then said.

"Okay, I'll adopt Nathan as my son," said Veinna.

"Very well, I have the documents in my case. Please prepare to bring Nathan to the court and it will be all complete. I will inform you when. But there're also laws that you must acknowledge and abide by as a legal guardian," said the man in black, smiling that this case will not last long and he no longer need to explain the rules. It was a fast and precise decision, no changing, that was what he liked.

"But there's one thing that I would like to add. I wish to keep Nathan's surname, Doyle. I respect his father and I don't hope any complicated conflicts will occur in the future," added Veinna. Nathan was feeling sick, something in his stomach was pushing his diaphragm.

"Yes, it is possible," the lawyer said. He didn't even care to know the reason of maintaining the surname, it was just only the fact that it needed more papers and longer procedures. But that all was just fine, as long as the payment's higher.

His hand on the door was getting looser. At last, he lost his grip and fainted. He didn't even remember he hit the floor.

Chapter Sixteen

EMERGENCY MEETING

Outside Nathan's room it was 10 a.m. but the room had gone long silent from the weeping and swearing. Natalie Collins had just boarded the Atitlan. Before that she was flown by a private jet from Australia straight to the aircraft carrier, which had joined the formation where the Atitlan had been in. The warship was owned by a woman, not the government or the military, just her. Don't be surprise.

She troublesomely switched to the ship where two heads of the IIO had boarded with the boy that had attracted so much attention and hard-work from both IIO and Ventures. Even the government and many secret agencies were trying to find out what had happened in the last few weeks. The events in the forest were rather shocking. But with the field of expertise in secret that the IIO had as an asset and the influence of politicians and big businessmen, the door remained sealed.

Despite the fact that Nathan Doyle was such mentally abused by Argent, the senior officer of hers, just a gap of authority separated them in status, power, rank and business. She had her rights to assemble an important meeting without informing them a month before, especially if she had a good reason or some emergency had happened. She had done it the moment the news hit her ears.

She made her way to the meeting cabin located in the center of the ship, it was the safest place. Guards saluted her although they didn't recognize her, but her authority to enter this place told them she was either a high-ranking officer or their boss. But for precise security measures, the other one demanded fingerprints matching, voice matching, a 17-figure password and a special key for access, which she didn't mind troubling herself with. This was not a negotiable protocol in the IIO for their leaders' security.

The door made a loud "click" as metal arms pulled back by hydraulic forces as if addressing her notably. She pushed the door and made her way along a plain walkway with zero furniture and no decorations. It wasn't only like that. The place was filled with electromagnet waves, which would make any metal object to stick to the walls. Weapons were not allowed when meeting. The key was aluminum.

She reached a metal doorway where two varnished oak doors stood in her way. The doors contrasted with the surrounding as if they shouldn't be there. She pushed the locked door, and a usual fingerprint detector under the handle panel verified who it was. It was the same system in the Balmorals Hotel. The last door obediently opened by hidden electrical rollers and the metal walls stopped radiating electromagnetic waves.

Beyond it, the area wouldn't be affected by the ship's gentle rocking in the ocean, it had been modified to prevent any interruption in the meeting. Rumours said it would be able to withstand a nuclear missile. The room's only furniture included a solid oak table, long and wide with comfortable traditional Victorian chairs. There were accurate clocks showing times from around the world, and a big elegant wooden, yet secure, box containing top-classified information. It was information that could bring down governments if mistakenly used.

Two men in their 40s and 50s sat there, showing no concern for her presence and offering no seating or a drink. She would not put anything in her mouth anyway.

Those were common rules, no verbal interaction other than giving vital opinions for some decision-making or missions during meetings. They were also asked to avoid the high-ranking officers from getting involved in private issues in meetings that could lead to childish fights, which have brought down many great companies.

"Hope I won't be bothering you all much, gentlemen," Natalie broke the silence and took her own seat beside Argent and opposite Norman. They nodded respectfully and acknowledged. Then they begin opening the profiles that her secretary wrote for her, which were edited twice to prevent the slightest mistake and to highlight points and clear motives.

"I received information from my agents that the Ventures are hunting a boy and we have him here. And I'm here to discuss that matter and the future plans for him and for us," she said.

Argent David, the director and one of the largest shareholders of the International Intelligence Organization looked at his first officer—the General Secretary and Advisor—Natalie Collins in surprise.

"You are not going to declare an emergency-class meeting. This type of thing isn't classified as emergency and could be arranged a week after. So doing this breaks the protocol. Explanation now!" demanded Argent David.

"I assemble you all for this meeting not only about the vital plans but also for the fact that you just told Nathan Doyle about Joe Pryor's real identity. Without any meeting with your advisor, this is important information classified as first priority. I'm not satisfied as your advisor," she said.

"Moreover, I just now know that Joe Pryor had been a spy for a long time, a few years. I don't like the fact that the organization is keeping this kind of information from me," Collins said. She was as cool as a cucumber.

"As already explained to Norman, if we keep letting him grieve for his coma-stricken friend, it is delaying everything, the plans and our process of tracking Ventures initiative and for him personally, his aunt. This is for him and for us," Argent replied as frustrated by saying the same thing so many times.

"But he's only 14! And what happened to Joe, who had been sent to on this mission. The files said non-dangerous level, and it almost cost him his life! You can't treat children like that!" she said, regretting a little for exposing her personal feelings.

Argent immediately exploited that. "Don't be overcome by your sympathy. If you don't like this kind of thing, then avoid being in this department, we are doing intelligence work and not child day-care. I reckon this type of things has happened in your experience and your field-expertise and you handled them well until now," he snapped and waited for an answer.

"Nothing involving on our side threatens the safety of children. I don't like to use children in missions. And you must be afraid that this problem would occur so that you hid the previous child-exploitation missions from me and Harvard, but this time things are too wild for anyone to cover up, at least not without doubt and suspicion." She waited for a while and continued.

"Our protocol had been stated that avoiding children under the age of 18 is one of the priorities. This may cause even more massive troubles until the MI6 and the British government is going to interfere and spoil our long-term alliance between them, they may not trust us anymore," she said. Her tone was serious and her advice will not be pushed away or ignored. These issues had involved the protocol, the recorder was under the table. It had been there for every meeting and everyone knew its presence.

"We have been advised to avoid it, but we can't. So we have to—No, we are forced to just accept what we have done. It was a golden opportunity. This is the largest connection in 10 years and the shareholders will be delighted and give us the permission to take risks in this kind of business, not what child-exploiting thing you're saying," Argent said. His tone sounded convincing and matter-of-fact.

"What business is so important that they desperately need a child to exploit the Venture's connection? Or did you want him to go back to school and watch for another suspicious child?" demanded the advisor.

"It's something more important and I'll have them written in the file for the next meeting. But the dangerous level will either be high or low, it depends on circumstances and how brilliant

Nathan is in handling tactical situations, and he'll go through sufficient and professional training before we make a final decisions and preparation for him to get involved in the new missions. These would be missions that no adult could be really useful even though they're trusted and experienced agents. We need the element of surprise," Argent continued.

"So you're admitting that the IIO is going to exploit him until a bullet goes through his head and he ends up like Joe!" She stopped for a while, going through the situation and finally said the best she could think of. "With the most toleration under certain circumstance, I'll only agree if it is for his aunt. He'll have the rights to decide and we must help him," Natalie said, letting the tension fall slightly.

"He'll surely agree right on the spot because I have plans that are certainly for his aunt's search and we are going to help him. But the plan also has benefits for us and the IIO. We help him if he helps us back with assisting us. It's the best deal and a perfect way of doing this, in conjunction with having a good plan. But it may be dangerous as no huge mission can avoid risk, but the training from our agents will minimize any risks to their lowest level," Argent explained.

"Although it's not dangerous or so that is what Argent claimed, we should be more concerned even with proper training. After all, the same thing may happen that has already happened on Joe," Harvard Norman cut in for the first time in the meeting, proposing his first opinion.

"Furthermore, Nathan is important to us, and as you said, he can help us get some momentum in finding Ventures' plans. This proves he is a valuable asset to us, so shouldn't we protect him even more instead of sending him on missions? If he is dead, we can't get any more information and the momentum will be as slow as the previous years," he said.

Argent David leant forward, comprehending about the new point made. The room was silent for the few moments.

"If Nathan is sitting there and doing nothing with the tag of 'valuable asset' pasted on his forehead, he isn't important to anyone. He'll even start blaming himself for not doing anything to save his aunt and would request us to give him the mission. And our momentum will be nothing more than insubstantial curiosity," Argent said, again sounding matter-of-fact.

"I will make a deal. Nathan gets a special training session, perfect assistance, psychology treatment and a well-planned mission, and make sure we help him to find his aunt. Nathan will work for us, not being exploited and every decision of his should be in the meeting for further discussion. And we'll find him a comfortable home instead in the adult quarters, which would do not good if the rumors spread," Collins said. She took a step back to see if there were anymore arguments. "It isn't the problem after all, I had long agreed on this," Argent said.

"And he will live in your niece's and nephew's home. It's better for him to have teenagers about the same age around," Natalie said.

Argent immediately widened his eyes as he had never been expecting such matters and quickly said. "I don't think that is significant for his mental aspect, he can have psychologists and a good home but not *my* relatives' home! I think that these things shouldn't involve them," Argent said, his tone slightly frantic.

"This is for his mental aspect and it is significant. We can't risk letting him make friends out there before he's ready, he could not even find any, anyway. We don't have any child in the IIO except him, not to mention one in a coma. And about his safety as well, the Ventures may have recovered the information then locate him, and we can never be sure that is impossible. Plus, the home for your relatives is in safe-house level and no one will ever figure out where we'd place him. It *won't* be dangerous!" said Natalie, verbally pushing her chief.

Argent couldn't make out any words for the moment, he was shocked and in the back of his mind, worried.

"You're so protective to your own relatives but how about the boy that risked his life and will be again risking his life so that we can track the Ventures down? A psychologist would also recommend this. Two companions would be perfect and this can give him hope, motivation and most importantly, recovery from his damaged emotion and mental strain. Just a little contribution from you wouldn't bother you much, would it?" Harvard pushed on, making his chief feel guilty.

"Nathan will only stay for two weeks, and then he is out of the house to the training grounds. If he causes any trouble before that, he'll be out early," he said reluctantly. He knew their plan, they wanted him to take care of Nathan as how he cared about his young relatives, so his safety and his position will be like the ones he valued. Companion and mental recovery were only excuses. Anyway, they just messed up his two weeks for a big plan, not a big deal.

Natalie Collins hoped she had done the best for Nathan Doyle, who she'd never met in person before but at least she felt better, now her self-conscience was forcibly acceptable to herself. By increasing Nathan's safety and influencing his well-being and the position in the IIO, this also controlled her chief's impulsive decisions and caused him to plan more effectively. He had said just for two weeks, but after the mission she will find other reasons to let him stay longer and, if possible, permanently.

The comfortable home and some other issues that she fought for Nathan was all she could grind out of this meeting. She could feel the tension and limits that she had pushed between herself and Argent. Anything more, it will certainly not work and would make a bad impression in front of the shareholders (the recorder was there) and other leaders of the IIO, and that would do no good to her or Nathan.

Luckily, Harvard Norman was on her side and that made things easier. Maybe he also felt what she felt for Nathan. She had confirmed one more time that she hate ill-treatment of children especially brave ones, like Nathan.

After a moment of silence, they dismissed themselves with hand-shakings that was one of the protocols. Collins passed Nathan's room and stood there for a moment, hoping he will appreciate what she had done for him even though he knew nothing about her. She prayed for him.

She then retreated back to the V.I.P. quarters. Her next flight will be at 6 a.m. to Russia, there she there would be meetings to attend to with other chief officers and surely, her industrial business to be addressed.

The formation of vessels sailed into the windy ocean, ready to respond if any possible threat occurs. But they were secret. The captain received the orders, change coarse to 192 degrees back to United Kingdom at full speed. The specific details and location were classified.

Chapter Seventeen

PRE-MISSION

When he sat there, there was an uncertain feeling in his heart that he couldn't be sure of. Was is grief, sympathy, anger or disbelieve? Maybe it was the combination of all.

He was in the miniature hospital at the ship. The walls were all white-washed metal and it seemed like a little more cramped than usual hospitals would be. A wardrobe stood in one corner containing hospital clothes, blankets and some emergency medicine.

There was also a monitor with a bag of liquefied medicine, which showed Joe's heartbeat, blood pressure and other measurements sitting dutifully beside its host. Tubes fed into Joe's mouth, nose, stomach and wrist, transporting oxygen, fluids. Wires were attached to measure. The soft *beep* of the monitor showed Joe's slow and regular heartbeat.

With a smell of antibiotic that radiated from the heavy bandages around his head, Joe surprisingly looked calm as if taking a rest, with his chest rising slowly and descending humbly. But the real condition wasn't that simple. He may be in a stable condition but still in a coma. Doctors needed to further treat the wounded part of the head.

Nathan was tired although he slept through the day after Argent told him who Joe really was. It hurt him deeply in his heart. This was one of the precious hours that Harvard reluctantly allowed him to meet with Joe. The days ahead will not be comforting and he won't be able to visit his friend easily.

Everytime he decided to talk to him, some kind of thickness or lump would stick in his throat and he would instantly go silent again, he couldn't do it. He had been like this for the pass half hour while he knew Joe would be listening. The boy was just unable to reply. But this time he forced himself on.

"Joe . . . It was entirely my fault," he sounded sobbing, but he held back the tears. "I shouldn't have gone out that night so you wouldn't have followed me."

He sucked in the air filled with antiseptic, clearing the tears that had flowed down his nostrils and throat.

"Are you still my friend, Joe?" he asked as if expecting him to answer.

"All those years before you came to know me, no one really cared about me in school except you. My so-called classmates would come if they needed help, but wouldn't care about me afterwards. The teachers wouldn't do more than their job. I don't know why it was like that. Maybe this is what they also thought of me.

"But you suddenly came and my life isn't lonely anymore, I also have the chance to get more friends with your help and you made me my day almost every time I was feeling down. We studied together, watched movies, swam and did many others things. I couldn't expect more, I didn't even dream of having a friend from a different year," he said, the memories flowed through his mind as tears spilled out. It was real, Nathan was introverted in such a degree that making bunch of friends would always be hard. Maybe it was the absence of his parents that made him like that. However, that only lasted for a few years until Joe became his first true friend.

"Someone betrayed our friendship. He is Argent, some kind of chief in a secret intelligence organization. He claimed that you were a spy working on his side and had been given orders to look after me. It isn't true, right?" he said, but he knew the real answer. He couldn't throw out any firm reasons why the scumbag will lie to him about this.

"You never mentioned your parents or where you came from. Is burning leaves one hobby you liked in your childhood? Or did you read this from a script? I'm confused, Joe. How can I be angry with you since you lied to me to protect me, although I was not aware of it until now?"

"You can continue to lie to me but I just hope that our friendship is real, pure, and innocent without any disguises. We will still be friends, I hope." He paused for a moment. "I know you don't like what you were doing, but were forced to get into it. But I have to tell you something." He swallowed hard.

"I'm going to do something you have done but this is even far more dangerous and if I'm not careful, it may as well cost me my life. I hadn't told them that I'll agree to do it and I still have no idea what it is. But it will be for my aunt. She was kidnapped and I need to rescue her. Will you forgive me, Joe? I'm sorry to do something you would surely dislike. I'm truly sorry." He held his breath and then let it go.

"Please understand my desperate situation that I'm in, you know I ought to do this. I won't be visiting you for the next few weeks or perhaps a few months because of training and the mission. If you were with me, I think you'd be a lot better than me.

"When I'm not here, don't feel as if I'd have neglected you. I promise after things had settled down, I will visit you everyday. Or maybe you can wake up from your coma. We will be friends again. You can even live with me and my aunt, far from this place."

He imagined Joe suddenly protesting and advising him no to involve himself in the missions and said. "Hold on, Joe. Be tough and patient," he said. The tears had stopped and his voice slowly returning to normal.

Nathan thought of what the worst could happen in the mission. "If I die in that mission, please remember me and that I'm always your best friend."

He hugged Joe gently while he laid his chest on his, careful not to hurt him. It was the little comfort that he needed the most, someone on his side. He would do anything for their friendship and most importantly. He knew that Joe would speak in his own words, without disguise and doubt. It seemed to be just a few minutes but half an hour had gone. He was going to be late. He helped cover Joe with the blanket up to his chest, making sure that at least he would be in the best comfort he could give to repay he friend's debt.

"Good-bye, Joe. We will meet again," Nathan said.

He stood straight and walked out, closing the door behind him. He made his way to Harvard Norman's office, ready to tell him about his decision and to face this new challenge. Nathan hoped he had made the right decision. This was a sharp one for his aunt's sake and to get back what belonged to him and his family—the sapphire pendant, not for the value of price but for the value of meaning. Argent David (Harvard told him his second name) was somehow surprisingly correct and had made fact-supported points.

However, the limited time given to him to comprehend what was left for him and how bad his life had become, it was cruel. It hurt him deep in his soul. The organization had everything—money in the billions, immense power, resourceful contacts, political influence, everything, but never Nathan's true trust. He really couldn't comply with them but for his aunt and his life, he didn't really have any choice. He had carefully made this decision the moment he cooled down from weeping and being angry, and the result was this.

When he told Harvard and Argent his decision, one tried to hide his sympathy and guilt but failed, another showed no expression as if he had been expecting this after all like a mastermind. Despite that, Nathan could tell he was satisfied and even more confident that before, as if the authority in him had been strengthened.

The ship docked at a private military harbour owned by MI6 and they made their way to Nottingham, a beautiful and great city. He still had no idea why they were heading there, but Harvard reassured him everything will be discussed in the car. It would be an official briefing like the one he had in the hotel.

They drove in the same white Peugeot they had taken to the Balmorals. Argent sat in another vehicle behind them, but he was too tired to notice the details. Harvard sat in the back seat with Nathan, while an agent drove the car-a professional driver who spoke only when spoken to.

Meanwhile, Harvard offered him some time to take a rest but Nathan defiantly refused, he needed to know what was going on next before anything else. Now sipping the coffee the agent gave him, he looked at Harvard rather innocently and calmer than angry.

On the contrary, that worried the man, shouldn't he be indignant or disliking him, but he showed no emotion neither of joy or sadness, just invisible tension and pressure building on his poor shoulders. Other children faced with this pressure may have just given up on themselves and gone crazy.

"I'm sorry about yesterday morning. Argent shouldn't be so uncivilized and had rather applied a bad manner in informing you the real identity of Joe, which even I recently came to know this," murmured Norman, deciding not to take all the blame himself.

Harvard had advised the man a lot of times, but Argent often ignored him. Harvard had done what he should and did not need to feel like that. It was Argent that needed to examine his own self-conscience.

"You no need to be worried, nor does Argent, it's my problem," Nathan simply replied. There was anguish and infinite tiredness in his voice. The wound on his arm must be hurting him again. He could make out the red lines on the skin of his neck were slowly fading and drying into scabs. Harvard paused for a moment and went on, even feeling guiltier after the sentence Nathan had just uttered.

"We are heading to Nottingham as you now know. The investigation in France will be addressed by experienced and trusted agents. In the city, you will be staying at West Bridgford with Argent's niece and nephew for two weeks. I can assure you that this is the privilege fought for during the meeting by one of your supporters, but I'm afraid I cannot tell you more about the person.

"They are nice kids and good-natured," he said. Then he leaned closer to him and said. They are a hell lot better than

Argent. You may not notice that they are Argent's relatives if I had not mentioned it."

"Why did he allow this?" asked Nathan. Allow them to be friends for him? For the first time, he seemed so shocked that made a little life seeped back into his expressionless and pale face.

"Yes, he said you need some companions before the plans," Norman said. *Or he reluctantly agreed because he was forced by his advisor*, he thought. "We need arrangements, information, preparations to make sure your mission will start and end perfectly and that takes time, and it has been the priority in our busy schedule," he added.

"You do not need to do this, Argent will not be happy with it," Nathan said.

Harvard Norman once again leaned closer to him. "Listen, Nathan. The leaders of the IIO are trying to help you, so just be nice and make friends with them, do it so that Argent can't threaten you badly before having a second thought.

"We are helping you from being exploited and giving you influence in this organization. Just appreciate what you have and maybe one day you can focus more effort in helping your aunt," he whispered into his ear.

Harvard gave him time to think and then continued. "You will have some normal life for the moment, schooling nearby and there's a football club for your interest. I advice you to enjoy as much as you can because the time will be hard after this fortnight. Please try to be happy because you need to pass the psychology test before any missions are allowed for you," he said and regretted. How can his self-conscience give him the permission to tell a boy to be happy after his aunt had been captured and was in custody of one of the most dangerous criminal groups? Plus, his best friend is in a coma and his future life uncertain?

I'm sorry, Norman said to Nathan in his mind, hoping he could know it. *I was forced to do something like this and please abide what I had said, it's for your well-being also. Since sadness will attribute nothing good except depression.*

"Other than that, you need to pass one of our tests before the mission for the Physical, Mental and Trust Level Clearance certificate. I know you don't need some of it but it cannot be excluded.

He was worried about Nathan, the boy seemed to be sitting there with his coffee lukewarm and masked with a worn-out look, slumped on the chair. He wondered how long he could take as the organization pushed on in the mission. It's a mission that will have high expectations of a teenager.

"On the bright side, we found a little contact that can potentially lead to the location where your aunt is being kept. It's involves a millionaire that mainly invested in technology and science research centers. And this mastermind also has legal businesses as well, but we can't find solid evidence because he's 'kept his hands clean'.

"We don't know the exact location but evidence and reports reveal sightings of your aunt and suspicious activities somewhere (they may be constantly shifting to avoid being tracked). We can't be sure until more time is given to the agents to confirm. We'll get you near him after the training," Norman said.

"Tell me more about Argent's niece and nephew." he asked. He didn't want to care about what his mission was first, at least not before his training.

"As I have assured you, they are very fine and good-natured kids and about your age. You can spend two weeks time with them to comfort yourself and look at the bright side of life. Maybe things haven't been that bad and I trust you can handle them well.

"If you have anymore doubt about that, I can tell that they also had lost their parents and they're never spoilt, they took care of most of their needs with their uncle assisting a little. They can understand what you feel and perhaps fit into your situation.

"However, you are not allowed to tell them some of your real identity and any of the mission, please remember. I'll give you something to look at and that will be temporally be your information of your false identity. This is for their own safety as knowing too much about the organization will bring problems to both sides."

He looked at Nathan who was already half-lying on the chair. He took away the cup.

"Get some sleep," he said. Covering the boy with his jacket and he looked through the window, as the same countryside scenery flashed by. He felt something, a kind of emotion towards Nathan. Was it sympathy or protective?

It's better not to think about it, the chief officers may lose their trust in him if they know that a single child could affect his decision-making and work, it'll be a negative effect to him. However, he insisted to himself that Nathan a brave person. He was a person willing to risk everything to save his aunt and friend, which was beyond the management of a Chief Executive Officer like him that sat all day in the office reading and signing reports. Or the worst part was sending agents to risk their lives just for a certain mission, he thought.

One more hour or so, and they will be reaching Nottingham. He had been there before, visiting Suzzle and Izle. Argent didn't feel pleased about Nathan's contact with them.

The hour was spent watching Nathan sleeping innocently but looked away when his emotions hit the peak or were getting a little more sympathetic than he expected. He must be careful of the driver's sight, just in case he reports to Argent. For the last meeting had triggered tension among the heads of the organization, it wasn't great news. Everybody would be suspicious and could lessen their trust in each other, including him.

Could Suzzle and Izle reassure Nathan to cheer up or get even worse? Argent disagreed about the plan also for this—after Suzzle and Nathan becomes good friends, she would try and stop Nathan from the upcoming mission and start persuading her uncle. He would have only two weeks with her but Argent could not dismiss this possibility. This conflict was going to be severe and he needed deep preparation for the following meetings.

Natalie Collins hadn't been so expert after all, the emotion and lack of experience had failed her real ability and intellectual and political intelligence. She may supply Nathan with influence from herself and Suzzle, the leader's niece, but it threatened her and the organization with political fireworks.

After all, the involvement of children in this operation had gone up to three dynamically. He needed to be careful enough to tender the conflict and handle the situation.

Chapter Eighteen

WEIRD HOLIDAY

THE CAR ROLLED INTO NOTTINGHAM as the sun roused brightly in the blue sky of the great city. It was 1 p.m. and Nathan managed to get sufficient rest to boost his energy back. The border of the city was marked by 18th century Victorian houses, which stood in stark comparison with the hustle-bustle of the city they embraced.

But as they waited, Harvard suddenly remembered something and told him, or he was waiting for the right moment. Harvard said that Joe will be known as a boy leaving the country for important reasons. He had told his old school. Nathan thought what Roberts might think of them.

The sun-baked, battered road slowly changed into black-fresh tarmac that had recently been coated. Coming to the end of the sole highway that led into the city, it separated into various branches of motorways of different sizes.

Nathan took in the concrete scenery and the variety of engineering styles that made up the city. A few Victorian houses littered the modern inventions. The traffic was moving well with office workers hunched in their chairs, kids at school.

Harvard Norman told him his temporally new home was located in West Bridgford, having a great view of River Trent and its great bridge construction. They noticed St. Giles Church and a small forest was nearby as they rode pass. The car exited the motorway and entered a street, quiet with a harmonious neighbourhood. A row of houses stood on both sides with lawns and a few senior citizens taking a walk after lunch.

The agent parked the vehicle beside a modern house. It was nice with glass panels occupying the front part as walls, showing the decoration inside of a carpeted wooden floor, a dining table, a homework area with a lamp. Silk curtains closed half of the view and there seemed to be no one at home.

Nathan noticed the car Argent took wasn't following them, they had separated earlier on one of those motorways. Harvard got down and Nathan helped himself.

Nathan wondered why the house occupied by Argent's nephew and niece by the name of Suzzle and Izle had such lapse of security, Harvard said. "Argent wanted to keep his relationship with his only relatives concealed from anyone else. He decided that being secret is the best security rather than locking them in a maximum security safe house. This is a safe house as well, but rather spares more freedom and air."

"Where's Argent?" Nathan surprised himself with asking about the person he called scumbag. He retrieved his little luggage containing his clothes bought by the agent (he couldn't just go back and get his possessions), and a few photos and money he brought to Edinburgh.

"He's in an office doing business. He's involved with wine collections. We do have normal legal business as well. Not to say that spying is illegal, it just has a neutral phrase in the law. The kids will be back by 3 p.m. so you have about an hour and a half to keep yourself comfortable and suit in." He looked at the agent for a while.

"Not to bother my agent from checking the security of this house. I will show you around," Norman volunteered. The agent nodded an awkward thanks to his boss.

Harvard led the way into the house with a few hidden passwords and fingerprints scanner panels to deal with on the way. He promised there weren't any cameras inside the house apart from the lawn and the rooftop.

While no-entry rules were not to sneak in the agent's quarters in the basement and some rooms on the top floor. Every part of the house was modernly designed. He first showed him the dining part and the kitchen, and the living area on the ground floor. Next, he showed Nathan the bedrooms and entertainment rooms on the second floor. It was impressive with a wide plasma television and play stations, but he wasn't in the mood to enjoy the little luxury. The third floor he wasn't allowed to enter without permission from the agent.

And lastly, there was an extra bedroom for him. It was neatly and immaculately furnished with a comfortable bed, a glass-made writing table and a PC with Wi-Fi service and a cute wardrobe. There was also a fine collection of fiction and encyclopedia books. Some modern paintings showing Europe's famous scenery hung elegantly with a yellow wall behind them, but there were no posters of popular bands.

Nathan left his luggage beside the bed, his only belongings for the moment. Harvard told him he would come back to visit him after he took care of some urgent issues. He gave Nathan some time to fit in and then left.

Nathan got washed and changed into simple attire. Perhaps everything will be fine and better than he thought all along. Perhaps he will have training, save his aunt on the mission and move to another place and cut off contacts with the IIO. He was sure his aunt will agree to take care of Joe.

The month after this was evidently going to be rough and difficult. But as Harvard told him, he can relax a bit for the moment. For his aunt's sake, he must hold himself together. Not to mention continuing on as well for Joe.

He switched on the PC and searched whatever information that could lead to his aunt's abduction. He found that recently a bank had offered her a job somewhere in France but she hadn't told him of this before. Could this be normal procedure for commercial banks searching for experienced accountants?

According to the website, his aunt didn't have an answer yet but it could be one of the reasons for her being kidnapped. He wasn't sure and not much evidence showed any appropriate conspiracy. He made a mental note to search for further information if he had the chance.

For the moment he searched for Joe's info but got nothing extraordinary—some Facebook posts information. Surely, the IIO hid them well from the world. He didn't know when he could really visit him again, or talk to him, but he hoped it will be soon. After an hour of searching, he made the final preparations to met Suzzle and Izle whom he will be staying with. If they were fine and kind as Harvard had mentioned in the car, perhaps the two weeks will at least be pleasant and comfortable.

He changed into nicer attire and brushed his hair, he didn't want to look like an intruder found in somebody's home or provide a bad impression on the first day.

Wearing a collared blue T-shirt and jeans, he descended to the first floor and sat there. He did not notice the agent watching him from a distance at the back door.

He finally realized that he was indeed hungry after missing lunch. He headed to the kitchen and a container with a note there—indicating some filling snack for him by Harvard. Honestly, Norman was far better than Argent, and Nathan liked him for showing concern, if he could only put aside his involvement and position in the IIO. He wolfed down the cheese tuna and mayonnaise sandwiches with salad, and then washed the container.

Just at the moment, he noticed a car pull up beside the house. The sound of closing doors indicated they were back.

After that, the inner door opened with Norman first to appear and then a teenage girl with shoulder-length blond hair about his age came in. then, behind her, a 13-year-old boy that quite resembled her followed. He was rather timid but smiled warmly at him. His sister, also smiling, looked to be more extroverted than her younger brother. They must have known about his stay before he came.

Nathan stood up from the sofa to address their presence. He smiled awkwardly.

"Ah, Nathan. It's good to see you better after the tiring journey. Both of them are Suzzle and Izle as I had said before. They will be looking after you as a guest for these two weeks, while your father will be at work with their uncle. He looks to like wine," Harvard said. He had come in from the door. The false identity had been pasted onto him and there will be no going back without them knowing. Nathan shook their hands. The three of them hadn't spoken since Harvard did all of the introductions.

"You will be schooling with them in West Bridgford Secondary School starting from tomorrow if you don't mind. I will give you all some time to adjust to each other. I still have work to do," Harvard said as he went into a room somewhere in the first floor.

For the moment, the three children stood there, wondering what to say. But Suzzle broke the silence first.

"It's nice to meet you, Nathan," she politely said.

"You too," he replied awkwardly. He had relaxed a bit by knowing Harvard hadn't lied about them being good-natured and friendly. However, the training and tension of the next two weeks kept him uneasy . . . And surely, some unease came from knowing about his abducted aunt and Joe.

Harvard said you are one of my uncle's business partner's sons. They're busy so he sent you here to prevent you from being bored," she said.

"Yes, something like that," said Nathan falsely. It wasn't anything like that. He had reluctantly read and memorized the script that Harvard left on his table earlier.

"I hoped you don't mind Izle for being quiet, he's a bit of a shy boy," she said as put a hand on her brother's shoulder. "Would you like some biscuits or tea, I can offer some," she asked him as she landed her bag on the sofa.

"No, thanks," Nathan replied, he was still full and didn't wish her to serve him.

"I will go and change, the TV's there, drinks are in the fridge."

Nathan nodded appreciatively and she and her brother retreated upstairs.

Harvard Norman approached from the room and carried a pile of files.

"I hope you will suit well with them. Have some normal life," he said.

Before Nathan could offer him some help with the files, he was already on his way to the car.

Nathan spent the evening chatting with Suzzle about his old school and sometimes about 'family'—which was stated in the script of his false identity, but that also made him fell a faint sour of sadness and defeat in his heart, sometimes until the extend that tears threatened to pour out of his eyes. She also said very little about her family. Izle stuck to his natural behaviour, only spoke politely and shyly when spoken to.

After that, he went to bed early. Harvard had already brought the books he needed for school.

It was a day where normal life started seeping back into him. Expected routines of school and sports came back, which was to his delight. The day passed quickly, with the minimum level of worry about his future. It wasn't that feeling of total relaxation or satisfaction, it was the feeling of appreciation, to be satisfied while he had the two weeks of normal life. He took in his own advice that depression will only deteriorate his health and make more of a mess of this situation.

To solve things, he needed to be calm and in the best condition he could make himself in. As a result, he chose to let himself be indulged in the timetables of school and free time at his temporally home.

His friendship had started pure and he didn't decide to use it to bring influence to him in the IIO as Harvard had advised. He couldn't address his self-consciousness to do this to a normal and rather attractive teenage girl, and to her timid brother that she held the main responsibility to protect him. He travelled a short distance with Suzzle and Izle to school. The agent was quiet but from afar, he looked like a concerned father with few words.

School was considered close to perfection and there was nothing more he would dare to ask. Harvard Norman had helped him with the documents that needed to be transferred from his old school and the other things needed for switching schools. He guessed: What would Roberts think of them after their missing at the tournament? But Harvard reassured him he had taken care of these issues.

With kind teachers during registration and simple advice of orientation, the students looked friendly. Some were already trying to make friends but the teachers smiled and told them to keep quiet. They didn't resist. He didn't enter any sports clubs yet because of his study for two weeks was classified as a short period of time. Perhaps after his training and the mission, he could switch back to his old school or go somewhere else.

It was a busy day, especially for him. He had new chapters to learn, old ones to revise and urgent projects that needed to be handed in. Other than that, he concerned himself with his social development in the school. He skipped half an hour of his lunch just to catch up with his homework and the full-blown questions from his new friends. The hard part was he was reluctant to tell lies about his identity and the reason of his stay.

School ended at 3 p.m. and he met up with Suzzle and her brother at the school gate, waiting for the agent to arrive. Technically, it was personal time given to them to do whatever they wanted to. Suzzle, as usual since his arrival, always broke the silence naturally.

"How's school? The students here are quite talkative and friendly, you must have had a nice day," she said, tugging her backpack firmly. Izle stood beside her, being rather a listener, nervous and silent.

"Thanks for your concern, I'm fine and like it here," he replied. Awkwardly, he asked. "Where's your class?" He was trying to make friends.

"I'm in the same year with you, coincidentally. It's just the next one after yours," she replied with a broad smile and seemed to like him. "If you're concerned, Izle's is in year seven, the second class after the third floor."

Surprisingly, Nathan asked. "Where does your uncle works his wine business?"

"It's in a simple office and wine warehouse just after River Trent. I rarely go there," she answered. But there was a slight difference from her earlier voice, which could be considered as significant.

It was a little metallic, hard and serious with a not-concerning expression. Her posture and face remained the same and friendly but the difference in her voice was unmistakable. Could Suzzle know Argent's another job since the agent was so strict in safety? He didn't want to know. Perhaps her relationship between her uncle wasn't good.

"Oh! Did you try out the nuggets at the canteen? It's my first recommendation. And the pasta tasted quite well," Suzzle suddenly said. Her voice burst into a friendly and extrovert question as if Nathan had not asked about anything.

"I'll try it out tomorrow, I was busy during lunchtime. I needed to catch up in my work," replied Nathan. He still felt some unease about the coldness of her a few seconds before. They paused for a moment.

"Actually, there is not much time that I can really share with you at my home. Do you want to take in the evening's fresh air in the park? I can arrange this for you if you want. You will be fascinated about the Trent scenery," she naturally offered. But he could feel something in her voice, hoping he'd agree to her suggestion.

"Sure. And thank you," he said, appreciating the offer. It was also better to keep him busy from the tension and worries.

Just at the exact moment, the agent strolled up to the car in front of them. Unlocking the doors, he fatherly urged them in. He's an unmistakable professional in his disguise. They went in with Izle and Suzzle, not waiting longer to declare their destination before home. The agent nodded as he had been expecting this, then quickly tapped something onto his Smartphone and sent an e-mail.

He controlled the steering and simply manoeuvred the vehicle onto the motorway. The traffic was surprisingly smooth even though during pick periods. With train services and wider motorways. The agent switched on his navigational device, which was attached on the dashboard, avoiding any possible traffic problems.

Nathan spoke less in the car, he didn't want Argent to know the contents of their chat. On the other hand, the driver's skills were admirable, turning complicated twists of small roads and wide highways with ease. He didn't mention that he was doing anti-surveillance procedures to avoid anyone following.

After about 15 minutes, they reached a clean river with its harmonious vegetation and various flowers. Surprisingly, it matched with the city's wooden and concrete scenery, perhaps the flowers looked modern as well.

The car parked at a distance away from the park on the roadside parking area. He unlocked the doors and led them down, stopping at one of the park's tables. He turned and said. "I'll give you 15 minutes, go on and enjoy yourself."

He said it with a cheeky smile as if a father had successfully tolerated his child's behavior. Suzzle urged Nathan and her brother towards the waist-height barrier shaping the outline of the stream. She seemed to enjoy her privacy without any of the tight-and-close surveillance and security.

They stood facing the Trent and its menacing bridge, the buildings and contrasting modern houses stood as a background far behind it. The sun was showing its best appearance, orange-red flames of fluid coloured the fine blue sky, the eye of heaven dipping half in the horizon beyond menacingly.

"It's nice, isn't it? I seldom have the chance to be here alone with Izle, my uncle is always not happy about any freedom that was allowed to me more than he gives," she said.

"It's beautiful. I don't see any other bridges back home except London's."

"This must be the first time you've come here. Do your parents work here? Where are they?"

She had hit the uncomfortable and critical spot. As he was forced to tell the lies that had been written and stated for him, a feeling in his stomach occurred. Maybe it was self-consciousness but he lied to protect her from the world of intelligence and secrets.

"He does insurance business somewhere in Scotland. He hired a maid or whatever better names he called to fulfill my daily needs. My mother was not with me when I was small, a train crash." Some of the details about him weren't stated down, so he can at least tell something true about himself.

Suzzle felt his long-accumulated grief and hers as well. She lowered her head slightly, too little to be obvious. "I'm sorry about reminding you. I didn't even know the real reason of my parents' death. At least you have a father," she murmured and forced a bittersweet smile.

There was a harsh and sour feeling building in Nathan's chest and a kind of thickness in the throat. Suddenly, she changed her extroverted emotion into a sad and desperate impression as if something bad had happened.

"My uncle always lies to me. Almost everything was personal and a secret to him but how about my own privacy? You can see this with agents pretending to be my father sitting there watching us with a high salary every month. Although I cannot confirm the truth, I know what my uncle does not only involve the wine business and he rarely mentions it," she said and made a paused, hesitant about the following words.

"Nathan, this is the first time since I'm alive that Argent lets his 'business partner's son' live with me! Don't treat me like a 3-year-old kid. Be honest, Nathan. I can see that you are a rather kind person. You don't like to lie, and I can hear something in your voice every time you do!" she said.

He opened his mouth to speak but nothing came out. Noticing Izle was already shocked by the sudden commotion with wide eyes. *He feared of something. He feared something that will be declared without approval.*

"You do not need to say anything. I'm not angry with you. Did something bad happen to you and your parents? What it something ugly that my uncle did to you?" She paused for a while and continued. "I'm rather more impulsive to understand than curious. Maybe I should let it be like this until it fades away. Knowing something that we weren't meant to know is always not pleasant.

"You have something to do with the things my uncle is in and I can see your reluctance and you don't like it. I don't really want to care who really you are or what you are doing, my responsibility is to keep you entertained for the fortnight and I know this without being told. I want you to be in the best comfort before leaving," she said quickly and the words poured out, making Nathan even more uncomfortable, he was meant to keep this things and his identity from her. What could happen if Argent knew about this?

"I tell you all this because I feel guilty that you were forced to read those things from a script and to convince me to trust you. But just understand that our friendship that just started is real, at least for me," Suzzle said.

"You can follow my uncle's instruction while you stay to avoid any trouble from happening, but please know that I know what you feel and whatever reasons that have forced you to lie are due to suffering and a torment. At least you can relax a bit when the agents and the bugs are not around. This is all I want you to know," she said, looking in his watery eyes.

She said the friendship between them was real but could Nathan really treat it like this? Or was he borrowing influence in the IIO for his own good? Just like what Harvard told him to do. He was too tired to think about that, maybe he was a bad person after all. *Sorry. I'm sorry*, he said in his mind to Suzzle, hoping she may receive his meaning.

"Thank you for understanding," he said with his feelings and emotions pouring out. It was only that that he could manage in the form of words. He avoided eye contact with his head low.

"Just promise me that you will not involve yourself in my uncle's job after you have finished what you need to," she said with an emphatic tone.

"I promise. I won't," he replied. But in his heart, he could feel the urging sensation that told him things will not be so easy after this. He had a *bad* feeling.

He had made a mental note and conclusion about Suzzle, she was not only attractive and brilliant, she was intelligent. She probably understood him more than he did. It looked like the head of the IIO's niece wasn't completely innocent.

Although the harsh and real facts in the conversation hurt him, but her understanding also gave him the warmth of comfort that he needed from a friend. He desperately needed a companion as one of the leaders that Harvard mentioned had chosen to put him here.

Or some cruel part of his mind started to tell him that they want him to be in good condition regardless, mentally or physically, for perfect presentation in the operations that will come. Or it was real. They had been brutal to do like this and cruel as one could argue. They forced him to make influence in the IIO by befriending the leader's niece and then gave him the best to make him their perfect agent.

They were changing him and succeeding. However, after he got back his aunt and the crystal, he will never step into their world again. But he had a significant doubt in it, which he couldn't be sure why or what.

After the long silence, Izle eventually cooled down and had alerted them that the agent was urging them back into the car. They all headed back and realizing the real motive of the visit to the Trent. That was something weird about Izle that Nathan had just noticed. Did he need to be in such fear when his sister told something to him without Argent's approval? And why he was so quiet? He didn't intend to know his for the moment, maybe he was too sensitive about the recent matters.

Chapter Nineteen

TIGHT SCHEDULE

"Nathan cannot go to the training, we are running out of time," said a man. He was wearing a black overcoat that was long enough to touch the floor, the menacing collars magnifying his eternal might.

He was sitting comfortably in a warm room. It was furnished with elegant wooden tables, chairs, cabinets that were handmade of the best rosewood by the finest carpenters on the continent. The room was large and spacious, decorated with a fine collection of paintwork from the late 18th century, which had been brought from an old museum with a high price of hundreds of thousands of pounds.

Argent David was in a large arm chair, sitting opposite the man whom didn't like to be addressed by his real name or more precisely—didn't like anyone to know his name at all. But Argent knew his and almost everything about his background and identity.

His nickname was the Executioner, and he owned hundreds of commercial plantations of different fruits and vegetables that stretched on for thousands of acres. The both of them radiated menacing political influence and power in the IIO. The meeting was secret and important, no secretary was allowed to know this. They had personally sent coded messages to meet.

"This is the problem, our schedule is late and now the impact is making itself known. We will have to solve this tactically, no more straightforward ways," David replied, his voice was so calm as if he was predicting the very genuine future and it was like a fortune to him.

The man who preferred to be called the Executioner looked at the Director of the IIO. It wasn't because he admired him, it was because of his self-confidence. He wanted to know what resources he had under his sleeves.

"Tell me the solution, Mr. David," the Executioner challenged him directly but showed no offense.

"You mentioned Nathan Doyle cannot go to training, so he doesn't need to go. This is not my problem after all and I had earlier considered the possibility of this kind of things happening," Argent answered in a flat tone.

"This is protocol and I'm sure you know it. Plus, Natalie Collins is a trouble finder, she won't allow this possibility to happen, she'll not even consider it. Think again," the Executioner said.

"Ah! You finally detected the source of our problems. Natalie Collins, the blond-hair-child-daycare-woman. Unfortunately, she's my foolish advisor. But I somehow remember why I chose her to hold this substantial responsibility. She is not so brilliant and I'm right. This is the world of intelligence and criminals. I chose her because of her straightforward characteristics. Not because I like it but because of the exploitation I can indulge in," he pronounced every word, savouring them.

"When I use tactics that on the surface seem to be directed at certain matters and to serve only one purpose, it actually serves two or more things and if they're brilliant enough, they implement the opposite function, in a paradox way. We just have to examine what the aftereffects could do and not what are the aftereffects. And about the organizations protocol, it is as simple as this. We will not break any of it arguably.

"Instead, Nathan is not going to any training or mission for this month prepared by the organization," Argent said proudly. He liked to say something about his coherent plans and slowly revealing them to his audience, he then absorbed the feeling of pride and the huge understanding that he gave them. It wasn't arrogance or anything bad, it was the authentic genius part of deduction and calculation that he had in him.

"Isn't Nathan going to the mission? And why are we not breaking any protocol? We will be sending him to a mission with no proper training and authorization. This is nonsense, you better explain what you are doing instead of playing words and facts with me. I had reached the limit of my patience," the man embraced in his big overcoat poured out the words. He seemed to be vexed rather than confused.

David had been enjoying every word he said recently and now comfortable with his confusion and demanding a reply. This showed that his acquaintance was shortsighted and liked him, although the words were unpleasant. It somehow made him look like a child frustrated by his homework, but disliked adults telling him the answer.

Other than that, the reason he chose this partner to discuss this matter was the same as why he chose Natalie Collins. They were one brilliant individual and one straightforward, yet powerful person, who both would make great and successful achievements.

Argent shook his head to protest, but he didn't show the slightest impression of offense. "According to my respective, Nathan's psychology is still unfit to go to any missions and he may not pass the test. So, he is not going to any mission authorized by the IIO since he can't pass the training in time. He will go to *our* mission assisted only by us and there are no rules and protocol as long as it achieves what we and the organization wants.

"Although we will not tell the IIO about this matter, the shareholders will not know this, we will use the very natural excuse of sparing Nathan a holiday as he is having with my relatives. And according to Natalie Collins, he needs a vacation and I'm just setting up another one for him. If you want to know what I'm saying directly, Nathan will go on a vacation but with one special task that is only known to us. On the other hand, his vacation can cover his identity very well, both from the IIO and the enemy," he said matter-of-factly.

The Executioner looked shocked by the preposterous plan. "What if the shareholders eventually find this out? What if Natalie Collins knows this? We'll be in dire trouble!" he said in a pitch that was too high and sounded uncertain.

Argent threw him a reassuring grin. "I'm not worried about the shareholders. First, once we get what we want from the mission, we'll earn a huge profit. I'll tell you that this mission is funded by the CIA and they will pay us well, and the money will keep their mouths shut and if we're lucky, they may encourage us to go on and ignore the troublesome protocols.

"And surely, if they still don't agree, which is not likely to happen, we can claim that this is an accident and we really don't know what happened. We will say that we had no knowledge of any potential danger in the vacation area that will possibly threaten anyone. Although they might suspect us and put that in the meeting's agenda, they will not have any evidence to put us in the court," said David steadily as if reading it from a file, his voice reaching a high pitch at the every end of each sentence.

"I know Nathan will only do such things if it is only for his aunt and it was agreed to in the briefing. So, what plan that the CIA cares about will involve the abduction of his aunt?" challenged the Executioner.

"It's a fair point. It does have some relationship with things the CIA and Nathan's interested in. The Americans want something from a millionaire company's files that they claim to be very important and threatens something to them. However, I noticed Ventures' agents are reporting some sort of files to the same computer as well. The agents under his authority are involved in the sightings of his aunt, and the millionaire must be associated in the abduction somehow. So, what the CIA and Nathan want is in one computer," Argent made the words out slowly as he replied calmly.

"And Nathan will download all of it during the mission and pass it to us," Argent went on. He simply said this as if it were an easy task. However, the plans he made will grant a high possibility of success.

"What if he fails to do it? And how sure you can be that the information of the abduction and what the States want will be in one computer? He can switch the files into another computer and place it in a different place. This is still unclear," the Executioner said and seemed to be less confused, but the annoyance in his voice could be easily detected.

"About what the States wants, we are very sure as agents found a secured line that sends information to him. We recovered a little of it that could let one know that he is guilty, but not enough to become evidence on the court. But if we have what he downloads and all of it, the millionaire is finished," Argent said.

"Therefore, the information is too important to him and he keeps it in a highly secured laptop, which convinces us that he didn't switch it into another device. He also brings it with him whenever he goes out of a country. And about the abduction, we also got a little information, but it's not specific enough to execute a search and we aren't completely sure that it will be in the same computer since it is not as important to him," Argent continued.

Argent smiled and went on. "Did you say he may switch the abduction info into another computer? But this isn't of much importance to me, while we won't mention this in front of Nathan. As long as we get Nathan to do the job, we can give an excuse after that," Argent said without a blink of an eye. There was no uncertainty in him and he was sure of his plans.

"But what if he agrees to get information that *only* involves his aunt as Norman told him in the briefing?"

"It will do no good to both sides. If he knows where his aunt is, the only people that will help him are us. We promised him to find his aunt only, not save her. We can make a fair deal with him. We get what we want, we'll help him and I'm not lying his time. With luck, the two files of information will be in one computer."

There was a long moment of silence. Argent was sure the Executioner was taking in and measuring his brutality and massive exploitation of the teenager. But it was for the good for both of them and the IIO. And if the situation were better, if they had more luck, Nathan will reunite with his aunt.

"This is the most complicated plan I ever heard. What if he fails, above all?" the man opposite Argent asked, the hint of uncertainty slightly heard in his voice.

"We lose our money, he dies and his aunt is gone forever," David uttered the sentence without much hesitation. "But I will support him with the best assistance and even without training, the chances of victory is seven out of 10. We had seen him escape several death traps that the Ventures set for him and I know he is very good in practical matters rather than theory," he said it in great confidence.

"Do you want me to make the preparations?" the man asked.

"It would be so kind of you but I had Harvard Norman to help me. You do not need to worry about his credibility, I have ways to keep him silent," Argent replied.

"Once again, what if Natalie Collins suspects something and investigates us. If she finds our real motives and have evidence to proof the conspiracy of sending Nathan to the-," he asked but was interrupted.

"You are the Executioner. If this happens, I'm afraid she will no longer be needed for her services as my advisor. Or more precisely, she will not have the chance to work for anyone again," Argent cut in without any extra thoughts and spoke quickly, making the point crystal clear . . . *He meant to kill her with a snap of two fingers if the odds started to switch sides.*

Silence occupied the place for a long moment, which seemed to drag on for a lifetime for the Executioner. The amazing yet brutal and cruel plan from David had intimidated him more or less. But he felt glad that a thought suddenly busied his mind.

"Something doesn't really make sense had happened a week before and it had been bothering me for a long time. I would like to ask you why Ventures wanted to electrocute Nathan in the pool in Edinburgh if they wanted him alive for the valuable information about the crystal?" he asked suddenly. It was the moment his heart started to fear about the complication of the issues.

"They want him alive and never once wished to kill him and you're right. I sent the orders to paralyze him to get him out of the water, but that was not more than to create a scene and experience that how serious the Ventures are in the matter although they won't kill him. It's all my fabrication so that he knows what the Ventures will do to his aunt if he doesn't agree to go on the mission.

"Actually, I want him to understand completely what the Ventures are truly like through actions and experiences and not only through words and advice. I want him to be urgent and serious in this mission so that he will succeed and his aunt will be saved," he paused for a moment and continued about a different matter. "Golem had personal revenge and the motive to kill Nathan and we don't want that to happen. I've kept him under tight custody and surveillance in the maximum security prison."

He waited for a moment and thought of if there was anything else they hadn't mentioned and discussed in this private meeting. When there was nothing he could think of, he once again reminded the Executioner to be cautious and not to make any mistakes or let anything undesirable happen, he then wished him good luck and said his farewells.

Then, at last, he dismissed himself and brought his briefcase with him. He made his way out of the mansion. He thought of what it would be like if he owned one and then drove back to Nottingham, feeling proud of himself for the brilliant plans he had come out with. There would be no mistakes and he was sure of himself.

Chapter Twenty

DEEP SEA MISSION

This was one of the few moments that Nathan felt something pushing and churning in his stomach. It was probably just nervousness and a bit of anxiety. This happened when the agent that lived with him suddenly broke the routine of the days that had passed. He told him that Harvard Norman was waiting in his office after school, and he must go there for some important issues regarding the mission.

Although the agent didn't mention the word "mission" because it was classified, he knew about it pretty sure. It was predictably a briefing as it was every time they met officially. The meeting was known to him suddenly when he was in the car on the way home from West Bridgford School. It looked to him to be planned perfectly in time as Suzzle and Izle needed to stay back at school for extra classes. They would be going home after the meeting.

Nathan stood in front of the door of Harvard's office. The agent had brought him into a modern building of a firm and into a small office. It was the standard construction of glass and concrete and steel, and inside the lobby was furnished with coffee tables, sofas. There were flowers in vases and wooden tables that held a pile of files. There were computers with receptionists hunched behind each of them.

He told him where he needed to go and left him. The nervousness was at its paramount, and he had a bad feeling as he always felt when meeting with one of the leaders of the intelligence organization. Since it was always unpleasant and shocking news every meeting, he thought positively that this was one of the better ones that will break its bad news frequency record.

Taking a deep breath of the cool air, he knocked on the wooden door with three numbers in silver that decorated it. After the three *thuds,* it immediately opened as if it had been waiting for the moment he stepped a foot into the place.

Norman stood there wearing a black office shirt with white strips, and black long trousers. He masked a cheerful impression on his tired face, looking like an exhausted parent looking at his son for the first time after the day's work.

"Nathan, I'm glad you were willing to come here quickly. I've important news about the mission. Come in," Harvard urged him with a hand signal.

Inside sat another man in his fifties, serious and experienced-looking with calm watchful eyes and grey eyebrows and blue irises. He didn't look surprised or insulted that most adults would have if working with a child. It was just the normal expression like a professional chess player would give when his opponent reached across the board. He gave a slight smile and nodded neutrally in acknowledgements of Nathan's arrival.

"This is Professor Archnon Winters, our chief of the MSC-D, Mission Specialist Consultation Department. He will be assisting and monitoring you throughout the mission," Norman introduced him.

A little colour had drained out of Nathan's face, he looked pale like he had a week before. Bad thoughts started to haunt him.

"Only one week had gone, why are you all talking about missions? I thought I'd have my training sessions next week?" Nathan said innocently, a bit of fear flavoured his voice.

"Sit down, please. I'll tell you the situation. Would you like to have something to drink?" Norman said as he took his seat opposite the professor.

"No. Thanks," Nathan said, declined the offer and sat down so that he could have a close view of the two men. The other side of the room was the working place of Norman, with a metal table supporting the heavy files and papers, cupboards and cabinets and a large floor-to-ceiling window showing the concrete background of Nottingham.

"I'm afraid to tell you there isn't any more time between now and the mission for training," Norman said, his words presented in a clear manner.

"No time? I thought you said I must go to the mission only after training," the words poured out unexpectedly. He was indeed shocked in the midst of relaxation and routine life that he thought he had for a week more.

"I need to tell you that this is the only chance we could have to reveal the location where your aunt is being kept. All along, we have failed to track the exact location of your aunt," he explained. Nathan wanted to ask why and decided to let him explain.

"Why that can't be after training? Why isn't there anymore time?" he said and knew the answer somehow.

"I'll tell you the reasons and details from now onwards, so please listen and you can ask whatever necessary you want after this," Norman said, he took a deep breath and started the briefing.

"Our agents had been tracking signals and satellite visuals about your aunt's whereabouts and they're not very progressive. But as I had said, there is no exact location and we can't search the whole area as big as a city. They had been switching your aunt into different locations once every few days, and when we get near it, your aunt's no longer there. This is the problem.

"If we can find out earlier where is she, there's no doubt of losing her and wasting time. And to do that, we need your help. I'll first tell you the details of one of the powerful individuals that had is highly suspicious and who we think was involved in the abduction of your aunt.

"I've found out a millionaire that invested in research centres. He had an unmistakable connection and alliance with the Ventures. I had told you slightly about him a week ago. He gave orders to the agents that are responsible for your aunt's custody. Evidence of the tracking signals from his computer indicates some sort of involvement. The good and bad thing is he always brings his laptop with him all the time whenever he goes. It may because of the valuable information in it, which is the reason he never leaves it alone. He will also need to give orders and make decisions immediately through the device.

"The good news is we will know where the computer is and the bad news is the files are very secure and we are lucky if we can even put our hands near it. The security break is out of the question due to the guards around him and his security system. With that, we cannot place any agent or you near him without being suspected and we have no reason," Norman added.

"Despite of the tight security, the only lapse of it where we can afford to place you and an agent near him is in this mission. This is the one and only opportunity for years. I'll have to tell you first that this millionaire had recently invested in international marine companies that research in deep-ocean creatures and ecology.

"They built a research centre in one of the deepest depth of the earth—Mariana Trench. In conjunction with a great project called Dark Rim. It cost them billions of pounds and it had just been completed.

"Fortunately, they allowed visitors annually starting from this year. It'll give us the chance to insert you in there. Only 50 people can visit the place a year. And we are uncertain he will be there. If we wait until your training finishes, it'll be next year. It's the only way we can get you near him in the easiest and fastest way," Norman said.

"I think they do this because of the recovery of the money of investors and to supply a sufficient modal for the project. With the good coincidence, this millionaire will be there for the opening ceremony where he will also be staying for a few days. We confirm he is there with the computer because of the e-mail signals he sent (he had reached the place this afternoon).

"Your mission is simple but not to say easy, you need to get to his computer in his quarters and download the files and we will supply gadgets for you," Norman said. He was referring to the files he had brought with him.

Nathan emerged himself in deep thoughts, understanding and trying to accept what he had just heard. *This is crazy, he said two weeks of rest,* he thought.

"What if the security is too tight? What if I fail?" he asked desperately. A small part of him had started to rebel, to decide whether to care about anything anymore.

"I'm sorry to tell you this. But this is the best we could do, this is the only shot we have. We will assist you but for the rest, you have to do it on your own and it must be the best and good enough," Norman said in a manner as if giving a motivational speech.

Nathan was uncertain and desperate. What about his aunt if he fails? In a few moments, responsibilities that a teenager shouldn't normally have had started to pile on his shoulders like boulders. His aunt's freedom counted on him, not to mention her life.

"When does the mission start?" he said after a long pause.

"Tomorrow. We will fly you to the harbour and from there you will take a submarine to the research centre. We had brought you and an agent tickets. It's a significant sum of money that hit the peak of the organization's budget. You're not going to refuse and make the efforts futile, are you?" Harvard said again and hated himself for pushing him on like that. He hadn't told him any declines were unacceptable by the IIO.

"I'll have to," he replied in a sour voice. A thought appeared to him. "This can't be true, why the IIO financed so much money to save my aunt?" he asked. It wasn't that he intended to decline the assistance, it was just to solve the weird sensation in his mind as if something were missing. They could be lying as well.

"If you are concerned, this mission is a multi-task type. As well as it contributes to the search of your aunt, it helps us and the organization, too. This millionaire by the named of Gata Harriman (it doesn't sound very nice) is suspected of possession of high-grade weapons illegally by many intelligence agency. This may be because of the location of the place—you surely can hide something in the deepest depths on earth.

"However, they have no solid evidence to prove that and substantial searches throughout the centre had been made, but none have found r anything close to it," he explained. The professor had already been briefed and he didn't mind to hear it again.

"The CIA is still very uneasy about something built in the Mariana Trench, which does not belonged completely to any nation and that means its internationally owned by its investors. He had the license to make nuclear plants only for electrical-energy-generating-purposes for the centre.

"But as I said, the intelligence agencies and governments are worried and fear the possibility of possession of weapons that could bring them down, including nuclear missiles. As a result, the investors, including Gata Harriman, gave them a chance to search the place to address the potential threat of national security, and they all had accepted it.

"The agencies wished to search again because of their previous futile effort to prove anything (which they really wished to find something to sue and imprison him than leaving the place empty-handed regardless whether any threat ever existed or not). But enough is enough, the government and wealthy politicians fear it may interrupt the alliance and businesses of the country since many millionaires are involved in this investment," he continued. He looked to Nathan was catching up or not.

"We are given a project to find solid evidence to prove that he is guilty. If there is another hidden nuclear facility, he will need a blueprint and he can't just dispose of it. There are procedures and I'm not going to tell you all of them, just know that he must keep it somewhere safe, if he really built more than the permitted number. Not only that the trading of uranium to run the plants could also be solid proof. If he buys more than he needs, it's enough to sue him by looking at his accounts and records.

"According to my analysis, he must keep this important information in that computer. The evidence could bring the end of his career and business if anyone in the government can obtain them.

"We are very convinced he keeps all of the information in one computer. And if anything goes wrong, a few clicks will instantly delete all the information, so nothing will ever reveal his plans or motives. Once you have all the information of your aunt and the nuclear issue, we can earn profits and get your aunt out of whatever miserable place she's at," he said confidently. He said it as if it were a clear-cut, perfectly planned mission, but Nathan knew he was only convincing him to join.

He thought for a moment. Could they lie to him and try to exploit him to get everything they want and then put him aside after this. The information about his aunt may not be in there as well. Anyway, if he keeps thinking about the negative possibilities, no one will ever save his aunt. If this was really a lie, all he could tell himself was he had tried his best about what he could do. It wasn't him that held all the alternatives. All he could do was hope that it all wasn't some kind of lie.

"What gadgets can you give me?" Nathan demanded, trying to put aside a sense of curiosity in his voice.

"There are some secret gadgets, one of our finest made by professionals in the Mission Specialist Consultation Department," the man in the room said for the first time as if waiting for his turn all along.

Professor Archnon Winters opened the briefcase on the table. It revealed four delicate items, a mobile-phone size tablet, a simple black plastic pen, an electronic watch and two magnets that attached to each other. A black, soft fabric with cotton padding supported the items and shaped their outlines. They did look very expensive but casual. They were the simple things that people used everyday.

"These items provide two functions, one that a person would expect and another that one could be the last to expect," Winters said proudly. He placed his hand over the four items like performing sacred magic. First, he took up the watch. It was black with strips with a high-tech and precise-looking number combinations that showed London's time.

"This tells you what the time is but it can hack any software and overwrite security lockers. Beneath the plastic strip, there are two hidden wires that need to be connected to the wires of the lockers or the casing as long as it is metal. The wires will then connect the lock to the machine and start overwriting.

"If the code and security is tighter than we predicted, there will be connections to our technology specialists on 24-hour shifts each day of the mission. They will find the way to hack through it. There is an indicator on the screen showing its progress," he explained. He then pulled the two stripes that were meant to secure the watch to the wrist, showing the two wires camouflaged beneath as a part of the design. He secured the watch back in place. Then, he took the miniature tablet without any manufacturing company name stated on it.

"I called this the electronic parasite. It can download information from any electronic device without leaving traces and you don't need to attach it to the socket as normal pen drives would need to. You don't need the power on as well. Just make sure two of the devices are not more than 20 meters apart and it will work." He paused for a moment. He was probably remembering how much time and effort he put in to create such invention.

"Just switch on the pinball game application and there will be a file called *parasite.* Activate it and the download starts until it finishes. The information will instantly be sent to the IIO headquarters and we'll provide feedback you whether it is useful or not.

"What if it's not useful and there are no more computers that I could download?" Nathan asked. He asked with some fear about the thought that he may fail.

"You must find more if that is possible," Winters said solemnly.

A silent moment seemed to drag on for a long time but Winters put it back into its home and retrieved the two cylinder magnets that attached together as if they were made to be twins. They were the size of a small finger.

"I did say that these wonderful gadgets served two purposes but only this one serves one. It exaggerates its own function, which is to provide magnetic force. Once you beat the pieces together hard and the next thing throw it near a metal object, they generate a scary magnetic field. All metal objects will be attracted to each other and stick as if they had been melted and harden into one piece, like the kind of power from the hospital's MRIs.

"The field will last for not more than five hours. I know that the research centre is 90-percent constructed out from metals and it's the last gadget you want to use. Causing trouble and suspicion is to be avoided. Also, make sure you don't wear anything made of steel," he said. His eyes focused in such concentration as a stern warning as if trying to hypnotize someone. That sent a shiver down Nathan's spine.

Winters then switched to the plastic black pen, it gleamed elegantly in the fluorescent light of the office, reflecting its modern construction.

"This pen can write but as well can give you vital surviving chances. Down in the deepest depths with water, millions of gallons surrounding you, what could happen? If the glass broke, which isn't that easy, but if it did, there's no doubt everyone will drown if they're not killed by the pressure first. But anyway, that's not likely going to happen and I don't intend to scare you.

"Maybe the water creates a leak and floods the whole place, if so, this pen can be your saviour. You'll need to pull out the tip and there's another tube containing liquefied oxygen that can supply you oxygen for five to 10 minutes. I hope you will not need to use this, but if you really need to, it'll help you to breathe and might enable you to survive a dire situation. He cleared the case after placing all of its contents and taking one last look at them.

"You will get them in your luggage after you reach the harbour. Don't lose them and keep them safe," he said. The words were rather a polite warning to Nathan.

Some cruel part in Nathan's mind suddenly urged him ponder. Why must he be the one to do this kind of job and not other agents? They also could do it because the files revealing his aunt's location were together. So they would also have what they want. But Nathan disregarded his lazy part and vowed that he would exert effort for his aunt's search. However, he needed to know why they must choose him over everyone else. "Among so many agents, why did you choose me? I'm untrained and inexperienced. Why not use other professional agents?" asked Nathan, trying not to sound unsatisfied.

"This is because of Argent's insistence. I personally did not recommend you. He said you offer an element of surprise and no one will suspect you. You can handle life-and-death-situations perfectly," Harvard said. It's not that he wanted to tell a child that he was so brilliant and then send him to a deadly mission. In fact, it was to give him hope so that he won't give himself up before anything starts. Nathan didn't seem bothered by the entire situation. "Can I say my farewells to Suzzle and Izle?" he asked.

"Yes. You will be travelling the next morning. The agent will meet you at the airport and we'll not make any unnecessary contacts to both of you from then on," Harvard added.

Nathan felt like a sponge full of shocking and unpredictable surprises of tensional news that could no longer fit in. He decided to have a good consideration whether to stop expecting routines for a few weeks. The breaking of frequency definitely brought a kind of sour feeling all around his chest. He wanted to go on holiday after things had settled down.

"I want to go back and rest," the words came out unnoticed.

"Surely, take some rest, there's a long day ahead," Harvard said friendly or at least tried to be.

With that, they dismissed and Nathan went back down to the car and travelled back with the agent so silently that he looked at him suspiciously. Nathan was trying to empty his mind for the night, he was going to the deepest depth on earth.

Chapter Twenty One

RESEARCH CENTRE

It was the day when wheels and distance played an important role. Nathan had started the day travelling from Nottingham by car to the nearest airport. He had grabbed a simple breakfast of garlic toast spread with butter and brewed milk with coffee. It had surprised Nathan that he had started to like the brown liquid, which supplied the awareness he needed for the start of a morning.

He and the agent met in person before had booked an 8 o'clock flight to the harbour in Japan, close to the Mariana Trench in the Pacific Ocean.

The agent that stayed with Nathan again sent him to the departure entrance in a fatherly manner, but said no notable farewells. He handed the luggage to the security checking area and masked a mock grin, and then said a simple sentence that Nathan knew was from Norman. "Be safe, and come back alive."

With that weird good-bye-phrase, Nathan made his way to the plane alone with not many other passengers present. He sat in the business-class seats and double-checked his number. The agent hadn't come yet but he somehow knew the four casual gadgets will be placed among his things, o his large bag passed the checks easily without a single doubt from the guards.

He was in early and it was only 7 p.m., and the anxiety had started churning his stomach into knots. Nathan took long deep breathes, calming his heart and the sour hot liquid pumping through him like adrenaline.

He did that without any necessary cessation until half an hour went pass. The passengers had increased rapidly and filled the seats with laptops and files cradled in their arms. The businessmen and companies' representatives filled in their precious time with either typing onto the keyboard furiously or sitting there staring through the window, looking into the far distance. They were thinking and planning future presentations or not believing there was time when there was no work.

The agent suddenly appeared to sit down beside him just before the last call before departure. Nathan didn't notice him moving from the door and that shocked him a little, but he didn't show it, not much. The agent wore a brown coat with a simple T-shirt inside and long jeans, he looked to suit the crowd more easily.

The surprising part was when Nathan looked through his casual make-up, which a person will not notice without looking at him for a long time. He eventually made out the features hidden behind. The man was French, pretending to be an English, and the bad thing was Nathan knew him and more likely to dislike him.

"Looks like I'm still your uncle and I'll be for a few more days, Nathan Doyle," the man said, his English was pure without any accents of his own country.

The agent was Fibiano, the one the dead man in the train asked Nathan to pass something to, the one who hated him for speaking in a rude manner to Harvard, he was also the man who secretly pinned him to the wall and warned him to mind himself in the Balmorals Hotel. Nathan wondered, among so many agents, he would have to work with this one. Argent David must be laughing at him now. Unintentionally, he swore silently to the boss.

"We'll be partners for the mission and if there's any personal inconvenience, I hope you will put that aside until the vacation ends," he whispered casually, setting his briefcase and laptop he brought in place. Nathan was too shocked to reply or further register the conversation. *Argent's mad*, he thought.

"Are you well, Nathan? You don't look very good," he asked. Fibiano laid a hand on his shoulder. Nathan wasn't sure it was a pretence of concern or not.

"I'm fine, thanks. It's nice to meet you, uncle," Nathan said in a normal tone. Faster than he could see, Fibiano pulled back his hand as if nothing had ever happened. He remembered Fibiano pretending to be his relative when they met in the gallery at Edinburgh and accepted the fact he was now doing it again.

"Why are you going for this vacation? You haven't told me yet," Fibiano simply asked.

"I wanted to take a rest," Nathan lied but both of them knew the word "vacation" was "mission" and just a cover for their identity.

"What about you?" challenged Nathan.

"I'm accompanying you there, your parents wouldn't want you to be alone," he said. Mentioning his parents actually hurt him but he didn't show it, he just knew that his false identity was the same he wore a week before.

"How was your stay in Nottingham?" he asked.

"Fine," he answered. But Nathan knew it was far better, he had made new friends and many more.

"Are Suzzle and Izle well?" Fibiano continued.

"They're fine," he replied.

Fibiano threw him a glance and took out a magazine from his briefcase. Their time was then occupied with either reading or throwing side glances uncomfortably at each other. Nathan knew well that if this goes on for a day or more, the people in the research centre will start suspecting them more than being an uncle with few words spoken to his nephew.

"I think you know where you are going. There will be a briefing on the ship," he said without looking up from the page. Nathan didn't answer him, he just nodded slowly.

The last steward came in from the main door. She was in her late twenties, wearing a red waist coat and black shirt with knee-length dress. She closed the large door of the plane and electronically locked it.

"This is the 231 on the first flight from U.K. to Japan non-stop. Please fasten your seatbelts," she said cheerfully.

After a moment, the 231 pulled out of the airport and moved onto the runway, it picked up speed with its turbines at full power and left the tarmac. The plane then soared into the air.

With the weather fine, the flight only took about five hours and they had crossed the immigration line and picked up their luggage. Fibiano urged Nathan and got into a cab, which he had hired earlier. The driver was local and definitely not an agent or anyone else close to it.

He was a large man with an unshaven chin, hoarse voice that could barely speak English or couldn't at all. He had a bald, shiny head and was foul-mouthed during his meaningless conversation.

The country's motorway was filled with impatient drivers and some merchants huddled in their little stalls. They were busy piling stocks of vegetables and meat. They reached a little harbour about 15 minutes later.

Fibiano handed the fare to him without demanding change and he got out as quickly as possible from the heavily tobacco-polluted atmosphere of the cab. The sun mercilessly tried its best to scald them, and sweat immediately plastered their shirts to them.

The harbour was in front of them with nothing to mark its border. Commercial and business-class cruises floated on the tide on one side, separating the weather-beaten and rusty local fishermen's boats.

Fibiano led the way to somewhere in the heart of the harbour and stopped near a ship. They boarded it. It was a black submarine, hundreds of meters long with hydro-blades protruding outwards. A shade was set up in front of its entrance. Almost instantly, a steward or someone else dressed in black overalls that absorbed the heat effectively addressed them politely.

"This way, gentlemen," he said, gesturing a gloved hand. He was definitely not local with his complexion or accent, perhaps Scottish.

He led them to the shade and walked across a metal gangplank with railings to the entrance of the submarine. They entered it, relieved from escaping the sun's glare. The area was stuffy with fluorescent lights that lit the cramped area.

He demanded their passports, registration identification and tickets. For a slight moment, Nathan feared that Harvard forgot to give him those. But Fibiano handed the documents for them both. The steward smiled and threw a few heavy cops onto the paper, leaving red ink of clearance sign and their company's logo.

"I hope you all will have a nice trip. Please proceed to the guest room. Thank you," he said politely while giving back the documents with both gloved hands and showing them the way.

"After they moved along the steel floor and reached a room with its door opened, a stewardess showed them to their seats. The steward left them. There were other passengers of scientists, researchers, wealthy families and workers. They were all busy with something else and didn't bother them. They settled down with their own luggage beside them and sat on the plastic seat screwed to the floor.

The stewardess handed each of them a pamphlet advertising the research centre and moved to the front, patiently waiting for another guest to come along. There must be another guest room for as Harvard said they allowed 50 guests last year.

Nathan knew the submarine had started to pull out of the harbour and descend as the stewardess' console beeped and she closed the door. She took a breath, glanced at a paper and prepared to talk. The lights dimmed for a moment and Nathan felt a slight humming and movement of the submarine.

"Welcome to our private submarine that will be on its way to the deep Pacific. The research centre is 1,000 meters below the sea-level. Although the conditions are harsh with no light and freezing cold temperature, there are special creatures that had not been discovered or had undergone special evolution processes. We have two research centres, one was built in the dark zone of the sea, which is 3,300 feet below sea level.

"Another centre has been built even deeper, in the Mariana Trench—the deepest depth on Earth. There are submarines that could connect them but we will mostly stay in the first centre, a slightly shallower place than the Mariana Trench. This is because we hadn't found much sign of life at such deep level. The two centres had cost investors $10.4 billion as we had to build them with metal and shift them piece by piece down there," she said. The amount of money spent surprised some people.

"I will now tell you about some of the process of the construction of the first research centre, the one which is not so deep. We started building it in 2003, which is 10 years ago. First, we sent special marine tractors and bulldozers that are used to build bridges to fix in supportive systems in place. These centres had to be constructed so that they will not sink or being battered away by the current," she said.

"Next, the special machines started to shape the landscape of the seabed to make the construction easier. They also hammered in another set of supportive systems to hold the foundations that they were building. Then they transported materials like stainless steel and concrete. After all the materials were in place, they set up the outer part of the centre and made it airtight, and then drained the water inside and washed the salt out," she then continued.

"Lastly, they built in the electrical systems and inner part of the centre. And last month, the first experiment had been carried out with safety precautions successfully. We had also launch a project called Dark Rim to detect undiscovered signs of life below the Dark Zone. Ladies and gentlemen can also refer to your respective pamphlets for a more detail information about the project and the centre. Do any of you have any questions?" she asked.

A girl no more than 12 raised her hand. She sat four seats away from them. "If there's no light down there, how are we going to see the fishes?"

The stewardess smiled and said. "There will be special lightings systems that will not affect the lives down there," she replied. The girl relaxed in her seat, imagining what she might soon see.

"Are there any more questions?" The people on board seemed to prefer to read their pamphlets. She waited for a moment and continued. "After this, we'll board another smaller submarine straight to the research centre. I hope it won't disturb your comfort much because this submarine is quite large and the air inside it won't allow it to sink farther." Nathan was peeking through the window, trying to see through the dark blackish water for any sign of life. But there was none visible. He wondered how deep they were going to sink and how much longer it would take.

They were approximately 25,000 feet below sea-level which made some of the passengers claustrophobic, being trapped in a slab of metal with millions of gallons of water ready to sink them. The only prospect to measure time was the continuous humming of the engine.

An hour ago, the stewardess said they will have to board two submarines, and the second one was much smaller than the first. It only held 20 passengers, the two stewardess and two captains. Nathan could see them through the window in the front with the controls and only a door separating them.

Just half an hour before, the process of switching submarines took a frustrating 20 minutes and a few complaints broke off. But now the cramped space caused them an intense sense of claustrophobia. They just were unaware that if the glass broke, it only took two micro seconds to make them disappear, not enough time for anyone to even notice.

After an hour of almost silent travel, the miniature submarine hit something quite hard, the sound of metal brushing against metal vibrated to their souls. Although it was just a small collision, paranoia and fear amplified it. Some of the scientists started to groan in terror and wished they'd never come.

The lights dimmed for a few seconds, exaggerating the claustrophobia and then everything became stable, the humming of the engine ceased, no more vibrations. A light on the far end glowed green, replacing the red one.

"We have reached the research centre, please unfasten your seat belts," the stewardess said, even she was relieved to get to safety, perhaps to the extent to consider whether to pass up her resignation letter at the end of the month.

She pressed some of the buttons on the panel of the door and stood up, then pushed it outwards. The door creaked loudly with vacuum sucking it back and then hissed white smoke as it gave up and parted company with the air-lock hinges.

Outside, a few workers in yellow jumpsuits equipped with helmets, belts and boots looked at them at such a calm state, as though they were experimental materials. Behind them was just a slab with a lot of circular metal panels, which shaped a hemisphere wall around them.

"Ladies and gentlemen, the captain has permitted landing. We'll proceed to the research centre. Please follow me," the stewardess said, regaining her composure. With the words of comfort, one by one, the people on board walked curiously through the open door and descended a few wet metal steps. Nathan was the tenth person off the small submarine with Fibiano right behind him.

Waterproof lights shone brightly from the ceilings. As he walked, he noticed the ship was docked on a wet platform with a hemisphere connected to the inside of the building. After it had docked there, the hemisphere shut off and drained the salt water out.

The line climbed down the yellow painted platform and made their way uncertainly towards the entrance with the workers in yellow leading. As soon as all of them had entered the building with the captains last, the worker tapped a few commands into the panel of the door, then the airtight metal shutters bolted and secured themselves with heavy locks.

It was the end of the journey from Nottingham to the Mariana Trench. They noticed another 30 people from another submarine were looking at them, as nervous as they were. After a moment to calm themselves and finally accepting the fact that they were safe even more than 3,300 feet below sea level, they started taking in the surroundings.

The whole place was indeed covered in steel and a small portion of concrete. Neat wires protected by rubber hoses hung along the corridors with control panels below them. Two metal paths each led to the right and ahead. There were two quarters about the size of houses in sight with numbers and codes printed on them that made no sense to Nathan.

Another woman looked to have taken charge of the guests. She was dressed in a white coat to her knees, and a T-shirt with black trousers. The woman wore thick spectacles in metal frames and told her guests she was a scientist.

"Welcome to our Mariana Trench Research Centre. This is Level 2, the Research Department. I'm Cecil Holmwood, the Chief Researcher in this centre and your tour guide. First, I'll just tell you the whereabouts of this place and skip the details for the moment," she said in a professional tone.

Holmwood led the way ahead and the crowd followed. "This is the Marine Geology Research Unit," she said as gesturing to the right where an immense length of protruding cuboids was. The good thing was at last the numbers made sense to someone who could refer to them.

"The other one is the Marine Genetic Research Unit. Here we complete experiments on bio-chemistry. They check whether the marine life had committed changes for a long period of time or something else like that," the woman said as she showed them a smaller box of metal farther up to their left.

She walked past the two metal cuboids and approached a separation path.

Ahead of us is the Marine Life Research Unit. We'll be visiting mainly that part afterwards," she said as she took a right turn, the left one path was totally sealed off by a metal door and she didn't mention or even look at that.

She led them to a corridor and turned left then waited for all of them to keep up. A wide metal cylinder with a panel glowing different colour of lights stood at the far end.

"We normally won't present this. It's only for visits for the curious ladies and gentlemen. We can see the scenery of the Dark Zone with our night visions," Cecil said. She then typed a few commands into the panel, which was attached to a wall.

After a minute or more, the metal panels that covered the whole side of the corridor folded and slid upwards into a hidden socket in the ceiling, revealing a blue illuminating glow with blurred dark blue images moving far away, each one with a small ball of light near it. The fluorescent lights dimmed. The crowd held their breath.

"The Dark Zone actually does not allow any light to penetrate and it's totally dark and ice cold with no plants that could survive. Although we can't see it with our naked eyes the beauty of its nature, the centre has night vision capabilities as I had mentioned. Normally, night vision will use a very limited amount of light and elaborate the image. This means it detects light from the bioluminescence of every fish in sight," she explained and paused for a moment.

"Bioluminescence is the production of light by living organisms and it's mostly for creatures far under the sea. The visions will use the very little amount of light that we could barely see with our own naked eyes to form out the picture of the fishes.

"Unfortunately, we can't zoom in or learn any of the creature's species or anything specific now, but in the research labs and the dome, which you all will see later, it can facilitate us with equipment and make explanations clearer and with live references," she continued.

Nathan looked into the glow and tried to make out the shape and movement of the figures, but none made any clear progress. The shadows of the creatures were somehow baiting him to take notice of all of them. If he had the funny idea of counting them, the black figures would swim around and eventually disappear and he would lose track.

The silent and calm figures with the soft yet striking illuminating blue somehow gave Nathan a sense of eternity, like everything around the world was no longer important. It was like the colour of crystal that Veinna gave him, now in a Ventures agent's hands. It was something Nathan couldn't ignore or decipher the real sensation. Beauty was the closest thing he could relate it to.

The woman waited for a few moments for them to enjoy or accept what was the thing were they looking at. Despite the beauty, her eyes barely enjoyed it as she had looked at this kind of boring blue light for 10 years.

She urged them on and proceeded to the wide and large cylinder on the far end. It connected the ceiling to the floor. It looked like an elevator, a big and weird one. She pressed a button on the cylinder. The doors slid opened into their sides and they all went in, it was big enough for 40 people. *Someone could stay here*, Nathan thought.

"This elevator is indeed unlike the ones you're all used to," she said after looking at their curious glances. "This lift is totally powered by hydraulic energy and water pressure. The sea water is pressured to push the lift up," she continued as she pressed a few buttons of code and hit the button with a number printed onto it.

The inner construction rose as it left its cylindrical shell behind to Level 1.

It came to a halt and slid open its two huge doors. They exited the cylindrical metal and followed their tour guide. The surroundings looked opulent and comfortable and, more importantly, gave enough meaning to everyone to know where and what the purpose of it was.

Ahead of them were two wooden doors leading to a large hall or something like that. On their right was a parallelogram construction of glass and metal. Inside it were about 40 computers and board games. And along the corridor, opposite it were rooms, a lot of rooms that were probably meant for them.

"This is Level 1, the Guest Unit," she said and stood there. We'll offer a rest time of two hours for ladies and gentlemen. I hope you may enjoy your leisure privacy and the best comfort we could provide. Please remember to retrieve your room number and card in the hall in front of the lift. There will be a reception area," she said and paused for more words.

"At 6 o'clock, we will provide a detail explanation and tour around the centre, starting from the Marine Life Research Unit. Before that, I would like to inform you about the computer and free Wi-Fi services and your respective rooms. I think we'll dismiss here," she continued professionally, delighted at announcing her guests as well as her own rest time. She walked to the elevator and pressed a button, then disappeared with the doors opened and closed.

After getting the room cards, Nathan and Fibiano went to their rooms. Nathan's was just after his, arranged side by side. He smiled at the teenager and entered his own quarters, not wanting to secretly discuss the plans about the mission, he may have been paranoid of bugs. Nathan entered his own room as well.

The room was spacious with a bed and a desk accompanying it. The bathroom at the side had the door closed. But the most attractive thing was the view of the Dark Zone, the soft illuminating blue, hiding blackish images of fishes each with their bioluminescence.

He looked at the luggage but he didn't notice it had been couriered to his room. The gadgets were casually placed among his belongings. He went into the bathroom and took a hot shower, washing away the tiredness of travelling and feeling a sense of unease, he knew the heat came from a nuclear plant as Harvard had mentioned in the briefing. He dressed casually after that, fresh and prepared to start his mission.

Then he looked at the screen for a long moment. The endless view and relaxation was calming, but then a thought occurred to him, pulling him out from the midst of something, almost vicious and with threats.

You come here to save your aunt and for your mission, don't be too relaxed because bad things will be happening soon.

Chapter Twenty Two

DARK ZONE

An urgent shiver woke Nathan up from the bed. He came to know that he was lying on his back. Jet-lag had gotten the best of him, but sleep had recovered some part of him. Only now he knew that they were using England's time in Japan since day and night weren't separated by the sun in the deepest depths where no sunlight could penetrate.

He noticed he was dressed in casual clothes after his warm bath and had slept there, the sheet beneath him, pillows unused.

The illuminating blue glow was still visible through the thick glass in front of him, the dark figures seemed to be never sleeping, never ever willing to let their guard down, which will be resulted in being digested by other fishes. They indeed were never in a vulnerable state, not allowing any surprise attacks from creatures in the Dark Zone.

Nathan supported himself on an elbow, then rose up and sat on the surprisingly comfortable bed. He only now noticed the digital clock, which was present on the wooden desk in front of the yellow lamp. It showed him the time was 5:57 p.m.

Only after quite a while of staring at the digits, he remembered they needed to continue their tour and meet somewhere whom Cecil Holmwood didn't mention. He scrambled for his jeans and shirt and wore a jacket over them.

Then, he headed for the door. Just in time for him, he secured the watch on his wrist and pocketed the other three gadgets. He opened the door quickly and calmed down his urging of feeling late.

There were a number of people that were hanging around, strolling across the mass number of identical doors. He let out a breath of relief.

"Almost late," a person said in a masculine voice. Fibiano stood at the wall beside him, probably the entire time. He was dressed in the same attire, brown coat and black jeans, presumably another pair of the same. The agent looked calm, with hands crossing each other, one leg standing in advance of another.

"I was sleeping," Nathan replied. He glanced around once more. "Where are the others and our tour guide?"

"They will be here," the French in make-up said. "I think they gave me the wrong room, the irritating blue light they claim to be night visions made me unable to differentiate dawn and dusk without a clock. And, aren't night visions supposed to be green? Whatever the thing was, it kept me awake the entire time. Did you find the button to shut the thing like the one in the corridor?" Fibiano continued.

"You should have asked the tour guide or just shut your eyes so nothing could irritate you," he answered, delighted by his reply. He had already started to cooperate and suit in with the French but he liked to make a little offense. But he soon regretted the counterattack.

"Better not talk to me like that or else I'll tell your parents about your behaviour on this trip, Nathan Doyle," he spat the words out like a teacher on report card day.

Nathan looked away, the French was cruel, tormenting him about remembering him about his parent's death. He was no better than when he was in the last meeting at the Balmorals, having him pinned to the wall secretly and whispering venomous words. He made a mental note of demanding a reason for his team-up from Argent or Harvard.

The elevator at the far end opened its doors with a *thump* and Cecil Holmwood walked towards the guest rooms.

"Good evening, ladies and gentlemen. Are all the guests here?" she said notably. She was cradling a folder in her left arm. She looked tired and her skin was pale without the glare of natural sunlight.

The crowd moved towards her, the eleven-year-old girl at the first, curiously masking her face. The others made a respectful distance, isolating the guide a bit.

"I think we will not wait any longer. The late ones can meet us in the Marine Life Research Unit as I announced earlier," Holmwood declared. "Let's move to there," she urged them.

The crowd followed behind like a herd of sheep. Fibiano and Nathan did as well, but always maintaining to be at the back. It could make it easier and not as obvious for them to leave the crowd as well.

All of them entered the gigantic elevator and descended to Level 1, the Research Department. They made their way along the corridor to the front of an identical cuboid. The guide tapped a few codes into a panel and the metal cover slid aside, revealing a glass door.

Nathan could see through the transparent glass for some activities. Beakers, airtight cages and chemical containers on lab tables filled the place, scientists and researchers hunched on their chairs, busy with either paperwork or handling a specimen on Petri dishes.

They walked through the work space of tables and specimens. "Please don't touch anything without permission," Cecil said, noticing one small girl's hands.

Nathan took in the black and soft specimen of the fishes in the Dark Zone, all dead with mouths opened wider than themselves. Born in the dark but died in light, pathetic souls. The scientists that were already tired with bloodshot eyes peered through microscopes and articles, either adjusting fine or coarse imaging or writing reports and theory or examinations. Some scientists sighed in tiredness as a result of an experiment ruined their long-made hypothesis and smiled when one came out with another. All realizing that one failed experiment could bring them closer to success, but how much further?

They headed to the middle of the unit, where floor-to-ceiling aquariums occupied the space. The lights near it were switched off, making the illuminating glow shining marvelously. But there was huge difference from these ones in his room and the corridor.

The Dark Zone fishes were more contained in the glass cubes and they could clearly make out the shapes, colours, sizes and physical characteristics of each of them. The fishes were all carnivorous and furious looking without knowing their future may be lying on Petri dishes or bubbling in beakers. All of them were dark-coloured and most were black. A bioluminescence hung from each of them.

"I'll show you all some common fishes and introduce their characteristics of surviving in the Dark Zone. The Dark Zone doesn't allow any light from the sun to penetrate into the deepest depths of the ocean. As a result, no plants will exist in such place. I'd told you were all in the first briefing.

"These fishes survive by eating and consuming each other, some regardless how big the size or their own size. But the doubtful part is if there are no plants, how do these fishes even exist in the first place?" Holmwood remarked.

"I mean that every food chain must have a producer, which is green plants that are capable of carrying out the photosynthesis process, making their own food. The common food chain in the Dark Zone actually involves the Twilight Zone as well, which is 200 meters below sea level, it is found above the Dark Zone and below the Sunlit Zone.

"The Twilight Zone allows a significant amount of sunlight and few plants will grow. There will also be plant planktons that are very small organisms and some are micro-sized. These less-vicious and non challenging species will go up to the second zone and consume plants for a period of time in the night. Then, they will descend back to the Dark Zone for resting or mating," she added.

"First, I'll show you the Black Sea Devil," she explained and pointed to a shiny fish inside the aquarium. The species was opening and closing its huge cavernous jaws, oblique mouth. Sharp, glassy and fang-like teeth were present.

"Black Sea Devils are hunters in the Dark Zone which use its 'fishing pole', also known as bioluminescence, the production of light by living organism to lure and hunt other creatures for food and sometimes for mating," she explained.

Then, her fingers switched to another fish, it was grey with a dorsal fin, black round eyes and a mouth not as large as the one before. It was the size of a football.

"This is the Hairy Angler. Its body is covered in long antennae to detect prey movement nearby. The male is about one-tenth of the female's size funny enough, not bigger than a ping-pong ball. The males of this Angler are particularly a parasite. It forms a parasitic relation with the female, attaching himself to her flesh, ultimately sharing her blood circulation and becoming a dependable source of semen, a liquid body consisting sperm and other fluids," she said.

"This fish also has a stomach that is capable of expanding to eat other even bigger fishes than itself. Other than that, very little is known of the Hairy Angler because of its deep habitat," Holmwood said, circling the fish's belly.

She pointed and held one hand over the glass, a fish which looked to be very long, with its tail dangling in the cold water. Fins lined the entire length of the tail. A bioluminescence was attached to the end of it.

"This Pelican Eel's most notable feature is its large mouth, much longer and larger than its own body. The mouth is loosely hinged and can swallow fishes that are bigger than itself but analysis of the stomach's contents shows that they primarily eat small crustaceans. Despite the size, they only have tiny teeth, which would not be consistent with a regular diet of large fishes," she explained, drawing an imaginary replica of the eel.

Cecil Holmwood then urged them to another aquarium behind them, both almost identical. She pointed at a slender fish. It was covered in small, silvery, deciduous scales and a large blunted head. Its entire body looked compressed.

"The Lantern fish remains within the Dark Zone during daylight hours but rises to the Sunlit Zone at night. They do this to avoid predation and to follow the migrations of zooplankton, which they feed on. Zooplankton is a group of plankton, an enormous amount. They return to the lightless depths during daybreak," she explained, gesturing at the pale-brown fish.

Then, the attention shifted to the last fish. It was a small slab of pink meat. Two fat little fins protruded from its sides, the eyes staring into the distance.

"This is the Sea Toad, found in the continental slopes of the Atlantic, Pacific and Indian oceans. The first dorsal fin is modified into a short bioluminescent lure which dangles over the mouth," Holmwood said.

She led them across the other side of the lab. The tables were placed with fishes on Petri dishes at the middle of attention from scientist. Bones, organs and slime were visible from the precise cuts on their bodies. The visitors whom mainly were scientists themselves looked surprised and attracted, while the others glanced in the opposite direction, as nausea haunted some of them.

"You all could also understand more about the inner structures of the fishes," Cecil said, as she regarded the researchers. She strolled slowly along the tables, giving an opportunity for the crowd to take in the wet, slime-coated insides of the fishes.

They reached the other end of the lab and exited the place, back into the illuminated corridor. She led them along the blue glow, passing a path to the right with a sealed door at the far end. She stopped beside an identical cuboid. She tapped in a set of codes for the metal and glass doors and they opened.

"This is the Marine Geology Department," Holmwood said as she entered.

The whole lab was set up differently. No fishes or any aquariums were present, just glass blocks holding rocks and minerals. Maps and landscape pictures underwater decorated the walls. A handful of computers and machinery beeped and worked. Similar-looking scientists sat on chairs and stools looking at eyepieces of weird microscopes or searching information through machineries.

She walked into the centre of the place where a hologram of the world's map was projected from a computer, it stood amazingly in front of her, twice her size.

"This unit researches for new minerals and landscape changes on or under the seabed. Our new project is to find an undiscovered source of petroleum and natural gases. Useful minerals were also investigated. But the most interesting part is the underwater volcanoes, which are either inactive or active. They are generally the main source of heat in the Dark Zone, which allows some species to survive," she said as she typed a few orders into the computer's keyboard.

The hologram of the world's map zoomed, only showing the entire Pacific with some lands, and concentrated to the Mariana Trench, below Japan, then formed a green image of the seabed.

"There's no light down there so I hope night visions will help us. As you can see, the black protruding, chimney-shaped columns are called vents. They were formed when hot water pressured through the seabed, making holes and forming the vents that are made of mineral.

"These vents spill mineral and gases like sulfur and hydrogen, richly feeding bacteria. The bacteria are soon consumed by tube worms. They are the long protruding pipes with plume of tubes which are supposedly red," Cecil Holmwood explained as she used an indicator from the computer to circle the images.

"These tube worms are mysterious because they don't consist of proper mouths or guts, they eat or digest as a proper term the sulfur-eating bacteria, known as partners that live inside their bodies. Moreover, eelpout, vent fish, blind crab and vent clams consume largely on these tube worms and celebrate the warm water. The creatures also grow faster than land-animals because of the rich nutrients of their food," she said, clicking on the keyboard.

Then she moved on to the collection of minerals that was kept in protective cube-glasses with labels of numbers and alphabets. Nathan couldn't take in more than the various colour and shapes of the rocks. Emerald-green, ruby-red, sapphire-blue, pale-grey, charcoal-black and many other colours a person couldn't really imagine.

The group then proceeded to the Marine Genetic Research Unit. They passed the corridor and made a right turn, which they didn't use before and strolled passed the submarines docking place, then walked to the left to the identical area they first saw the moment they disembarked the ships.

It was the most boring part of the tour, with test tubes full of brightly-coloured chemicals, beakers bubbling above Bunsen burners and sealed conical flasks in glass containers. Scientists were taking specimen and blood of the poor Dark Zone creatures and wrote reports from these tests.

At last, Cecil Holmwood led them back to the elevators and rose to Level 1. She told them that there will be a meeting with visitors for the opening ceremony soon.

"Ladies and gentlemen, you could have your dinner at the Halls after the opening ceremony at 8:30. It will be conducted by our valued investor—Gata Harriman whom fortunately has the time to spend with us," she announced. *Gata Harriman, the millionaire with the weird name,* Nathan thought.

He remembered the elevator connects three floors, Level 1 and 2, but she didn't mention what was on the third level. It must be the staff quarters where Harriman will stay his private quarters there, he will probably sneak in there when the time is right.

"The presence of the opening ceremony is compulsory because we have prepared a very nice dinner and delicacies for ladies and gentlemen. Please be there before 8:30. Thank you," she said quickly. Feeling relieved as if had just finished handling a herd of kids, she headed back in the same manner to the elevator and disappeared.

It looks like Nathan will need to get to Harriman's quarters during the dinner. It was the only period of time to be sure that the millionaire wouldn't in his room.

Just for a long moment he stood there, the other people were either entering the entertainment unit or retreating to the guest room. He wasn't sure what was missing, it wasn't any of his gadgets.

The thought came immediately to him. *The Frenchman Fibiano was missing.*

Chapter Twenty Three

CREATION OR DESTRUCTION?

Nathan nearly yelled at the Frenchman 30 minutes later when the first sight of him reached his eyes. He had been searching for him for more than half of his rest time all around the level. As a result of his failure to find him before, he admitted the fact that Fibiano must have remained in one of the Research Units.

"Where had you been?" demanded Nathan. They were in the Guest Unit near the Entertainment Area when the Frenchman approached him.

"Looking around the place, I indulged myself in looking at the fishes on Petri dishes," the French answered casually. His simple and not concerning tone caused Nathan to throw him a look of disgust and anger.

"I've been looking for you! Why didn't you tell me or leave me a note?" Nathan asked. If someone didn't understand the situation properly, it could sound like a demanding father questioning his son if the voice was a bit tougher.

"You're 14, my dear. I reckon you're able to take care for yourself without grown-ups around for a few minutes," Fibiano said in a pitch that was too high. A few visitors that looked like parents masked a smile and a few shook their heads. Nathan blushed, his cheeks uncontrollably growing red and hot.

Then, a thought came to him, instantly extinguishing the entire blush. *You researchers wouldn't even grin if you are a*

14-year-old spy in a mission that involves your aunt's life. How would you feel if your team-mate increased the possibility of being captured?

"I'm just worried. Please don't treat me like I'm still small," replied Nathan. However, he secretly threw him a *you-are-an-idiot look.*

Fibiano saw that and the invisible tension between them rose, but the agent suddenly smiled and relaxed his shoulders, then particularly broke the long silence. "Let's get ourselves seated in the Hall, the opening ceremony starts in a moment.

"There will be seafood and other nice dishes. I hope you will have a limit for those because your mother told me you're slightly allergic to seafood," he said with concern.

Nathan walked to the Hall quietly, not addressing the conversation anymore. His weak part had been terribly exposed for a long time and kept being the primary target for Fibiano's counter-material in either big or mild arguments. *What's wrong with him? I just asked him where he'd gone. He really hates me, more than I thought.*

Fibiano masked a steady grin with nothing more than curiosity on his face. The Frenchman followed what seemed to be his nephew towards two large oak-doors, elegantly carved in flower patterns and coated in expensive wood toner, the spirit still flavoured the air nearby. One of it was opened and a desk covered in red cloth stood a few paces away.

Nathan stopped beside the table, a doorman or that's what he looked like with coat beneath the standard-like white clothes and ironed black trousers just stopping to reveal the hard-polished shoes, his hair was immaculately brushed with gel.

He wrote his name and got his table number, and then made his way into the space between opulent tables with wine glasses, white clean tea cups and plates on the top of white linen cloths. The entire left side of the Hall was made of re-enforced glass, the illuminating blue glow with dark restless figures swimming freely, luckier compared with the ones in the labs.

The other side was decorated with portraits or pictures of the millionaires that were larger than themselves. On the front part,

VIP tables stood before a stage below microphones paced apart at equal distances. Scientists and visitors were filling up seats and chatting with what seemed to be a soft, polite manner.

His number led him to a table at the middle on the left, a two-seater and close to the glass, at least within a few steps of reach. He sat down on the embroidered cushioned chair and knew who was opposite him before Fibiano took his seat.

"Nice place," Fibiano praised. "It's just the blue light that should be shut out," he murmured. Nathan preferred not to bother him with any more than the slightest and neutral of acknowledgements.

"Our opening ceremony starts in a moment. Ladies and gentlemen, please be kind enough to have patience," a man in coat said via one of the microphones on the grand stage.

"Uncle," Nathan begun, Fibiano looked at him. "Can you please stop mentioning about my parents?" Nathan said. His voice had been set to the softest tune and the vulnerable part of him had come out. He hoped the French would agree, if not, he wasn't sure if he would walk out of this place or not.

"Nathan, I'm just reminding you about something important during this period of time to be good and behave well," Fibiano replied. Nathan thought he would still continue to torment him with sweet-poisoned words and disagree to his request.

He froze as he leaned forward, so close until his breath could be felt. "You can't go on like this. You're vulnerable to verbal situations, especially questions about your family." He looked at him and let the words hang in the cold air.

"If one of the visitors or researchers or even Cecil Holmwood has a conversation with you, it must have to be something like an introduction and your family. You will need to tell your identity to them as my nephew," he held his position, refusing to use any words involving "mission" or false".

"If I even slightly mention about your real family, you will flinch and turn your head away, filled with emotions and uncertainty that wouldn't be of any importance during these few days.

"How would they think about your weirdness when they possessed a kilo of radioactive uranium illegally? You may think this little issue isn't even worth to be suspicious of by any normal people, but they aren't normal. You ought to treat me like your real uncle and that you have parents alive as written in the files," Fibiano continued.

"Your test had already started the moment you boarded the Atitlan in Edinburgh, the unofficial one. How did Suzzle come to know your lies such easily? Because she smarter than any of you classmates. She's experienced and you know who her father is.

"I admit I don't like you, maybe even to the extent of hating. Nevertheless, you are a liability and an asset of surprise. If you keep on acting like this, whatever element of surprise will be gone, and even worse, changed into a negative suspicion on us. And if this mission is compromised, we die.

"As a result, we must cooperate and I want to continue my career. You better understand well," he said so silently that Nathan strained to listen even though not more than three centimeters separated them.

Fibiano leant back and seemed to relax like if he'd been gossiping. He laughed to the extent where people near them looked at them and then ignored them. The professional agent couldn't risk of any amount of suspicion. From far, an uncle telling his nephew something weird and funny then laughing, leaving his nephew shocked and rooted on the seat, *how natural.*

"Our ceremony begins now. Ladies and gentlemen, please take you respective seats," the stage man said, waking Nathan from the shock. After a minute or more, the place settled into perfect silence, the lights dimmed, leaving one shining on a microphone attached to the top of the stand on the grand stage.

"I'll now present our very honoured guest, one of the most willing and generous investors for the Dark Rim Project, Gata Harriman," the worker said and immediately hurried to hide on the back stage. There was applause and hand-claps.

The attention was passed to a man walking up the red-carpeted steps to the front stage, his eternal might radiating throughout the Hall. Gata Harriman made the last few paces and reached for the microphone.

He was dressed in grey padded waistcoat and a neat black tie, his trousers were striped with dark and light variations of grey and black. The millionaire looked both English and Russian, and it suited him name very much.

"I wish my honoured and welcomed visitors and workers a great evening. I feel very lucky and appreciated the invitation to carry out a speech for so many founders for the opening ceremony of the Mariana Trench Research Centre and the preposterous project—Dark Rim," he started the speech.

"The nature in this world, our mother of nature, will never be completely discovered. It leaves us with the mystery and anxiety to uncover one curiosity and then another. You may treat butterflies and paddy fields as an endless gallery drawn by nature and reckon the deepest depths of the world so mysterious.

"Nevertheless, every part of nature has its own beauty, regardless of how deep. I, with the cooperative and generous list of investors, have taken the first step to uncover the beauty of Mariana Trench, the deepest depth on Earth," he said. He had a motivational tone and gestured a welcoming hand to his right. The guest followed his gaze to the immense piece of glass separating them from the millions of gallons of water, the menacing illuminating deep glow looked to fulfill its very rights to attract notable attention.

"Once I had a dream, when I was probably 6 years old. It was a dream to build a fortress in the deep sea," he said and smiled. His pause invited the audience to laugh for a moment before he continued.

"I didn't build a castle for civilians, because a research centre is more appropriate. My dream is no longer any simple one when the project and construction of this place hit 10 billion American dollars. My wealth yet doesn't fulfill the needs of financial aspect. But my previous dream motivated me to go on, to give nature a few more admirers. I funded, planned and had various researchers study the marine life. And at last, the great engineers and architectures of Japan and other international companies fulfilled my vision to construct my dream world.

"Nevertheless, without the help of the generous and nature-loving investors, nothing would be true today. I thank them for the financial help. I wish more ladies and gentlemen had already seen what our research centre is capable of and when the project starts, it will be tested to its limits," he spoke eloquently.

The worker behind the stage appeared, his hands holding a sliver tray with an electronic device about the size of a chocolate bar. Gata Harriman took it and flicked a switch, and a green light glowed from an indicator.

"I now officially, representing the investors, start the project, Dark Rim," he said. His finger pressed on the green button.

Immediately, the dark figures outside swam eagerly and circled around a point with perfect timing and distance apart. A light source had attracted them. Since the fishes used bioluminescent to lure prey, the foreign light bulb that was much more powerful than their lights had indicated a very big prey. It tricked them into a pursuit that created a united march. The scientists looked impressed, but knew the trick behind the curtain.

After 10 seconds, the bulb died, not disturbing nature anymore. Harriman returned the remote control and descended down the stairs to his table. Another worker took over the stage.

"Thank you for being willing to commence our ceremony. Now, we will have our opening dishes," he said and paused.

Instantaneously, waiters and waitress rushed to the tables with plates on silver trays and served them to each table. They opened the metal cover. A shell food, a few big oysters were served on ice.

Vegetables like carrots and cabbages exaggerated the oyster offerings. A perfectly sliced lemon was placed carefully on the sides of each plate. A saucer stood beside it, filled with some kind of spicy sauce.

"This is a dish of fresh oysters carefully chosen from the sea coasts of Japan and sent directly here to maintain their freshness. Please use the lemon to enhance the taste and your appetite. For a more outstanding taste, you may dip a small amount of ginger with garlic marinated with a few sprinkles of rice wine. Enjoy," the man on the stage said and went down.

Gata Harriman had joined the guests on the front tables and chatted, picking his shell food and chewing it in measured mouthfuls.

Nathan took one and sucked the oyster out of the shell into his mouth, it was big and filled almost the whole of his mouth. Then he chewed it. It felt like soft rubber, the juice of freshness and salt flavoured his taste. He finally ate the entire slab of grey meat and washed it down with water. Fibiano looked at him curiously, not even touching his plate.

"What?" Nathan demanded.

"Are they nice? They look like giant creatures," Fibiano murmured. The Frenchman seemed to have forgotten about the conversation a few minutes before. They were supposed to treat it like a joke. Perhaps that was why Fibiano laughed just after he said something that could kill them, in order to cover any suspicion.

"Taste it yourself," Nathan said. He squeezed the lemon onto his dish and picked another oyster, disengaged it from its shell and dipped it into the sauce. It tasted sweet-spicy. It had been marinated for a long time and it warmed in his stomach.

Gata Harriman was moving around, chatting randomly with scientists. Nathan suddenly felt nervous and something was rushing in him, hot blood with adrenaline.

He didn't forget to always look around and measure how much attention was focused on him. If it was minimal, he'll try to excuse himself and get out. Then, he'd travel to the millionaire's quarters and get the job done.

Just as he finished the opening dish of shell food, Harriman surprisingly paid enough attention to the boy and his uncle to walk over. Nathan thought Harriman was just passing by but when he pulled an empty chair to their table and sat down, this couldn't be an accident. *You got to be kidding me.*

"Do you mind if I join you for a while," he asked the two of them.

"No, I don't," Fibiano replied. He didn't look as nervous as Nathan but was equally surprised. A man with hundreds of millions of dollars, not fewer than 10 villas around the world, a couple of bungalows that he barely lived in, a fine collection of sport cars and the one whom invested in a $10-billion-project was asking permission to sit in front of them. Nathan suddenly remembered something.

"So, you're one of the youngest people to be in the deepest depths in the Pacific, probably the only teenager as far as I know. It's nice to meet you," he said in a perfect manner. Surprisingly how his tone consisted of no arrogance.

Gata Harriman extended a hand. It only contained one gold ring and his handshake was perfectly business-like. Nathan stared at it longer than he intended, and then hesitantly shook it. He had accepted the fact that the millionaire wanted to have some conversation with them the moment his hands touched the chair.

Fortunately, he had even earlier considered that everything was possible and something like this wasn't that shocking since much worse things had happened to him over the past two weeks. Anyway, he needed to be a kid with his uncle. And meeting someone so wealthy would be a big thing. A very big thing, so some length of nervousness was required.

"Nice to meet you," Nathan replied. He could now clearly see the probably English-born-Russian. His hair was neatly combed with immaculate clothes that would need an accountant's three month's salary to buy with discounts.

"So, what makes you come here with your—father?" Harriman started.

Fibiano looked to be completely in control and acted professionally to mix his emotions of a millionaire meeting his nephew in person. But deep inside his heart, there was doubt and undisguised fear and worry about his team. He hoped he could remember and abide what he had advised him of before the opening ceremony.

"He's my uncle," Nathan replied without hesitation. "We are here on a holiday, to see some species in the Dark Zone. If we're lucky, maybe some newly discovered ones," Nathan answered naturally, really inserting himself in the conversation.

"Just holiday? Nothing more than a boy full of inspiring hope?" Gata challenged. *If you want to know one thing, I'm going to flank you in jail and pull my aunt out of her misery when I get to your computer. And it's all because of your involved in my aunt's abduction. Idiot!* Nathan thought.

"I had a dream when I'm 5 years old. It's like yours. Maybe one day I'll build a resort in the Atlantic," he said cheekily.

Gata Harriman broke into a laugh, attracting attention from visitors. Fibiano tried to join but looked very unnatural, anyway a normal uncle should have been that way.

"Where do you live? Sea-lover kid," Harriman asked after the humour in him died down.

"Central London. A home of absent parents," Nathan replied. This was one he should say given it stated that in the files. A trickle of shiver and grief ran up his spine but he showed not the slightest sign. He hoped he was real and convincing enough.

"Your parents are always busy, like me. So try to understand them," he answered in a harmless tone. *My parents aren't like you, if they stored a handful of uranium in my house, I'll blame them,* he thought.

Nathan didn't reply nor did he start a new topic. After a moment of silence, the millionaire stood up and shook both of their hands. "I appreciate this simple conversation and hope we'll meet again," the millionaire said.

After Harriman had strolled to another table, too far to notice them in detail, Nathan slipped out the miniature tablet from his pocket. He had switched it on long before the millionaire came to sit with them, hoping it was near enough to pick up a connection.

And suddenly, like a gift of coincidence, he voluntarily came near him for a period of time. Professor Archnon Winters, the chief of the Mission Specialist Consultation Department, had introduced him about the tablet's hidden function.

When he switched on the pinball application and activated the file named *parasite*, it will download whatever files from electronic devices in range. It must be either his mobile phone or something else.

Whether it is useful or not, he waited for Harriman to engage in another conversation and then read the feedback. It was a single **NO** written in a very small size. For a brief moment of consideration he had a thought that Gata Harriman was not guilty and only build this research centre for an innocent purpose like he said, ". . . to make a first step to uncover the beauty of nature . . .".

However, the millionaire had no reason to store something so important into his mobile phone that could cause him a life of imprisonment if it fell into the hands of the police. As Harvard Norman had said, everything important will be in his computer in his quarters, including Nathan's aunt's location and information.

He pocketed the tablet while the main dish was served. It was salmon marinated in Japanese teriyaki sauce, grilled until the juice inside seeped out.

Despite his previous good appetite, he had a lot more important issues to contend with on this vital part of the mission. Fibiano hadn't said anything more than praising and protesting the dishes after the millionaire had gone. He naturally took a bit to avoid any possible suspicion. Why would a hungry boy go elsewhere just after a delicious dish had been served? Yet, since all of his concentration had been prioritized to his other senses, the food seemed tasteless.

Then, he excused himself to the toilet. He didn't want Fibiano to know his plan, not before he finished this.

He walked out of the Hall, passing the scientists whom were chatting and made a final glace at Gata Harriman. *I'm coming to save you, aunty*, he thought.

Making one last check on the gadgets, he took a deep breath and braced himself, calming his nervousness and heading to his real destination. Level 3, into the millionaire's quarters.

Chapter Twenty Four

ELECTRONIC PARASITE

The sense of nervousness and anxiety was far more powerful and influential than Nathan had ever expected. The space of the elevator was not enough from satisfying his claustrophobia although 40 people could easily fit in. What if the pressure that worked the lift failed? What if armed guards suddenly burst in and captured him?

Time was ever slow as the elevator descended to Level 3. He had used his watch to activate clearance to this level effectively. Now the only thing to measure the seemingly slow progress was the number indicator above the two closed doors.

The lift stopped, producing a *thud* and the locks of the doors disengaged. The first sight of Level 3 was slowly revealed as the doors slid apart. Nathan imagined guards with guns noticing him and immediately pulling him to the office or cell while his feet dragged uselessly on the floor. But nothing happened. No one else was present.

There was a corridor with no rooms leading the way to the front and it ended with two separating paths. A single artwork of the Eiffel Tower decorated the far end. It was designed to be as lifeless as possible, certainly it wasn't for the visitors to come here, everything seemed not welcoming.

Nathan walked out of the lift, and proceeded uncertainly along the bare metal walls. He heard the lift doors shut gently behind. When he reached the T-junction, a sign indicated a left turn will bring him to the staff's quarters.

There was a door to the left, electronically locked and Nathan had the watch that could help him but the right-hand path wasn't blocked by anything. It led to the far end and turned to the left, disappearing from sight.

For a brief moment, Nathan considered which path would he choose and came to a thought, maybe a coherent one. A millionaire, building his own research centre in the deepest depths on Earth had decided to live in the staff quarters? Don't be ridiculous!

He turned to the right, the one not indicated by a sign. Nathan clung to his hope and bare instincts that Gata Harriman's computer was where he was heading. It would be a waste of time to return and start all over again.

He walked slowly to the end, the left twist of the path had two wooden doors and a single panel on it. He looked around. There wasn't any visible surveillance camera so far. Immediately, he unsecured his watch for the second time, exposed the hidden strips and contacted them onto the surface of the metal panels.

The red light on it was still, glaring steadily at its intruder. For a moment, he fought back the desperation to ram his knuckles onto the doors and resisted to accept the worrying fact that the IIO's technology couldn't compete with the centre's wizardry.

For about a minute, the red light remained unchanged. It was like a gift when it dimmed and a welcoming green light took over the indicator, Nathan nearly made out a victory yell but instead just breathed out in relief. His mission had just started.

He secured the watch back and pushed open the two wooden doors, surprisingly modern with metal hydraulic arms supporting his direction of force. It creaked and hissed as the magnetic restrains desperately released as if it failed to hold back the intruder from their master. He took in the opulence of the quarters.

Beyond the doors were the finest series of living area and an office, both separating without marked borders. Leather sofas stood around a low glass coffee table at the front of the room.

A broad varnished wooden table about five meters long was placed behind a piece of floor-to-ceiling glass that illuminated a blue glow. The table was shining in the glow and clean without the sign of any crowded documents. Files were kept very neatly on small rack holders and spaced equally. A laptop stood on the right end of the massive wood, folded.

There was other notable furniture as well, cabinets, lamps, armchairs and even a million-dollar chessboard in the room. A small door presumably led to his bedroom with a private living space and a spa. Nathan stepped in and closed the doors, his shoes making no sound as he walked on the soft carpet worth more than he could ever imagined.

Suddenly, all his attention and determination were concentrated towards one focal point. It was the one computer in this whole room. He let his legs guide him towards the notebook and got behind the table then sat on the cushioned-chair, which Gata Harriman used since he arrived. The doors shut automatically. It was a device specially made for the millionaire by the Apple Company, then modified to maximum security and to his needs.

He fished out his miniature tablet for the second time and activated the pinball application's parasite file. The process began, unmeasured and unknown. Although Professor Archnon Winters told him that it would work perfectly within 20 meters of range, he decided to make it much less distance between them.

He fixed his glance on the screen, waiting for any feedback but also applied some sense to his hearing, tracking any presence outside.

The tablet he held in his hands looked bigger than usual, its importance exaggerated by the time passing. The feeling of someone approaching the entrance was intensifying every moment, something like when he and Joe were burning the binds in the warehouse with Golem somewhere outside.

He wondered if the files in the form of electromagnet or neutrons were feeding into his tablet, then transmitted to the IIO's headquarters. How many files had been sent? And more precisely, how much longer would it take?

Minutes passed by and he began to wonder whether this gadget would work or not, or had it even started? Maybe he should switch on the power but Winters told him it wasn't needed, just the need to be within range.

After what seemed an eternity, the tablet's screen lit, a feedback of a simple bolted phrase. **NOT ENOUGH**

What was happening? Was his aunt's information not complete or the nuclear evidence? Which one wasn't enough? Nathan felt desperate and more frustration accumulated within him. He had risked so much and the result was this.

He held back the temptation to take the laptop and leave with him but that certainly won't work. Gata Harriman would search every inch of the centre and get it back, then secretly eliminate him. He gathered his thoughts and possibilities about how to solve this situation. There weren't any more computers and electronic devices. Perhaps this was as much as the millionaire had brought with him.

But any of those thoughts vanished as he heard footsteps approach. Who was coming? Wasn't Gata Harriman eating his dinner and chatting? Or he had noticed his absence and somehow figured out where he went and brought armed guards with him?

Nathan quickly searched for any cover he could conceal himself. The whole place was opened to sight and he doubted the sofas would provide any use. He quickly made his way to the door that probably led to the millionaire's bedroom.

It was locked and there wasn't enough time to hack it using the watch. He heard the *sound* of the panel, the doors had been unlocked. Harriman would be inside in a few seconds.

At last, he went back behind the board table and crouched below it, hiding and hoping the worst would not happen. The design of the table provided cover from the door. Gata Harriman would just retrieve the files without coming behind the table or just make a phone call in a private place. Why would he come in to use the computer while the main course of the dinner was just served?

The doors swung opened. He couldn't hear any footsteps as the soft carpet had covered any of it. But there were two masculine voices. One he knew as Harriman's and another unknown to him.

The English he spoke was clear without any faint accents. They made their way to the coffee table, he could hear their voices amplifying as they got nearer. The doors once again shut.

"There's a problem that I need to report to you," the unknown voice said. It was deadly serious and business-like, without emotion.

"What it is?" demanded Harriman. He was impatient and annoyed but some worry and uncertainty failed to be hidden in his voice. He was somehow like a child being questioned.

"It's regarding the international uranium trades. Something went slightly wrong but I'd fixed it. I just want to report it to you and authorize the changes," the voice said.

"Tell me more. Sit," he said. Nathan could hear the fabric as they sat on it. Nathan let out a breath of relief silently, his luck was so far so good. He wasn't going to be found hiding under the table. It wasn't only embarrassing but it would cost him his life.

"The CIA and Interpol was interfering in almost all of our exports and imports. They are suspicious with our trades but don't know about anything detail of the uranium," the unknown voice said again.

So, Harvard Norman had been right all the time, they were involved in illegal nuclear-weapons after all. It was just he failed to find enough evidence from the computer.

"So, what was the big deal? They had always been like that and we have managed to make them return empty-handed," Gata Harriman said. He had started to feel annoyed and angry. The arrogance in his voice was totally opposed the speech that he made not more than 30 minutes ago. To protect and discover nature, dreaming to build a castle underwater. *Well, this hypocrite was trading uranium.*

"We noticed some of the CIA agents peeking on our cargos at the harbour. We couldn't take risk so our men killed all of them and relocated the stocks. It will take time and our client won't be very pleased. Plus, the killing will make them confirm the relationship of us to the Ventures. It will make things harder to deal with," the voice said.

The Ventures, they held his aunt. He was somehow relieved that the IIO didn't lie to him about the fact. Gata Harriman had a connection with them.

"Tell our men to tighten the schedules and security. We need to get this done in a month," the millionaire said. His confidence had slightly decreased, probably worrying about his uranium project.

"All right, where do you want to relocate the stocks? And there will be some financial problems too—," the voice continued but was cut off by the millionaire.

"Do your job and send me the files to sign, if the problem is only about money, it will not bother me much. Just make sure there will not be any evidence and traces left behind. Do you understand?" Gata said.

"Yes, sir. If there is nothing else, I'll dismiss myself," the voice said. The voice took a few steps but stopped as his boss asked him something.

"Hold on for a moment. Have you checked the backgrounds of the visitors properly?" the millionaire asked.

"Sure, sir. I've double-checked. What is the problem, sir?" the unknown voice asked.

"I'm still afraid that the CIA or whatever intelligence agencies will be suspicious. Anyway, I want you to re-check the list again," Harriman blared out his command and paused.

"Please don't make any mistakes or exceptions, don't be bothered to delay the schedules for a while, just do it completely. That's all, you can leave," Harriman said. The unknown man left without saying another word. The doors opened and shut. The millionaire let out a sigh of tiredness.

The man sat on the sofa, silent and worrying something might eventually go wrong. He would lose all his power and wealth. It wasn't that he will be going to jail, he had contacts and influence all over the governments and criminals like the Mafia.

If anything really went wrong, the worst was just being changed into a different identity and moved to another country. If he kept his head low and did nothing to provoke the police, they will eventually leave him alone although knowing his whereabouts. Just the lifetime of surveillance was unavoidable. But was that even life? No, he will not fail. He will kill anyone that got into his way.

For the long moment, Nathan thought that the millionaire wasn't going to leave and somehow chose to use his laptop and the silence made all of those possibilities even more tense and worrying.

He prayed and hoped for the best. It wasn't only concerning his own life, it was also his aunt's life. He needed to make sure that the IIO get his aunt out and wasn't really cheating him and just using him completely for their own good.

Gata Harriman stood up from his seat and headed for the door. He needed to talk more to the visitors and somehow see through their pretence if there was any. He had a very remarkable conversation with a child not more than 14 and he was daring enough to speak like that to him. Anyway, he liked his guts.

He pushed opened the door and left his quarters. There were people waiting for him in the Hall and he couldn't create any sense of suspicion among the visitors. He wasn't really sure the intelligence organizations had really given up from inserting their undercover agents in the centre. To be honest, there were more than 50 kilograms of radioactive uranium in there and a dozen illegal nuclear reactors.

Nathan counted a minute and then sneaked out of the large area of the room. He silently looked outside to trace any presence of the unknown man or Harriman. When he was sure that there's none. He followed his previous trail back to the Hall. He needed to be careful not to meet anyone else outside the lift on Level 1.

When he got back to the Hall, Fibiano was just finishing his main course. Gata Harriman was chatting and laughing. Despite the conversation that he just eavesdropped, the millionaire was really good in pretence as if nothing happened at all.

"What had you been doing in the toilet? It took you so long," Fibiano asked as Nathan approached. He was not acting like the uncle he should be for a moment, keeping his voice low and trying to sound natural. The agent surely didn't want to let any people know his partner had left the place.

"*Nye.* I was just wandering around the area. I like to look at the fishes," Nathan replied, equally natural. He took his seat. The salmon was cold and the sauce sticky. Anyway, he ate the remainder of it. It didn't taste as good as he expected, maybe he lost his appetite. It wasn't weird after he was able to eavesdrop on a deadly conversation about killing and uranium that could result in his death.

"Look at you food, it isn't hot anymore. It's a waste," Fibiano said, trying to sound annoyed. Nathan somehow knew what the French was thinking. He knew that he had gone somewhere dangerous, anywhere but not the toilet. His expression must have slightly given him away.

Nathan didn't answer him. He took in his new surroundings as he ate the fish, which seemed tasteless and grimy. Gata Harriman was having one of his last conversations on the last table and retreating to his VIP seat. No one else was looking at the boy and his uncle. That was good.

He had been thinking since he made his way up to the millionaire's quarters. His mind passed through the thought. *What if there isn't any important information in his computer?* He flashed back the scenario of his first minutes in the research centre, while Cecil Holmwood introduced the various part of the place to the visitors. She brought out everything she knew about this place.

They were only allowed to visit the first research centre, the stewardess had said during their journey in the submarine. One was built higher up in the Mariana Trench while another even deeper down the sea depths. Neither Gata Harriman nor Cecil Holmwood didn't mention about the other research centre. Whether the Chief Research was involved in the nuclear trades, it wasn't as important as any other things that he needed to be concerned with. Anyway, the millionaire could have told her to keep quiet.

Why was it like that? Something like that was really worth talking about. It was their company's pride to build such a remarkable place. That's of course unless it was the place that stored with something illegal and dangerous. A dozen kilograms of uranium was considered even scarier than drugs.

He didn't miss out the fact about the secret door at Level 2. The one she wouldn't even tell them not to enter under any circumstances. Why let people notice that the door even existed?

Why would she? It was locked and then sealed by the highest technology they could afford. They didn't know about a teenage agent in their centre. He had been somehow worried that they could find out about him as the millionaire told the unknown man to re-check the list of visitors, but he trusted that the IIO had covered them well enough. It wasn't requesting to go back will help. He finished his dish and put down the fork and knife quietly.

The door must lead to the other research centre. The stewardess mentioned that the two centers were connected by submarines and he had excluded the idea to sneak on one of the ships. It was too dangerous and risky. Anyway, he was very sure he would not have a chance. So the door was the one possibility that was left to him. Get through it or leave empty-handed. Take it or leave it. There was no time to waste, he had the watch.

A waitress came to collect the plates. Another served the last course. It was a cup of fruit drink. Watermelon, lemon, strawberries and many others he couldn't really taste, blended together and iced. It was surprisingly refreshing and cooled his throat. Even Fibiano had temporally forgotten his undercover identity and praised it in his mother tongue, but soon regretted it and became a bit paranoid.

The rest of the ceremony was boring and Fibiano's mobile phone rang. He retrieved it from his pocket and looked at something on the screen and then typed a few sentences on the touch screen.

"Nathan, your mother is calling. She has something urgent to tell you. Let's find somewhere private to talk," Fibiano said. His voice was deadly serious and Nathan knew he meant that Harvard or someone from the IIO was making contact with them. He had no doubt that it was regarding the information he sent to them.

They both pretended to be worried and headed out of the Hall, walked along the expanse of identical rooms and then entered the agent's one. It was checked and presumably safer than Nathan's. Fibiano went in first and looked for any intruders, then asked Nathan to close and lock the door. The room was identical as his one.

Fibiano took out his laptop from a makeshift hidden compartment in the toilet, which he made himself, and then switched it on. The French returned to his room and put the computer on the bed. Nathan followed him. He logged in and typed a series of passwords and activated the maximum security systems. And lastly the French made a secured connection to the IIO headquarters.

The tired and almost friendly face of Harvard Norman appeared on the screen. His eyes were bloodshot and the bags under them were purple-black. He looked to be awake for more than 24 hours. Behind him was Professor Archnon Winters, monitoring a computer. He didn't take a lot of notice to their presence, probably too busy. Nathan sat down in front of the screen.

"It's nice to see you Nathan. This connection will only last for five minutes so I'll only briefly tell you the situation here, only ask questions after this," Norman said through the speakers. "The information we had just received was indeed not enough. The first one you sent us was irrelevant and I'm sure it's from the cell because the phone numbers were frustrating," he added.

"Let's talk about the second attempt. It also wasn't useful but everything seemed to be just incomplete. Gata Harriman stored only one part of the information in his computer. We found the location of you aunt. She will be located somewhere in the suburbs in southwestern England. It may be easy to search without making the public suspicious.

"But about the man, the crazy millionaire has a few hundred kilograms of uranium and 12 illegal nuclear reactors in his research centre! However, we only have the evidence of the quantity of the radioactive stuffs but not the blueprint of the illegal nuclear plants and where he got all those dangerous things from," Harvard Norman said, then paused. Nathan breathed out in relieve that they had known where his aunt was. He's going to make sure they kept their promise.

"I've eavesdropped on a conversation between Harriman and an unknown person. He said something about some sort of uranium trades and stock relocation internationally and the killings of the CIA agents. He also said something about tightening schedules," Nathan quickly said, using the opportunity of the pause.

Professor Winters looked up from his computer and stared at him, equal tiredness written on his face. "What did you just said? You mean Gata Harriman wasn't just buying uranium but selling it out of the country? We can confirm that he is processing the uranium and then exporting it. Oh my goodness! What a mess!" Winters murmured. He looked older and more worn-out than the last time they met.

"You already had all the things you need. Now get me out of here and find my aunt. That millionaire is going to jail!" Nathan said. He was relieved that his mission had been completed. But he was wrong as three pairs of eyes locked on him like a teacher making a mistake. "What? What's wrong?" he asked.

"Nathan. Your mission hasn't been completed. You heard that the psychopath is exporting nuclear materials, probably to terrorist and maybe it's to the Ventures. You have just heard that we only have half of the information and that's not enough to put him in jail.

"However, there's no information regarding the uranium trades and you said he mention the word 'international'. This is already involving national security issues globally and we don't know anything more about the trades. How much? Where are they? What you've just told us is an incomplete and unrecorded conversation. You need to get more information," the professor said again.

Nathan couldn't believe this. "You said you'd find my aunt and get me out of here. I have already done what I could and what you told me to do. We had made a deal!" he said. But for a moment, he remembered what he had thought of during his dinner in the Hall a few minutes earlier. *What about the door?* Anyway, he's tired.

"Nathan, can you imagine how many people will die if they used those nuclear missiles. A dozen governments will be threatened. The millionaire had just loaded a nuclear tank! We may arrest him right on the spot but we will not know where the other part of the information will be stored. We don't know where the uranium is that he sold.

"He may even delete them before we could put him into custody. Maybe it's not even in this research centre. If we don't find it out earlier, lots of people will die," Harvard spoke after a long pause. The time indicator on the screen showed that there was barely two minutes left.

Nathan had watched the world news when an earthquake struck Japan in the year 2012, triggering at least three nuclear reactors to leak in Fukushima Dai-chi. People died, the ones who survived got cancer and others will have abnormal babies for the rest of their lives. The sight was terrible. He suddenly realized how serious this matter was. Another half a minute had passed.

"What if the millionaire didn't store the information in this place? And he is now re-checking the list of visitors. Our covers may be blown off!" he said.

In the back of his mind, he knew he would be agreeing to help the IIO once again, he couldn't watch so many people die because of his decision. When we come to know of lots of people dying, we feel sad and sympathize with them. But if people died because we didn't help them, the story is different. You couldn't live with yourself for the next day. You will keep blaming yourself for the rest of your life.

"About the cover issue, you do not need to worry. The IIO had been very careful and there isn't any possibility they will suspect an uncle and his nephew. We have to assume that the millionaire stored the information in that place since it was more secure than any safe house in the world. We can't risk him deleting that information. Remember, psychopaths will do anything to hurt others.

"I had just sent an emergency team a few kilometers out of your area. They will not suspect anything," Harvard convinced him. The clock showed only 30 seconds left. The faces of the two leaders of the IIO looked even more stressed and tired.

"Whatever you say, I'll try. After this, make sure you help me find my aunt no matter what happens. I will not help you the next time, this is my last time," Nathan made himself clear. The two exhausted men smiled and a little colour seeped back into their faces.

"Thank you, Nathan. The world owes you its gratitude," Harvard said. "Fibiano, give him everything he needs and avoid any possible suspicion."

"Yes," the Frenchman replied. They all spent the last 15 seconds looking at each other. Nathan knew well that if anything went wrong, it will cause him and his "uncle" their lives. The two leaders of IIO may be looking at them for the last time and they knew that pretty well.

"See you again, Nathan," Professor Winters said. The clock ticked down to the last second and the connection cut off. That left Nathan and Fibiano staring at each other. "I will go tonight. Once and for all," Nathan said.

Chapter Twenty Five

UNAUTHORIZED PERSONNEL

He waited. It was 11 p.m. now and he was tired. Jet lag hadn't completely released its grip yet. He needed silence tonight but there were a few scientists working late and visitors chatting outside the corridor. Nathan didn't want anyone else to know that he had exited his room in the night. Not when he was going to attempt such a dangerous mission.

Nathan had managed to persuade Fibiano to let him complete the job all on his own. They had agreed that if Nathan was captured, Fibiano will use the information they had just downloaded to bargain with Gata Harriman. Harriman wasn't going to know that the files had been sent. If that happened, what he will know was that the boy's uncle had information that will put an end to whatever career and wealth and they threatened to send it. The IIO had promised to temporally keep the files confidential.

The clock was now showing 11:51 p.m. Luckily, the scientists were getting back to their own rooms and vacating the corridor (he could hear lazy footsteps). He was really tired and had to ask Fibiano to prepare two cups of coffee for him. The drinks were no doubt drugs to him. Ever since he drank a little in the car to Nottingham that Harvard insisted on, he wanted more of it.

Nathan went to the toilet and washed his face. He then changed into a tight black sweatshirt and jeans. By tying the ropes, it will give him easy movement. He fitted on black trainers and pocketed all the gadgets in safety within easy reach. He no longer felt tired and knew that by morning, the lack of rest will make itself known. It would be a postponed sleep attack.

He opened the door and looked outside. Nobody was present. The door to Fibiano's room was shut. He wasn't going to knock it, attracting whatever attention may be unpleasant. He somehow knew the French wasn't sleeping and wouldn't accidentally do it. He was trained and experienced. Nathan suddenly regretted this, didn't he promised to himself that the previous risk was the last?

He remember that if Fibiano went and was caught, the information overwrite system will need a series of computer codes and skills and then a 20-figure password to open and send. The French insisted that none of those codes would be written down in paper, he claimed it to be risky and madness.

After a few silent arguments, they had agreed with equal reluctance that Nathan will do the job. It wasn't that Fibiano feared the millionaire or his security system. He actually felt excited as if something was urging him to go and that boy was interrupting. It's was probably because he's a passionate spy.

Nathan made his way to the left end of the corridor and got to the lift. The lights had dimmed and probably the Hall was vacant. He took the lift to Level 2, where the sealed door was located.

The Research Department was equally silent but something in his mind kept coming back. *You are an intruder and if you get caught, hope that Fibiano wins the false bargain.*

The place was dark with only dimmed lights. He strolled along the Marine Life Research Unit, the one he didn't recognize before because of the identical cube and cuboids of metal. It stood stationary there, silent, but if there was any activity inside, he couldn't tell. The glass panel along the corridor was still illuminating the blue glow, the dark figures swimming in freedom.

Nathan was careful not to relax, he walked close to the walls. If anyone approached, the shadows may give him enough cover to conceal himself. He came to a right turn and there it was: The metal door with lights blinking on it. There was another alternative left turn that will bring anyone to the Geography and Genetic Units, but he wasn't interested in either of them. He wondered what was beyond the door.

Careful to notice and check his surroundings, he quickly unsecured his watch and placed the hidden wires onto the metal console, which demanded a series of passwords. It took about probably three minutes and the thick air-lock door's disengaged then slid aside, creaking on its own weight. Probably, the IIO had increased their 24 hours staff to work the watch, knowing that time will decide between life and death. But for the moment, it wasn't that critical, and that helped a lot, too.

On the other side was a big circular white object about three stories high and with a wide expanse of white metal. The ceiling was also whitewashed with pipes and wires tied neatly and lights shining down. Nathan could only make out a little part of it.

The two sides of the cylinder made out two paths that could bring him elsewhere. Was this the nuclear reactor? Surely this wasn't the illegal ones. The CIA agents that came for the first time to check must had noticed this heavy-looking door and demanded to know what was inside. The anxiety and nervousness had no longer disturbed him, perhaps his tiredness had covered most of his worries.

It wasn't that he wanted to know what Gata Harriman had legally, he wanted to find the illegal ones then download the operating systems files and the location of the uranium exports and send it. But where could he go anymore?

Fibiano had told him that while he was missing on the first day, he had sneaked into the workers' quarters on the same level as the millionaire's and found out nothing interesting more than papers and accommodation. So, that left out this remarkable door.

He entered the place and the door automatically shut behind him. The whole place was an expanse of whitewashed metal walls and a bunch of neat humming machinery. The wide cylinder gave him two choices whether to take the right or left path. He had to be aware of surveillance cameras and guards, he regretted choosing black overalls as this place was all white! But he noticed a few machines that were grey, convincing him his costume wasn't that contrasting and stupid.

He let his instincts lead him, he chose the right lane, probably because he was a right—handed. But the two seemed 100 percent identical and none of the design could easily distinguish the difference. He hoped it wasn't like that afterwards, he could fail just out of confusion.

The whole cylinder thing could actually fit an entire building, after walking along the whitewashed corridor, which the wall was also some part of the circumference of the cylinder, nothing seemed to be changing.

After walking for a long time, he noticed that the other side of the cylinder that he first saw. But that wasn't a big change as another cylinder ahead continued into another circumference. There were a whole lot of round circles. So these are called nuclear reactors? What was so great about them?

He continued his journey with nothing changing, the humming of the machines guiding him. But then something changed. There were footsteps. He heard two pairs of boots clinking onto the metal floor.

He froze, there was nowhere to hide and he doubted the machineries of the corridor will give him any cover. What he was going to explain when they found him? I was just taking a walk? He had just hacked through their security door!

He ran back, trying to minimize the sound of his trainers hitting the metal, hoping the little humming of the reactor could cover the sound. He knew very well that Gata Harriman had asked his man to re-check the list of visitors and he should still be suspicious by now. He might as well kill him before Fibiano could try to bargain.

There was still a long way ahead but thankfully the circumference of the cylindrical reactor gave him cover and as long as he maintained a good distance between the guards, they will not see him.

He went back to the spot where the big cylinder was in front of another identical one. They were not attached or connected to each other. Nathan walked between them to the other side. If he chose to take the left path from the very start, he would have ended up here, there wasn't a big difference.

He hid behind the second cylinder, or the nuclear reactor protected by big slabs of metal and concrete. The footsteps got nearer. What if they decided to take a turn and found him there? Perhaps he could just start moving along the circumference of the reactor and play hide and seek. It wasn't funny, losing meant death and winning meant a second chance.

But they didn't, the sound of boot stomping the ground loudened and then decreased in volume as they walked passed. Nathan had avoided them with him crouching behind wires and machineries, which were grey and attached to the cylinder. The men wore biochemical suits of white and yellow overalls and each was carrying a baton, attached onto their belts. Each of their wrists was strapped with a metal bracelet and they wore white air-lock helmets. The sight gave him a sense of concern.

He suddenly understood that he had just entered a nuclear plant wearing sweatshirt and jeans and thought he was so safe. What if there was a radioactive leak? He could die in half a day, painfully and then he would hope that the millionaire would end his life faster.

But that didn't stop him for long, he continued on his way. He somehow regretted having come to this scary place. Gata Harriman didn't have to necessarily store his information in this plant and this route didn't have to lead him to the illegal plant. But with all the places already checked, it left this place the most possible alternative.

Either heading back and doing nothing or going forward, there's no time to waste. He moved forward and along the second reactor's circumference and then the third.

Occasionally, there were guards or workers, all of them wearing the same metal bracelet, he wondered what these bracelets function was. He sneaked passed the workers easily. The suits they wore made their movement slow and clumsy but his jeans and sweatshirt provided easy movement.

There were almost six or five reactors and although his lack of knowledge about nuclear plants, he was sure that one piece of uranium that was the size of an adult fist can easily supply a whole city with electricity for 24 hours. So why did Gata Harriman need so many reactors to power his two centres?

The extra reactors couldn't be illegal because the CIA agents would have instantly noticed them as they had checked throughout the place. He might have some machines that needed a lot of energy.

Nathan continued his way forward and then the repetition of cylinders and circumference changed into a straight corridor, which worried him. If some of the guards approached, footsteps would tell him that he's already too late. He was terribly exposed.

There was also another similar air-lock door. He hacked it easily and passed through it. But there was also something spectacular on this side, the glasses on both sides of the corridor showed a lot of water and steam. It was probably an inspection area. Above the water were turbines and the steam rose to turn them, activating the dynamo and producing electricity. The sight was somehow spectacular, how much heat was needed to boil tons of water?

He continued, and the doors shut. Those glasses seemed to be stretching out for about a few hundred meters with the corridor. He understood that this exposure was scary but it was the only way he could proceed deeper. The inspection area ended and there were rooms around it, with one more path leading somewhere else.

He peeked inside one of the rooms, there was a glass room at head-height. It was full of men in white overalls hunching over monitors and surveillance inside the nuclear reactor. He couldn't hear any sound and it was probably sealed with an air-lock. But he could imagine the busy sounds of discussion and reports with radioactive and electrons monitors beeping around the room. The place was probably a control point.

The other rooms were almost the same with only size and a few words or codes making a difference. He continued towards the path that led deeper into the plant. A room at the far end showed a sign that was the only one that could make him happy.

EXTRA PROTECTIVE WEAR

He used his watch to hack open the sealed door and got in. There was no one around luckily. He took in the surroundings of the place. There were metal cabinets and a few benches for the staff to sit on.

He opened one of the cabinets. It wasn't locked. Inside was a variety of sizes of white overalls. He took the smallest size and put it on. The process was frustrating to look for the right suit to fit his body and finally with some effort and patience, he'd done it. The suit was very bulky and heavy but comfortable with the temperature okay. Earlier on, he had removed all his gadgets and placed them in the external compartments that served as pockets made on the suit.

He looked like one of the workers now, just his size was different. One could argue he was a small person. He found a helmet and sealed it airtight. An air filter started working as he put it on.

He also noticed the metal bracelet around his wrist like the other workers. He touched it with his gloved hand and found something to activate it with a twist. A single red light indicator blinked. He didn't know what its purpose was but looking exactly the same was vital.

He returned to the corridor and sealed the door behind him. No one had seen him and that was a good thing. He would want to proceed somewhere else but suddenly, a red light blinked on the wall with a loud deafening sound. It was an alarm!

Could Fibiano have attempted to enter the place and was caught? But as guards roamed out of the doors of the rooms, he knew their attention was fixed on him. How did they know he was here? It must be the suit and the metal bracelet. He regretted about it, trying to be safe but being captured would be signing a death letter.

They all surrounded him in a semi-circle formation, their batons out and a light was flashing from it, a blue artificial colour. He ran through the corridor leading deeper into the plant but there were guards there as well. He was trapped in the corridor. He tried to look for a weapon or the baton on his suit but there was none. He felt desperate.

The guards moved nearer to him slowly and he could imagine the smiles behind their tinted helmets. One of them swung his baton towards him and Nathan dodged then counterattacked with a kick to the head. He had learned some martial-arts as well at school and maybe this could be an advantage.

All of his movements were slow because of the bulky protective wear but he hadn't the time to remove them. His kick was no more than a tickle to him since he could not move easily and not much momentum to bring more force, and the man's suit protected him as well.

This time another guard joined the first man and both struck out their batons. Nathan managed to side step it and they missed him, but he soon knew how painful it was when the blue devil-like light hit him. Another guard that was surrounding him with Nathan back to him cunningly jabbed the baton into his back just below the lungs.

Nathan felt a burning and shocking sensation passed through his body to his brain. It hurt him and something seemed to absorb all the energy out of him. He groaned and knelt down, the pain was menacing like electric or something strong.

Why didn't the suit protect them from these blows? And why didn't his suit have the baton? Perhaps it was because of the type of suit. The suit he was wearing was the scientist-type while he guards' ones were prepared for battle.

One of the other guards came forward and once again jabbed his baton into Nathan's side, causing him great pain with the weird energy current. He couldn't take more of this. He collapsed onto the floor but the guard didn't take off the baton until a minute passed. This man was very cruel.

The pain had made him unable to stand or even sit, he lay there helplessly as the cruel guard, probably the leader, communicated through his speakers and ordered for the guards to escort him somewhere. The others went back to their respective posts and the alarm stopped.

Did Fibiano know he was in trouble? And how was he going to know? It may be hours after this and with his absence that will make him know that something had gone wrong and that it will be too late, by that time Gata Harriman may have ordered to kill both of them quickly and silently. Why hadn't they talked about this a few hours before?

They dragged him into one of the rooms, the biggest one that was presumably the control point. The other scientists looked at him through their helmets, they still didn't know about him much. They didn't know he was 14 years old. And perhaps Gata Harriman will release him and tell him to shut his mouth up. He wasn't convinced about that. The pain remained in his bones.

But there was a little advantage about his capture. He finally knew where the hidden nuclear plant was. For the moment, the wall of the side of the room was identical to the rest and no one could tell the difference, as it was all whitewashed, polished metal.

But the chief guard took out something like a remote control and typed a series of codes into it, he then pointed towards a part of the wall. He pressed a green button. Unbelievably, a part of the whitewashed wall moved a few centimeters back and then slid aside to reveal a path to somewhere else, probably to the illegal nuclear plants. The other workers didn't as much glance at the change as if nothing had happened.

How brilliant was it, placing the hidden entrance in the control point, most likely the first place the CIA agents would search and demand for information regarding the plant. No one would as much as make a glance towards the part whitewashed wall that was actually the door identical to the original wall. But in truth, it was what all the agencies around the world were finding, including the IIO.

If he hadn't been arrested, he wouldn't know the location and couldn't even possibly enter with so many guards around. But was he going to live much longer to tell where it was?

The two guards dragged him inside the wall with another two following behind. The chief led the way. The special part of the wall then slid to conceal the hole.

The path inside was almost claustrophobic with only a very contained spaces, and everything was white including the lights and the floor. They walked a few meters and descended steps, a lot of steps to somewhere undesirable.

Nathan didn't know where exactly they were bringing him, but he was sure it must be the hidden plant. He hoped they will not just kill him and dump him together with the nuclear waste. But with five armed guards escorting him, he wasn't very convinced. Perhaps something much worse was about to happen to him. His instincts were yelling to him and his dear life.

Chapter Twenty Six

BLACKISH WATER

His stomach churned as they forced him down the steps. This nervousness was o one he never felt before. No one really could have explained the exact feeling but now he started to experience it. It was the true fear of death.

Some part of it told him what would be his thoughts before death. The pain from the electrical batons had worn most of his wits out of him, but as all his weight had been roughly supported by the two strong men in white suits, his strength slowly returned.

The steps had ended and they needed to walk down one of the most plain and lifeless corridors. It stretched on for about 100 meters and sometimes they changed direction. No alternative of routes, just one single dead path.

They approached a metal door and the chief took out a card to overwrite it. As they passed through the doorway, Nathan took in the massive insides of the plant. This illegal plant wasn't like the one he just seen, white and with grey of machineries and huge cylinders. This was immense and over five stories high. The reactors in their shells of concrete and metal stood there.

A lot of metal platforms with railings gave access around the machineries and even more workers in suits were walking or busy with some sort of technical work. None of the men noticed his presence or that of the five guards. Even if they noticed, they didn't bother. They probably had been high-paid and told not to bother with anything else except their work.

They dragged him to the far end and descended one by one in a line using the steps built on metal supporters and secured by barriers. After descending another five stories, the height of the huge reactors, to what he believed was the ground floor of this place. They walked on a few paces more along a series of air-lock rooms with wide glass barriers in front at head-height.

The guards stopped in front one of those. They suddenly they let him go. Nathan scrambled to his feet and stood upright, almost losing balance. "Strip off the protective suit," the chief guard said in a metallic accent.

Nathan suddenly remembered and regretted that all his gadgets were in the pocket compartments of the protective suit. He couldn't lose them.

Before that, when they were bringing him out of the legal nuclear plant, he thought he was going to die. They probably just needed to drag him to a place and used a loaded gun to do the job. Nathan didn't think firearms were allowed inside the plant, one single inaccuracy would blow the whole seabed.

But if someone asked you to remove the clothes he was wearing, they wouldn't kill him so fast, at least for the moment. Which millionaire would bother worrying about a cheap, protective suit when he was far too busy doing illegal work to sell uranium for billions? He thought of an idea.

"I can't. I'm naked. I just left my clothes in the room where I got changed," Nathan said. He pretended to be in total fear and uncertainty as he spoke.

The man paused for a moment. He probably was hesitating whether to use the baton and cause more pain for the troublemaker boy. Here's this boy getting himself into a nuclear plant and now this.

He communicated again through his speakers, which Nathan couldn't tell anything about it. They may be planning to change their minds and just kill him. After a while, one of the guards walked away, climbed the metal steps and headed somewhere else.

After a few minutes, the same guard (probably) returned with a pair of trousers and a weird jacket. He threw them onto the floor in front of Nathan. "Get the suit off and put these on, right now!" the chief said again. Nathan could imagine the man's being face contorted with anger and frustration beneath the tinted glass.

"But I'm naked. I think you don't want to see me without clothes," Nathan said. It was hard to mix the feeling of fear and embarrassment and then present them out to men that could kill him on the spot with their bare hands.

One of the guards struck out his baton and attempted to hit Nathan. He flinched, preparing to let the weird current run through him again. But before the guard could even barely make the move, the chief raised a hand into the air.

It was surprisingly a signal not to hurt him. He thought the man was cruel and even electrocuted him even though he was lying on the floor a few minutes ago, but now he chose not to hurt him. What was really going on?

The chief moved forward and used his card to opened one of the air-lock doors. The door hissed and slid aside, revealing an empty room about 20 meters wide. There was a rectangular glass barrier at head-height. Nathan didn't know what they had stored in the compartment before, but he just ignored the bad thoughts.

"Get inside and change. Not more than one minute. If you try anything under your sleeves, I will personally kill you and throw you together with the radioactive waste. Do you understand?" the chief asked again in the same metallic tone, but there was a slight difference in his voice, it were as if something had reached the limit and any trouble would make him pull out a gun and use it.

"Yes," Nathan answered, trying to be scared. The guard didn't answer and he walked himself into the room. The door hissed and closed behind him. One minute. Looking through the head-height glass while standing unstably on his toes, the guards were looking at him. It was an advantage to him that they chose this room. They only can see the upper part of his head but not his torso or legs.

He quickly throws all the gadgets onto the floor and stripped off the protective suit. He took off the helmet. It took him about half a minute. With luck, he remembered the buttons and air-lock zips and how to remove them.

Then, he used 20 seconds to get dressed in the white trousers and the jacket. He didn't bother to undress his jersey and jeans as these pieces of clothing could probably let them know he was lying to them. They may collect the suit and find out what he had previously worn and then get angry.

He didn't want to make them angry. Or worse, they will check what he had with him and confiscate the gadgets. He used the remaining 10 seconds to pocket the four gadgets into the new pockets safely but within easy reach.

Suddenly, he thought about using one of his gadgets and then to make a run for it but how? But it would certainly not work. They may lock him here until the oxygen ran out and watch him die.

Just as he pocketed his last gadget, the door slid opened and one of the guards looked at him, letting him knew that he will give them no more troubles. He followed them like a silent yet loyal dog. The guard didn't look surprised as he took in the 14-year-old boy. Probably he had already known somehow or didn't bother his age or who he was.

Nathan didn't waste any more time, he quickly followed him out of he room back into the custody of the five guards. Two of them held him and they proceeded along the identical air-lock rooms until they reached a bigger one.

More guards, about 10 men in suits, were standing there, but one of them was slightly isolated. Nathan couldn't make out his face behind the tinted glass but he knew he was powerful, even held more authority than the chief guard. He could know from his body language, the legs stood steadily as if the place belonged to him, with one in advance of another with a hand at his left hip.

The guards left him and another two held him. The man in suit that was probably the boss. He urged them to follow him into the bigger room. Only the two guards and Nathan followed. The air-lock door slid aside and shut behind them.

The room was lit by lights built into the ceiling, a few controls, monitors and computers with machineries surrounded by office chairs. A glass wall and another air-lock door led into a smaller room.

The man removed his helmet, revealing a fair skin, hair cut short and combed with gel and the Russian-English look. The man was the millionaire, Gata Harriman. He sat down onto one of the office chairs, the guards remained standing, but let go Nathan's arms as the millionaire threw them a hand signal.

"It's so nice to meet you, Nathan Doyle. You are no doubt a remarkable child," greeted the wealthy man. "At first, you said you wanted to build a centre in the Atlantic like I'd made mine in the Pacific, but I'm now telling you, although I'm not sure you were lying or not, you will not succeed or even have the chance to attempt it. I'm going to kill you with pleasure," Gata Harriman continued.

"You are a hypocrite! Idiot!" yelled Nathan. Then, he swore at him, the worst sentence he could ever speak out. He had quickly made up his mind, if he really died, the last thing he will do was to spit in the millionaire's face.

One of the guards suddenly drove the baton into his back. He groaned in agony and doubled over, and then his knees hit the floor. The men in suits pulled him upright roughly, not giving any chance for him to recover.

"You have a very undesirable list of swearing words but I'll let you yell and say whatever you want to grant your last wish, isn't this so generous? But first, I must ask you a few questions. You will tell me everything correctly and I had known some of it but I'll still ask.

"You can be obedient in the last moments of your life and die quickly but if you don't abide what I said, you will die slowly, pathetically and with the worse experience of suffering. Do you understand?" the millionaire said, his tongue flickered like a snake spitting venom. He was actually venomous, in words.

Nathan didn't answer him and one of the guards struck him with a fist, hurting him. "Yes," Nathan reluctantly said. Getting another electrical shock won't do him any good.

"Good, Nathan. Very good," Harriman said slowly. "Who and what sent you here?" he asked. His voice was expressionless and Nathan wasn't sure he knew about the IIO or not. But he could maybe try and lie somehow.

"M16," lied Nathan. Gata Harriman smiled as if he'd done something cute. Nathan expected the guards to thrust their baton into him but they didn't.

The psychopath then threw another hand signal towards the guards, immediately, the both of them dragged him towards the doorway of the smaller room and opened the air-lock door. Nathan resisted but the grip was too tight.

They threw him in and sealed the door. Were they going to see him suffocating as the oxygen burned out? No, he could predict it was something much worse.

In the room, a single black metal case about 40 centimeters cube was attached to the wall. The room was otherwise empty. Nathan looked through the glass, and glared at the millionaire. The guards then took their places behind one of those monitors, waiting for orders from their boss.

"Very well, this is your second chance," Gata Harriman said through the speakers. "I'm still demanding the right answer," he continued, barely looking in his direction.

"The IIO," Nathan said. Just as he predicted, the millionaire stood up and clamped his gloved hands with not much sound. He worked for Ventures and there was not much doubt he knew the IIO.

"You're truly remarkable. So, they're involving children in intelligence. What a transformation!" he exclaimed. "So, how did you hack through one of my security doors? You must need something with high technology," he asked.

This was what Nathan was worrying so far. Did he actually know how he did it? If he even mentioned the gadget, they will search him and everything will be confiscated. His last hope would be distinguished.

"My uncle helped me to get the door opened," he answered naturally.

"What did he use? And please don't lie to me, he's not your uncle."

"A card or something else like that. It must be a duplicate or something," he said.

Harriman seemed to be satisfied with his answer. He returned to his seat. "You both are so brilliant. Just the agent with you was a bit coward, sending a much younger boy to finish the job. But unfortunately, you both are going to die. I've sent men to hunt and kill him. Anyway, did you use the card to get anywhere else or overwrite any other security system?"

Nathan couldn't tell him about his attempt to download all the files from his computer. Fibiano may have dealt with him about the bargain but things were different now. The psychopath would kill him immediately if he knew about that. He may even cheat Fibiano using his recorded voice.

"No," he said but he needed to make it real. "But I would like to hack your whole research centre," he added. He hoped it would satisfy the psychopath.

The man smiled. "You don't have the chance to do so," he said. "Anyway, I'll not waste any more time and assume that you came here to get evidence of my illegal nuclear plant, but what makes you enter that legal nuclear plant?"

"There's no where else to go," he answered.

Gata Harriman frowned with an eyebrow. "You are so clever and brave as well. It's just that when you activated the metal locator on the suit, your mistake means my survival. Why would you do like that?" he asked. The man now seemed cheeky as if winning a lost game.

"I just wanted to look identical," Nathan answered in a simple sentence. He knew that actually none of them had won any game. It was the IIO that won. He's going to die, the man will go to a life of imprisonment.

Gata Harriman laughed. "I think this is the end of our conversation. I will always remember you," he said as if leaving a good friend.

One of the guards then pressed a button.

Inside the smaller air-lock room, water began to flood the place. Nathan gasped. The water was ice-cold. They're going to drown him alive! Just about 10 seconds, it had risen to his ankles. He looked around, finding for the water source, a pipe or something, there must be a hole.

Almost immediately, he saw gushes of water breaking the surface, it was highly pressurized, a drain or something spilling water onto the floor.

Gata Harriman looked, his eyes were filled with joy and satisfaction. Nathan's fear and worry even made him laugh. He couldn't know what the guard thought about this torture. Their impregnable visors didn't give out any expression.

Then, just as the water level reached Nathan's neck, he ordered the guards to stop the flow. Nathan stood shivering on his toes, breathing rapidly. The freezing water was failing him. He wasn't going to die like that, was he?

"I've forgotten to ask you something. You must be grateful that I'm spending my time on you, a pathetic creature. What is the last thing you want to know?" the millionaire asked.

It was useful if Nathan survived whatever plans he was making but anyway, even if he died, he wanted to know. "Where did you store your uranium to be exported, the illegal material," he asked.

"What a good question. If anyone else asked me them, I'd personally kill him or her but you are different. I want to play games and I have to treat you fair. There's a compartment as big as a warehouse in this plant and it's not far away from here. Air-tight locks and sealed with an electromagnetic force. You can go there as a ghost," the psychopath said again.

Nathan waited for him to order the guards to increase the water level and drown him alive but nothing happened. Harriman waited.

"Aren't you going to kill me?" Nathan asked, still standing on his toes. The water had numbed his whole body and the cold was piercing into his bones. Suddenly, he felt tired. He must be the verge of hypothermia. The extra clothing did not do much to hold back the coldness.

"Do you remember what did you said when you just entered this room?" Gata Harriman said. "I don't like people calling me hypocrite no matter what I've done. I said before I'll let you die peacefully in the water if you're in perfect obedience. You lied and swore at me once," he said. The man then signaled one of the guards and he flickered on a switch.

Nathan expected water to rise but nothing happened. "Do you know what this switch can do?" He pointed at the glowing red light beside the switch he had activated. "Do you see the black cuboid at the side of your room? Do you know what is stored inside the black box?" the man said slowly.

Nathan froze, not by the cold but by his last sentence. He will not die of cold, not by drowning but by something even worse.

"Yes, Nathan. It's a fist-sized piece of radioactive uranium," he said. "This button can expose it, the illuminating green glow. Do you know how long it takes for the workers to transport that rock? Procedures after procedures and someday I hope I can use it against somebody and now you are here," Harriman continued. His finger was hovering over the red devil-like button and Nathan gasped.

"Please, don't! Kill me with a gun! I don't want to die like that! Please!" Nathan begged. Every composure and pride had been let away even before he died. He had been embarrassed and now mentally tortured by fear and threats. But soon the physical torture will followed up. *Oh, God. Please take my life now!*

Gata Harriman, the millionaire, the psychopath, his finger hovered even more over the button, he looked tempted and the malevolent smile on his face was filled with ideas like a naughty, crazy child. He then shifted his attention toward Nathan and looked for a long moment. The boy was begging. This was exactly what he wanted before he died.

Nathan continued to beg him, tears were already spilling out. He remembered what he had watched on the news.

The massive destruction of the area around the four leaking nuclear plants in Japan just in the aftermath of the earthquake and now he was going to be one of the plant workers. The difference was no one was going to know how he died. They will throw him together with the nuclear waste and not even the greatest intelligence agency like the IIO could risk finding him. He will die and be buried by nuclear waste.

Even if he guards felt sympathy and tried to help him, they will not stop the psychopath from pressing the button just less than a centimeter from his finger. But like a miracle, his hand disappeared from any where near the button.

Gata Harriman laughed as if he had succeeded in a prank. Nathan looked at the millionaire. *What the hell was he doing now?* He suddenly knew it, he cheated him, there was no uranium inside the box, he had lied.

"Nathan. Ah! I really liked to see you like that. I won't kill you that way. But anyway, there is uranium in that box and this button really opens the box, do you know?" he said.

Harriman signaled the guard and he flickered off the green switch beside the button that could kill Nathan. Both of the lights dimmed and then died down. He then regained his composure and then made his last series of chuckles.

Nathan silently swore at him in his heart and vowed to kill him. *How could he do this to a child?* For the moment, he wanted to revenge him by telling him what he had downloaded and sent, and watch as the millionaire went crazy, but that was too risky and will do nothing good. In just two flicks of the switches he could kill him almost slowly and with great suffering. The less the psychopath knew the better.

"But I'm still killing you the other way. I'll drown you alive. You had said your last words and now it is the time. But please remember, Nathan. I like you and that is true," he said and almost sadly, he signaled the guards. Immediately, the water inside the small room began to rise and then filled the place.

Nathan choked and breathed in and swallowed water into his stomach. He coughed and struggled in the water. But after that, he relaxed and closed his eyes. The buoyancy of water supported him into a half-float, his hands dangling like fins in the water.

"That's for all for the moments. Remember to pick his corpse afterwards. But for the moment, we have to get the man named Fibiano and then kill him using the radioactive way," the millionaire said. Nathan overheard it.

The millionaire's voice was dead-serious and business-like. Just after the sentence, they switched off the power and exited the room. The water level remained. All the lights had died into darkness and a little glare came from the window outside.

Chapter Twenty Seven

CELSIUS AND JOULE

Nathan opened his eyes. He tried to adjust his vision to the dark and then examined the whole room. His breath was starting to burn out but he still could hold on for a moment. He swam down to the floor of the room. The water was blackish and he couldn't make out anything. The water was really cold and he continued to shiver, feeling every wave of coldness pierced through his bones.

Anyway, he felt lucky the millionaire didn't use the uranium to kill him. He then found the hole that let the water in.

He still remember the a radioactive uranium was just a few meters away from him, separated by solid concrete and metal, but he was sure it would not leak. The hole was covered by metal grilles, he could feel them. The grilles stretched on for about 40 meters wide and 20 meters in length. He felt lucky it wasn't a pipe of something smaller, which he couldn't use to escape out of there. *But where does this passage lead?* It wasn't the time to think, this was his only escape route, take it or leave it.

He felt out of breath and he scrambled for his pockets. He needed to be careful and if he dropped the pen the IIO gave him, he's finished. He felt for the tip and pulled it, breaking the pen into half, there were two tubes, one bigger filled of ink, which he was sure and another smaller one filled with concentrated liquefied oxygen.

He held the smaller tube and pushed it into his skin and flesh, found an artery in the left wrist. He pushed something on the top of the tube. Immediately, the air pressure inside the tube increased, pumping the liquid into his blood.

The red blood cell's haemoglobin mixed with the oxygen, forming oxyhaemoglobin that will supply his body with oxygen. But there was still a lot of liquefied oxygen inside his blood and Professor Archnon Winters said it will last for 10 minutes.

He felt he was still out breath and suffocating but the professor he trusted said it was normal because the brain kept sending signals to the lungs to breathe without knowing the blood had enough oxygen. He just needed a moment to hold back the temptation to breathe and then everything went back to normal. A minute had passed. Nine more were left.

He somehow knew that there wasn't only liquefied oxygen inside the tube but also a little of liquefied nitrogen or other chemicals that could slow down the use of oxygen, not creating any possibilities of hyperventilating. He also needed to be careful not to breathe hard for 10 minutes or else—hyperventilating, the feedback of too much oxygen in the blood would kick in and he had no paper bags to calm it.

He felt for a strong grip between the grilles and held it with both hands. He positioned his legs so that they touched the floor. His body was now in a squatting position. He kicked the floor, propelling his body back with his grip on the grilles. Nothing happened. He had felt for any screws but there were none, so his chances were higher, they were probably just hammered in. He pushed and pulled back harder and felt a little movement. He was succeeding. Another minute passed.

He yanked and kicked even harder and felt satisfied as the grilles came loose. But the hole wasn't actually very big. By force, he could make his way slowly downwards. He went in head first, using his hands and legs to scramble the walls of the passage. The algae made it even harder and sometimes he slipped, losing his grip and balance.

He was afraid of being stuck in this horrible passage, full of algae and dirt. But it probably wouldn't happen. The green algae and slime made out less friction between him and the walls.

Where could this hole lead? But he decided to think about that later, when he's safe. The passage twisted into another direction.

After about five minutes of kicking and scrambling, he saw light at the far end, a white glow. He kicked even harder, his fingers scrambling for grip on the grimy walls. As he got nearer to it, he smiled. He almost had died by radiation exposure and drowning but for the moment, he was safe. His skin and joints seemed to be frozen as every part of his body felt numb and hard. He continued shivering.

How would Gata Harriman react if he found no body and a loose grille in the room? He will not take any chances, he will search this whole passage and kill him. That was why he needed to be fast. Nothing could measure how long the guards will come to pick up his imaginary corpse and gasped. Another two minutes had passed.

More light shone as he proceeded along the slime-coated walls. He finally got out of the passage that widened into a pool or something as big as one. He broke through the surface and was careful not to be overjoyed, he breathed in the air slowly, it was stuffy in the place. He didn't feel nausea or anything else telling him something was wrong. So he continued to breath. The liquefied oxygen in his blood must have just finished in time.

The water was as cold as it was in the room. He had a sense he will die of hypothermia, a bullet, or drowning. He vaguely took in his surroundings. The place was covered in a cylindrical whitewashed metal tunnel. Water flowed around him with not much current around his waist. There were lights lighting the way. What was this place?

One end was locked by some sort of round metal and he didn't want to use his watch. If it was dangerous, he may die. He somehow had the feeling about where he was. This was a part of the nuclear plant.

He continued the path on his left-hand side. The water was at chest level now and cold but slowly receded as he walked. He knew his body temperature was dangerously below the normal level and anytime, he will pass out and die.

This whole place was identical and he wasn't sure whether it was his hallucination or not. Just as he thought of giving up and dying in the water, he felt heat inside the water. Maybe he was going to die after all, his body was now so hungry for a warm bath and he was dreaming about it. How pathetic was he? He had been threatened to die with a fist-sized piece of uranium just a few meters away or forced to drown in the cold blackish water, and now this. He could tell that his body was giving up and he was dying.

Anyway, he continued forward, whether the heat was a hallucination or not, it was comfortable and warmed him and gave him hope. The water level dropped to ankle-height and he saw a little steam coming from the way forward. So this couldn't be any hallucination, he touched the floor and felt warm water flowing.

To make more feeling come back to his numb body and limbs, he laid down onto the warm water, the little current splashing against his shoulders and feet. He felt good, like some sort of spa he never experienced before. After a few minutes to regain his strength and cease his hypothermia, he stood up from the warm water and continued.

He suddenly remembered something, Fibiano! They are going to kill him using the uranium. He recalled what Gata Harriman had said before leaving the room. He had escaped for the moment and was now leaving his teammate alone to die in such horrible way. No, he would save him no matter what it cost.

He had been too clever and even stupid enough to activate the metal bracelet, which was a location detector for every worker to look identical to one another. But it had the opposite effect, it was as if he had been holding a neon-light sign showing his presence. Gata Harriman shouldn't want any worker to enter his nuclear plant without knowing their whereabouts.

Above all this nonsense he had been thinking about, he should underline the main problem that led to all this, he shouldn't have entered the nuclear plant at all. The millionaire would not have known about their presence and the IIO had covered them well enough. He had personally blown two agents' cover just by a twist of fate and a bad decision.

If anything happened to Fibiano, how could he live with himself? He may save a lot of people but he had indirectly killed one. He made a decision, if he could do something to save the Frenchman, he would have to do it. He owed him.

Nathan was sure if Fibiano was the one to enter the plant, he will come out safely without any harm or gain. There was no way he could get into the control point and get behind the hidden doors.

As he continued, he felt the water's temperature increasing steadily and the steam was billowing and interrupting his vision ahead. The water around his feet was about 40 degrees Celsius and up to his ankles. If the water was waist-height or even higher, he wasn't sure that the spa idea would work and he couldn't continue without burning himself.

The steam was now rising from the water below him. It must have passed 40 degrees and he could feel his skin being scalded. He now understood the flow, the way he was heading was hotter and hotter, but he couldn't turn back without wasting half an hour.

He broke into a run, the steam was scalding his eyes and skin and the water was boiling his feet. He thought of removing his extra clothing but knew it won't help much, may even let the steam enter much easily and scald him more.

More steam ahead, the water increasing steadily in temperature. How was he going to continue if the temperature came to 50? There was no way his legs could stand this kind of torture. He noticed a lot of steam ahead. The water remained at ankle-height.

The cylindrical passage way widened into a big area like the size of the Hall. There were metal platforms with metal steps and built-in ladders connecting them. On the ceiling, a few big turbines had been spinning very slowly, pushed by the billowing steam. Just at the top of this place was a ventilation system to get the extra steam out.

The water was still increasingly getting hotter. It was about 45 degrees. Nathan suddenly came to understand something. He was in a nuclear plant. The kind he saw in the legal inspection area and now he was in the one to be inspected. But surely this was in the illegal plant. They were just starting to heat the water using the nuclear reactors. He could see a steady stream flowing out at the end and another sucking in water.

Just all of a sudden, big metal panels shut the way behind him. He gasped. There was no retreat and he was going to be boiled alive. The water was even boiling furiously. The nuclear reactor must have taken time to heat the ice cold water from the Dark Zone but was doing its job very successfully. He studied simple physics and knew how nuclear plants work.

First, they used uranium in the reactor and it made some kind of chemical reaction that caused the radioactive particles to separate from each other, producing heat, an enormous amount. That was called fission.

Basically, all compounds undergoing chemical process to either separate into a simpler form or join two types of particles called elements that create heat. However, when it came to uranium and fission, the heat wasn't going to be a comfortable spa. There was another way called fusion—joining particles or something like that. There will be water around the nuclear reactor, pressurized to prevent them from boiling although the temperature had reached 100 degrees Celsius. Who wanted their nuclear reactors to be shaking and steam billowing inside? It won't succeed without a massive explosion or a miracle.

And now finally the water was released from pressure and flowing to the turbine chambers. It was hot and boiling.

Nathan counted his dead line, he had probably a minute if he was lucky. The water will be 100 degrees in not more than 20 seconds. He needed to get his feet out of the water.

He looked around as he ran, ignoring his scalding feet and ankles. There was a platform above, just at the side of the place. A built-in metal steps led the way. He reached it in 10 seconds, climbed it in 20 to the platform.

He now saw that there was also a glass just above him. It was probably an inspection area. What if one of the guards or crazy scientists saw him? Would they save him and switch off the reactor or ask all their friends to watch the show?

Or even worse, they will bring a file with them and state down the variables and make a hypothesis, treating him like a test subject. No one was there or patrolling. The guards must have been busy locating Fibiano. No one had come to pick his "body" from the room.

But that won't happen as long as he had all his limbs and the gadgets. He got up the platform and then found metal steps leading to a higher platform. He was surprised that the turbines looked so menacing just as he came closer.

The water was boiling and more steam billowed from below. If he had been down there by now, he will be a human stew. But he had another thing to worry about. The steam, it was hot and killing him and the humidity of the air rose, making it harder to breath. The sweat trickled down like streams descending a slope.

He looked around for an exit and saw a door at the far end one story above him. He raced for it for his life. The steam was increasing and filling the whole place, the turbines rotated faster and faster. He climbed another series of steps that doubled once over each other and got to the highest platform. The inspection glass was beside him.

Then he ran towards the door while scrambling for his watch. He quickly exposed the hidden strips and placed it on the metal panel. It took about five seconds and he got through it and shut it behind him. He was lucky it wasn't bolted.

He will be alive for the moment. It wasn't so bad after all. Luck had been in his favour but the odds were stacking against him more and more, until he was almost breaking underneath the enemy's good odds. The more he went on like this, the more luck played its role.

Chapter Twenty Eight

DEATH LEAPS

The air conditioner was okay and he felt relieved as cold air surrounded him. No one was around so far. He needed to get to the uranium storage room and somehow copy down the locations of the export.

Gata Harriman may have already exported some of it but there was still a lot left. He probably wouldn't ship it all at once, what if his uranium-trafficker got caught? He must also find a list of the exports' location.

Nathan noticed a puddle of water and sweat below him. He was indeed very hot. He didn't waste time to recover. After things settled down, he will reunite with his aunt and stay somewhere else. But he needed to be alive first.

There were two paths to choose from. Where will he go now? Nathan took about few minutes to gather his thoughts and knew that he was terribly exposed. If one of the guards came patrolling, he had lived for a moment to die later.

Nathan chose his right-hand path and walked the metal passage and continued his mission, which he thought was so far failing. He will need something to bargain with Gata Harriman like the information of where his uranium will be exported or something like this and he will stick to the same plan. Send it, and then let him know he hadn't. Bargain and threaten him with a non-existing threat. The psychopath deserved something much worse than that.

He came to another door at the far end. Again using his watch, he hacked through it easily. He recalled the incident when the guards told him to strip down his protective suit. It seemed to be a lifetime earlier. If he really did without all of his gadgets, he wouldn't have survived in the blackish water even though he found a passage out.

The door led to the place that he first came into the illegal plant. So this was a roundabout after a few threats of death. He stood on one of the metal platforms and took in again the shape of the nuclear reactors surrounded by thick and solid metal and concrete.

Pipes and wires brought in signals, electricity and water to be heated and then transferred to the turbine chambers. He saw the door that will bring anyone to the secret passage leading back to the legal plant's control point.

The workers never once looked at anything except their work and the path they will use ahead. That was good. *Continue to concentrate as you all should be* thought Nathan.

He noticed that there were guards all over the place, but then he made an observation that they weren't only guarding the place. They were also guarding the workers. That was why all of them wore the metal bracelets, they were location detectors. Perhaps they were somehow forced to be slaves and didn't ever intend to help the psychopath to process the radioactive uranium.

He needed to be careful. However, all of the workers' protective suits made them look baggy and bulky and any chase will favour Nathan. Plus, their visors only stretched on for about 140 degrees, limiting their vision. The impregnable screen also made vision not as clear as normal, he knew this as he wore the suit before. He doubted there were ear protective devices, so they couldn't likely hear his movement well.

Everything was good except for one concern. What if the nuclear reactor leaked? But he assumed and for the first time put his trust into the psychopath that the workers had all ensured safety procedures and measurements and a nuclear leak was the last possibility. It would do Harriman no good as well, if there were a leak.

Nathan remembered the answer for his "last wish" just before he "died" and Gata Harriman answered it in complete arrogance and pride. Gata had said that the nuclear storage was somewhere near this place inside the nuclear plant. He had limited the area of search so effectively that Nathan just needed to scan around to look for the chamber.

Behind his back were the turbine areas, to his left were the rooms he used to change his clothes and on the far end a large storage compartment was locked with an air-lock seal and solid doors. And these doors were more solid than any others, at least it looked like that.

The shocking problem was the size of the chamber, it was big. How much nuclear power did Gata Harriman have? This was madness. And one more thing, he needed to enter without any protective gear. And how was he going to enter or even get near it?

Nathan observed the platforms and the ground. There were guards all over there. The 10 guards the millionaire brought with him were patrolling and monitoring the area. There was no way he will get passed them. The lower platforms were full of workers and guards, it will be a miracle if he could walk across invisibly.

That left the highest platform, just above the reactor. It stretched all the way to the far end where the chamber was located. No guards were present up there. There may be during their normal shifts but now they were hunting Fibiano. Nathan wished he could be clever enough to hide somewhere and not just being dragged out of his room.

Nathan remembered what the psychopath said just before he went out of the room, leaving him in the water and darkness, he said to use the nuclear radiation to kill Fibiano. He needed to work fast. The problem was there weren't any metal steps that could bring him to the highest platforms. There weren't any ladders nearby, either. The ones in the middle were useless. The one on the far end wasn't guarded but how could he reach it in the first place?

Nathan looked up and around for any footholds that could assist him to that safe place, out of anyone's sight. There were pipes and wires in metal holders. Nathan doubted if the wires could hold his weight and that left the pipes.

Above him, two blue pipes each as thick as five centimeters were tied to each other. They then led to a turn that was leading even farther away to his left. But there was another pipe horizontally out a bit farther. The distance was about three meters and he must jump to reach it, get on the pipe and continue with another red pipe to get to the railings of the highest platform. There was no time to waste, no other possibilities to get there unseen.

Nathan removed his extra clothing and left the weird jacket hanging on the pipes above him. No one will look up and their visors limited their vision, he hoped they would not notice him as well.

He undressed from the weird trousers. He then tied the two pieces of dangling wet fabric together that was supposed to cover both of his legs. It was long and strong enough to be a makeshift rope. He swung one part of the trousers up over the pipes above him and retrieved it. Now the makeshift rope could be tied. He put them into a tight knot. Then he jumped and his hands caught the pipes, he grabbed them. He then levered himself and lay on his stomach on the pipes with his legs parallel.

Slowly, he tried to balance himself and stood on the pipes. They were only a little wider than the length of one of his shoes. He positioned himself so that his side was facing the way ahead and he needed to move sideways.

He grabbed the tied rope and move in a parallel way along the pipes for a little safety precaution. They were strong enough to hold his weight. He moved sideways until the platform under him turned away. Now nothing was below him except a hard grey concrete floor three stories underneath.

He continued to move sideways, not caring about the concentrating workers and the dreaming guards. When he got to the point where the pipes turned in another direction, he once again saw the two pipes tied together. They were identical to the first one ahead of him. Three were meters ahead, horizontally placed. He would have to jump and grab it with both hands, and then climb up slowly, if he failed, he will either have the chance to drop on one of the platforms or the concrete floor below.

He left the makeshift rope behind, it was no longer needed. Bracing himself, he aimed and powered his leg muscles. His body was airborne for the moment. He concentrated on the pipes that were approaching nearer and nearer to him. The pipes struck Nathan in his chest and he scrambled for a grip with both of his arms. All the breath was knocked out of him. He inhaled reluctantly and failed. His legs were now hanging just a few meters above the railings of the platform below and if any workers looked up, they would be astonished.

He quickly levered one leg to get hold of the pipe and then another to balance himself. He sat on the pipes between his groin and then looked at the next pipe. Two more jumps to go. He was sweating and salt and water dripped onto the platform, but no one noticed.

Nathan carefully stood up again, facing the next pipe that was also horizontally placed. This pipe was two meters away and painted red. It was slightly lower than the one he was on. But then he knew the ones he did before were easier, but this one would be a little harder so he thought about it a little longer.

This pipe transported hot water. It was under pressure so that it wouldn't boil but was nothing less than 100 degrees. He could see a little steam above the pipe. If he had done it that way earlier, hit it with his chest and used his hands to hold it for grip, he would scalded himself and the pain would have forced him to let go.

He needed to land on his feet and only his feet. And then only one meter separated the pipe from the railings of the highest platform.

Nathan hesitated for a long moment. There was no way he could go back. He aimed his body towards the railings of the platform and jumped. He stomped both feet onto the red pipe, he heard a hiss as the soles of his shoes burned under the heat. A drop of sweat dripped onto it and it hissed again, boiling it instantly into steam.

Nathan quickly jumped off the red pipe the moment he landed, propelled over the railings onto the platform. He was safe for the moment.

He used 10 seconds to calm his heart, he thought a heart attack was coming but it didn't. He smiled to himself. *This mission is crazy! Did Harvard Norman do these kinds of things before he laid his butt onto the Chief Executive Officer of the Elite Division chair in the IIO? I'll need to be alive to ask him that.*

He continued his way along the platform. Beneath him, more than 100 guards and workers were busy with their work and they didn't notice his presence. He ended up on the edge of the platform and used the metal steps that no one was guarding, which he had seen earlier.

This was reality. He climbed down the steps to the end of the ground floor and hid behind a pile of metal boxes as big as small ship cargos. The guards' backs were facing towards him or looking at the work going on above the platforms. This was good.

He easily used his watch to hack the large doors in front of him. The doors opened. Nobody cared and he entered silently, and closed it with a button. There were guards inside here as well.

He hid behind a metal holder that held big concrete and metal boxes with codes written on them. The fluorescent lights lit that lifeless place. There were three guards patrolling but they didn't look around much. It must be Gata Harriman's command to carry out frequent patrols and they were now bored. The metal boxes will provide cover. This was the uranium storage room and he knew what was inside the boxes. The numbers were the coordinates or country codes.

Although he couldn't find out the locations of the uranium that had been exported, he could at least get the coordinates of the uranium that will be exported. By luck, they may use the same place to dock. He knew how serious it would be if he failed to find the locations of the uranium, both his and Fibiano's covers had been blown into bits already and staying longer will help nothing except Harriman's torture plan.

But how would he download all of this information? These weren't electronic files and he didn't have the time to borrow a pen and get a paper to copy down each code, especially with so many guards around.

Nathan passed behind a guard that was patrolling, j but he didn't hear a sound with his protective suit on. The first metal holder stored about 20 boxes. He brought out the phone the IIO gave him, took a nice photo and proceeded to the second and did the same.

The guards were so ignorant and didn't even notice his presence until Nathan thought that his job was the easiest. There were about five rows and Nathan took a photo from each of them.

But this time, it was different. One of the guards was just coming to the last row as Nathan kept his phone out. The guard saw him, remembered what his boss had said and yelled. He scrambled for his baton but Nathan ran forward and made a kick to the solar plexus and he staggered back. He couldn't have done that if he wore the bulky suit.

The alarm had already been raised. The guard took only a few seconds to recover. His suit must have taken most of the impact. But two more guards were rushing towards Nathan, their batons already out. They were just like jogging towards him with their bulky and heavy protective wear.

Nathan looked around. There was another door just behind him. He had been surrounded by the men and he could choose to fight his way through, but that won't help. They had probably alerted the guards outside and where would he run?

He quickly used his watch to hack the door and prepared for the men's assault but they were pathetically slow. The guard who he had kicked recovered and ran towards him with his baton.

Nathan temporally resigned from his work and held his arm out before the guard could strike, he then easily manoeuvred the man's baton and drove it into his gut. The guard groaned and dropped to his knees. That was what he felt like when they did that to him.

Nathan took the baton with him and secured the watch back to his wrist then entered the door. He watched as the remaining guards were equally surprised to find a boy that had just hacked through two of the doors they were supposed to guard, and then they desperately tried to stop him with their shouts of pursuit.

The air-lock door closed, shutting out the noise of the guards. The door led to a large cargo elevator, probably used to transport the nuclear cases to the submarines. He didn't know where it could bring him, but there were only two buttons on the entire panel. One was to seal the door and another to order the lift to a floor.

He pressed the button, a number one printed on it. The lift moved, very slowly indeed and finally stopped. The doors slid aside. He walked out of the metal box. It revealed whitewashed walls and a lot of doors to rooms. The place looked lifeless and must have been to accommodation area for the workers and the guards.

Just to make sure that the guards won't be able to use the lift, he placed the baton between the closing doors. The doors slid towards each other and hit the baton, then opened again and would do the same for as long as it took for someone to come and fix the problem.

He then thought. *Why would a lift in the uranium storage led to the living place of the workers?* Gata Harriman was insane. However, he remembered that the lift had only one button that one could really operate . . . The lift will only lead anyone from the uranium storage to the accommodation area but not the other way, it was a one-way ticket. And if he had pressed the button on this floor, it must lead to somewhere else except the floor of the illegal plant.

And to enter the illegal nuclear plant, they could use the well-hidden door on the wall of the control point of the legal nuclear plant. This was how he fooled the world's best intelligence agencies. He may be psycho but also clever as well. He may be a psycho-genius.

He took out the phone he used to take the photos and removed the memory card. Then he activated the parasite file in the pinball application and waited. The phone won't probably download anything inside itself but when its own memory card was outside the phone, like a foreign agent posting threats, it will download the files in it as well. It's the converse concept. He attached the card back into the slot.

The feedback was a "GOOD JOB. I'LL GET YOU OUT NOW". He didn't know how to contact the IIO other than that so he typed a message into the phone stating that he and Fibiano are in danger and their covers had been blown to pieces, he then demanded them to immediately do whatever that could to help them.

He saved the message and deleted everything except the note and the photos. He then removed the memory card once again and used the tablet's real function.

He hoped they will check the things he sent again. He proceeded ahead, finding his way out where he could bargain with Gata Harriman using the false threat and make time. He knew that they could change the coordinates if they knew he got the photos. But Nathan doubted that Harriman will have so much time to reset his plans. Anyway, if he wanted to bargain with the millionaire, he would need something to bargain with. And this was the only thing worth trying.

Chapter Twenty Nine

BLUE LASER

Nathan walked along the mass expanse of rooms and doors leading to showers, game compartments and kitchens. The place was virtually empty with no one else around. Gata Harriman must have ordered them all in a tight schedule to catch up on the plans he had talked about with the unknown man in his quarters a few hours ago.

He also had Fibiano to find and possibly save. Nathan was quite sure that the Frenchman must have been hiding well. Why else would the millionaire send so much of his guards to keep searching for him if they had already got him? The re-checking of the list of visitors didn't need such action. But where could Fibiano hide? Nathan had a plan in mind. He needed to get back to the Guest Unit in the safety of numbers. There were scientists, researchers and other wealthy visitors that will indirectly make the millionaire think twice before hurting him once again. The public exposure was too much of a risk for him with the intelligence agencies spying on his every move.

He assumed that the millionaire still had no clue about him sending the information of his future exports, and the amount of his uranium exports from his computer, and the photos respectively. But the guards at the illegal plant may have seen him taking photos and if the news got to Harriman's ears, he'll go crazy.

Then, he ought to wait for the IIO to do something. He hoped the IIO would do something that would bring them out of this insane Mariana Trench Research Centre. He also hoped to imprison Gata Harriman in the world's highest security lockdown.

As he found his way out of this place, he noticed there was an office area that led to an exit. There was an unlocked door, but no other way that could lead him elsewhere but to the accommodation rooms. The place was furnished with blinking monitors and office instruments.

He needed to pass the office and get through the door to somewhere out of this place. However, that wasn't as easy as he thought. The office was filled with about 40 scientists with their disheveled hair and dirty coats. They were being looked at by 20 guards, all equipped with electrical batons. The men were still in protective suits. They surely had no time to change their clothes. Harriman must have been so paranoid to guard the scientists like that.

He wondered what was now happening in the Guest Unit. Will the visitors be held in such a manner? Would they be huddled with each other so closely that they could feel each other's breath and fear? He hoped the psycho wealthy man wouldn't go to such an extent. He made up his mind to get by the guards, he thought of some effective ideas. It was nothing less than revenge. The crazy guards were still wearing their metal bracelets but he didn't notice any metal objects on the scientists. Metal bracelets, they were all metal! He smiled. He had one gadget that he had not used. He brought out the two magnets that Professor Archnon Winters had given him and separated them. He hit them together as hard as he could and that made a metallic *clink.*

The guards heard that obvious sound and seemed to be alarmed by a potential threat. But that didn't bother Nathan very much. He rammed opened the door and exposed himself fully to them. The guards were surprised by his presence and wondered why an idiot 14-year-old boy would try to be a hero. Or they wondered why the boy just gave himself to armed guards who outnumbered him by 20 to 1?

The men in protective suits didn't care about the reason anymore, they had been given orders to get anyone in their custody regardless of age or any condition. Failure will bring them devastating results. They brought up their batons and charged toward the teenager.

Nathan aimed for a solid looking file-holder cabinet at one corner and swung the two magnets toward it. The two magnets attracted the metal cabinet and stuck to it. But that was only the beginning of the story. The guards suddenly felt some kind of invisible force pulling their metal batons and forcing them to release their only weapons. All the batons flew magically towards the cabinet and attached to it as if they were made to be together.

The guards looked bewildered. Just at the moment, the metal bracelets around their wrist were attracted by the same field of magnetic force. In a few seconds, they were absorbed by the invisible force like a black hole in space. All of them crashed into the metal cabinet in a heap.

The scientists looked at him and for the moment, silence filled the entire office. A heap of injured men in white suits were crumpled around the corner, the cabinet in the centre of them.

Then, the men and woman that worked for science and research their entire lives screamed and roamed out of the door behind Nathan and the one at the other end. They got no where else to go unless someone could operate and get control of the submarines on Level 2.

In a few seconds, the commotion ended with the last shouts from the shocked scientists. The office was emptied at once, apart from the abandoned furniture and computers and the heap of guards.

Nathan didn't care about them anymore. He proceeded to the open door at the far end and got out of the office. He shut the metal door behind him with some of the guards yelling uselessly at him.

He had been in this place a few hours before. It was the place when his mission officially started. This was the Level 3 of the research centre. The corridor in front of him will lead him to the quarters of Gata Harriman and the path to his right will bring him to the elevator.

Fibiano had been wrong. He said that the staff's quarters stored nothing more than documentation and accommodations. Although the elevator would not bring them to the illegal plant on this level, there had to be a way to get to that level on it. He had been cheated by the special function of the lift just like the other intelligence agency agents.

Nathan wasn't going to the millionaire's quarters, there's nothing more he could take. Instead, he headed for the elevator and stuck to his original plan. He used the lift to get to Level 1, the Guest Unit.

There were more people there and he thought of his next move and tried to figure some clue about his team-up's whereabouts. He believed it was the only safe place for them in this entire place.

The lift that could easily fit 40 people descended slowly as the water pressure outside the walls decreased. The doors slid aside to reveal the huge wooden doors to the Hall, which is where Harriman had given his world-class hypocritical speech about discovering the nature of the Dark Zone.

Instead, he possessed a warehouse of uranium, an illegal nuclear plant, and was exporting nuclear materials. He was even using some of it to play a cruel game with a child. It was all madness from a cruel psycho. Harriman was really a bastard.

To his right was the illuminating blue glow behind the glass, which was holding back a few hundred million gallons of sea water. The light no longer gave him any relaxation as he knew how much danger this place was for all of them. It was just a normal fluorescent glow just like the idiot thing Fibiano had said.

He made his way down to the wide space that housed the entertainment area and the rooms of the visitors around it. He passed the Hall and peeked inside, there was no one around and the lights had been switched off.

The guest rooms were, as always, silent, too. The parallelogram-shaped entertainment area was lit in a dim yellow glow. No one was in sight. Not the guards or any visitors.

He remembered the time now. It was bedtime and it was supposed to be midnight to them. Could the visitors have been captured by the guards and held somewhere else? Had Fibiano managed to hide himself or was he just in his room? That wasn't a possible alternative place to hide, and the guards must have checked his room by now.

He continued his way between the entertainment area and the stretch of identical guest rooms on his right. He must admit that the whole place looked abandoned and creepy with no sign of life at all. Somehow it all looked like a broken down factory.

But just as he walked to the edge of the parallelogram of glass and the last of the rooms, he heard the sound of a child sobbing silently and boots stomping onto the metal floor. He crouched down near the parallelogram and looked through the glass.

The end of the Guest Unit was filled with the visitors he had seen the moment they boarded the larger submarine. The men in white suits were looking at their every slight movement although no one was barely moving.

About 70 visitors were huddled together and 30 guards were present. They were armed with the same electrical batons. At the farthest wall was a single piece of glass covering the whole back of the level. It illuminated the same blue with the dark creatures swimming in freedom, not bothered by the tense scene occurring inside this centre.

The visitors were no longer welcomed guests. They sat on the floor with their legs folded, the girl that was not more than 12 was the one who was sobbing, and swallowing tears back into her throat. Her mother was patting her back and doing what she thought was calming her, although she was barely holding herself together.

Nathan looked around for the French for a minute among the visitors but failed to locate him. He was sure about that. Nathan had looked precisely at the faces and body size of each of the shocked men and women, but found none even looking close to the French.

He also spotted Cecil Holmwood, their tour guide and the Chief Researcher among the crowd. So, she had no knowledge about anything illegal before this.

Nathan was starting to convince himself again that Fibiano hadn't been captured as three gunshots broke the silence. It came from behind him. He felt two hot bullets race passed him and another sliced his left upper arm.

He dropped to the floor and clutched his arm, blood was gushing out from the wound. He wanted to run and escape from the firing line, but there wasn't his choice to choose anything now.

He turned and saw Gata Harriman holding a handgun, sulfuric smoke billowing out of the muzzle. The millionaire had shot him in the arm. Two guards in white suits accompanied the psychopath. They must either have come from the Hall or from the lift.

The crowd had panicked and the guards were yelling and getting them back under control. The two bullets that missed Nathan had struck the glass at the far end. It hadn't broken, probably bulletproof, but there were web-like cracks around the holes where the bullets had hit. No one else had been hurt.

The pain washed through him now. He could feel it as the metallic coldness and throbbing climbed all the way to his neck and torso. He expected the millionaire to kill him immediately just as he intended, but he didn't.

The psychopath really looked crazy now, he probably knew now that the photos of the metal cargos storing radioactive uranium had been sent. He could decide to choose another location, but that had probably been planned for years. It would take too much time.

Gata Harriman walked forward and dragged Nathan's good arm. He forced him into a half-stand and continued dragging him toward the crowd. He then threw him onto the floor. A line of blood made a trail. *Why had the millionaire chose to keep me alive?*

The crowd was looking at him, the nearest visitors curled into a ball as if they could get as far as they could from him and protect themselves. The psychopath looked at him with madness in his eyes.

"Did you take the photos of the cargos?" he asked nicely, but Nathan could sense he was keeping the last of his wits to maintain his authoritative composure. He already didn't mind to let the world know about his illegal uranium.

"Yes. So you are going to kill me now," Nathan replied in a weak tone. There was no reason to deny it. It looked like he didn't have the energy to spit in the man's face before he pulled the trigger, but looking at his reaction as the plans that took years to plan crumbling in front of him was enough satisfaction.

"Did you send the files? Where is the other agent?" The millionaire ignored his last sentence. He held the gun loaded with live ammunition beside him, ready to use it.

"Yes. More than it needs to put you in jail for the rest of your life." He swallowed back his breath, the pain was devastating and he wasn't sure if the bullet had really cut through any major blood vessels or not. Blood was pooling on the floor around him.

"How would I know where Fibiano is? You said you'll find him. So you failed," Nathan continued, he found himself breathing very fast, his heart was beating in his chest and flying out. He knew he's was going to die and hoped that Fibiano could survive and make sure the IIO really saved his aunt.

The Russian-English man smiled and brought the gun up in his direction but didn't aim well, his psycho level was at its paramount. He was staggering as if high on drugs.

"You bastard! You ruined my plans! I can't believe my plans have been ruined by a 14-year-old boy? You somehow escaped from the tank. I should have killed you with the uranium. Die!" He pointed the gun at his forehead at point-blank range and reached to pull the trigger. There wasn't much Nathan could do apart from watching uselessly at the black eye of the muzzle. He waited for an explosion and a bullet flying out that will mark his end.

But that was when a man in a white suit beside Gata Harriman acted with incredible speed. He was surprisingly fast, although wearing the bulky protective suit. The man grabbed the barrel of the gun and manoeuvred it so that the muzzle was away from Nathan. Gata Harriman pulled the trigger half a second late, although he still didn't understand what had happened. Another bullet was fired. It was stopped by the glass illuminating the blue glow. Spider web-like cracks stretched on from the hole shaping the bullet about a meter in radius.

If the glass didn't hold, they'd perish in a few millions of gallons of water in two micro seconds. They'd probably be killed by the pressure before anything.

The man in suit then twisted the gun in Harriman's hand so that the muzzle faced the floor and made another 90-degree spin together with the psychopath's wrist.

Nathan heard bone cracking and the joints of the millionaire's wrist dislocating permanently. The man in the suit then took his own electrical baton from the loop of his belt and trusted it into his victim's side.

Gata Harriman yelled agonized both by his broken wrist and the weird current Nathan himself had experienced before. The man that saved his life then put a final kick to the side of Harriman's head and the millionaire slumped down onto the floor.

He raised the gun and hit another man in a white suit that accompanied Harriman earlier. His visor cracked and the metal struck his forehead. The worker fell to the floor in a heap beside his boss.

The unknown man then took off his helmet and threw it and the baton to the floor. He was Fibiano, the man that the millionaire had been looking for was just beside him. That made Harriman looked even more stupid.

The Frenchman waved the gun at the other 20 guards and warned them to stay back and lie on the floor on their chests. Nathan was already losing consciousness and looked at Fibiano with unfocused eyes.

"Are you okay?" he asked. He pocketed the gun and took out a piece of clean cloth from one of his pockets and helped to tie a tight bandage around Nathan's left upper arm. At the same time, he kept an eye on all the guards.

"Where did you get the suit?" he only managed to speak out the sentence. Fibiano ignored him and continued his work. Nathan groaned as he pulled the knot tight.

The visitors looked at them uncertainly. One moment, men in white suits were pulling them out of their beds with batons in their hands and another moment a boy not more than 14 was shot and dragged by the man who made the opening ceremony's speech. What the hell was going on?

Fibiano helped him to his feet, there was still blood trickling down to the floor. "We need to get out of this place. Hold on! Nathan," the Frenchman said as he put a hand around his shoulder and performed a human crouch transport technique.

"I've informed the IIO about our blown covers," Nathan wheezed. "Don't talk too much. You're wasting your breath," Fibiano replied.

They walked slowly toward a wall beside a door to the guest room. Fibiano gently helped him to sit with his back leaning against the wall.

"There are three bullets in the glass and that thing is not going to hold for long. The bastard Gata Harriman had deactivated all automatic systems because he thought they were bugged. Unfortunately, it included the emergency system. I'm going to reactivate them to get the metal binds down," Fibiano said quickly and handed Nathan the gun.

"Watch the guards. I'll be back in a minute. Do not pass out, Nathan," he said and looked for a reply. Nathan just took the gun with a hand coated with blood and nodded. His other hand went limp and put pressure on his upper arm.

Fibiano wasted no more time. He headed to the corridor where Nathan had come in and turned left to get to the elevator.

Nathan glanced at the guards that were still lying down. Some of them were looking at him and the gun and some at the fallen millionaire. The visitors kept silent apart from murmuring prayers and whispering to their friends like insane people.

That was the moment Gata Harriman struggled up and raced for Nathan. He looked totally wild, not far from looking like a man escaped from a psychiatric hospital. He used both of his hands and grabbed Nathan's neck. Nathan felt his air supply being cut off.

Nathan didn't have the time to use the gun, he was already losing consciousness and the sudden assault had surprised him. The millionaire cursed him with an unknown language, not English, not Russian.

Gata Harriman then shook him like a punching bag and rammed his head and body again and again onto the wall behind him. The bandage had torn away and more blood began flowing. The man's eyes were devil-like and only focused on the boy he wanted to kill with his bare hands.

The gun had been dismantled from Nathan by the vicious blows and skipped to somewhere on the floor. But the crazy man didn't bother to get it or even notice it. He continued to grab for Nathan's neck. More consciousness was seeping out of him and if someone or Fibiano didn't help him fast, he would pass out in a few moments.

Nathan tried to release the grip of the man from his neck but it wasn't possible, the man's hands were strong and his broken hand was in a weird angle and broken, but that didn't stop him from using it. Nathan saw black clouds forming at the edge of his eyes.

But it was at that moment another *crack* thundered through the area. He saw Gata Harriman's head burst out a ball of blood from two holes on both of his temples. He instantly released his grip and fell to the floor like a machine's switch had been flicked off.

Nathan ignored the black dots forming on his vision. He used his last bar of energy to look around. No one had fired a shot. The gun hadn't been used. It was from the glass at the end of this level.

One of the bullets had been pushed by the tremendous pressure of the Dark Zone and it powered in a parallel line towards and through Gata Harriman's head. He soon managed to focus a little and noticed a line of water spraying from the just-vacant hole of the glass.

It wasn't spraying, it was powering as far and as fast as it could. The pressure in the Mariana Trench was more than eight tons per square inch. The line of water was just in front of him. If anyone walked past the line, he would be cut into pieces by the pressure.

The cracks around the hole widened. But a red light in the corner of the ceiling started to blink just as Fibiano hit the emergency button somewhere. A metal panel had lowered down to conceal the whole piece of glass. The line of water was cut off and the hole and cracks sealed once again.

Nathan looked at the corpse of the millionaire in front of him. Gata Harriman was no doubt dead. The bullet that had been fired from the hole was much faster than any gun could shoot and had passed through his head. The pool of blood from Nathan's arm and the dead psycho's head was widening.

Nathan retrieved the gun as soon as the black dots around his vision cleared. He waited until the Frenchman came back to him. Fibiano was shocked to see the millionaire dead like that. He didn't ask how or when, though he wanted to.

But the questions will come later. They didn't know whether there were other dangers waiting for them and it was time to leave the place. Fibiano helped Nathan to his feet and got the gun from the floor. The guards and visitors were no longer concerned about them, they were shocked by the death of the millionaire.

They then slowly limped toward the elevator and Fibiano pressed a few codes and used some of his own gadgets to hack the system. The lift ascended to Level 4 and they got out as soon as the door slid aside.

The place was covered by metal and just as big as the Hall. "Where are we going? Aren't we're using the submarine on Level 2?" Nathan asked as Fibiano helped him to walk. "The submarines are too slow, we will go faster. This is the emergency departure of the centre. I'll get you out of here, with enough blood in you to live," the Frenchman said.

They walked toward the center where a big slab of metal was built from the floor to the ceiling. He opened an air-lock door and helped Nathan in. It led into a pod about the size of a small room with bare seats, a fire extinguisher and simple monitors and controls. Re-enforced glasses acted as windows, but offered no view.

Fibiano got in and closed the air-lock door behind him. Nathan wanted to ask him about the other visitors but he knew they will be safe for the moment. The guards couldn't kill them with the batons and why would they? Their boss was dead and there were no orders anymore.

Nathan slumped onto the seat lazily like the times he felt tired after school. The Frenchman hit a few controls and pulled a red lever. Immediately, the pod shuddered and ascended towards the surface. Nathan looked at the monitor showing how deep they were below sea level and started to pass out as the numbers dropped.

In a few minutes, the emergency pod broke the surface of the sea in the waters off Japan. The sky was dark and a few distance lights shone. They were likely from the faraway cities or harbours. He saw Fibiano making contacts with the emergency team and the light slowly dimmed. He heard the sound of beeping machineries and murmurs of Fibiano communicating with the authorities.

He suddenly felt comfortable and whatever pain had travelled out of him as if the wound didn't exist. Nathan closed his eyes and passed out.

Chapter Thirty

REST DAY

Nathan was lying on his back in the white room he believed was a hospital somewhere when he opened his sleepy eyes. There was no psychopath and no one else in the room. Beeping machineries of monitors told him his breathing rates were buzzing around him.

The bed wasn't as comfortable like the one in London, the one he had left a long time ago, but that wasn't important. He'll make sure the IIO gets his aunt back like the deal they made with him before he got himself into the mission.

Harvard Norman had been sitting with concern written on his face beside him when the first consciousness seeped back into him. The pain didn't leave him completely but the morphine drip stuck to his arm had lessened the throbbing sensation.

The Chief Executive Officer of the Elite Division in the IIO came personally and under some official circumstances. He insisted that Nathan to lie down for a moment while he briefed him with the new timeline going on to his just-ended-mission, and about his aunt and other things.

Fibiano had managed to tie a tourniquet around his wound while he waited for the 24-hour-a-day Japanese Marine emergency team to get them to the trauma centre by helicopter.

The Frenchman had also donated blood to him. The blood-test procedures had been done just a day before the mission and that saved time may have kept him alive. Although he felt a weird sensation of with the Frenchman's type A blood pumping around his body, he owed his thanks to the team that saved him twice.

Looking at his bandaged arm, he wondered why the Frenchman hadn't stop Gata Harriman from firing the first three shots. That was maybe because the agent didn't expect Nathan to be there and the millionaire's brutal action hadn't been expected.

And how he could move so fast in that suit? He soon got the answer himself. The suit they all wore had been either bigger or according to their own sizes. The Frenchman's suit was slightly smaller than his actual size, making movement even more flexible and easier. The bigger, the baggier the suits were. And Fibiano was using the opposite fact to work in his favour.

The hospital then graphed back his half-torn bronchial artery and applied whatever was necessary to prevent further bleeding and infection. The IIO asked them for a clearance and to get him onboard a jet back to England. He didn't take notice of that because he had slept through the remains of the night and for the entire next day.

He was in a hospital in Nottingham at night. The agent that saved his life didn't make any contact with him from that moment onwards. Not waiting for any thanks. It wasn't needed and he knew it. He wanted to ask someone where was Fibiano, but he knew it would not do anything much. Their mission had ended and there was no reason for them to meet again. He knew very well the last time he saw him was when he was hunched in the controls of the emergency pod until Nathan passed out.

Nathan had told Harvard Norman about the details of his mission and everything about the things he knew including the uranium. The man gasped as he mentioned the torture. He also mentioned about the backfired bullet from the pressure but Harvard already knew that from the forensics and Fibiano's report. The French had probably made out the reason before anyone else.

One of the great leaders of the secret intelligence sat on the chair beside him and was looking at him with concerned eyes. Nathan lay on the bed with an elbow to support him and demanded answers to the questions he had wanted to ask.

"Where is my aunt? Had you found her?" Nathan blared out the questions. He still felt weak and his voice was taking energy from him.

"You do not need to worry about that. As I told you before, she is somewhere in the suburbs of Cornwell and we are sending our elite teams to locate her, it'll take time. But we'll continue and keep improving the search. You had helped us and we no doubt will repay you," Harvard said and paused for a while.

"There's also a little compensation for you, we'll pay you an amount of money into your bank and we won't care what you do with it. But I must remind you not to buy too many drinks. Would you like to know about the millionaire and his ruined plans?" he asked.

"I don't want your money. Just get my aunt back no matter what. So, just for my interest, how much uranium did the dead millionaire lose after he died?" he said.

"You're right, the millionaire is in Hell now with two holes in his head and a dislocated wrist. The good news is we found all the uranium that would have been exported. It was in the illegal nuclear plant, the one you took the photos of. We didn't expect you to be caught and the photos you took were less useful, but it still helps a lot. We can investigate further on about the locations of the exports and what the psychopath was planning after all.

"We recovered some data on the uranium that had already been exported. The ones Gata Harriman with the unknown man said in his quarters. International police and authorities have managed to confiscate many of them, but there were three locations unfound and we're still working on it.

"Above all, you are the one that helped the most and you risked your life. The IIO and whatever people in the world have to thank you, although we can't declare you identity or even our agent's existence." He looked at Nathan for a while.

"About the first research centre, it had been shut down. The second research centre that is deeper in the seabed actually hides the illegal nuclear plant and almost all of Harriman's information," Norman said. He stopped and thought about something for a moment and continued.

"What do you want in return, apart from your aunt and the money?" Harvard Norman asked. "I want Joe to live with my aunt and me as soon as possible. And I want to visit him for the moment," Nathan answered.

That reminded him about his friend. His friend may have lied to him but it was to protect him, he knew that the friendship remained real and pure, no matter what Argent David said. He had never blamed Joe for that and long ago hoped he will get better and eventually wake up from his coma.

"You can visit him after you're better and when the doctor says so. Isn't there anything else?" Harvard asked again. His voice changed into a slightly different tone.

Nathan had something else. However, he didn't want any of the agents of the IIO to know it. He missed them both but involving them with his mission and his life will do them no good. It was better to keep them away.

"No," Nathan replied. He knew very well that his voice had changed and his tiredness was devastating. He wanted to rest and sleep until the morning.

"If there's nothing else, Suzzle and Izle are waiting for you in the lobby. You can talk to them for as long as you can tonight, but just don't get too late. They need to go to school tomorrow," Harvard said.

"Argent David allows this?" asked Nathan. Norman knew his thought a few seconds earlier but didn't mention it.

"Yes. Why not?" he replied as it was an obvious question. He stood up from his seat and said his standard farewells and told him not to worry too much for his aunt then he exited the door.

The shoulder-length blond hair Suzzle came in with her face in half delight and half concern. Izle followed in and said his awkward hellos. They both wore T-shirts and jeans.

"Nathan! What happened to you? Your arm . . . Does it hurt?" she said as she sat at the small portion of his bed beside him.

The bandage was large and the nurse disagreed with pulling his left sleeve down. Izle took the seat Norman was sitting in a few seconds earlier.

"Hi, Suzzle, it's nothing. It got cut," he lied. He understood that his false identity as a businessman's son coming to stay with them hadn't changed, although Norman didn't mention it just now. However, he had handled a mission pretty well . . . despite the metal bracelet. They were expecting him to follow orders without reminders, what a change!

Suzzle David knew he had lied but she didn't show it. She had also seen through his false identity the moment he stepped into her life, but chose not to make his life harder. He doubted the IIO knew about this.

"Your neck . . ." she murmured again. Nathan put a hand to his bruised neck. The wound had been made by the fingers of the psychopath as he tried to strangle him to death.

Suzzle moved forward unexpectedly and hugged him. She was careful not to make it too hard on his injuries. "I'm so worried about you. You do not have to tell me where have you been, but please, quit the stuff you're doing with my uncle. Promise me, please," she whispered into his ear, not letting her brother hear a word.

"Yes. I'll get out of this as soon as they find who I want," he answered, equally silent. She hugged him longer and he could feel her warm breath on his neck.

After about a minute, she retreated and wiped her eyes. They chatted about everything, from the new things in West Bridgford School he had studied for about more than a week, before Harvard Norman called him to his office and marked the start of his early mission schedule.

They didn't mention anything about her uncle or Nathan's life. Izle was still as quiet as Nathan expected. He only answered when asked and spoke when spoken to. Nathan wondered for a while why he was like that and what had happened in the last 13 years of his friend's brother. He didn't ask or make any sign about that. It would not do anything good.

Suddenly, Nathan felt heavy. It wasn't physical but something in his heart disturbed him. He knew very well that Suzzle and Izle, two of the best friends he could ever have like Joe, that it would be the last time he will have the chance to see them.

After the IIO made their deal and he got his aunt back, they will have no reason to meet again and no way to regardless. It was just as the same for Fibiano. Harvard Norman had scheduled their last meeting.

After two hours of chat, they had nothing more to dig out and comment on, and Suzzle asked about Nathan's life. "What about you after this?"

"I'll go back to London. We can e-mail each other or add me on Facebook. We'll still be friends," Nathan said, but he knew very well that Argent David will monitor and cut off any contacts between them in the next few hours. This last time was the final time.

"Yes, Nathan. I'll miss you." She knew what he thought but didn't hide it. She leant forward and kissed him in the cheeks. "Always friends no matter what . . . I'll never forget you," she whispered.

Nathan blushed and smiled at her, his exhaustion had been forgotten. "Good-bye, Nathan," she said with a voice barely audible and stood up slowly from his bed.

"Good-bye, Suzzle. And you, too, Izle," he replied. Izle just smiled and waved his hand, friendly enough to show his meaning silently.

They moved to the door. They all exchanged looks and Suzzle looked at him for a long time. Nathan made out again her nice blond hair and her friendly look, and then looked one last time at her cute brother.

They smiled to each other and Nathan knew it was the last time they would meet each other as the door opened and shut. The door closing was his last glance of Suzzle and Izle. He felt his heart rate slow and he wanted to be alone for a while just like he was now.

Nathan stared into the distance through the window. A tear flowed from his eyes down to his shirt. He had another two good friends in his memory. He had loved Suzzle, Izle and Joe, and they were either gone or in bed. He wanted them to be happy and hoped to talk with them, but he knew he couldn't.

Nathan switched off the lights of his room and retired to sleep. He still had one thing he forgot to tell Harvard Norman. He wanted back the crystal his father had passed to Veinna and she had passed to him. He desperately needed it now. But the new friendships would always be a part of the thing that accompanied him during all future bedtimes.

Suzzle, Izle, Joe . . . they'll always be friends.

THE END OF BOOK ONE